THE PROPHECY TALES:

AWAKENING

I hope you enjoy the journey!

Acie Lynn

ACIE LYNN

ILLUSTRATIONS BY KYLA CLARK

WAYFARING ARTISAN PRESS

ISBN: 978-0-9905383-0-1
LCN: 2014948170

Print book layout by eBooks By Barb for
booknook.biz

DEDICATIONS

For Eric, my unwaveringly supportive husband,
who tells me constantly, 'You don't know how to fail.'

For my boys, Austin and Cade, who inspire all my greatest laughs.

For Mom, my loudest cheerleader.

For Gerald, Darla, Kyla, Rianna, Wes, and Haley, who lived through
and loved all my stories, even when they were bad.

For Judy, who taught me to love, no matter what.

For Dad, who taught me to dream.

For Grandma, who taught me a faith that sustains me.

For Grandpa, who taught me what not quitting really means.

To all my family and friends I didn't mention individually,
you helped sustain my dream even when
others would have given up on me.

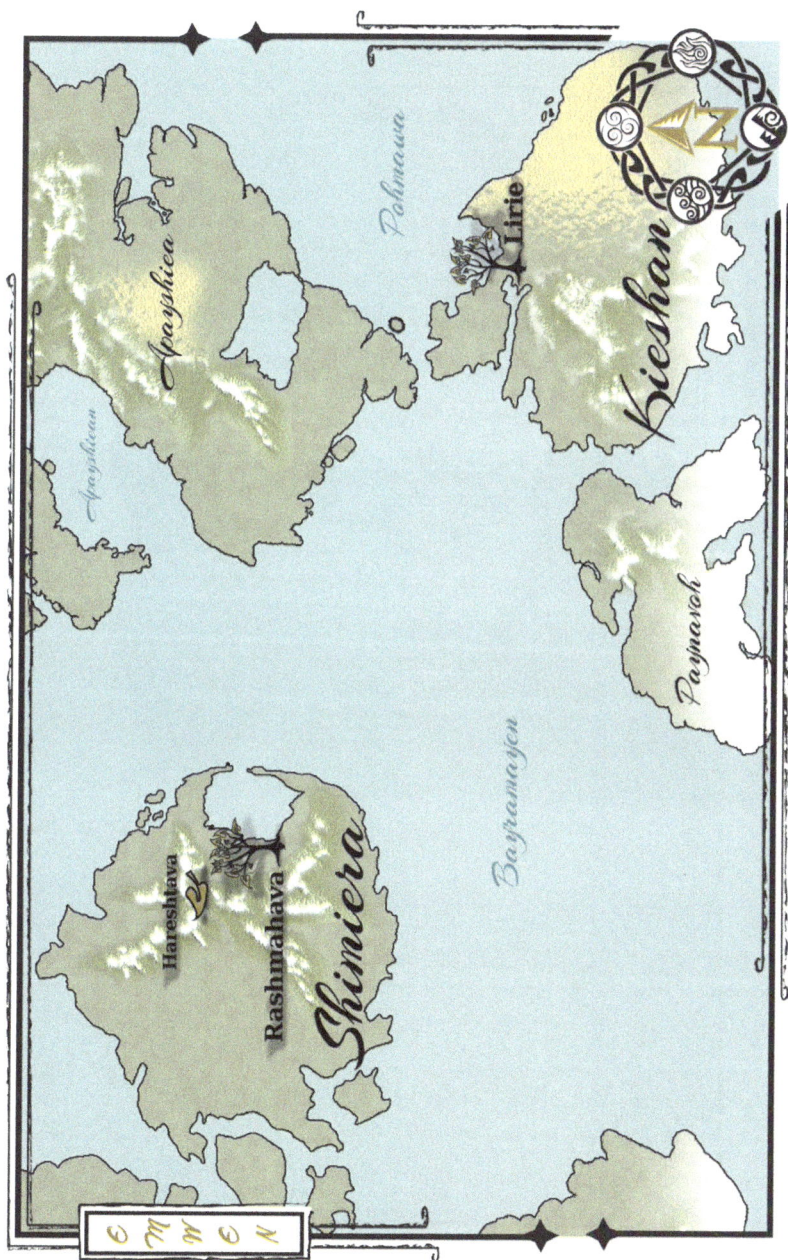

CHAPTER ONE

If prison could be beautiful and, in it, family could be found, Mayven was sure fate had granted her such a boon. This apartment had been her prison, a necessary one perhaps, but prison nonetheless, as long as she could recall. Love had been her keeper and destiny her sentence. Fate—the keeper of the keys—was unlocking the doors at last. However, Mayven found the cost was more horrifying than the thought of a life spent in servitude to a destiny she had never wanted and still didn't understand.

Today, it felt like heaven and all its contents weighed on her young shoulders. Prophecies, destinies and hopes of a world she had never really seen weighed against the life of the man who represented the only family she had ever known.

Mayven studied the building across the street, admiring the broad branches of the willow tree that were artfully curved around the exterior of the trunk. The smaller leafy branches twisted together to form a living railing, the fluttering leaves dancing softly in the slight summer breeze. Along the path of the broad, leafy walkway, crystal windows—bright round portals of glass—caught the last rays of summer light, making the massive trunk of the tree appear as if it were studded with brilliant gems. Behind the windows, as the light grew dimmer, the warm glow changed the gems into radiant orbs. Between the windows, doors seamlessly opened and closed. Except for the crystal pads marking their locations, one would not recognize the doorways that silently slid open after a series of buttons were pressed on the crystal displays. The doorways had no permanent openings but instead appeared and vanished into the wide expanse of the massive tree upon demand.

Mayven's gaze traveled upward to where the last of the windows stopped and the bower of impressive branches spread out above the willow tree's trunk. Larger, upper branches arched across the street below, twining with the branches of her own home and forming walkways above the street that created a green, living archway. The walkways' railings were the artfully twined smaller branches of the wide limbs on which several birds perched, begging passersby for crumbs of bread.

The full leafy top provided bountiful shade for the walkways below and in its abundant arbor birds of every size and description had built homes. Mayven smiled as she watched while they, too, came home to rest in the nests cradled in their treetop home. But soon Mayven's reverie was broken by the harsh sound of a wracking cough in the room behind her. The tranquility of the scene outside her window no longer soothed her raw emotions as she continued the argument that had driven her to stare out the window.

"I don't have to lie to be old enough to work; others just have to assume I am. You have always said don't lie. I already understand that." Mayven's voice rose an octave with each word. "I just want to help! Why won't you let me?"

Mayven turned and stood, hands on hips, glaring at the withered figure of the man she had loved her entire life. He had raised her, sacrificed everything for her, and now he would not allow her to help him. Without him, she would be alone. He was the only world she had ever known.

Mayven's fury boiled over. "You always remind me that you are not my father or my family, Payin. You can't stop me from going. I only have two years until I am of age. I look old enough, you said so yourself."

"I know I'm not your father, Mayven, and yes, you may do as you please. However, you know, because I have taught you as much, that your abilities for the next two years are nearly useless. You can only use them in a classroom. The binding that holds your magic in check is not released until the day of your birth at the age of majority after you have spoken the oath of *hsmakda*. You may have everyone believing you are of age, but you can't lie yourself and change the truth; so the fact remains that you're a child."

"I could lie. I could change it to be true," Mayven pleaded wistfully.

Payin smiled weakly, his eyes filled with tenderness. "But you won't, because you wouldn't dishonor me in such a fashion. You know that to lie changes so much more than just your age. It will change who you are. I love that you love me so dearly, child, but one life is not worth the life of an entire world."

"And how can I change the fate of an entire world?" Tears spilled down Mayven's cheeks as she repeated again a question she had asked her whole life. "I'm only me."

Payin took a ragged breath. "In time, Mayven, you will know. Perhaps sooner than you think."

Mayven, blinking away tears, turned back to the window, noting that the sun had faded. Shen sapling lights glowed in the early twilight, casting glowing pools along the glass-like rock streets of Rashmahava. Mayven studied the shen lamps, a tingle faintly touching her skin even at this distance, as if the night brought them more to life. Mayven felt the familiar pull of the natural magic the shen saplings used to cast their light. As a child, Mayven named them talking trees. Every time she and Payin had managed an outing, she had insisted she felt them talking to her. The older she got, the more fearful she had grown of them, due to Payin's continued warnings against following wherever her magic led her.

Mayven heard again his quiet insistent warnings. *"Mayven, one day you will be able to go and explore shen trees, and many other things. For now, you must remain distant from all that calls you. Don't let things that pull you to them guide your steps. You do not know enough to understand the consequences. Be careful."*

Mayven sighed. *Yet another love-placed bar on my necessary cage.*

Very few pod vehicles now rushed silently along the streets. Those that did were service vehicles for trash or transit; no one in this district had the station or the money to afford a luxury like a pod vehicle. Just beyond the window, the thick, broad branch of the willow housing Mayven's apartment complex served as a busy pathway up from the streets below. Mayven watched wistfully as people passed by the window. Mayven sighed, lowering her gaze to the sink in front of her, and tried to wrestle her wayward emotions under control.

The lump she kept trying to swallow would not diminish as anger and grief warred for control. Mayven turned from the window to check on Payin again, when she heard the shuffle of his shoes across the floor. Payin's dark gray eyes were sunken into his skull above his high cheekbones, his feet unsteady, and his tall thin body bent. However, Payin waved Mayven off as soon as she started across the room to help.

Mayven, her arms dangling uselessly at her sides, watched him totter across the floor then settle himself at the table that grew from the floor of their living home.

For an instant, anger won the war inside her as once again questions filled her mind. *Why can't I leave this house? Why must he insist that no one ever see me? I feel useless. I can translate things. I can find a job doing that. Then I could afford a doctor to heal him. Why won't he let me help?*

Mayven's thoughts raced frantically around her head until tears threatened to course down her face once more. She took a deep steadying breath, knowing it upset Payin to see her emotions out of control. Mayven felt the cool touch of the tree's natural magic sink into her body from the soles of her feet as she waited for Payin to seat himself and her own raging emotions to settle.

When at last the thoughts in her head had calmed themselves, and Payin was settled at the table, Mayven took a seat next to him and took his hand in hers. She felt the feeble strength in his body through the touch of his hand. Instinctively, she gathered the life-force of their home around herself, pulling in its strength, using the lines of magic that connected all living things to create a deep well of strength within herself.

Mayven felt the comforting strength of the tree fill her, and she willed it into Payin, pushing it out from herself along the connection of their joined hands. Pleading with Payin silently as she gazed intently into his eyes, Mayven released the strength she had gathered, sending it to Payin. Payin simply stared back at her, his lips dry and cracked, a sad replica of a smile etched across his gaunt features.

Their sparsely furnished apartment was only one of fifty housed inside the massive oak. Mayven knew the tree was taxed to its limit to support the life that it cared for, but she shifted the strength she had gathered to Payin, feeling it leave her in a tingling rush that coursed across her skin.

Payin shook his head feebly. "I'm ill, Mayven. I think it is bad, and I can't afford a doctor."

Mayven sucked her breath through her teeth and closed her hand over his, trying to still his words as tears pooled in her eyes.

Payin took another ragged breath. "You will need your strength, child, in the days to come. Don't waste it on someone old like me."

Mayven felt a knot choke her as she shook her head, tears spilling down her cheeks. "It will be fine, Payin. I'll find someone. Don't give up. I don't need what I lend you. I'll be fine."

But even as she said it, Payin quietly rejected her gift of strength as he returned it to her in a rush that warmed her skin. The return of the magic left her tingling from head to toe before it coursed unused back into the tree through the soles of her feet.

Payin sighed heavily. "I can't find one who would treat me, given my lowly station. I know you count on me, child, but my time grows short and there is much you need to know." Payin looked down at his thin hands a moment. "Your family was murdered when you were an infant. The reason they were murdered is because of the mark you hide beneath the band I make you wear every day. Your mark, like everyone else's mark, represents your magical ability. Your magic is the greatest magic our people possess. Our government seeks to control anyone in our world who has great magic."

Mayven's body stiffened, and her breath caught in her throat as her mind stuck on only one word. *Murdered.* She had begged for the story of her parents and family her entire life and now, here in this awful moment when she was losing the last person in this world she was connected to, *murdered* struck her like a blow between the eyes.

Payin stopped speaking to cough, a deep hacking sound that caused his already pale features to go ashen. He gripped the table with shaking hands as spasm after spasm wracked his body. Mayven rose quickly from her chair and brought him a glass of water, which he gratefully gulped. Smiling weakly, he waited for her to be seated and gathered her hands in his.

Mayven raised her eyes, shock her only emotion, as she waited for the rest of the story.

"You must let no one know what is beneath that headband. I was entrusted with your secret by a group known as Niesha. They asked me to raise you as my child. I have done so with great joy."

A lump rose in her throat and tears spilled down her face as she instinctually patted his hand, trying to comfort him. Unable to grasp the details, her mind clung to the only thing that mattered right now, keeping the world she knew intact.

"I know you have. I love you, Payin. Please, we'll make you better. I'll find money somehow. You'll be fine, you'll see."

Mayven again tried to transfer her strength into Payin, but he refused, letting it return to her unclaimed. Mayven gritted her teeth in frustration as she tried again. *He can't expect me to do nothing. He can't leave me like this.* When he rejected her attempts again, Mayven jerked back from him, thrusting her balled fists into her lap.

Payin looked at her, his gray eyes ringed in dark circles, his cheeks sunken. He took a slow ragged breath. "I'm afraid not, child. You need to accept that some things are meant to be. Please, what I have to say to you is important. Listen carefully. The illness I have ravages more and more people every day. Everyone who becomes ill eventually dies. Even the wealthy are becoming ill. Our government wants you to believe it is a sickness that can be cured. However, it is a symptom of our world dying and a problem only someone of your abilities can correct."

Mayven nodded but didn't speak, for the lump in her throat was making it hard to breathe. Confusion, anger, grief, and a sense of betrayal left her uncentered. A whirlwind of emotions assaulted her senses as she tried to focus on Payin's next words.

"Niesha is a group of people who are trying to make things right in our world. They understand the greater importance of your magic. They know you have the power to correct what is wrong. But those who serve Niesha are hunted by an organization known as Adamdavas." Payin once again paused, taking a ragged breath and another long drink of water.

Mayven took the glass from Payin and refilled it.

"Adamdavas is the real power behind the Shimiera government," he continued. "Adamdavas has convinced the Shimiera government that, if they can control you, they can fix all the problems that are plaguing our world. You are the answer to our problems, child, but your destiny is not to be controlled by anyone."

Mayven felt the familiar chains of her unknown destiny tighten as Payin spoke. Anger, fueled by fear and doubt, made her hands shake as she returned the glass to the table in front of Payin.

Payin took another long drink. "Among the many nations of our world is another nation called Kieshan. Niesha has headquarters there. One day, someone from Niesha will find you again. They will want to take you there. You must go with them so you will be safe. They will guide you to your true destiny. In the meantime, you must never reveal your xodieha. The symbol of our people reveals the level of magic we possess. It is like a birthmark, and yours must never be known until you are free of Shimiera."

Mayven's anger began to boil. *What is the difference? Controlled by Adamdavas or guided by Niesha, my life will never be my own. All I want is Payin to be okay.*

Another spasm of coughing overtook Payin, and Mayven had to steady his hand so he could drink from the glass before he could speak again.

"Until Niesha is able to find you, and in the likely event I die before you are an adult, you will be required to go with a payjik to the orphanage. Mayven, you must promise me that you will never reveal your xodieha to anyone. It will be an easy thing to make others think you don't have one. I work at the hospital, and I know the story you must let others believe." A brief look of sadness and fear flashed in Payin's eyes.

Mayven reached out to comfort Payin, clasping his gaunt hand in hers.

"You have seen the news reports. There are more and more children born without a xodieha. The news reports that these children live. However, they all die at birth. You will be an orphan, and your caste will make you untouchable. No one will want to touch you to prove or disprove your lack of a xodieha. All you must do is let them assume you don't have a xodieha. You must also promise me that when Niesha does find you, you will go with them. Promise me, Mayven."

"I promise, Payin," Mayven answered. Rising from her chair, she threw her thin young frame against him in a fierce hug.

"You can't die. You can't leave me here alone. What will happen to me? Why did you wait until now to tell me about my parents?" Mayven pulled back from Payin, gripping his face between her hands. "I need to know more."

Sadness, guilt, and regret mingled in Payin's gaze. "I did what you needed when you needed it, child. You would have gained nothing by knowing how your parents were taken from you. In your lack of knowledge, you were allowed a brief time of joy. Hang onto that when I am not with you. This world will change you, Mayven, if you let it. Be strong enough to learn and grow. Be wise enough not to shut yourself off. There is much you are meant to do with your life."

Mayven jerked back from him, angry that yet again he spoke of a destiny he would not define and a responsibility she didn't want. "I don't want your destiny or your plans for me. I want you to be here with me. That is all I need."

"There is more to this world than just you and I. Mayven, I have told you many times that you are never alone," Payin rebuked her gently. "The creator, Dsohoay, is with you always. He is the author of your life, your destiny. He is a father who will never leave you. If you remember nothing else I've ever taught you, remember that. Perhaps this is our maker's way of showing you why you must want things to be different."

Mayven no longer cared if her emotion made Payin upset with her as she let her tears fall unheeded down her cheeks. "I am not interested in a god who would take away my only family to teach me a lesson, Payin."

Payin sighed, looking at her with sadness. "When I am gone, you are to go to the landlord and tell him I died and that you have no other family. He will call a payjik to come and collect you and take you to the orphanage. When the payjik comes, go with him willingly."

Payin smoothed her cheeks with trembling fingers, wiping her tears.

"You know the first rule of magic. You cannot lie, because it changes reality. You need to have your power and your xodieha. In this lie, you must be very clever. Let them come up with the lie. Let them assume they know the answer. Those who will assume the answer will spread the lie for you. In this way, you have never altered anything by lying. You have only avoided telling the truth."

Payin started to say more and broke into another coughing spasm.

"Don't talk anymore." Mayven blinked away tears as she gently put the glass to Payin's blue-tinted lips. "You need to rest. Please, Payin. You need to rest."

Payin shook his head weakly, gasping for breath. "You must become adept at letting others create a lie for you. Your power is so great that if you ever lie, even to yourself, even for a moment that lie can change everything. Remember that always. Never be afraid of being completely honest with yourself, Mayven. Someday it will make all the difference."

Mayven nodded mutely, barely able to breathe as tears streamed down her face. Payin pulled a thin tattered hanky from a pocket and wiped her face.

"Now, child, enough crying. Smile for me, sweet one, then off to bed with you. I will see you in the morning."

Mayven gave him a trembling smile and hugged him fiercely before walking across the room and entering behind the thin curtain that separated her room from the rest of their little one-room apartment. Mayven listened as Payin shuffled around the kitchen, his movements often punctuated by the sounds of gasping breaths or wracking coughs. Mayven soon found her angry thoughts centered on Payin's comments on Dsohoay. *Why does Payin have so much faith? He is dying. If this god of his is so powerful, why doesn't he make Payin better? Dsohoay is just as cruel as Hsdaie if he lets Payin die to teach me a lesson.*

Mayven stared at the ceiling angrily. *I will not dishonor Payin. I will do what I can to set things right because that is what he wants of me. I owe him that much. But I want nothing to do with his god or his religion. It isn't any better than the religion that follows Hsdaie.*

Hours of listening to Payin's ragged breathing and hacking cough and her mind racing through all she had learned, and all she hadn't, finally drove Mayven into exhausted sleep.

The next morning, she woke to find Payin slumped over the table, his eyes wide and sightless and his body cold to the touch.

I thought I had more time. Mayven gently smoothed back the long lank strands of gray hair from his face and closed his sightless eyes. Wiping roughly at her face with the sleeve of her shirt, she took a seat in the chair next to Payin. Mayven stared at Payin's beloved face, memorizing every line.

He looks like he is sleeping. Compelled to check, Mayven reached out and touched him once more. There was no stirring of breath or bone and Mayven's sobs erupted loudly in the silence as she drew her hand back. Curling her legs against her chest, Mayven hugged her knees and cried until she was breathless, all the while staring disbelieving at the end of her world as she had known it. At length, Payin's instructions entered Mayven's thoughts, and she rose shakily from the chair and exited the tiny apartment.

Mayven cried the entire way to the landlord's apartment but once outside his door she wiped her tear-streaked face with a sleeve and followed Payin's last instructions to the letter. A few short hours later, a payjik in his copper tunic arrived and marched her out the door.

One last look over her shoulder gave her a brief glimpse of two members of Gayied, the city guard, dumping Payin's lifeless body onto a stretcher before hauling it to the pod van outside marked *Rashmahava City Dump*. Dread filled her, and her stomach knotted as she found herself picturing Payin's body tossed carelessly on the pile of garbage at the dump like carrion for vermin to feed on.

There will be no pretty paktwatm or flowers for him, no seedling to plant to honor the only man I have ever known as family. Turning her eyes forward and trying to ignore the pain in her arm from the cruel grip of the payjik, she silently vowed that never again would anyone she loved be forgotten and treated so cruelly.

Mayven stumbled as she rushed barefoot along the stone paved streets next to the tall man in his copper uniform. She was well aware that if he didn't have to be touching her, he wouldn't. *Untouchable, I should have that written on me somewhere. I went from low caste to no caste because my family died.* Now, like the criminal her birth had made her, the payjik's gloved hand closed like a vise around her arm, restraining her as if she were accused of a crime.

"You have no business out running the streets. You don't have a marsa, you have no family, your only good to this world is that you can serve. Remember your station, gutter rat, it will make life much easier for you where you're going."

He looked down at her briefly, his face tight with a cruel superior smile, until it thinned into a hard line as he took in the wide, plain, silver band across her forehead.

"Why do you wear that ridiculous headband?"

Mayven remembered what Payin had said and knew she couldn't answer his direct question. Stumbling to keep up, she remained silent. When she didn't answer his question in time, he stopped, jerking her around to face him.

"Don't act like you have some kind of place in this world. I asked you a question, orphan. Answer me! Why do you wear the headband?"

Mayven felt her heart slamming against her ribs as she struggled against the command in his voice, the magic in his order pulling at her and compelling an answer. She lowered her gaze to her bare feet, her tongue wetting her lips as she tried to come up with a way for him to come to the answer on his own. The whispering glide of pod cars racing along the smooth, glass-like rock streets filled the silence.

"You are one of the deformed, aren't you? No wonder your father kept you hidden at home. You don't have a xodieha." The payjik's nose wrinkled, and his lips peeled back in a grimace.

Mayven felt relief flood her at his quick assumption of the lie she had needed him to believe. Her first lesson was learned. Proper attitude and behavior would lead those willing to put themselves above others quickly to the right assumptions.

The payjik jerked her roughly around as he started along the street once more. He seemed to understand she wasn't going to try to run from him, so he loosened his hold on her arm so that his hand barely touched her sleeve.

Mayven glanced up at him out of the corner of her eye.

"Don't think you will hide your deformity from the headmistress at the orphanage. I will tell her what you are," the payjic said, observing Mayven's furtive glance.

Mayven lowered her eyes to the ground in front of her once more, and her hand clenched into a fist by her side. The payjik had fleshed out her lie without her ever saying a word and would pass it along. But still the thought that now she would be even less than she had ever been before grated. Payin had always told her one day she would be able to show the entire world how great she really was.

Mayven roughly rubbed her fist across her cheeks to hide her tears. *I will make him proud of me one day. I will find a way to be great.*

Lost in her thoughts, Mayven blindly followed the payjik to the orphanage located in the poor business district at the end of the Fisherman's Wharf. The sound of the ship yards and the stink of fish filled the air. Delivery pod trucks lumbered silently by on the rock-paved streets while pod cars rushed to and from, delivering passengers to work or shopping at the various businesses along the narrow crowded lanes.

Mayven paid the busy sight little heed as her eyes fastened on the place she would live until she was declared an adult. The massive oak tree was ten stories tall, its girth equal to half its height. The yard, nothing but hard-packed dirt, was enclosed with a stone fence. In the yard, lines of children shuffled out from the massive oak and across the barren yard to a tree, a twin in size and height, at the far back corner of the massive hard-packed compound. Mayven noted the looks on the faces of the older children, defeat and acceptance for the majority of them. But she also noted that there were a few, better fed and better clothed, who wore looks of superiority and cruelty on their faces as they marched ahead of the others. The children, some barely old enough to walk, were all but ignored by those who commanded them into lines and marched them across the yard. Mayven noted that it was the youngest who still looked longingly up at those around them, seeking a comfort she was sure they would never find.

Just inside the open gate was a small pen where children stood huddled together, some barely old enough to walk. Next to the pen a woman at a long stone table looked them over with a cold critical eye. Her expression plainly said that the plight of these poor creatures was of little consequence to her.

Mayven was marched through the gate and unceremoniously deposited inside the pen with the other children as her escort turned to the woman. The children around her shuffled around to make room in the crowded space as Mayven turned to watch the payjik speak to the woman at the table.

Another payjik quickly joined them, dragging with him a half-starved girl with hair white as snow and the most amazing eyes Mayven had ever seen. Mayven was captured by her eyes, the center of the iris shone a bright, clear, almost surreal silver and along the outside rim a jet black ring with small lines traced inward halfway to her pupil.

The girl struggled hard against her less-than-gentle handler, who picked her up bodily and dumped her into the pen next to Mayven. The morning light was beginning to shine bright, and the summer heat and humidity rose quickly as the numbers of children in the small holding pen grew. Soon the sweat from the children gathered in such a small space was staining their clothes and the smell of so many unwashed bodies brought tears to Mayven's eyes. Outside the pen, Mayven watched as other children, already housed here, were periodically marched to and fro in the yard, all the while their keepers shouting at them.

The girl with the white hair now stood crushed against Mayven in the corner of the pen as she alternately stood on first one foot and then the other. Mayven looked down at her feet and noted the ground beneath where she stood was stained dark with the blood from her raw, bruised, dirt-covered appendages.

"What happened to your feet?"

The girl shuffled again to her other foot, leaning on Mayven heavily. "I tried to get free of the payjik by resisting and dragging them. It really is a brilliant plan except, well, I have no shoes. I didn't put a lot of thought into that apparently. I'm Amalayna, what's your name?"

Mayven couldn't help the wide smile that stretched across her face at the younger girl's impetuous reply. "My name is Mayven. Why is your hair white?"

Amalayna lifted a lank rather dirty lock of silver white hair. "Oh, this? It happened the last time a payjik tried to bring me here."

A puff of dust swirled around them as children shifted to make a tiny bit more space for the newest addition to their group. Amalayna teetered and leaned heavily on Mayven as she was jostled about. Mayven reached out, wrapping an arm around her shoulder to steady her.

Amalayna smiled. "I tried to use my magic to escape. I didn't know then that payjiks have wards to prevent their captives from using magic. I tried to portal out, and the recoil from the failed attempt stunned the payjik so I could get away, but it turned my hair white." Amalayna flipped her hair over her shoulder with a flourish and tilted her chin back with a grin. "I kinda like it."

"Why don't you portal now then? No payjik touches you."

Amalayna lifted a brow, her face lined with sarcasm. "They have this pen warded. I've already tried. I can't even gather enough magic to move across the pen."

Mayven felt a bit in awe of Amalayna, her eyes roaming her new-found companion. She had willingly come to this place as Payin had instructed, but this girl had fought hard to get away and apparently succeeded once. Mayven felt sadness grip her and lowered her head as thoughts of Payin threatened to overwhelm her resolve to follow his instructions.

"What's the matter?" Amalayna regarded her with an owlish expression.

"I'm good, don't worry." Mayven blinked, clearing tear-blurred vision.

Amalayna snorted. "I wasn't. I figured that if you give up and die in here, it just leaves a little more for me to eat. They don't feed you much in these places." Amalayna's features took on a wise sadness. "That's why all the older kids who already have their apprenticeships are glad to move out. They like the food they get when they earn money for their masters."

Surprised, Mayven stared at Amalayna.

"Oh, don't get me wrong. I'd miss you. You've already been nicer to me than anyone has, ever. But, really, I want to live long enough to get the heck out of this place." Amalayna shrugged casually.

Mayven felt dread settle in her soul. This was what life would be like from now on. Struggling to survive and fighting for the smallest scraps. Life with Payin had not been easy; she had struggled. They had worked hard to put food on the table and pay rent. But they had always had each other.

Mayven looked down at Amalayna and noticed that, underneath the brash bravado, she was failing. The combination of the heat and tight quarters were sapping the last strength her emaciated body possessed. Amalayna's grimy face was streaked in rivulets of sweat that revealed an ashen countenance beneath the dirt.

Mayven wrapped a protective arm around Amalayna's shoulder and shoved some of the other children back to give her a little more air. The sun, nearly at its zenith now, had increased the heat so much that the air was thick with humidity.

Mayven was grateful when at last the woman at the table rose and opened the gate. She and the payjiks lined the children up in front of her table.

"I see society is burdened with yet more of your kind. Well, nothing for it but to get you all in order." The woman rubbed a finger over the bridge of her nose.

She started at the end of the line farthest from Mayven and began pacing her way along the line. Each child had a payjik behind them, their hand firmly on a shoulder so they were unable to escape by means of their magic.

The woman sniffed now and then, holding a long-fingered hand beneath her nose, as she passed several children.

"The rules are as follows: you will address me as Jayben Tavadar. I have earned the title of Jayben and expect it to be used without exception when addressing me."

She stopped and turned to face the children, looking down her long nose, her eyebrows raised in question.

"Yes, Jayben Tavadar." The children spoke in unison.

A smirk pulled at the corner of her mouth before her face returned to its stony mask, and she began to pace along the line again.

"You will wear your marsa you are given here every day and never remove it. It is your identity and your tracking device. We will know if you remove it. You will do as you're told without question. You will never speak to anyone above your station unless you are spoken to. You will never look directly at anyone above your station. Because many of you," she glanced sidelong at the youngest children, "are very young, you will find that you will be here until you are of age to complete school and sit for you apprenticeship test. None of you will be leaving here until you have reached the age, or approximate age for those of you unsure of your birthday, of adulthood at 150 years, when you are allowed to take the oath of hsmakda. Your restraints on your magic will be released, and you will sit for your apprenticeship test."

Mayven's heart sank.

"Unfortunately, that means I will be responsible for some of you for quite some time. It would serve you well not to test me." Jayben Tavadar sighed deeply as she glanced sideways at the youngest children.

Mayven felt anger choking her as she watched the woman strolling along the line from the corner of her eye. Her clothing was not rich but it was decent. Her skin was soft from lack of any real hardship and her form well filled out; she hadn't missed any meals.

Mayven clenched hands at her sides as she bit her tongue to keep from speaking. *Jayben Tavadar acts as if our mere existence is taking something from her. I wonder if she has ever had children of her own and eaten them.*

"You will be given a bed, a blanket, and a new set of clothes once a year. You will be required to make sure your clothes are always clean and in good repair." Jayben Tavadar ticked off each rule on a long finger as she paced. "If you damage them, lose them, or they are stolen from you, they will not be replaced, and you will be docked meal privileges."

Mayven couldn't stop the hiss of anger that escaped her lips. Jayben

Tavadar, walking directly in front of her, paused at the sound. Jayben Tavadar slowly turned until Mayven could see her own reflection in Jayben Tavadar's highly polished boots.

"What is that I heard?"

Mayven remained silent. Her tongue nearly bled as she fought to control the temper for which Payin had so often scolded her.

"I was speaking to you. What was that noise I heard?"

Hard cool hands gripped Mayven's chin, tilting it up.

Mayven carefully released her grip on her tongue. Avoiding looking directly into Jayben Tavadar's eyes, she replied, "I said nothing, Jayben Tavadar."

Mayven instantly regretted her words as she heard the sarcastic tone in her voice. Immediately the hard cool grip on her chin vanished as Jayben Tavadar applied the palm of her hand to Mayven's cheek.

Mayven's head rocked to the side as her ears rang. Blinking hard to control the tears that threatened, Mayven once again lowered her gaze to view her reflection in Jayben Tavadar's boots.

"You will get off easy this time. This is your first day. But should you ever speak to me or anyone else in such a tone again, I'll have your tongue removed."

Mayven felt relief at Jayben Tavadar's statement but then fear as she noticed that Jayben Tavadar's boots hadn't moved from her sight. Again, cool hard fingers forced her chin up. Mayven felt Jayben Tavadar's gaze lock on her face.

"You're the one who is deformed. You don't have a xodieha. You are low even for an orphan." Jayben Tavadar's hand dropped from Mayven's chin as if it were a scalding pot.

Once again staring down, Mayven watched as Jayben Tavadar stepped backwards out of her line of sight. *I'm too contaminated for even my gaze to touch her. Well, that should make me properly invisible.*

As if answering Mayven's private thoughts, Jayben Tavadar continued, "You're beneath even other orphans. You have no status. No value. You will never again speak in my presence or utter even a sound. If you do, it could cost you your life."

Mayven felt dread spread through her. The challenge in the woman's voice meant that she would try very hard to make it so Mayven would violate just such a decree.

Mayven kept her eyes glued to the ground. A muffled whimper drew Mayven's attention. Amalayna began to crumple, and Mayven surreptitiously sidled closer in order to support her swaying form. Jayben

Tavadar droned on for a few more minutes. Then another woman started at the farthest end of the line and began pulling out marsas with two fingers from a large metal box and handing them to the payjik behind each child.

Mayven studied the marsas. They were beyond plain. Utilitarian, silver chokers with plain onyx crystals that hung from the center point of the narrow band. They were snapped into place by the payjik.

Each child was turned around and the payjik scanned the onyx stone with their engaohnie crystals. There was a beep, then a corresponding flash from the onyx. The payjik would then gratefully shove the child back into the pen and leave.

When they got close to Mayven, she quickly got on the opposite side of Amalayna and continued to support her with a shoulder until she was dropped back into the pen. When Mayven had her marsa in place, she entered the pen and shoved her way toward Amalayna.

"What is with these marsas? What are they for?" Mayven wrapped an arm around Amalayna's slight shoulders.

"They are collars to control you." Amalayna gave a feeble swipe at the rivulets of sweat coursing down her face, her earlier bravado conspicuously absent. "They allow them to track you and disarm your ability to use your magic unless directed otherwise. The Jayben has the ability to release the controls on our magic once we are assigned to apprenticeship. But the tracking device stays our entire lives. Orphans are slaves, Mayven. We will never be free."

Mayven felt horror and fear collide into a frozen knot that settled into the center of her chest. *How could Payin think this was best? He lied to me my entire life and now this?*

The last of the marsas were handed out. Then the children were divided, girls and boys, and marched into separate shower rooms. Mayven removed her clothing as ordered then reached with trembling hands for her headband.

"That one is to keep that headband on at all times. I don't want my eyes to be violated by seeing her naked brow. Besides, we will never get her apprenticed if she is shown to anyone with a naked brow." Jayben Tavadar addressed a woman who sat at a low table next to the shower room entrance.

Mayven lowered her hands and struggled to hide her smirk as she locked her gaze on the floor and dutifully dropped her clothes in the bag. She stepped into a stall with Amalayna, and Jayben Tavadar turned a knob at the far end of the stalls. Water shot from the shower head in

brutal, ice cold jets. A dingy rag and a bar of soap was flung into their shower stall, and Mayven struggled to retrieve them while supporting Amalayna.

"The person in your stall is your shower partner from now on. You will share the soap you were given and the cloth. You will be required to shower each night before bed. Your soap is to last you for a month. If you should run out of soap, you will be charged a meal to replace it," Jayben Tavadar pronounced.

The water was thankfully warming up as Mayven quickly lathered the rag. She began scrubbing Amalayna, who now shivered uncontrollably as she clung to the wall of the shower stall.

"You will have fifteen minutes for a shower every night. So don't dawdle, ladies."

Mayven rubbed soap into Amalayna's waist-length hair and down her emaciated frame then left the bubbles to sit as she quickly lathered herself. When both of them were covered head to foot in bubbles, Mayven took Amalayna in her arms. Standing beneath the pounding shower head, Mayven ran her fingers through Amalayna's hair to rinse out the soap. Then she leaned Amalayna against the wall and rinsed her body and had barely finished her hair when the water was shut off.

A thin rough towel was tossed at them.

"This is the towel you will share with your shower partner. When you are done drying, you will be given your set of clothing. You have three minutes."

Mayven dried Amalayna first, then herself and, shivering, they made their way to the table at the end of the shower room. A woman stood at the front of the table and measured their feet and height. Then they were handed boots, thin socks, and a set of plain brown breeches and tunic.

Mayven helped Amalayna dress in the small ante room. Mayven's own clothes were barely buttoned and she had just stomped her feet into the boots that were two sizes too large when Jayben Tavadar's hand clenched in her hair and jerked her head back.

Mayven closed her eyes so she wouldn't be looking at the woman. Pain from the pull on her hair and awkward angle of her neck made Mayven again bite her tongue to remain silent.

"Why are you helping this girl? Did you think I wouldn't notice? If she wants to live, she will find the will. Otherwise, let her die."

Rage flared in Mayven's breast at Jayben Tavadar's cruel words but she struggled to compose herself.

"You are forbidden from assisting her any further. She will get well or die and save us all the trouble of caring for her."

Jayben Tavadar released Mayven with a shove. "Besides, if she dies, you will have one less person to wait behind for food."

The group was lined up and marched into the cafeteria. Mayven was placed at the back of the line. Mayven studied the child in front of her as her heart broke. *He's only a baby.*

The little boy was thin. His hands, which should have been chubby with baby fat, were bony from lack of proper food. Barely old enough to walk on his own, he stood staring down at the floor, his shoulders bent and thin frame shaking. Mayven's study of the child was interrupted by Jayben Tavadar.

"Orphans are casteless, slaves, refuse of society." Jayben Tavadar stared down her long nose at Mayven. "But you are lower than all of this pitiful lot. You are so low fate denied you a xodieha. You are deformed, an abomination. As such, your rank is beneath even the infants. You are to remain the last in line for anything. Is that understood?"

Mayven's teeth grated loud in her ears as her fists ground into her thighs. From the corner of her eye, Mayven watched Jayben Tavadar smile broadly before striding toward the front of the line, shoulders back and chin up.

Mayven felt her stomach clench at the smell of food and realized it was nearly six in the evening and she hadn't eaten all day. The rag, towel and bar of soap were rolled into a wet bundle beneath her arm, causing her clothing to soak through and her body to shiver.

But the demands of Mayven's body were quickly ignored as she watched Jayben Tavadar purposely shove Amalayna, making her stumble and fall.

The other children ignored Amalayna and stepped over her as the line moved forward. Amalayna struggled to rise and get back in line. Mayven watched, helpless, her fists clenched at her sides.

When Amalayna was knocked to the ground for the third time by one of the older children, Mayven almost stepped forward to help. Amalayna stared straight into Mayven's eyes and just barely shook her head no before her eyes darted sideways.

Mayven lowered her gaze and, looking up from under lowered lids, she followed Amalayna's glance. Jayben Tavadar stood, arms folded beneath her breasts, staring directly at Mayven, a cold tight smile on her face. Mayven turned her gaze back to Amalayna and stared into her silver eyes, willing her strength.

Mayven felt a tingle prickle across her skin as she continued to stare at Amalayna. *Amalayna, get up. Please get up.*

Mayven felt the tingle increase, then a rush of heat passed through her body, followed by a chill that left her light headed.

Mayven stumbled a little as she followed the line in front of her forward. Her hand reached out and touched the wall of the cafeteria. The smooth surface of the oak tree's wall felt warm against her palm. It seemed to spread through her, chasing away the chill and soon her mind was clear once more.

Mayven sighed as her strength returned as she leaned gratefully against the wall a moment. Then remembering Amalayna, Mayven quickly looked ahead down the line to find Amalayna on her feet and staring at her. Mayven frowned in Amalayna's direction, and Amalayna quickly joined the line again.

When Mayven received her portion, it was barely more than a spoon full, the dregs of the entire meal. But tired and grateful for even such a meager dinner, Mayven turned to find a seat. She was directed to a small round table in the very corner of the room, far removed from all the other children.

Mayven sat down and stared into her bowl at the congealed lump of food. Sighing, she took a bite.

"Please pay attention to the news. As always, you will be required to write an essay on how your existence is impacting our society," Jayben Tavadar said.

Mayven nearly choked on the bite of food in her mouth at Jayben Tavadar's words. At the front of the cafeteria, a large crystal screen came to life as a well-groomed anchorwoman for the evening news began to speak. "The illness that is plaguing our nation has spread drastically, often killing many of those afflicted. The result is a rapid increase in the number of orphans now being housed by the state. The drain on the nation's resources to find a cure for this illness and the increased cost of care for the orphan population has the nation's budget stretched to the limit. Council elders are now instituting a curfew for lights out by ten bells every evening in order to conserve on power usage and cost."

Mayven listened absently as the woman droned on, but her attention was caught again as the announcer said, "There has been a motion approved by the council to have all those recently orphaned interrogated as to their involvement in the deaths of their families. It is believed that there may be some connection to the illness and the survival of the orphaned children. Questioning is to begin immediately and will be conducted by the Gayied."

Mayven barely swallowed her last nibble of food as fear settled in her stomach. The Gayied's reputation was not a good one. She had seen results of how they had interrogated Payin over the years. *There is no way these younger children will survive.*

Then Mayven's attention was drawn to Jayben Tavadar as she marched along the rows of tables. Mayven's hands shook with anger. *Perhaps this is exactly what they want. Less of us to feed or care for. Only the strong survive.*

Mayven's thoughts were interrupted as a group of Gayied entered the wide double doors of the cafeteria, their leader stepping up to Jayben Tavadar, who pointed out the children just recently received. Mayven noted the cruel smile on the vile woman's face as she pointed her out to one of the hard-faced leader.

Mayven, Amalayna, and all the other children who had arrived that day were marched from the cafeteria, Jayben Tavadar at the head of the line. They walked through the wide hallway to the front door and out across the hard-packed dirt yard to the school building. Inside the school, they were seated in the auditorium. Three of the Gayied were lined up in front of the group and the rest of the eight-man unit each picked a child and marched them up onto the stage where they were seated in a line of chairs. Mayven felt bile rise in her throat as the Gayied picked the youngest children first, lining them up in the chairs and standing in front of them as they removed black onyx crystals from their belts.

The guard directly in front of her flinched as the crystal was applied to a little boy's neck and he began to scream pitifully. He paled, his eyes bright as he blinked back tears. As the little boy's cries escalated and his guard shouted questions at him, the man in front of Mayven finally broke and turned around. "He is just a baby! What could he possibly do to anyone?"

Mayven wanted to scream her agreement but managed to remain quiet, her hand surreptitiously clutching Amalayna's. The hard-faced leader turned slowly away from the screaming little boy to face the guard in front of Mayven.

"He is an orphan. His parents died, and he did not. There is a reason why, and I will know it. If you cannot do your job, leave."

Mayven fought down the urge to vomit, her forehead breaking out in cold sweat as the little boy now curled forward in his chair, whimpering. While the two men of the Gayied argued, Mayven looked at the stage, her eyes taking in the children there and willing them to be strong. She focused on it with all her concentration. The children's screams grew less strident, and Mayven sighed quietly.

The hard-faced man sent Mayven's guard away and turned back to the little boy. Mayven watched helplessly, unable to stop the torture, but determined to help the children withstand it. She gathered strength from the living building and transferred it to the children onstage in a constant stream. The continual concentration and work it took to sustain them cost Mayven more than she realized. When she and Amalayna were called to the stage, they were the last of the group to be interrogated. Mayven, every muscle in her body trembling with exhaustion, stumbled on her way up the stairs before taking a seat in front of the hard-faced leader.

Mayven stared up into his beady obsidian eyes and knew he enjoyed the pain he inflicted. Mayven recalled the times Payin would return home, his face ashen, decorated in a network of tiny cuts. Around Payin's thin neck rested a gruesome necklace, created by an onyx crystal like the one the hard-faced leader now fondled tenderly. Jayben Tavadar sat like a person at a play in the front row, her hard thin mouth stretched in a sinister smile as she waited for the inquisition to begin.

Mayven's attention was caught by the voice of Amalayna's inquisitor. Mayven's eyes were riveted on the onyx crystal he now held only inches from Amalayna's thin throat.

"If you tell the truth, the pain will stop. How did your parents die? Did you kill them? Did you poison them and make them ill?"

Amalayna stared up at the man silently. He pressed his lips together in a thin smile then touched the crystal to Amalayna's throat. Amalayna screamed.

Mayven was so busy lending her strength to Amalayna, she wasn't ready for the pain that assaulted her mind. The crystal was hot against her neck, but it was nothing compared to the mind-scorching pain in her head. Claws tore at her brain, and Mayven could feel the presence of something dark and cruel inside her mind. It tore at her, ripping through memories as they flashed before her eyes and instantly Mayven understood the danger. She closed her eyes and clamped down her mind, focusing on only one thing; the face of the man in front of her. She memorized every line, wrinkle, scar and discoloration in his face. She focused on it so hard that soon the pain in her head was almost nothing.

Then the hard-faced leader stopped. He stared at her, his eyes prying into hers, trying to figure out how Mayven withstood him. When his eyes slid slowly up to her forehead, a flicker of something flashed through his eyes, and Mayven felt fear slice through her like a knife. He studied Mayven's face for a long moment and turned to face Jayben Tavadar.

"Why does this one wear the headband?"

"She is a deformed one. I don't want my eyes offended by her deformity," Jayben Tavadar replied.

"Did you check her forehead yourself? You, of all people, should be aware of the xohdieha we are looking for. I hope you would not, in your zealousness to insure putting each child in their proper place, overlook such an important inspection."

Mayven's eyes locked on her feet, afraid that if they saw her face, they would see her fear as she waited an interminable amount of time. At length, Jayben Tavadar reiterated, "I checked. The child is deformed. She has no xohdieha. I make her wear the headband as a mark of shame."

Mayven felt a sudden flash of magic assault her. Jayben Tavadar had lied. She had broken the first rule of magic, and magic was trying to make Jayben Tavadar's lie the truth. Powerful magic sent burning pain into Mayven's head. Mayven closed her eyes and clenched her hands on the arm of her chair as she resisted the magic that assaulted her mind and body, trying to change reality to make Jayben Tavadar's words the truth. At length, the burning stopped and Mayven, exhausted even more under the assault, sat trembling in terrified anticipation of what would happen next.

"Obviously it is her deformity that protects her from my questioning. She has no magic, so that means she could do nothing to cause her family's death." The hard-faced man's mouth turned up in a mocking smile. "Perhaps they died of shame. I know I would if my child were born deformed."

Mayven clamped down on her tongue, the wish to retort almost overwhelming but then Amalayna's screams began anew. Mayven concentrated hard on Amalayna, trying to provide her with protection from her inquisitor. The longest hour of Mayven's life was being forced to watch Amalayna undergo the inquisition while she sat helpless in the audience. Ignoring the exhaustion that already made every muscle in her body tremble, Mayven used her magic to help Amalayna withstand her inquisitor. Forcing her eyes open, Mayven stared unblinking at Amalayna and transferred strength through herself from the tree and into Amalayna. When at last the inquisition was over, Jayben Tavadar was nearly crowing with delight as Mayven and all the other children marched across the yard, their faces pale and features streaked with tears.

Mayven, her body weak and exhausted, was now the one being supported by Amalayna.

CHAPTER TWO

Varn glanced quickly in the mirror as he raked his fingers through his long copper locks, trying to get the waves to conform to some semblance of order before he had to meet with his uncle. Giving up, Varn tied back his hair, using the four small braids hanging down from either side of his face, fastening them into an intricately made silver clip at the back of his head. The braids, each one representing a year of service as a master mage in the historians' guild, now contained the rest of the thick, shoulder-length waves.

More points lost with the coach. Uncle Demok had best have a good reason requiring me to blow off a professional maygis team practice. Varn gave his uniform a brief once over, deciding that the rumpled state of his royal purple tunic and less-than-pristinely-pressed breeches would have to do. Grabbing his gym bag from the bench beside him, Varn raced out the door of the locker room and burst through the wide double doors of the gym, housed in a collective of aspen trees, as he ran toward the lot where his driver stood next to a pod car.

"Laydak," Varn acknowledged.

Laydak nodded, spoke a single word, and the side of the pod split open. Varn stepped inside the vehicle, taking a seat next to the man waiting for him, his expression grim. A moment later, Varn felt the tingle of magic over his skin as the pod car began to move. Throwing his bag down on the seat beside him, Varn turned to his companion. "What news have you heard? What has Uncle Demok so excited?"

Varn's companion gazed back at him, his dark eyes filled with a mixture of excitement and dread. His wide full lips set in a grim line, making the lines around his mouth stand out.

Varn raised a brow. "I assume you know something, Arrok?"

Arrok's chiseled mahogany features remained grim as he crossed thick muscled arms across his broad, deep chest. "We've located Payin. We think we may know the location of the Language Master."

"Why are you not ecstatic at this news? I don't understand?" Varn's knees bounced, drumming his heels against the floor.

Arrok sighed. "Payin is dead. She can only be one of two places, and we have tracked Payin back to his residence. She wasn't there."

Varn's mouth went dry with fear. His legs stilled. "Can we intercept her before she is delivered to the orphanage?"

"We are heading over to meet your uncle Demok. He is supposed to let us know if they were successful." Arrok leaned forward, elbows on his knees, and looked up at Varn.

Tension curled up Varn's back and shoulders. From the corner of his eye, Varn watched his best friend's massive shoulders roll restlessly as he, too, wrestled with tension. Though considerably shorter than Varn, Arrok's solid, muscular build, wide shoulders and stocky frame gave him an intimidating presence, even without the benefit of height. Varn watched as Arrok repeatedly traced a finger across one dark eyebrow.

"Has the governing council heard the news yet?"

Arrok turned to face Varn. "I saw them call in three of the top Gayied captains. There may be some news. Kalohdak is surely notified by now."

Varn rubbed at his neck as he turned to stare out the window. "Now it's a race to see who finds her first. We need to control this situation. Does Uncle Demok have any ideas yet?"

Arrok shook his head, and the car fell into silence.

At length, the car pulled up in front of the guild house. Varn, without pausing as he customarily did to admire the twelve-story maple tree, rushed through its open front door and followed the curving hallway three doors to the left. Walking through the office door, Arrok close at his heels, Varn jammed a button on the keypad to lock the door as it closed behind them. Varn didn't take a seat, instead leaning a hip against the wide desk growing from the floor.

Arrok, sitting in a chair at the front of the desk, thumped his heel against the floor nervously. Demok stood behind the desk, back to Varn and Arrok, as he talked in clipped sentences on his engaohnie. Varn massaged the tightness in his neck. *Ordinarily I go to this office to relax and unwind.*

Varn often found refuge in his uncle's office. The floor was the only space in the room that was free of the clutter of memorabilia from some outing or adventure. The walls were lined with shelves of pictures with Varn and Demok, Arrok and Varn, and even his sister Layla and her husband Hardak. Knick-knacks seemed to occupy every square inch of shelving in the room.

However, if one looked close enough, they would notice that what appeared to be knick-knacks were artifacts, some very rare and valuable. Varn gently pushed a rather ancient scroll out of his way as he raised his leg to rest his thigh across the corner of the desk.

At last, Demok ended his call and turned to face them, his normally cheery countenance pale. "I have news, but I can't say it's good. Arrok, I need you to go and control whatever information you can filtering into Kalohdak's lieutenants. Varn, you need to get to the orphanage. It appears the Language Master has already been taken there. She is young and unaware of the power she possesses. If frightened, she could use it in such a way as to identify herself. We need to activate our operative at the orphanage. We won't be able to get her out if she is already checked in."

Demok paused for a long moment.

"I need you to activate your ability. Actively seek the Language Master. It will form a connection to her. You unfortunately will then, as you already know, be aware of and even feel all she feels. But your gift, while revealing her to you, conceals her from everyone else who seeks her and protects her from others using magic against her. As a seeker, it is your gift, and curse, but we need a way to be certain she is safe."

Varn paused, searching his uncle's gaze for a long moment, finding sadness momentarily present in his normally lighthearted gaze.

"You have always forbidden me using my gift to find a person for that very reason. Because it connects me to them intimately. Why now?"

Demok planted his palms flat on the desk and stared down at the hard surface for a long moment before standing erect again and looking Varn in the eyes. "I never wanted you to feel the connection in case it could cause you pain. Now we have no choice. If she is being harmed, we must know. If others are using magic against her that could harm her, she has to be protected. The only way to do that all the time is through your magic and by connecting you to her. She is, unfortunately, out of our reach for now. We have to ensure we don't lose track of her again."

Varn shot a glance at Arrok, who returned his look with a raised brow but said nothing. Then, in unison, Varn and Arrok started for the door.

Demok's voice stopped them both in mid-stride. "The Gayied have been notified to interrogate every orphan who is brought into the orphanage. The Shimiera government believes that they are the cause of this spreading illness. I'm sure Adamdavas and Kalohdak are behind that assumption. I need you both back here tonight."

"Is there time to get there before the Gayied do?" Varn swallowed hard, his mouth suddenly dry.

Demok nodded mutely.

"I will keep her safe, Uncle. You work on a way to get her out of there. Contact Shayrok and let him know I'm on my way."

Varn took his car. Arrok jogged to the transportation station on the corner as they exited the guild house. Questions filled Varn's mind. *She needs training. If she is imprisoned in an orphanage, how is there any hope for our world?*

Varn felt the minutes tick by, feeling more like years with their leisurely pace. The orphanage came into sight, and Varn's heart sank, *Why didn't Payin just listen? There is no need to send this child to such a place. How will she survive this?*

The desolate landscape made his heart ache. When he stepped out of his car, it was all he could do not to race up the walk to the main hall but he managed to remain in control as he sauntered to the school building. Entering into the building's wide entrance, he made his way down the hall two doors to the right. Varn stepped through the door of the school room and was immediately confronted by a wide desk at which sat a middle-aged man with warm brown eyes. In the semi-circular room, the desks and seats were arranged auditorium style beyond the desk and the topmost row had wide oval windows that were set in horizontal to the floor at the top of the room.

Varn didn't bother with pleasantries as he took a seat on the edge of the desk. Leaning in close, his voice barely audible, he asked, "Where are they holding the interrogations?"

Shayrok Tamada's round pleasant features and slightly balding head usually gave the short man the look of a jolly professor, but know his face was marred by horror and sadness. "In the auditorium next door."

Varn nodded with satisfaction. "Good, that is close enough to be able to tune in on the Language Master. Have you seen her yet? What does she look like?"

Shayrok nodded. "The payjik who brought her in called her Mayven. She has been singled out already. She wears a headband. The head mistress, Jayben Tavadar, is convinced it is because she is deformed. Jayben Tavadar thinks she is without magic."

"Jayben Tavadar won't think that for long if I can't conceal Mayven's use of magic. I need to concentrate fully. You need to see that no one comes in."

Shayrok nodded and removed himself from his seat, offering it to Varn. Shayrok stepped to the door, listening intently for sounds coming from the hallway as Varn sat down. Varn closed his eyes, tuning out awareness of all things around him and concentrated solely on that he wished to find the Language Master. Varn rejected his usual ways of connecting to the object he was hunting. He had never seen her, so he could not concentrate on her face. He had never studied her, so he could not link to her through knowledge or understanding of her ways.

Varn simply connected through sensing her magic. He closed his eyes and concentrated on the most powerful magic he could sense in the room beyond the wall. When Varn found Mayven, the touch of her magic was raw and powerful. The attracting force of her magic was like a magnet that pulled Varn from his seat and had him leaning against the wall, his palms pressed into the smooth surface and forehead resting between them. The pull toward Mayven was so intense Varn felt his muscles vibrating with tension as he struggled to remain unmoving. Every fiber in his body wanted him to rush out the door and into the auditorium next door.

Instead, Varn focused his mind on one thing only, tying his adamie to that of the faceless, mysterious Language Master on the other side of the wall. Varn felt the connection settle into him like a line being tied to his chest and anchoring itself somewhere in the vicinity of his ribs near his heart. Then he felt a surge of power feed back through the line and knew he had set the connection just in time.

The power of the magic Mayven used felt like volcanic heat radiating across his skin, scorching him alive. The physical pain was so intense Varn barely controlled the urge to scream. Mayven was using an immense amount of magic. Varn felt the line connecting his seeking ability to Mayven's magic vibrate as it channeled the magic she gathered and used through him to its intended destination, effectively concealing its true source. Varn, unused to the vast amount of power coursing through him, felt Mayven's adamie light his every nerve ending on fire. Varn crumpled to the floor, his palms still pressed to the wall and tears streaming down his face.

Shayrok started to step away from the door but Varn waved him back. The longest hours of Varn's life were spent that afternoon on his knees, struggling not to scream. Varn couldn't think or breathe, he could only exist in a world of scorching pain. The magic Mayven used had to go somewhere. Varn understood that hiding her meant he served as the conduit for her power instead of it coming directly from her. But it took him longer to realize he could use that same power to boost his own abilities.

Varn scoffed at himself as at last the scorching pain eased. *I should have thought of that earlier.*

As if sensing Varn was at last in control again, Shayrok asked, "Is it over? Have the Gayied finished?"

Varn shook his head grimly. "No, it just took me a while to handle the feed back. I'm afraid the Gayied are being very thorough."

Shayrok's shoulders slumped. "Unfortunately they always are."

Varn stood on shaky legs. "I should go. She is protected. Test her tomorrow, warn her. It is all we can do for now."

Shayrok nodded mutely as he stepped aside and let Varn exit. Moments later, as Varn was leaving in his pod car, he watched Jayben Tavadar exit the school at the head of a line of children. Varn averted his eyes, though the pull of his magic was almost overwhelming.

Varn groaned as he struggled against the pull toward the object he was seeking, *To find her now leaves her unprotected,* Varn repeated to himself like a mantra as he ground his teeth with effort.

The further he traveled from the orphanage, the less intense the pull toward Mayven. However, Varn could still feel Mayven's physical exhaustion. When Varn once again stepped into his uncle's office, he poured himself a drink of Iresta and slumped, exhausted, into a chair.

"Did you make it in time?" Demok questioned.

Varn raised a weary brow. "She is as protected as my magic can make her, but now I have to avoid that orphanage. To see her means I have found her. Only as long as I'm seeking her can I remain the conduit for her magic and her shield. Seeing her releases my protection. You will have to be the liaison to the orphanage now. Shayrok will need you."

Demok nodded and leaned back in his chair as he stared out his office window. "Varn, you may find her time at the orphanage difficult for you. She is going to go through a lot. Orphans are never treated well."

Varn studied his uncle a moment. "You couldn't find a way to get her out?"

Demok sighed, avoiding eye contact with Varn. "I tried, but how would it look to adopt a deformed child in our position? Furthermore, who would believe a family member would claim her if she were deformed?"

Varn ejected himself from his chair. "You're telling me she has to endure that woman and that place for two years?"

Demok sighed. "It's unfortunate she is not with us now, but she will still be useful. She may learn a lot while she is there. There is a reason for everything, Varn."

Varn's hands clenched, his gaze locking with Demok's. "Is that what she is, a thing to be used? She is a child." Varn began pacing, his mind occupied with every speech he had ever heard about his duty to destiny and suddenly old resentments flew from his lips. "I can't believe this! You are so blinded by your desires for what you believe destiny has planned that you don't even try to help her. You just let her stay there and say it's for her own good?"

Demok faced Varn, his arms crossed over his wide chest above his slightly protruding belly. "I never said it was for her own good. I said I couldn't get her out."

Varn snorted. "You didn't have to. Isn't that always the reason you accept defeat so easily?"

Demok raised a brow but didn't respond to Varn's accusation. "I think you need to take over the duties at the hospital. Volunteering there is our best listening post for what is going on. The casualty list is growing. I have been noting a trend. I started recording the xodiehas of the patients who are dying and the surviving family members. I need you to review the list and see if you notice anything."

"Trying to distract me won't work. What are you up to?" Varn demanded.

Demok's mild expression altered, his brows drawing together as he pulled himself erect, his paunch flattening and face flushing. "I'm not distracting you. I need to be the one to deal with the orphanage and that means you need to deal with what I have been doing. I've already sent the information I gathered to your engaohnie. We have to track what is going on."

"Mayven can't help us until she has been through hsmakda. So we should just get on with business as usual, no need to concern ourselves with her problems, is that it?" Varn winced, the sound of his teeth snapping together loud in his ears.

"I am not oblivious to what she will go through. But, practically speaking, we have to know what we are up against and what we will need her to help with first. I don't have time for your tantrums. No one is being mistreated. Things are simply what they are, and we must do the best we can." Demok stepped around the desk and into the middle of Varn's path. "Since being at the orphanage will require you to come in contact with the Language Master at some point, you must now do what I was doing. Helping out at the hospital. This is not a request, Varn."

Varn stopped pacing inches from Demok and nodded his head with a jerk. "Yes, sir. But she has a name you know. Her name is—"

Demok raised a hand to silence Varn as Arrok stepped through the door. "Even if you know her name, I think Arrok shouldn't know."

Arrok nodded in agreement with Demok. "I work far too closely with those who are searching for her. It is best if I know as little as possible."

Varn ground his teeth, knowing his uncle was right but resenting being silenced, so he changed the subject. "What did you find out?"

"I overheard enough to know that they didn't find her." Arrok stopped next to Varn, planting his feet wide apart and crossing his arms over his chest.

Varn heaved a deep sigh, his hands raking through his hair and knocking it loose from the clip that held it in place. "Do they suspect she is anywhere in particular?"

Arrok shook his head. "I think we're safe."

Varn looked down at his feet, contemplating the events of the day. Sleep was not going to come easily tonight.

Arrok stepped away from Varn, headed to the door. "I need to get back to the council hall. Kalohdak declared a state of emergency. Everyone is supposed to be searching for her. I can't be missed."

Varn grasped Arrok's hand firmly as he embraced him with his other arm. "Thanks, my friend. Be careful."

Arrok gave a rueful smile. "I always am. It's you I worry about." Then with a brief wave to Demok, he left the room.

Varn, once again alone with Demok, announced, "I am going to the hospital for a short while tonight. I have a friend who works there and can begin to gather some information. I don't foresee much sleep tonight."

Varn ignored the look of concern that flashed across Demok's face and, before Demok could question him further, he left the office and returned to his car.

A short while later, Varn entered the hospital housed in another group of aspens not far from his gym. He made his way inside and past the front desk in the wide foyer. The floor was the smoothed tangle of white, bark-covered roots of the aspens. The walls, inside and out, were the joined trunks of the aspens. The roof, like his gym, a net of branches curved together above them that supported the domed ceiling constructed of clear hardened plant fiber known as ktelpie. Through the clear ceiling, a view of the twin moons hovering in the early evening sky overhead could be seen through the movement of the aspens' quaking leaves.

Varn, absorbed in his own doubts, paid little heed to the remarkable engineering and beauty of the natural design of the hospital as he headed into the depths of the maze of hallways created by the joined trunks of the largest grove of aspen in Rashmahava. Instead, his mind was consumed with finding Karshadem. Though he had proclaimed that he would work this night, Varn acknowledged inwardly that it was a need for some reassurance that his faith was not misplaced that brought him to the hospital this late. *I hope he has answers, a way to help me see Dso-hoay's plan in this disaster.*

The thought raced through Varn's mind, leaving him shaking with the memory of scorching pain and the overwhelming feeling of fear. Varn shook his head to clear his thoughts and proceeded at a faster pace down the long corridor to an office the size of a large closet. Without knocking or asking entrance, Varn stepped into the small room and found his friend leaning back in a chair, casually sipping a large, steaming cup of pahfie.

Karshadem greeted Varn with a warm smile. "I'm glad to see you."

Varn, accustomed to Karshadem's knowing attitude, did not acknowledge his friend's greeting and instead launched directly into the issue that scorched him to his very soul. "Dsohoay is a loving and merciful God, is he not?"

Karshadem smiled indulgently as he leaned forward and set his mug on the desktop in front of him. "You know the answer to that, Varn."

Varn's mind flashed back to earlier that evening. "Do I? I say it because I have been taught that, but how do I reconcile what I've been taught with what he allows? I have no idea how to justify this latest travesty, Kar."

Kar laced his fingers together as he rested his arms on his desktop, his eyes searching Varn's face. "What has brought about this crisis of faith, my friend?"

Varn dropped his gaze from Kar's, resting his head in his hands as he too leaned on the desk. Taking a steadying breath, Varn launched into a brief description of the night's events. When at length Varn's voice trailed to silence, Kar leaned back in his chair, his face etched in sadness and understanding. For a long time, no one spoke, Varn began to wonder if Kar didn't possess an answer either.

"It's easy to blame the workings of Hsdaie on Dsohoay. We so often see Hsdaie in our world far more than we pay attention to Dsohoay. It is our nature to see the bad, the dangers, and the horrors of our world. Those instincts have allowed our people to survive but they work mightily against our faith, eroding it to nothing for those without the foundation of a deep and abiding relationship with our creator."

Varn, heaving a sigh, started to speak, but Kar silenced him with a raised hand. "Hsdaie is in this world far more than Dsohoay, not because Dsohoay doesn't care, but because we are a fallen, broken people and hate to be reminded that we are capable of horrible things. When our lives are examined under the light of absolute goodness, we all fall horribly short. Because of that, we avoid searching out Dsohoay's comfort and council. We cut ourselves off from the author of our lives and make it easy to view life's tragedies through a hardened eye."

Varn interrupted. "I don't want your platitudes, Kar. I want to know why these things are allowed. Dsohoay could change it all with a simple word and yet everyday people are suffering and dying in pointless misery. How is that able to be reconciled with a loving and just god?"

Kar regarded Varn with quiet dignity and unruffled calm. "What is allowed is what we choose. If the choices, choices made of free will, should impact others and cause pain and harm, those choices cannot be unmade. Dsohoay will never take our free will. He can minimize the damage done or use the situation to bring about understanding or a closer relationship with him through that event but he will never mitigate a choice made of our free will. Hsdaie is the author of our pains and tragedies. Dsohoay, in his goodness and mercy, makes those pains and tragedies bearable by using them to draw us to him or by using them to guide us to our true destiny. We have narrow vision, Varn. As mortals, we love, live, and envision our lives as all there is to creation, but there is a much larger picture and its strokes are much broader than the small marks our lives make on that canvas."

Kar reached across the table, grasping Varn's forearm in a kind but firm grip. "However, all the little strokes of our lives, good or ill, make up those broader strokes. We can't know where all our tragedies and misfortunes fit into the bigger picture. It is a test of our faith to find reassurance in his unchanging nature in order to believe that Dsohoay will never let the evil that works in this world prevail."

The room faded into silence for a long time as Varn stared into Kar's serene countenance. Varn studied the lines of the aged and beloved features on the face before him, acknowledging that not all those lines were created by age. The scars of more inquisitions by the Gayied than Varn could count glowed pale against Kar's weathered features.

Varn sighed. "You have more faith than I. You have lived through horrors I can only imagine and yet you never get discouraged in what you see going on around you. I want that, Kar. I want to know that there is a reason for all this. I want your certainty. I need it."

Kar took another long sip of his pahfie before he replied. "I still question Dsohoay, Varn. But faith allows me to understand that I can't know all the reasons why until I am reunited with him. To find my certainty and faith, you must first seek out and cling to that which you want to have faith in. That is a journey that is never easy. You have long had a child's faith. Now you are being called to grow that faith to that of an adult. You are being asked to extend that faith to include things you can never understand. You are being asked to trust that all things will work to the good of our creator and the only one who can give you that faith is the creator himself. To gain that faith, you must seek out Dsohoay. You know where to find him. I am honored that you seek my guidance, but your questions can only be truly answered by the one whom you are questioning."

Varn straightened in his chair, heaved a sigh of resignation and changed the topic. "I am now taking over Uncle's job here at the hospital. Would you mind going over the information he has gathered so far?"

Kar regarded Varn for a long moment in silence then, accepting his change of topic, began to review the details of Demok's work. Several long hours later, Varn left the hospital and traveled back to the guild, his mind occupied not with the details of his new assignment but with the weightier issues of his initial conversation with Kar.

Varn lay in his room, staring at the ceiling.

"What is the purpose of this, Dsohoay? Why is she still so young and our world failing so fast? Why is there no way to free her from where she is? What is the purpose of her suffering under the hand of Jayben Tavadar?"

Varn's questions fell into silence. *I am questioning the one I want to understand and he remains silent. Doesn't a relationship have to be two ways?*

Then in answer to Varn's verbal and unspoken questions, a small brilliant white ball appeared in the air above his bed, bobbing, as if on some unseen breeze, between the end of his nose and the ceiling above him.

From the small ball of light, a voice like that of a crystal bell spoke into the silence of Varn's room, "Yes, a relationship has two ways, but you have had the *road closed* sign up. Dsohoay doesn't knock down road blocks unless asked to."

Varn regarded the Nifen, Dsohoay's tiny messenger, with vague unease. "I have not told Dsohoay not to speak with me."

Peeling trills of laughter like the sound of many tiny bells filled the small room before the Nifen replied, "But you have not invited him to speak either. Dsohoay does not barge in. That is bad manners. He only goes where he is invited. You have now sent the invitation, and I am here to relay his answers to your questions."

Varn sat up so abruptly that the Nifen bounced off the end of his nose as the sheet that covered him pooled around his waist. Varn felt a scowl tighten his features as he stared at the tiny ball of light. "Well, what is Dsohoay's answer?"

The Nifen brightened. "There are many ways to answer those questions. The first is, she chose to be there. She went willingly with the payjik who transported her there. It was her free will."

Varn interrupted the Nifen, his tone harsh with anger, "She had no idea what she was going into. She has been protected her entire life. Couldn't you have intervened on her behalf?"

The silence stretched on for a long time as Varn stared at the Nifen until his eyes began to water.

"Free will is free will. Dsohoay says he will never interfere. When she is ready to call on him? He will come."

"She may not even know him, and if she does know of him, she may be unaware she can call on him or that she should. How is this good?" Varn threw his hands up, letting them fall with a thump into his lap.

The Nifen became more brilliant, its light now filling the room.

"All things work toward the good of my people. What will come of any of her choices will be for the good of my people."

"And what of her? Will she just be a tool you use to get your ends or does she matter?" Varn questioned.

The Nifen blinked out, leaving the room in darkness, making Varn temporarily blind as a booming voice seemed to echo through to the center of his bones, "None of my children are forgotten. I am with her, even if she doesn't know me."

The silence that followed left Varn uneasy as he laid back down to stare up at the ceiling, his eyes now adjusted to the dimness of his surroundings. Varn eventually drifted to sleep, his dreams haunted with the bright bouncing figure of a Nifen that kept asking him riddles he couldn't answer.

CHAPTER THREE

Mayven forced her body forward one heavy step at a time as she followed Amalayna into the dormitory that would be their sleeping quarters. The room was a semicircular curve along the outside wall of the tree on the fourth floor. The narrow flat platforms that served as beds grew up from the floor, looking more like tables than the dish-like bed that Mayven had in her home with Payin. Next to each bed were a pair of hooks. The beds where someone already slept had threadbare towels hanging from each of the hooks. No other personal items adorned the living quarters, and the occupied beds were neatly made, though the ancient blankets and mattresses did nothing to make the beds look more inviting.

The line in front of Mayven stopped.

"These are your sleeping quarters. Choose a bed, and it will be yours until the day you leave this home." Jayben Tavadar turned to stare down at her newest charges. "You will make your bed each morning after you rise. You will be up promptly at five each morning and in bed no later than ten sharp. You will address all other adults here as mistress or master."

Jayben Tavadar marched up and down the long room as she spoke. She didn't look at any of the children but instead at some vague point far above any of their heads. "You are never to have any contact with the boys except at meal times and during work and if you are given a rest period during lessons. Tonight is the only time you will ever be in this room before nine. The empty beds have bedding and a pillow folded at the bottom of the bunk."

Jayben Tavadar stopped in front of Mayven, her booted feet just at the edge of Mayven's lowered gaze. "I suggest you take advantage of this privilege. You will begin your lessons to earn your keep tomorrow."

When Jayben Tavadar's feet had left her line of sight, Mayven followed Amalayna to two unclaimed beds that sat side by side at the back corner of the room and they began to make their beds. Stretching their threadbare sheets over the ancient, flattened madra pod mattresses, they paused when Jayben Tavadar spoke again.

"If you don't succeed at your lessons and cannot earn your keep, you will be dealt with severely. I suggest you all keep that in mind."

Once the door was closed behind Jayben Tavadar, all the children gratefully collapsed onto their beds, pulling their thin blankets up over them and falling almost instantly asleep. Mayven, however, carefully hung her wet towel and wash rag on the hook by the bed and tucked the soap up under the mattress.

Though exhausted, Mayven remained awake, staring up at the ceiling for a long time, wondering why Payin had thought this was the best place for her.

It was dark outside when their dorm mistress roused them from sleep and marched them all to breakfast. After breakfast, they were lined up and marched across the barren dirt yard to the neighboring building inside another giant oak and delivered to their school master.

Mayven watched the school master as he stood in front of the class and assigned them each their seat. He was short, round, and slightly balding, but his manner was warm. Mayven instantly liked him.

When he came to her at last, he glanced at her headband only for a brief moment then, with a smile, pointed to her seat. Once everyone was in their place, he turned to the blackboard.

The blackboard hung on the wall in a frame that had been grown from the wall of their living building. The school master wrote on the board in a broad flourish. "My name is Master Tamada." He turned to face the class, a genuine smile brightening his features. "Where you are all sitting is where you will sit every day until I assign you to your apprenticeships. Apprenticeships begin when you are old enough to speak the oath of hsmakda. There are some of you who will reach that age sooner than others. Depending on your aptitude, even if you are of age, you may be kept back until your abilities are trained enough for apprenticeship."

He walked down the center row all the way to the back of the class where he stopped next to Mayven. She breathed in the smell of fayen fruit and fresh-baked bread.

Mayven smiled. *I think I just found my new favorite smell.*

"All of you, however, will be here a minimum of two years. You must know, understand, and be able to use the basics of adamie—magic, as the uneducated call it."

Class began with the basics; adamie had three types. Adamha, natural magic, used by all living plants and animals on Emwen. Adamie, speaking magic, used by their race, the Hato. The third was adamsah, singing magic, used by those Hato working with their trade.

They learned the guilds, their uniforms and structures and how each of them would be tested for their talent to know which guild they would serve. Mayven was most interested in the levels in the guild.

Unlike society, the guild didn't care if you were an orphan. You advanced according to your talent and your service. If you were talented and hardworking, even as an orphan you could become a Master Mage in service to a guild.

Mayven went to break, her mind reeling with delight. She marched in line behind the other children around the yard's perimeter as she reflected on every conversation about school she'd had with Payin. *Why did Payin forbid me from going to school? I could have found a way to serve in a guild and made money to make him well.*

Sadness overwhelmed Mayven, sealing her throat with a lump as she blinked back tears. It was the touch of Amalayna's thin hand that brought her back. Mayven smiled as Amalayna danced around her.

"Mayven, I don't know what you did yesterday, but I feel fabulous!" Amalayna jumped up and down, her booted feet raising dust in the yard as she hopped in a circle around Mayven. "You must not be too deformed. You even healed my feet."

Mayven's arm snaked out, and her hand snapped closed like a trap on Amalayna's wrist. Mayven yanked Amalayna to a stop at her side.

Glaring into Amalayna's silver eyes, Mayven said between clenched teeth, "Will you please keep your voice down? I don't need the attention. I would like to live to get out of here too."

Amalayna paled, making her naturally dark skin look ashen as she whispered, "I'm sorry, Mayven. I didn't mean to be so loud."

Mayven kept a tight grip on Amalayna's wrist and marched her around the back of the building out of sight of everyone. "I don't know what my gift is. I don't know my talent. I seem to be able to do a lot of things. But I was taught that the magic I can do will get me killed."

Amalayna's dark skin turned a paler shade of gray.

Mayven continued, "I have a xodieha, but I can't show it to anyone."

Mayven stared at the younger girl's face a moment, then, taking a deep breath, she released her wrist. "I shouldn't have told you that. You knowing could get me killed if you tell anyone. I have to trust you now, Amalayna."

Silence stretched between them for a long moment then Amalayna shrugged before hugging Mayven with thin bony arms. "I guess I better not say anything then. Hey, what is that boy doing?"

Mayven followed her pointing finger to find a boy who sat hugging his knees and rocking. Walking toward him, she heard the sound of his quiet sobs grow louder as the chime on the clock tower from the center of town marked the hour of nine bells.

"Why are you so upset?" Mayven inquired as she knelt next to the boy.

From his size, Mayven had guessed his age to be close to that of Amalayna. When he looked up, however, the mustache on his upper lip said he was older. Crystal blue eyes regarded her with a wary expression.

Mayven reached out and wiped tears from his dirt-streaked face. "Why are you crying?"

The boy hiccuped before answering in a cracked tenor, "I have to take my apprenticeship test today. It's the third time I've taken it. If I don't pass this time, I'll disappear like all the others who don't pass."

Mayven's brow furrowed, and she looked over at Amalayna. Already Mayven knew that Amalayna seemed to get the way this place worked.

"Why would he disappear?"

"I don't know, it's just what happens." Amalayna shrugged, looking at the boy with pity. "No one knows where the kids go who don't pass, but they are never here when morning comes."

Mayven sighed. *Why does everything have to be so unfair? There has to be something I can do.* Anger made her teeth clench. Her hands trembled as she took the younger child's hands in hers. Looking into his eyes, she said, "You'll do just fine on your test. Calm down. Have faith in yourself. You know enough to pass, and tomorrow you will be off to your apprenticeship."

The air around the three seemed to crackle, and adamie curled around Mayven like a blanket as she felt it race up through the soles of her feet, tingling across her body and then flowing like warm water from her hands into the boy she wanted so desperately to comfort.

The boy's clear blue eyes grew wide as he stared at Mayven.

She smiled back at him. Then, rising from her knees, she helped him to his feet and wiped his face with her sleeve. "Now you'll be fine. Do you believe me?"

The child nodded mutely as Mayven continued, "What is your name?"

"Xietak."

"Well, Xietak, come and find me after school and let me know how your test went."

The boy's mouth trembled but he smiled and then raced around the corner. Mayven smiled also but her smile quickly faded as Amalayna yanked on her sleeve. Mayven turned to face the child and found silver eyes boring into hers.

"Why bother asking me to keep a secret for you if you are going to help every sad story in here? How do you know he won't tell someone what you just did? What *did* you just do?"

"I don't know what it is I did. I just spoke to him and assured him of his abilities. I don't know what it does. I just know that if I talk to people it seems to help."

Amalayna shook her head. "You'd better stop that. It won't take someone long to figure out it's you. It never does."

Mayven felt a chill run down her spine at the younger girl's words, then shook it off. "Are we late for class?"

Amalayna slapped her hand against her forehead. "We're in trouble now!"

The two girls raced back to the front of the school and through the front doors. As they took their seats, all eyes were on them. Mayven felt the scrutiny worst from Master Tamada. Putting her head down, she stared at her desk. He cleared his throat then carried on with class.

"I have a quiz. This is one of several that you will take while here. These quizzes serve as a way to gauge your talent so we can place you in the proper apprenticeship."

He handed out crystal tablets. On the screens were several lines of writing. "Please write your answers on the paper I provided you. I need you all to translate these. If you can't, please leave the corresponding line blank."

Mayven twirled her stylus absently in her hand as she stared at the page of writing in front of her. Her eyes read along the lines slowly at first as she tried to sort out the meaning of the letters. Then, like a puzzle piece finally snapping into place, she understood and quickly wrote down on her own paper what the text on her crystal screen had said. This was the fourth test of this type, and she had passed all of them. But this last one had been the only real challenge, and she was the only one who understood it.

Proud of herself, Mayven folded her interpretation as instructed and handed it back to Master Tamada when he came for it. Mayven felt relieved she had passed the test. The bell rang for lunch, and everyone filed out of the room. Mayven was about to follow the rest of the class when she was stopped by Master Tamada.

"Mayven, may I speak with you a moment?"

Mayven felt fear settle into her stomach as she stopped at Master Tamada's desk.

He looked up at her, his features drawn into a deep frown. "You wrote this, did you not?"

Mayven looked at the paper he held in front of her and re-read the lines she had written and nodded. "I did."

A sigh escaped her teacher's slightly parted lips. "Please close the door and take a seat."

Mayven felt her stomach knot as she slowly crossed to the door, placing her hand against the panel on the wall and closing it. She then returned to a desk directly in front of Master Tamada and sat down. He slowly got to his feet and, circling his desk, leaned against the front.

His arms crossed over his chest, and his eyes burned into Mayven's face a long silent moment. "I am sorry that you are here. Sorrier, I think, than you will ever know."

Mayven felt the knot in her stomach grow and the urge to race for the door built like a tidal wave that drew every muscle in her body into taut watchfulness.

"You've translated something that only one person in every generation is ever able to translate. Your talent is huge and unique, and now I know the real reason you wear that headband. You have a talent with languages."

Mayven suddenly felt sick as bile rose to her throat and her eyes darted to the door. She glanced back at Master Tamada and then the door again.

Master Tamada raised a calming steady hand. "I don't wish to harm you. I want to warn you. You must never again translate the language I gave you today. Translate every language given to you but never that one. If anyone, including me, hands you anything with that language on it, pretend you cannot read it. Do you understand?"

Mayven froze as confusion entered her mind. Her eyes searched Master Tamada's and found nothing but concern etched in his warm brown gaze. The knot suddenly dissolved, and she nodded slowly in acknowledgement.

"I will periodically have to hand out these tests; sometimes in front of Jayben Tavadar. You have now seen and gained a knowledge of this language. You know how it feels when you see it. Is that correct?"

Mayven nodded again, afraid to speak.

"When you are presented with this language by anyone, claim ignorance of it. It's for your safety. You will be able to get an apprenticeship because of your talent but this language must never be translated by you. Now, because I kept you after class, I will tell Jayben Tavadar it was because you were late. Which is true. You were."

Mayven nodded again.

"You will receive a punishment. Take it without complaint and never mention the conversation we just had to anyone. One more thing, Mayven, watch what you say to others. Your words, more than anyone else's, carry the most powerful of adamie."

He stepped forward and crouched down in front of her, looking up into her face. "I know what you did for Amalayna and for Xietak. One other teacher and I have been watching for someone like you a very long time, so we can protect you. She noticed the change in Amalayna and Xietak. She questioned him when he passed his exam."

Mayven's hands began to shake at Master Tamada's last sentence, and she clenched them into fists in her lap to conceal it.

Master Tamada laid a gentle hand on her shoulder. "You have nothing to worry about. Xietak didn't say what you had done. My friend guessed more from his change in behavior, and Amalayna's sudden health. However, you must learn to harden your heart in this place. Most of those you will meet here are broken and so beaten that they will do anything for anyone to gain more for themselves. You must learn not to be so eager to help or to trust. Do you understand?"

Mayven listened to his words that so closely matched what Amalayna had said and felt her heart sink to her feet as she nodded slowly.

"Mayven, please don't be upset. Take the two you have helped under your wing. You have gained loyal friends for life with the kindness you have shown them. I know because reading others is my talent. But as much as you may want to, don't ever do for anyone else in here what you did for them. It could mean your life. Do you understand? Can you trust me enough to listen?"

Mayven blinked back tears and breathed in the smell of fayen fruit and bread. "Yes, Master Tamada. I understand."

He smiled at her kindly, then patted her arm. "Now out to your friends. I think Xietak has something he wishes to tell you very badly. I will make sure everyone thinks I was scolding you. Please don't mention anything else, ever."

Mayven smiled at him and rose from her chair. Master Tamada walked her to the door and, with a kind smile on his face, whispered low, "Look like you were just in trouble."

Mayven lowered her gaze and tried to fix her face into a sad expression as Master Tamada opened the door, saying loudly, "Don't ever be late for my class again. Is that understood?"

Mayven didn't look up at him but nodded mutely as she stepped into the hallway. Just outside the door, Amalayna stood with Xietak in tow. Once Master Tamada had left them, Amalayna turned to face Mayven.

Xietak spoke first, his voice cracking even in a whisper with his excitement. "I passed my test. I don't know how you helped, but you did. I start my apprenticeship in a few days, as soon as they find someone who will teach me."

Mayven smiled. "I'm glad. I know you will do very well. You are very talented. You just need to believe in yourself."

Mayven felt adamie race over her skin with the few words of encouragement she had just given, and Master Tamada's words came racing to mind. "Xietak, I am glad you are getting out of here. But you must never speak of me or anything I may or may not have done to help. It is very important, okay?"

Mayven waited anxiously for the span of a heartbeat but Xietak just smiled. "I promise your secret is safe with me. I won't forget you either. If you both will try and meet me at break times behind the school, I'll bring you food from my apprenticeship whenever I can. You have saved me. I will do whatever I can to help you."

"You take care of yourself." Mayven wrapped an arm around Xietak. "We'll be fine. It won't take us long to get out of here."

"I believe that." Xietak smiled at her, his eyes full of teasing laughter. "But you do realize you are probably the oldest orphan in the place. How old are you anyway?"

"I'm not sure."

Xietak and Amalayna both regarded her with raised eyebrows, saying in unison, "And you hadn't already found an apprenticeship before you came here?"

"I was never allowed to go to school."

"Oh," was Amalayna's and Xietak's joint reply.

The three walked out into the afternoon's stifling heat and straight into Jayben Tavadar.

"You are to meet me in the yard after class," she announced, her eyes bright with malice, then marched off across the yard on long gangly legs.

Mayven spent the rest of the day quiet and contemplating the punishment she would receive. Jayben Tavadar would relish a chance to find fault in her, Mayven had no doubt in that.

When the last bell rang, everyone exited the school and were stopped in the yard. The students were lined up with the newest orphans in front and each class in succession behind them. Mayven was placed in the center of the front line.

Jayben Tavadar stared down her long thin nose, a hard tight line where her mouth had been and eyes gleaming with delight. She motioned for all the teachers to line up, facing the children in the yard then began to pace between the two, her head swiveling to face first the children then the instructors.

"It has come to my attention that my orders have been ignored. I made my wishes," she paused directly in front of Mayven and pulled her from the line of students by the collar of her shirt, "regarding this abomination clear. You are not to assist her or aid her in any way. She is to either fail or succeed on her own." She paused for effect, her eyes raking first the students then the teachers. "Anyone caught assisting her in any way answers to me."

Mayven suddenly felt sick. Her stomach lurched to her throat as she forced her face to remain impassive. The collar of her shirt pulled tight around her neck as Jayben Tavadar yanked her around to face the line of instructors. The sudden lack of oxygen in Mayven's lungs had nothing to do with Jayben Tavadar's death grip on her collar; instead it had to do with the pair of warm brown eyes locked on hers from the line of instructors she now faced.

"I will not tolerate any of my instructors not reporting when this child interacts with any other student in this school." Jayben Tavadar's voice rose an octave as anger and disgust dripped from each word. "I expect an honest and full report of her daily activities." Jayben Tavadar yanked Mayven around again to face the other students. "This girl is an abomination, filthy, disgusting, and lower than any other orphan here. She is so low she must hide her deformity with this headband." Jayben Tavadar pointed at Mayven's headband with a trembling finger. "I don't want this abomination to taint any of you other children. I want all of you to succeed and make the best you can of your lowly position in life."

Jayben Tavadar's voice changed from harsh to entreating. "Associating with her will damage any chance you will ever have. Please listen carefully. She is not to be helped or comforted in any form by any of you."

Mayven watched the faces of the other children and saw eyes glittering with anticipation, all except Amalayna and Xietak. Mayven shuddered in realization as the words of Master Tamada raced through her mind once more. *You must learn to harden your heart in this place. Most of those you will meet here are broken and so beaten that they will do anything for anyone to gain more for themselves.*

Mayven was yanked around to face the instructors one more time as Jayben Tavadar's voice once again changed to cold and threatening. "It appears that I must make an example even among my instructors. You must also be educated on how conniving and insidious this child is. She can get to even the most loyal and dedicated among you."

Jayben Tavadar released Mayven's collar then stepped in front of Master Tamada. "I am sorry you were seduced by this child."

Jayben Tavadar's voice, now sweet and laced with regret, didn't match the cold delight displayed in her narrow gaze. She crooked a long thin finger at Master Tamada and he stepped forward, his warm eyes focused squarely on Jayben Tavadar's narrow face.

Mayven swallowed hard and clenched her tongue between her teeth as she waited to see what vile thing Jayben Tavadar would do next. The wait was short.

Jayben Tavadar called forth a student from the graduating class. He marched through the ranks of the students, his broad shoulders shoving others from his path. His face displayed haughty arrogance and wide cruel lips curved in a smile as he stopped in front of Jayben Tavadar.

Jayben Tavadar smiled warmly at the student, and her voice was laced in pride as she addressed her audience. "This young man is an example to you all. He has passed his apprenticeship test on the first try and has been accepted into the Gayied. The city guard has gained a valuable member who will do very well."

Then Jayben Tavadar turned cold eyes on Master Tamada. "I'm sorry you must be singled out, however, you didn't advise me properly of your student's wayward activities. I cannot have even a loyal teacher such as yourself be swayed by her vile ways."

Mayven's stomach lurched as Jayben Tavadar's cold fingers curled under her chin and tilted her head back. Mayven lowered her lids to avoid looking into her eyes.

Jayben Tavadar's voice hammered at her fraying nerves as she said coldly, "You may look at me this time, girl. It is the only time you may do so. I need you to see I mean what I am about to teach you."

Mayven opened her eyes and stared up into the cold glare of Jayben Tavadar.

"I am teaching you a lesson you will need to remember for the rest of your miserable existence." Jayben Tavadar's breath fanned Mayven's face. "You can expect no aid or quarter from anyone. You are alone in a way none of these other children will ever know. I am preparing you for the real world, and one day you will thank me for it." Jayben Tavadar's voice rang with superiority and pride. "So you need to pay close attention to what happens to those you influence to help you. It's your hands that are dirty with their suffering."

Jayben Tavadar released Mayven's chin, and her bony fingers dug into Mayven's shoulders as she held her in place. Mayven stared wide-eyed at Master Tamada as he faced the student Jayben Tavadar had called forward.

Mayven felt Jayben Tavadar's hot breath on her neck as she hissed into her ear, "You should feel shame that you caused such a good man to suffer. He is far better than you. Watch how low you have brought him." Addressing everyone, Jayben Tavadar pronounced, "I want you to see the remarkable talent of this fine graduate, and the consequences should anyone else aid this creature before me."

With a nod from Jayben Tavadar, the student spoke three short words, and Master Tamada crumpled to the ground, his eyes wide and lifeless.

Mayven's control snapped, and she yanked from Jayben Tavadar's grip and spun to face her. "You didn't need to kill him."

Jayben Tavadar's cruel face lit up as if someone had granted her a wish. "You now will see what a real talent can do. I told you never to speak in my presence, did I not?" She looked at the young man she had called forward. "Teach her a lesson."

Mayven suddenly felt fiery pain engulf her entire body. The pain seemed to dive inward through her skin and coalesce in the pit of her belly. Mayven crumpled to the ground and clutched her stomach as shrieks ripped from her throat until it was so raw she could no longer make a sound.

The students stared at first in delight, but then even the harshest among them began to send questioning looks at Jayben Tavadar as Mayven continued to writhe silently on the ground. The teacher's faces were impassive, but several sets of eyes flickered with pity as Mayven's torture continued.

Jayben Tavadar, realizing the tide was turning against her, released Mayven with a wave of her hand then turned slowly to eye each of her audience individually.

"This world is harsh," she said, her voice soft and laced in regret. "The lessons I must teach are sometimes harsh, but I teach these lessons for your benefit." Jayben Tavadar waved a dismissive hand in Mayven's direction. "And for hers. Everyone has their place. It is best you learn now to stick to your own kind, where you belong." Jayben Tavadar addressed Mayven, her voice kind, her eyes icy-cold. "I think you have learned your lesson. Get up, clean yourself, then report to the cafeteria for dinner."

Mayven struggled to her feet and staggered toward the orphanage as Jayben Tavadar continued to address her captive audience. Mayven, still in shock, ran shaking fingers over her skin. Though every nerve still screamed that her flesh was seared to cinders, she was relieved to find her body physically intact. Mayven stumbled to her cot and retrieved her soap and towel before stumbling into the shower room. Without removing her clothes, Mayven stepped into the shower stall near the faucet and, cranking it open, stood face upturned under the pounding icy water for several seconds before bathing her clothes and herself.

Mayven's breathing tore at her raw throat as, beneath the pouring faucet, she let the tears she couldn't shed in public course down her face. She supported her weight on her arms as she leaned against the shower wall and felt the cooling warmth of the living building flow into her body and soothe her ravished nerves. Mayven drank in the strength, grateful for the healing that coursed through her, glad that even Jayben Tavadar could not stop the buildings from doing what they could to support the lives they sheltered.

As Mayven's senses returned to normal, she stood erect quickly, realizing that if she returned to the cafeteria completely healed, Jayben Tavadar would be suspicious. Mayven exited the shower and used her thin towel to dry her clothes.

Walking into the cafeteria, still damp from her shower, Mayven took her place at the back of the line. When it was her turn to hold out her bowl, she was surprised to find that tonight she had a full serving of food. Mayven looked up at the server from beneath lowered lashes and mouthed the words, "Thank you."

Taking her seat at her solitary table in the corner, Mayven kept her eyes lowered on her food and ate in silence. Mayven silently hoped

Jayben Tavadar was done with her lessons for today. Her hope was dashed as Jayben Tavadar stood up from her table in front of the cafeteria.

"You all now witness how well behaved the abomination is. She can learn. Please, children, don't make it necessary to educate her or any of you on this again. When dinner is done, I want everyone to report to their head mistress or master for your nightly chores."

Mayven stared at her now-empty bowl and waited until last to go forward and deposit her bowl in the pile. As the lowest in rank, Mayven's daily chore was the dishes. It was not hard work, just dirty and monotonous and it took every minute until the bell sounded for lights out.

The monotony gave Mayven plenty of time to relive her first day in her new life. Mayven's heart ached with sorrow, at times her grief causing tears to fall into the dishwater. She knew now in vivid clarity what Master Tamada had meant; she could trust no one. She had to guard Amalayna now with extra care and make it seem as though they were not friends. As Mayven carefully put away the last of dishes, she sighed deeply as she silently ticked off another lesson learned; hardening her heart was going to be very difficult.

Exhausted, Mayven stumbled her way up the stairs to her dorm and sank gratefully into her cot next to Amalayna. Without a word, Amalayna laid a tiny hand against Mayven's arm, and they both drifted to sleep.

CHAPTER FOUR

V arn sat in Kar's office at the hospital, going over the day's casualty list. The illness was spreading far beyond the reaches of Rashmahava or even the borders of Shimiera. Kar was busy relaying reports he had received from Lirie and several other nations that indicated the same alarming information. People were dying by the hundreds, and there seemed to be no cure.

Kar waved at the screen on his desk. "Every report is the same. The government here, in Shimiera, has created the myth that orphans are causing it. However, the truth is the balance of adamie has begun to shift too far toward the control of Adamdavas."

Varn raked his hands through his hair. "How long can this go on before the damage is irreparable?"

Kar sighed. "I don't know."

Varn recalled his conversation with the Nifen the night before. "I went to the source. I questioned Dsohoay, but I didn't get any answers. The Language Master still has two years before she is of age. Then she has to figure out how to correct this mess. Do we have that kind of time?"

Kar shrugged, his scarred face lined with worry. "I can only have faith. I don't know the answers."

Varn snorted. "Admit it, you're worried—"

Varn's sentence was cut short when his words stopped and were replaced by a strangled scream. Varn looked frantically down at his hands to see if he was on fire. His senses were suddenly consumed in pain, as if someone had doused his entire body in acid that was scorching through his every nerve.

Taken completely by surprise, Varn now lay on the floor, his body curled into a ball as he screamed. Varn tried to reason where the pain was coming from. He tried to find something to distract him as he wondered if this was what it felt like to die from the sickness ravaging his people. Time seemed to stop, frozen in one horrible, unending moment of agony, and it took Kar placing a hand carefully on his shoulder before Varn registered that he felt something besides pain.

Kar's arms curled around Varn's shoulders as he gently lifted him from a puddle of his own vomit and urine. Varn barely registered the words Kar spoke as he struggled upright. "Varn, I had to silence you. You started screaming. I called Demok. He is going to check on the Language Master. You need to get up and go with your driver. I have to clean up in here before someone starts asking questions. Do you understand?"

Varn nodded mutely and struggled to his feet. He shook his head, trying to clear it but the sudden movement made him dizzy. Varn planted a hand against the wall to steady himself. Taking a slow breath, he looked down at his filth-covered attire.

Kar opened his office door to let in Laydak.

"Do you have my gym bag in the vehicle?" Varn inquired.

Laydak nodded and exited the room as Varn, grasping the chair's arms for support, slowly sat down. Moments later, Varn's driver reappeared and Varn looked up. "Thank you, Laydak."

Varn quickly changed, his body still weak and unsteady as he struggled into his gym clothes. Varn exited Kar's office and stepped out the side door next to the closet that served as Kar's office. In the alley, Laydak opened the pod vehicle and Varn stepped in, collapsing into the seat as he mumbled, "Take me back to the guild house."

The words had hardly left his mouth before he slid sideways into the seat, unconscious.

Varn felt a nudge on his shoulder and opened his eyes to see Laydak looking down at him. "We're here, Jayben."

Varn nodded and exited the vehicle. "I'll not need you the rest of the day. Thank you."

Laydak nodded and, returning to the vehicle, drove off. Varn turned and faced the guild house. Taking a deep breath, he walked through the doors and into his office. The afternoon was spent compiling the information he had gathered from Kar. When at last Varn had it organized, he opened the two lists side by side on the crystal display on his desk.

Varn scrolled through the reports as dread created a knot in his stomach. The obvious direction his research was taking him sent chills down his spine. Varn pulled up the first report and ran a finger down the list, his eyes scanning the names and abilities of each person on the list labeled *deceased*. Varn then pulled up another list next to it labeled *surviving family members*. He examined them side by side and compared the talents associated with the survivors against those of the deceased.

Varn sighed heavily. *The conclusion is inevitable. Those who survive have the greater gift of adamie. They require more adamie to survive and so more is taken from those who are weaker.*

The door to Varn's office opened. Looking up, Varn greeted Demok with a grim smile. "I have news, and it isn't good."

Demok sighed heavily as he took a seat. "That makes two of us then."

Varn raised an eyebrow as he took in his uncle's expression. Demok's usual bright gaze was filled with sadness, and the lines around his eyes and mouth deepened with sorrow instead of the usual easy laughter. Varn asked, "What happened?"

"After Kar called me about what happened to you at his office, I assumed it had to be something to do with the Language Master so I went to the orphanage. Shayrok was murdered by a student at the orphanage under orders from Tavadar."

Varn rose from his chair, circling it to reach his uncle, then laid his hand on his uncle's shoulder. "I know he was your oldest friend."

There was a brief silence before Demok continued, "There is worse news. Tavadar did it in front of the entire orphanage. She blamed Mayven, saying he aided her."

Demok shifted in his seat, his hands clenched in fists on his knees. "Tavadar was notified by the Gayied that someone was protecting Mayven's group from interrogation. Tavadar discovered that Shayrok was in his classroom at the time and blamed him. In order to keep in good standing with the Gayied and Adamdavas, she made an example of Shayrok. The added bonus was blaming it on Mayven, then torturing her when she spoke out against Tavadar. Her torture is what you felt this afternoon in Kar's office."

Varn closed his eyes, taking a slow breath before asking, "Is she all right?"

Demok made a sound halfway between a laugh and a groan. "I suppose she is as all right as anyone can be who has been tortured and forced to watch a murder."

Varn stepped away from his uncle and slammed a fist on the top of his desk. "Is there nothing we can do to get her out of there? We need her safe, and we need her trained. I spent the afternoon reviewing the reports from here in Shimiera from Kieshan and at least six other nations and it's all the same. Our people are dying, those with the weakest magic first. It's like the stronger adamie is drawing too much away from everyone else and those who are weaker are just wasting away. We don't have two years to wait."

"I feel your desperation and frustration." Demok sighed, then stood and rested a hand on Varn's shoulder. "My comfort comes in knowing Dsohoay has perfect timing. What must be done will be done when it is the proper time."

Varn spun to face Demok, his anger and confusion boiling over. "I don't have such peace on this subject. Men, women, and children are dying by the hundreds and you say Dsohoay has perfect timing. I would think perfect timing would involve not letting people needlessly die and suffer. Especially the one he has ordained to fix this awful mess."

Demok closed his eyes, the pained expression on his face making him seem every day of his age and more. Varn felt his conscience pain him and was about to apologize when Demok spoke again. "I know that it is hard for you to understand. It is for me also. However, faith is what will see us through. There is a purpose behind what happens here. Time is not up until we all have breathed out last breath."

"I suppose if there is only one of our people left when the prophecy is fulfilled it is still enough." Varn's momentary twinge of conscience was forgotten. "Well, that's comforting. I suppose we should all be grateful."

Then, without letting Demok respond, Varn marched out of his office, leaving the guild house and heading for the gym, not bothering to call Laydak, whom he had given the afternoon off.

CHAPTER FIVE

The next day, before lessons started, Mayven snuck behind the school and spoke briefly with Amalayna. "I have to stay away from you, Amalayna. I'll not have you be Jayben Tavadar's next lesson for me. You're never speak to me in public or acknowledge I exist. When you meet with Xietak, you must tell him the same."

"I'll risk it, Mayven," Amalayna stated, her features resolute. "You're my friend. I won't abandon you!"

"Amalayna, listen to me," Mayven pleaded as she grabbed her by the shoulders. "We can find secret ways of talking, but everyone is watching and listening. You have to appear like you don't know me. You have to treat me in public like everyone else. In two years, we'll be out of here and it won't matter, but for now I don't want you to talk to me. Ever."

Amalayna looked up at Mayven, her wide silver eyes brilliant with wisdom beyond her years. "You're brave and right, too. But be warned, us acting like we aren't friends will only make Jayben Tavadar a little less hard on me. She knows you have helped me before. She will try to make you want to again."

Mayven nodded and sighed heavily as grief and loneliness suffocated her. Then she gave Amalayna a quick fierce hug. "But a little of her harassing you I can handle. Watching her kill you to teach me another lesson, I could not."

Amalayna gave her a bright, slightly fierce smile. "So then we are a secret society of two who must hide our friendship in public. I like it! I feel like a secret agent."

Mayven smiled as her friend gave her a jaunty salute and turned on her heel and marched away without looking back. Mayven waited until the bell sounded for class to follow around to the front of the school and file in behind the others. When she walked into her classroom and saw Jayben Tavadar at the teacher's desk, she was grateful that Master Tamada had not set Amalayna anywhere near her.

The first order of business conducted by Jayben Tavadar was the translation test. The only language she presented to the class was the one Master Tamada had insisted Mayven never translate. She had listened to his warning and stared blankly at the screen like the others, though what it said rang clearly in her mind.

There is one who will come and reveal the lies. The truth will set us free.

Mayven stared at the cryptic message for the full ten minutes given to complete the task, fascinated with what the obscure passage could mean. When Jayben Tavadar collected each of their boards, Mayven kept her eyes lowered.

"Well, it's obvious you're of no importance," Jayben Tavadar pronounced upon finding her slate empty as all the others.

This became the mantra for everyone regarding Mayven. She sat through class each day, absorbing every ounce of knowledge she could glean from her lessons, while to Jayben Tavadar and the students she seemed not to exist.

Mayven struggled daily to ignore Jayben Tavadar singling out Amalayna over and over. Then, at night, when the rest of the dorm was asleep, Mayven and Amalayna would share silent conversations in sign language before falling asleep.

Months passed, Jayben Tavadar stopped baiting Mayven by tormenting Amalayna. She decided, based on Mayven's lack of reaction, that Mayven had apparently lost interest in protecting Amalayna. It also helped that Jayben Tavadar discovered Amalayna was a very powerful transportation mage and would eventually bring her great credit. However, for Mayven, the torture continued unabated. Young children new to the orphanage seemed drawn to Mayven, and she found it difficult to convince them to stay away from her until one out of the new children would be singled out to teach Mayven a lesson. When at length Jayben Tavadar got bored with that game, there were always extra chores of the vilest nature that needed to be done and often Mayven went to bed long after the other children.

It soon became a rare thing for Mayven and Amalayna to have any silent, late-night talks. Though, thankfully, Jayben Tavadar had decided Amalayna was no longer a way to torture Mayven, she still found ways to pick at Mayven that left scars on the heart Mayven could not seem to harden enough not to care about those around her.

Jayben Tavadar seemed to know instinctively how best to try and break Mayven. On one particular morning, the opportunity that presented itself at last put the final callous over Mayven's battered heart. The chores had been assigned for the day and, because today was the teachers' off day, the students were given assignments to last all day. Mayven was assigned the nursery.

Mayven gratefully entered the section of the orphanage all the other children avoided. The others hated caring for and cleaning up after the tiny, wailing waifs. Mayven hummed to herself as she finished the last of the baths for the infants and toddlers and began gathering bedding to wash. The children, now in the play area, were confined to play pens or huddled in groups to entertain themselves, as the dorm mistress ignored them. Mayven quickly collected the linens and headed for the laundry area. On her way back, she encountered Jayben Tavadar.

Mayven's voice instantly fell silent at the furious expression on Jayben Tavadar's face. The familiar cruel fingers latched onto Mayven's shoulder and marched her into the nursery, where Jayben Tavadar confronted the dorm mistress.

"Why is this urchin humming? What have you done to make her life so enjoyable she is happy about it?"

Mayven watched fear instantly blossom in the dorm mistress' eyes as she replied, "I've done nothing. Perhaps she has finally learned to accept her station, Jayben Tavadar."

Jayben Tavadar's fingers dug even more cruelly into Mayven's shoulder. Then, from between clenched teeth, Jayben Tavadar pronounced, "I would think she would have the decency to be properly humble and silent and not inflict anyone with the knowledge of her presence if she had truly accepted her lot in life. Wouldn't you agree, mistress?"

Mayven watched a fleeting flicker of pity in the mistress' eyes disappear under a hard mask. "I would think she would have learned by now, Jayben Tavadar."

Jayben Tavadar's voice became soft as she stated, "You take the rest of the day off. I will oversee this abomination for the rest of the day and see if I can't get her attitude properly under control once and for all."

Mayven felt fear coil in her stomach as she looked around the nursery. *Surely even Jayben Tavadar wouldn't hurt one of the infants.* Mayven instantly decided that no matter the provocation she would be as silent and remorseful of her existence as possible in order to protect them.

Jayben Tavadar's hot breath fanned Mayven's cheeks as she leaned closer and whispered, "I want you to go to each of the children and write their name and the clan they belong to, according to the xodieha they are marked with. Then I want you to bring that list back to me."

"Yes, Jayben Tavadar," Mayven stated, surprised she had kept her voice steady.

A short while later, Mayven placed the list in Jayben Tavadar's outstretched palm and surreptitiously watched as she reviewed the list, then walked around to each child to verify Mayven's notations were correct. *She wouldn't want to harm an orphan who could elevate her status.*

Mayven felt rage nearly choke her as she struggled to maintain her composure. Jayben Tavadar came back to stand in front of Mayven moments later and proceeded to outline her list of duties for the rest of the day. When Jayben Tavadar finished speaking, Mayven began to work, keeping her eyes downcast to hide her fury.

Mayven's neck ached and her head throbbed from the tension as the morning dragged by while Jayben Tavadar scrutinized even Mayven's tiniest actions. Mayven refrained from comforting or soothing the children, terrified that if Jayben Tavadar were to decide that Mayven favored one of them what may happen to them. In the end, however, her caution was for naught. Mayven had made it through the majority of the day and was beginning to hope she might escape from Jayben Tavadar's scrutiny without incident.

"I see you do this job with care. You leave nothing undone or half finished. You take pride in it. That leaves me to wonder which of these poor children have fallen under your wicked sway." Jayben Tavadar spoke from behind Mayven, her hot breath stirring Mayven's hair. "I've watched all day. You have made sure not to favor any of them, however, I think you do. I think you favor them all. I think you hope to raise them up to follow you. You want them to be corrupted to believe that you matter. So you make them all feel kindness toward you. I think it's time I changed that."

Mayven kept her expression carefully blank but her heart continued pounding like the wings of a caged haeden bird against her ribs. Fear for the children's safety snaked down Mayven's spine as she kept her eyes properly lowered to the floor.

Jayben Tavadar's long fingers snaked out and clamped cruelly around Mayven's jaw, forcing her chin up. "Look at me!"

Mayven prayed her eyes did not betray her fear as she opened them to look in the glacial narrow gaze of Jayben Tavadar. The cruelty reflected there sent ice to the core of Mayven's being as she waited for the pronouncement that would undoubtedly harm one of the innocent children in Mayven's care.

Jayben Tavadar stared down at Mayven for a long silent moment. Then her mouth curved into a smile that somehow made her expression even more sinister. Releasing Mayven's chin, Jayben Tavadar reached out a hand and nonchalantly pointed at an infant in the bed next to them. "Get me that."

Mayven wanted to scream, *Child, she is a child*, but with supreme effort remained silent as she gently lifted the sleeping girl. The infant curled against Mayven's chest, her cheek soft and warm in sleep.

Jayben Tavadar looked down the length of her long nose. "Beautiful, isn't she? Shame that she is so unwanted, so unnecessary to life as to be in this orphanage."

Jayben Tavadar squared her shoulders and raised her chin in a righteous tilt. "I am simply trying to protect you and all the other children here. You must learn. You have no place in society, you have no future but to serve others, and you must learn to accept this and expect nothing more. However, in your service, you must not seek to ingratiate yourself to those you serve or have them thankful to you. You must understand it is simply your place and station, nothing more. Hand me the girl."

Mayven's hands clenched protectively around the infant in her arms as she instinctively took a step backwards. Jayben Tavadar's hand snaked out and landed with a resounding slap against the side of Mayven's head, making her vision blur and ears ring. The other children, startled by the noise, woke with a start as the room began filling with the sounds of their cries. Jayben Tavadar yanked the child from Mayven's arms.

Mayven reached out to the girl, who was now crying hysterically at the rough treatment, and Jayben Tavadar spoke in a cold authoritative voice, "You all will be silent, still, and watch."

Mayven felt the compulsion of Jayben Tavadar's voice roll over her and the magic that bound Jayben Tavadar's words lock her mouth closed and her eyes open. Mayven stood frozen in place, her arms outstretched toward the child in Jayben Tavadar's arms. The infant stared back, her expression locked in a silent terrified scream as tears spilled from unblinking eyes.

"I have tried to be gentle with you, Mayven," Jayben Tavadar cooed, her voice silken and her eyes cold. "I have tried less hurtful and difficult ways to demonstrate my point about your position in life. Your refusal puts what I must do next squarely on your shoulders. I want you to understand this and take it in. You will forever be responsible for what I must now do to get you to understand your proper attitude and place in life."

Mayven felt sobs she could not voice strangling her as she fought with all she had to free herself of Jayben Tavadar's commands. Just as Mayven felt the bonds begin to slip, Jayben Tavadar pronounced her sentence. "This child should never have existed."

Mayven felt the magic in the room that locked her and all the other children in place rebound and coalesce around the child Jayben Tavadar held at arm's length. Simultaneously, the terrified screams of the children erupted into the silence, and the child in Jayben Tavadar's outstretched hands vibrated violently for several seconds, then disappeared.

Mayven's knees gave out as bile filled her mouth and the contents of her stomach emptied itself onto the freshly washed floor.

"Silence!" Jayben Tavadar roared above the cacophony.

The room once again fell silent as she reached down and yanked Mayven to her feet.

Mayven let her body hang limply in Jayben Tavadar's grasp as Jayben Tavadar spoke in a low harsh tone, "You will clean up your mess, get these children back to sleep, and never forget what can happen to anyone you think you can influence. I will be watching you every moment of your miserable life here. I had best never see you so much as smile at anyone in this orphanage again. You now know what words can do, and I have no problem demonstrating the point again."

Jayben Tavadar released the collar of Mayven's shirt, letting her fall into the puddle of her own vomit before turning on her heel and exiting the room. As soon as Jayben Tavadar was gone, the room erupted into terrified cries once more. Mayven spent the rest of the evening calming down the children and getting them back to sleep. When the mistress of the infant dorm returned, Mayven noticed that she didn't remark on the now-empty bed.

Mayven took careful note and learned her final lesson from Jayben Tavadar—life is fleeting and fragile and the right words can make you never exist at all. The callous over Mayven's heart was fully in place. She went about her duties with a robotic and stoic resolve. She closed her heart away, determined never to let anyone else suffer because of her. It worked very well.

Soon, no one ever even took the time to try and hurt her. It was as if she didn't exist at all. Mayven never spoke, looked, or smiled at anyone in the orphanage again. She spent her days diligently pursuing her studies and her nights lying in her bed, silently signing to Amalayna. In daylight, she never acknowledged that Amalayna existed. Jayben Tavadar was convinced.

Jayben Tavadar, having taken note of Amalayna's extraordinary gift with teleporting, was soon promoting and favoring her. Mayven acted as if she didn't notice. Amalayna took it all in stride and, whenever possible, passed on the benefits to Mayven in the form of extra food. Amalayna now could come and go without so much as a passing interest from Jayben Tavadar, so convinced was Jayben Tavadar of Amalayna and Mayven's separation.

The shift in Jayben Tavadar's attitude toward Amalayna was a relief to both Mayven and Amalayna, making it much easier for them both to meet occasionally in secret behind the school with Xietak. He brought them food and small gifts of warmer socks or shirts they could wear under their baggy attire. Mayven watched as Amalayna and Xietak grew closer with each passing day and smiled each time he brought her a gift.

Mayven always left them early on some made up premise or another so that Xietak would have time with Amalayna in private. Then, as winter began to change to spring, Mayven noted a subtle change begin in Xietak. He still came and visited often and his devotion to Amalayna was still slavish, but his conversation was darker and laced with a fear Mayven could almost taste.

"I think tomorrow I would like to spend a few moments with Xietak alone," Mayven said to Amalayna after one of his visits. "I think something is wrong, and he is afraid to tell you. Perhaps he will tell me. Would you mind if I spoke to him for a while before you came to meet with him?"

Amalayna signed back, her eyes wide with gratitude. "I'm glad you noticed. I was going to see if you could speak with him. He is changing. I don't think I like it either."

Mayven nodded and signed back, "Tomorrow then. Goodnight, little sister."

Amalayna smiled back and signed, "Goodnight, sister."

Mayven laid staring up at the ceiling long after Amalayna's breathing had slowed to a quiet steady pace. Mayven sighed as again her last conversation with Payin flitted across her mind, and she wondered if Niesha was ever coming. Mayven turned on her side and watched Amalayna's sleeping face as she went over again how she would take Amalayna and Xietak with her when they asked her to leave.

The next morning, before school, Mayven slipped unnoticed behind the school and met with Xietak. He stood in the dark shadows where the stone fence met the towering bulk of the schoolhouse.

Xietak's eyes studied the yard behind Mayven. "Where's Amalayna?"

"I asked to speak with you alone a moment, Xietak. I hope you don't mind."

Mayven watched relief flicker across his face for a brief second. "I'm glad you did. I needed to tell you something, but I didn't want to scare Ama."

Mayven felt tension curl up her spine, leaving a dull ache at the base of her skull. She waited anxiously as Xietak gathered his thoughts before he spoke again.

Taking a deep breath, Xietak looked into Mayven's eyes. "It turns out my gift is in high demand. Whatever you did for me on the first day I met you released my ability and it has impressed my guild leaders. I've moved up fast in the ranks at the guild."

Mayven smiled brightly. "That's good. I'm glad for you."

Xietak's eyes became frantic, his face stark with fear as he insisted, "It is and it isn't good. I have access to information others don't, which is good. It's bad because now I know more of what is going on, and I don't know how to help you."

Mayven's brow wrinkled in confusion. "Me? What about me?"

"I'm a technology mage now. My gift is the ability to manipulate magic to make new technology. They have been having me work on a tool that will harness the ability to detect a person's gift in a device. It's the same talent Master Tamada had. The device will be able to test people and discover their talent. They have been using this gift on women, girls, and girl infants."

Mayven felt a knot forming in her stomach as the import of Xietak's words settled in her mind.

Xietak was pale, his lips trembling. "They know who they're looking for is female. They are linking this to some prophecy they have discovered, and they are going to start testing more of the population as soon as the device has finished the first test phase. They're looking for a woman who can translate the most obscure languages. They call her a Language Master."

Xietak was trembling now, his face ashen. "I tried to build in a flaw but every time it has been discovered. Thankfully, they don't know I'm the one creating the flaw." Xietak looked at her, his eyes pleading and filled with desperation. "You're my family. You and Amalayna are all I care for in this world. I can't believe my gift is going to harm you. I promise I'm trying to find a way to stop this but before I knew what they were having me create, I had nearly finished it. I'm so sorry!"

Mayven took Xietak's hands in her own. "Do what you must to save yourself. I'm good at taking care of myself. Don't put yourself at risk for me. Someone has to be able to look after Amalayna, and I know you love her. Do what needs to be done. I'll figure something out, I promise. Besides, they will never look at an abomination."

Mayven felt adamie curl around her body and travel through her palms to Xietak.

"I'll not let you command me to abandon you." Xietak guarded himself against her magic. "Not after all you've done for us. I'll find a way to fix this." Xietak pulled his hands from Mayven's and a smile instantly created a mask over his face as he looked over Mayven's shoulder. "Hey there, Ama. I thought you were standing me up today."

Mayven watched Xietak and Amalayna a brief moment as Xietak forced lightness into his conversation. Then she turned from them and quietly blended back into the milling crowd in front of the school.

Mayven didn't reveal all of what Xietak had told her to Amalayna, agreeing that Amalayna needed to be protected. As the weeks and months passed, however, it was obvious that Xietak changed more with each meeting. Mayven continued to meet Xietak alone, trying to reassure him that everything would work out fine. Each time, her reassurances seemed to calm him but then he would return the next time even more agitated.

Varn

CHAPTER SIX

Two years of constant connection to Mayven was exhausting. Every day, Varn fought his nature not to go to her. Even when sleeping, his dreams were haunted with finding her. Never was there relief from the constant connection that tugged at him. Every day, some new pain was inflicted on her that he felt.

Mayven's most intense suffering bled through her emotions and left him aching to comfort her. Distraction had become his only relief. Maygis practice and games for Shimiera's professional team, his duties as instructor at the guild, and working with Kar kept his days full. At night, there was no distraction. Often, Varn found his dreams haunted by a faceless woman begging him to save her.

Just such a dream woke Varn tonight, his body drenched in sweat and heart pounding in his chest. Varn rubbed the palms of his hands in his eyes, trying to dispel his latest nightmare. Then, the sound of the bell on his room door drew his attention.

Varn stumbled from bed, blindly searching for his engaohnie to unlock his door. Through sleep-blurred vision, he tapped the unlock button. Varn's door slid open, revealing Demok standing in his doorway, a wide smile wreathing his weathered features.

"You're not allowed to look so cheerful. I haven't even had my pahfie yet." Varn staggered to his bed and collapsed into the thick mattress nestled in the dish-shaped frame growing from the floor of his room.

Demok laughed heartily and stepped through the door, letting it close behind him.

"I brought you pahfie." Demok held out two steaming mugs.

Varn sat up and gratefully accepted his mug, cradling it in his palms as he breathed deeply of the savory aroma wafting from the cup. One scorching sip later, Varn looked up at his uncle.

"What brings you here so early?" Varn eyed his uncle's cheery expression warily. "And what've you got to be so abominably happy about this early in the morning?"

Demok leaned a hip against the small writing desk across from Varn's bed and took a careful sip of pahfie. His eyes studied Varn a long moment then took in the rumpled bed. "Mayven sits for her apprentice-ship exam today. I thought you would like to know."

Concern flickered across Demok's face as he took another long pause while sipping from his mug.

"You haven't been sleeping well?"

Varn followed Demok's glance at the disheveled bed and, catching a glimpse of his face in the mirror at the bottom of the bed, noted the gray shadows beneath his eyes. "You could say that."

Demok stepped forward, clasping Varn's shoulder with one hand. "Well, hopefully today will end that. You get ready for the day. I cancelled your appointments and got a substitute for your class today. I assumed you would want to pick up our newest apprentice yourself."

Varn looked up at his uncle and found himself almost on the verge of tears. Relief flooded through him like a tidal wave. Varn lowered his chin to his chest and took a deep breath.

Demok squeezed Varn's shoulder once more. "I'll see you downstairs then."

The door closed silently, and Varn rose from the bed and headed to the shower.

A short time later, Varn sat quietly in the back of his car, watching out the window. Every moment brought him closer to the orphanage and the pull from Mayven grew more intense. Anxiety made his heel drum against the floor of the vehicle. When the orphanage at last came into view, Varn had to take a slow breath to calm down.

The buildings hadn't changed much from the last time he was here. The yard around the orphanage was still hard packed and barren. The children marching in lines across the yard still looked either beaten or hardened into cruelty. *I wonder which one she will be, beaten or cruel?*

Varn exited the car and went to wait with the others guild mages who had come to retrieve their new charges. The wait was interminable. Then, at last, Jayben Tavadar stepped into the foyer to announce that they were free to go and interview the graduates.

Varn filed down the curving hallway behind the others and watched as they stepped into the classroom where the graduates waited. *Two years of waiting are about to be over, and I don't know whether to be happy or vomit.*

Varn felt her on the other side of the classroom door like a magnet. He felt like he knew her as well as she knew herself and yet he was nervous to meet her face to face.

Varn shook himself mentally. *Get a grip. She's just a child. She doesn't even know that I know all she's been through. This isn't some lovers' reunion.*

Taking a deep breath, Varn stepped through the classroom door and instantly his adamie indicated who she was. She sat arrow straight in her chair, her lashes lowered and hands folded in front of her, yet from her came an energy that vibrated along their connection so fiercely that he was astonished no one else noticed it.

Varn felt her scrutiny intensely, though she never looked directly at him. When he called her name, she rose from her seat and calmly proceeded him from the room.

Varn walked silently toward the interview room, his senses acutely attuned to the girl who trailed behind him. He felt adrenaline racing through his veins, making his heart pound. The excitement of finding the object he was seeking always left his with an adrenaline-induced high. But instead of the customary release of connection he had longed for over the last two years, the adamie that linked him to Mayven had changed. He no longer felt the intense pull toward her. Instead, he sensed an awareness of her emotions, as if he could almost read her mind. Varn stood aside at the interview room door and let Mayven pass in front of him. When he stepped inside the room, the door slid seamlessly back into place as he motioned for Mayven to take a seat.

He studied Mayven's slight form. Lack in her life was written all over her. Mayven was tiny, as were most orphans from lack of good nutrition, her clothes so large on her frame that they hung in massive folds. The boots on her feet were much too large, as was evident in the fact that she nervously shuffled her feet inside them. Her hair hung down her back in a thick, lackluster ebony braid and her hands, which tapped nervously on the tabletop, displayed broken dull nails and red, calloused skin.

When Mayven raised her eyes, he was struck first by the remarkable shade. Deep-set, almond-shaped, amethyst orbs framed by raven lashes beneath thin, ebony eyebrows regarded him unflinchingly. Her thin oval face displayed high cheekbones, Cupid's bow lips, and a small aristocratic nose that divided her large wide eyes. Her rough, alabaster skin stretched taut from lack of food and care over a strong chin and delicate jaw.

If I didn't already know her real age, her size alone in that oversized bag she is wearing would convince me she was only a child. Varn realized he was staring when her eyebrow arched in question. Shaking his head, he lowered his eyes to the screen he held in his hand.

Scanning the information briefly, he said, "Mayven, I'm Varn Amal-vadar, Historian Guild Master Mage, eighth year."

Mayven looked down at the table. "I counted your braids, master."

Varn concealed a smile. *She doesn't like people to think she's stupid. Her spirit is still intact.*

"I am taking you into the historians' guild for training. Do you have anything you need to gather up before we leave?"

Varn glanced up in time to see her conceal an ironic smile as she answered, "I'm an orphan."

Varn nodded as he tapped the screen he held. "We'll take our leave then."

Varn watched her from the corner of his eye as they strode out of the school and across the yard. Her eyes never left the ground, though her posture, including her head, were stiffly erect. When they stepped out of the gate, her eyes raised and she turned to look back, a small tight smile displayed on her full lips.

Varn nodded to Laydak, who waited on the curb next to a pod car. Laydak opened the side of the vehicle with a word, and Varn motioned Mayven inside ahead of him.

Varn settled back into his seat as the silence inside the vehicle stretched on for several long blocks. Varn studied Mayven as he wrestled with his next step. *How is she going to react to what I need to tell her? She is very beautiful.* Varn shook his head, trying to clear it of distracting thoughts as he looked out the window.

When he looked back at Mayven, he caught her studying him, her eyes filled with questions that were quickly masked by a clear, blank expression that turned her eyes into nothing more than remarkable gems in her lovely face. *I need to do something. I don't need the distraction of a pretty face, too much is relying on my success in aiding her.*

Varn sighed and straightened in his seat, smoothing his palms across the neatly creased breeches he wore. "Today is the first day of your apprenticeship. I'm going to go over a few things with you regarding that."

Varn picked up a satchel on the seat next to him. Rummaging inside, he took out a thin flat engaohnie just larger than his palm and handed it to Mayven.

"This is yours to keep. I'm sure you recognize it. This engaohnie is your communication device. It is the means for the guild to reach you, your apprentice master to reach you, and the way you can track your bank account, bills, receive news and contact anyone you wish to speak with. The applications needed for your apprenticeship are already loaded. There are several applications. Some are for class schedules, your study guides, text books, and personal applications you may need, including your bank account. The application for your bank account only needs to be activated by you."

He watched Mayven for a long moment as she used a small finger to flip through different screens on the device then tuck it into the pocket of her oversized breeches. Watching her reminded him of the next order of business.

"We are going to meet with my assistant at a shop not far from the guild. She will be assisting you in purchasing your personal hygiene items, a wardrobe that will include undergarments, shoes, and four uniforms along with other items. Afterwards, she will also take you to a salon to have you made presentable. One uniform will be a dress uniform you will be required to wear to all guild functions. The other three will be basic daily uniforms you will wear as long as you are employed in the service of the guild. The cost of these items you will see deducted from your pay, along with charges for room and board. The remainder of your earnings are yours to do with as you please."

He watched her face as he waited for her response.

An expression Varn couldn't quite register flickered across Mayven's face then vanished.

"We pay our apprentices very well," Varn continued when she didn't speak. "Your deductions, except for room and board, are taken out on an incremental basis. You will receive a detailed itemized receipt of all the purchases today, and you will see the balance decrease as your payments are made."

Mayven didn't respond, her eyes studying the scenery beyond the window. Laydak pulled the car to the curb outside a row of expensive shops

Mayven looked out the window then down at her clothing. "I don't think I need clothing of this quality if it will take me months to pay it back."

"I think I know what is best in this instance." Varn dismissed her objections quickly. "You'll be serving wealthy and elite clientele in your new position. You will need to look the part. If you want the position I have apprenticed you for, the makeover you seem loathe to endure is required. You cannot serve wealthy clientele in an exclusive business looking as you do."

Varn watched her pale cheeks color a faint red as her head lowered to stare into her lap. He felt a twinge of conscience, knowing in part he was deceiving her. She did need to be properly dressed, but the complete truth was she could be adequately dressed and presentable for far less than he was about to have spent on her. The door opened, his assistant looked into the car, and Mayven stepped out to join her.

As his car drove away, Varn thought she would not be hurt to have a small benefit of the inheritance that was rightfully hers. After all, it was really her money he would be depositing into her bank account as a "bonus" for agreeing to the internship that would help pay for her makeover.

Varn settled into his seat, knowing he had left the project in capable hands. He stared out the window as he tried to ignore the string that seemed to have tied itself to Mayven and pulled him in her direction with increasing strength the farther he got away from her. *I don't understand. My magic usually releases after the object I'm seeking is found. The connection to her is now stronger than it has ever been in the last two years.* Varn sighed, making a mental note to speak to Demok.

A short while later, Varn stepped into his office at the guild house inside a giant maple towering six stories above the immaculate streets at the center of town. Varn scanned the room before approaching the mini bar to the left of his broad maple desk and pouring Iresta from the crystal decanter into one of two matching glasses. The highly polished floor was bare, the walls held several large paintings, all of which depicted some natural outdoor wonder. In front of the desk were two large chairs with a low table between. Behind his desk were a large, comfortably padded chair and a wide oval window horizontal to the floor, its crystal glass polished to gleaming and unadorned with curtains. On the desk was one neatly stacked pile of folders in a bin. The rest of the apprenticeship applications he had yet to complete.

Sinking into the chair behind his desk, Varn admitted he was grateful he had, in effect, given himself several hours to figure out how to approach Mayven about his true reason for picking her to apprentice. *Besides the obvious, her talent fits the guild to perfection.*

Demok strode through the door, closing it behind him, and took a seat across from Varn. "Have you told her yet? Where is she?"

Varn smiled at his uncle. "I haven't told her everything yet. I have her out with my assistant, getting her properly dressed."

Varn tried to avoid adding, *I need time to get a handle on this strange attachment I feel for her.*

Demok, however, seemed to read Varn's mind. "You already feel it, don't you? The attachment to her."

Varn's head jerked up as he stared questioningly into the kind, familiar, blue eyes. "What do you mean?"

Demok smiled at him his sun-worn, wrinkled countenance, displaying love and understanding. "I know what you are feeling because it was foretold in the prophecy. She is to have a protector who will find her, guard her, and lead her to the path of her destiny. It was far too coincidental that you were born with the gift of seeking and tied so closely to her family. I long suspected it was to be you, however, I am surprised it has gotten so strong already."

Varn fell back in his chair, his hand shoving roughly through his copper hair as he absorbed what his uncle had said. "How come you never told me that part before? Is that why you didn't want me to have to use my gift to seek her?"

He watched his uncle's face become serious and his kind eyes darken. "It's never wise to reveal to a player in destiny their role until they discover it themselves. In order to try and fulfill what they think it is, they may try to force it to happen with disastrous results. Yes, I was afraid that by seeking her, the connection would create a problem. You, however, seemed to manage it well up to now."

Varn carefully searched his uncle's face. "How do you know that, Uncle Demok?"

"Because it's happened before."

Varn heaved a sigh and leaned back again. "I accept your reasons. I just don't know how to tell her."

Demok's voice was kind as he replied, "Start with the basic truth, and the rest will reveal itself in good time. I'll advise, however, that you don't reveal to her what she truly is until she is safely away from this dark country. Knowledge is power, and incomplete knowledge is dangerous."

Varn felt the familiar weight of responsibility he was reluctant to carry settle its heavy weight on his shoulders. Shoving himself erect, Varn paced to his window and, leaning against the frame, stared outside, not really seeing the lovely spring sunset that colored the sky in shades of pink and orange.

"You have a grave and great responsibility but nothing that is asked of you is given without reward," Demok continued, his ancient voice gruff and laced with kindness. "Dsohoay honors those who honor him. Do what must be done, and all that is to be will be as it should."

Varn smiled as he looked over his shoulder at his uncle. "You talk in riddles, Uncle. Perhaps it is you who should take her out of here and educate her. After all, you seem to know more about it than I do, and you'll be leaving with us."

Demok's gray head shook, his face wreathed in a kind smile as he replied, "I am far too old for it, dear boy. Intrigue, secret societies, taking down of corrupt and evil governments, and secret networks that whisk people to freedom and a new life, these are all adventures of a young man. At nearly 500 years, I'm afraid I no longer qualify. I'm going home to retire, not educate a Language Master. It's your turn to pick up that torch."

Varn listened to the familiar argument and shrugged as he turned to face the window again. "I don't think she is old enough to do what the prophecy says she will."

"She is only ten brief years younger than you, boy." Demok laughed and walked around the desk to grip Varn's shoulder. "You know that better than I do. You have made a monument to the date of her birth and the death of both your parents and hers, which you make larger with each day of your life. Are you too young for what you are called to do? Aren't you the one who reminds me constantly that at 160 years old, you are already an adult and capable of taking care of yourself?"

Varn rested his head against the cool, clear, crystal of the window as he murmured, "She just seems so young, so naive, and guarded." He once again looked into Demok's eyes. "One minute you can see her vulnerability and fear, the next she has this hard shield up and all you can feel from her is this anger that burns like a raging inferno. I have felt her every emotion for the last two hours. That has taken some getting used to, I might add. I am used to feeling her location but her emotions are an entirely different arena. Only occasionally did I feel what she felt in the last two years. Now how she feels screams at me constantly. She is good at hiding behind the mask she has created but when she thinks no one is watching, she is so lost and fragile looking."

Demok sighed. "As you would be, if you had lived her life. You know what she has suffered better than anyone else. But she is not damaged beyond usefulness. You would not feel the connection to her you do if she were."

Varn felt the stab of a familiar guilt prompting him to ask yet again, "Is that all she is to Niesha, useful? A means to an end? Hasn't her life been enough pain and sacrifice?"

Demok wrapped his arm fully around Varn's shoulders. "As I have told you before, dear boy, she is useful because that is her destiny. The prophecy foretold it long before her birth. However, what she is beyond that is her choice. And yours."

Varn's head snapped up, and he straightened out of his uncle's embrace. "I feel her, she is close."

Demok nodded as he resumed his seat on the opposite side of the desk. "You need to tell her. Tonight."

Just then the door swung open and the smallest, fiercest tornado Varn had ever witnessed blew into the room in the form of a tiny, violet-eyed beauty.

Varn watched her breathtaking almond-shaped eyes flash with amethyst fire as she stormed up to him and jabbed him squarely in the chest with a tiny finger. "What do you think this is?"

Varn's brows raised in surprise and question as Mayven spun in a circle, displaying herself in explanation. Varn felt panic radiating from her. Fear of being noticed, fear of being unable to hide. *Fear created by a life of abuse in an orphanage.*

"There is no way I can be unseen, looking like this," Mayven snarled at him.

Varn looked at his uncle, only to discover him hiding a smile behind his hand and his crystal blue eyes dancing with mirth. Varn rolled his eyes and turned to face the kata who stood before him, her claws and teeth bared in fury. Upon inspection, Varn smiled and agreed that she would have a hard time blending in looking as she did.

Her hair had been cleaned, polished and restored to a healthy luster and hung in deep, thick, blue-black waves well below her waist. Her formerly rough hands and face had been restored to healthy, smooth, satiny alabaster perfection. But it was the display her clothes made of her body that set his own blood pumping and made his heart too loud in his ears.

Her purple satin tunic was full across the top with a wide square collar that displayed delicate collarbones and magnified the intense color of her eyes. Beneath her ample bosom, her blouse was fitted in pleats that hugged a taut slender belly and impossibly tiny waist, where it tucked into a neatly creased curve-hugging pair of black breeches. The breeches did nothing to hide a firm, heart-shaped bottom. Nor did they disguise the length and pleasing form of a well-muscled pair of legs that disappeared into pair of tiny, highly-polished set of boots.

Varn's errant and racing mind registered that, on any other woman, the plain silver headband and utilitarian marsa may have detracted from her appearance. However, on Mayven, they only served to enhance the simple elegance of her attire and focused his eyes on her neckline, making him wonder about the vision he might behold if only one or two of her buttons were not so neatly fastened.

Suddenly Mayven's delicately booted foot stomped the floor. "See what I mean? What have you done to me?"

Varn, his cheeks red in consternation, cleared his throat. "I've only done what is done for every other apprentice, provided you with your uniform."

Mayven glared at him, unconvinced by his reply. "I'm sure that I look nothing like any other apprentice in this building."

Varn managed to stop himself from confirming her suspicions aloud as his eyes roamed over her one more time. When his gaze returned to her face, he found a muscle jumping in her jaw and wide eyes drilling into him.

"I suppose if this is how I must dress, then so be it." Mayven tugged at her collar. "May I please be seen to my room? It's late, and I'm tired."

Varn's eyes snapped to his uncle's face when he heard him try to disguise a chuckle with a very unconvincing cough. Varn ground his teeth together as he glared at his uncle then, forcing composure into his features, he turned back to Mayven. "Follow me."

Varn stepped into the hallway. The core of the tree where the life rings were most dense housed a hollow shaft and a platform created from the wood of the tree itself that moved up and down the tube, serving as the elevator to the six floors of the historians' guild. After pressing the elevator call button, Varn stood silently next to Mayven, watching her from the corner of his eye. She stood straight, her arms crossed beneath her bosom and her chin high and eyes locked on the crystal display above the elevator door.

When the door opened, he stepped in and pressed the button for the fourth floor then cleared his throat. "I've verified your bonus is ready for transfer into your account, minus the itemized charges you will see in your banking statement for the items purchased today. The bonus will cover all of today's expenses with a fair sum left over. Activation of your account on your engaohnie is acceptance of the apprenticeship."

From the corner of his eye, Varn registered her nod of understanding before he continued, "In the morning, your hair will be braided in the standard two-strand braid required of all apprentices. You will need to make sure you have your engaohnie with you when we depart tomorrow. You will find the application for your otal pass already loaded on your device. The cost of the monthly pass will be automatically deducted each month. Please activate that account tonight as well. You will find the cost of the pass listed in your itemized deductions once you activate your banking account."

The elevator was silent, however, Varn clearly read from Mayven an unreasoning fear. With each passing moment, the fear increased. In response to that fear, her emotions changed to anger. *She is angry because she is afraid and doesn't know how to deal with this new place.* Varn felt his forehead wrinkle in confusion. *Why does she hide behind anger?* As the elevator slowed to a stop Varn shifted to view her better from the corner of his eye. *Because fear makes her feel out of control. Anger gives her fear direction.*

The elevator came to a stop, and Varn followed Mayven out of the elevator, trying without much success not to stare at the graceful sway of her hips as she walked ahead of him. Discovering he suddenly had no control over his eyes or thoughts, Varn stepped to her side and led the way along the passage curving in a circle around the inner core of the building four doors to the left of the elevator.

"May I see your engaohnie, please?"

Varn winced as much from conscience as pain when she slapped the device into his open palm. He touched a picture on the screen and a box popped open on the display as he explained, "This application is your own personal entrance pad into your apartment. There is a manual override for maintenance purposes, however, unless it is an emergency, your room will never be entered without your permission or without access to your personal device code. When you tap unlock the first time, the device will ask you to enter a six-digit code three times. Make sure it is the same code each time and that it is a number you can easily recall but others will not easily guess. The only other code to this room is the maintenance code, which is changed every six weeks. You are assured your privacy here."

Varn handed her the device and waited as she punched in her code and the door slid open. He walked in to find her packages from the day's shopping laid on the bed. He let her look around the room as he continued speaking. "Your morning and evening meals are included in your 400 venay for room and board. This first month will be prorated, due to you starting halfway through. Your payment receipt will show you your mandatory ten-percent deduction to the guild house and other than your monthly rent, the rest of your pay is yours. All apprentices start on a salary here of 1,100 venay a month. Do you have any questions?"

Mayven turned to face him, and he purposely locked eyes with her to avoid his gaze wandering as she replied, "No, thank you."

Varn nodded and stepped back into the hallway then struggled to control his pulse all the way back to his office. When the door to his office closed behind him, Demok burst out laughing in great heaving gales as he held his arms across his ribs and tears streamed down his face.

In between great guffaws, his uncle stated, "You should have seen your face. Even without my talent of reading people, I could feel your reaction to her. Tell me you left the poor little thing in one piece, nephew."

Varn flung himself into his chair and almost snarled at his uncle, "Don't be vulgar. She is fine, if I am not. Did you not see her? She is exquisite. To think that was hiding under all those rags and grime."

"I am sure that you'll find no problem wanting to be around her," Demok pronounced, punctuated by another round of low chuckles.

Varn slapped his hand against the desktop, making a loud resounding crack that cut his uncle's chuckles off instantly. "I don't need this kind of distraction. I have a dangerous and important job to do. Being distracted by a lovely face is not conducive to good business."

Demok, his eyes now serious, stated, "Business is not all she is to you, Varn. You know that. You may find trying to relate to her on that level will cause you more difficulty than admitting what is obvious."

Varn sighed and began to rearrange the stacks of papers on his desk.

Demok asked quietly, "Did you tell her who you are, who we are, why she is here?"

Varn shook his head as he continued to thumb through the piles on his desk. "I'll tell her. I only have two weeks before the next exit is arranged. She'll go, I promise. She'll be out of here, along with you and me, in two weeks' time."

Varn avoided speaking of Niesha and all things related to his destiny, or hers, on their way to Mayven's apprentice location the following morning. Varn walked with her down the broad avenue to the otal station. At the station, he showed her how to activate and use her otal pass, where to find the listing of otal locations on her device, and explained to her that she would probably at times still need to call for a pod car to some locations in town.

Varn hid his smile while watching her wide staring gaze take in the sights and bustle of Rashmahava's main otal station. Housed inside a massive abhietie tree, the sheer volume of portals, passengers, and activity explained without words the reason this particular otal station was located inside the largest tree on their planet. A total of twenty high-capacity otals ringed the perimeter of the massive living building. In the center of the station's highly polished, gleaming floor grew a giant square information desk with a total of twenty different registers, all of them with a line. The ceiling towered high above their heads and stained glass windows allowed dappled light to filter in, coloring everything it touched.

Varn took her arm and led her around the wall to a portal locked in place by two crystals inserted into a pillar, one on each side of the massive blue disk that served as the otal to the uptown business district. Varn took out his engaohnie, tapped the screen, activated his otal pass and passed the screen in front of the crystal on the right of the portal. He stepped through the portal and waited on the other side until Mayven joined him a brief moment later. When they exited the uptown otal station, Varn again watched Mayven's reaction as they began strolling through the wealthiest business district in town.

Museums, boutiques, coffee shops, even restaurants displayed the elite touches provided by shops that waited on the most well-heeled among their society. Varn took her elbow as he guided her through the crowded streets until they reached a shop marked as Translations & Authentications, Inc. Stepping through the door, Varn released her elbow and put a slight distance between them as her nearness and the scent of her jasmine shampoo caused his pulse to quicken.

A tall thin man with a rat-like countenance exited an office located at the opening of a hallway off to the right of the entrance. His beady, black, narrow eyes roamed over Mayven appreciatively, and Varn instantly stepped closer to Mayven's side as he locked eyes with the man. "Takmar, may I introduce your new apprentice, Mayven."

Mayven's turned to appraise Takmar with a smile, but then her face closed off almost instantly and her smile disappeared.

Varn felt her discomfort and anxiety transmit itself to him through their connection. Unconsciously, he placed a hand at the small of her back.

Mayven stepped closer to Varn's side then reached out a hand to greet Takmar. "A pleasure to meet you."

Only Varn could have told from her smooth delivery that she was anything but delighted to make the man's acquaintance. Varn closely tailed the two as Takmar showed her around the shop, explaining her job and duties as his apprentice.

The shop resembled a museum with wide, glass-fronted, display cases whose solid wood tops served as counter top. The living cases, growing up from the floor, held four shelves each and circled the entire room. The only gap in the continuous surface was for the hallway to the office. Behind the counter, from floor to ceiling, were more display cases lining the walls filled to capacity with scrolls, books, and odd pieces of parchment. Perpendicular to the wall cases and attached to two rings, one that circled the room above the upper most case and one on the floor, was a moveable ladder that allowed access to the highest cases. The middle of the shop held a bright, thick, vividly colored rug and several well-cushioned chairs and small tables.

Mayven seemed fascinated by her newest surroundings and asked numerous questions about items she discovered in the cases while Varn kept a wary eye on Takmar. Takmar chatted continually and, all the while, his beady eyes took every opportunity to leer at Mayven when he thought she wouldn't notice.

Varn, however, noticed and the tension that vibrated along his connection to Mayven caused the muscles along his shoulders and neck to tighten. When the last of the tour was winding up, Varn blocked Mayven from view by inserting himself between Mayven and Takmar as he said, "If she is okay to handle the counter, I have some business to discuss with you, Takmar, if I may."

Varn was well aware that his tone and manner indicated Takmar didn't have much of a choice, though Takmar replied, "Certainly, follow me."

Varn glanced at Mayven and gave her a slight nod as she stepped behind the counter. Then he followed Takmar into the office and closed the door before rounding on Takmar and saying in a low hard voice, "I'm going to make something perfectly clear right now, Takmar. She is off limits. If you so much as leer in her direction ever again, if you suggest, or insinuate anything improper, if she so much as feels slightly uncomfortable in your presence, you will deal with me."

Takmar fell into his chair behind the desk and inclined as far back as the chair would allow as Varn leaned across Takmar's desk.

Varn smiled coldly. "I can personally assure you that if I so much as get a hint, and trust me, I will know, that she is uncomfortable in your presence there will be such small parts of your carcass scattered over the Baksadie Mountain Range that even the carrion eaters won't be able to find you. Have I made myself clear?"

Varn continued to lean over the desk until Takmar replied in a shaking voice, "Absolutely."

Varn smiled widely, relieved to have the matter resolved and settled into the chair on his side of Takmar's untidy desk. "Now onto guild matters. You will be able to keep all the earnings she generates over the 1,100 venay a month that is her salary. From your portion of the proceeds she creates, the guild will receive ten percent and you have the rest free and clear."

Takmar turned from frightened lecher to sly business man in the blink of an eye as he asked, "Do you think she will be able to generate that much income? I don't want to be paying for her without any income on my part."

Varn resisted the urge to laugh aloud as he smiled congenially at Takmar. *If he only knew who and what she really was, he would never ask such an insulting question.* Waving casually at the screen on the wall next to Takmar's desk, he answered instead, "I think she already has her job well in hand."

Takmar glanced at the screen and watched, fascinated, as Mayven easily handled three very wealthy customers. Takmar turned his now greedy gaze back on Varn. "I'm sure she is going to be an asset. However, just to clarify, all the extra income she provides is mine to keep?"

"All but the ten percent owed to the guild, yes," Varn reiterated.

Takmar's face split in a wide smile as he reached across the desk to shake Varn's hand. Varn took the man's hand in his and stared him down. "Just remember what I said. So much as uncomfortable in your presence ever again, and you will have a lot worse to worry about than your share of the income she generates."

Takmar swallowed convulsively, and his eyes slid away from Varn's gaze after he stuttered an affirmative reply. Varn stayed a short while to observe Takmar's behavior. Then, satisfied the man clearly understood the limits of his contact with his new apprentice, Varn stepped gratefully back outside into the warm spring afternoon.

Varn checked his engaohnie when the alarm sounded and the screen lit with the reminder of his maygis practice. Taking the otal station back to the guild, he retrieved his gym bag and gratefully called his driver to take him to the maygis arena. The combination of the now constant connection to Mayven that tugged at him every second of the day and the attraction that set his nerve endings on fire whenever he was within five feet of her, had created a tension in him that he was grateful to find a release from.

Varn watched the arena come into view and once again admired the workmanship that had shaped the collective organism of this group of aspen into the remarkable bowl-shaped arena before him. The trees' quaking leaves waved in the gentle spring breeze, shimmering like sunlight on water. The bowl their magically merged trunks created formed the outer wall of the arena. As Varn stepped through the wide entrance, the floor gleamed pale and smooth beneath the glow of shen fabric lights hanging from the ceiling. Beneath his feet, the merged and smoothed surface of the collectives many roots were polished to a glossy shine and echoed each hurried step he took toward the locker room. The roof above, created by the interlaced branches of the aspen, supported the thick clear hardened fiber of the seaweed fiber called ktelpie.

Varn had no difficulty admiring the savvy ingenuity of the workmen who had created this arena. He admired each ingenious creation that had made it possible and the beauty of green filtered light through the hard clear ceiling, and he understood fully the advantages of aspen being the best trees to use for just such a building. The aspens' most remarkable trait being their ability to proliferate made buildings like hospitals or arenas easily expandable. However, today his admiration was cut short in his wish to remove from his mind the distraction created by another more diminutive beauty that it was his sworn duty to protect.

In short order, he was on the bouncy two-foot thick mat that covered the arena. His thin, light-weight shoes with rubber bottoms caused the mat to squeak as he bounced anxiously from one foot to the other. Varn had exchanged his breeches for a soft one-piece sleeveless outfit, its form-hugging material ending just above his knees. Ten feet above his head hung the magically suspended court. Four balance beams twenty feet long lined the outside parameters of the court, the ends of each beam never meeting, for the court's length measured twice their length and the courts width triple their length.

Varn watched his teammates meander from the locker room as he swung himself up to the nearest beam, launched himself into the air, deftly catching the nearest knotted rope. There were a total of eight such ropes on each side and twelve on each end of the court. Beyond the ropes, suspended an additional ten feet above the lower beams, around the inner portion of the arena were four more balance beams. At either end of each of the beams, a single rope then four sets of two parallel uneven bars placed just above and at the center point of each balance beam. At the very heart of the arena, a bright silver hoop suspended at the center of it all. The hoop suspended magically thirty feet from the arena floor.

Varn deftly swung around the course, throwing his body through the air, concentrating only on the task at hand, not plummeting to death or serious injury onto the padded floor below. The last of his team finally appeared from the locker room. The coach called him down from the course. The team was divided four players to a side, and the coach lined them up on the lowest set of balance beams.

Varn caught the heavy leather ball as the coach tossed it into play. Then the action began. He wiped from his mind any other thought than helping his team get the heavy leather ball under his arm through the hoop, rising an additional foot each score, at the center of the maygis ring. The end of play sounded as Varn's team scored the final point, a total of fifteen required to end the match, and the coach pulled Varn aside on his way into the locker room.

Varn wiped at the sweat pouring from his face as the coach asked, "What were you thinking about up there today? You need to do that in the next league game."

Varn instantly, upon the reminder for his utter focus, noticed his connection to Mayven begin to pull at him again. Varn let out a deep sigh before muttering, "I was trying very hard to not think of anything but the game."

"Well, it seemed to work. You should do that the next time we play," the coach remarked, slapping Varn roughly on the shoulder.

Varn gladly occupied the shower for longer than usual, then exited the arena to find his driver the only one in the parking lot. Nodding to Laydak, he stepped into the vehicle and ordered transit back to the guild house, then leaned back in his seat and closed his eyes.

Dinner at the guild house had already passed, and the apprentices were busy in their evening classes when Varn arrived. Taking up his seat behind his desk, he sent a message to Mayven's instructor to have her report to his office after class then settled back in his chair to sip at a goblet of Iresta two fingers deep as he stared out his office window on the city lights of Rashmahava. Several long moments passed, then the door to his office opened.

Without turning around, Varn said, "Good evening, Uncle."

A chuckle responded to his welcome, and Varn slowly turned to face Demok, who was helping himself to a liberal portion of Iresta.

Demok took his drink and sat down opposite of Varn. "Have you told her yet?"

Varn stared into his drink a long moment. "No, she is on her way here after class in order to discuss the matter."

Varn watched his uncle's face as Demok nodded in approval. Varn leaned forward and carefully set his glass on the desktop. "I want you to stay while I speak with her."

Before Demok could answer, Varn rushed on, anxious to explain his reasoning, "I need you here to push the matter. This damnable connection to her makes me loathe to give her any kind of news that upsets her, because it feeds back on me with such intensity I can't seem to focus on anything else."

Varn stood, scooping his glass from the desk top, and began to pace his office in long restless strides. "I can't function with this connection to her." He sipped the deep red liquid, savoring its sweet heavy taste followed by the sharp after bite. "It makes me act irrationally. Today at Takmar's shop, I nearly took his head off because he was ogling her. I'm sure she could have handled it, but her defensive reaction to him set off this reaction in me I almost couldn't control."

Varn planted his feet wide apart as he stood staring at his uncle, a pleading look etched in every line of his face. "How am I supposed to be any good to her when I'm distracted by all these emotions this connection keeps throwing at me? I'm a man. I'm not made to handle this illogical moody ocean women deal with."

Varn watched his uncle try valiantly not to laugh and finally realized he would get no advice if he didn't give permission to let Demok enjoy the joke. "Go ahead, enjoy your laugh. Then you had best answer me before she gets here."

Demok burst into gales of laughter. At length, he pulled himself together, though his eyes still danced with laughter. "She is not intending to send you those emotions. You just have not learned to limit the information you get from her unless you want to know more. I have no practical knowledge of the process, but I will explain the theory for you."

Varn nodded earnestly and listened then practiced for the next hour as he waited for Mayven to arrive.

Shortly before she was due to walk through the door, Demok turned to Varn. "Her proximity may make the feedback harder to filter at first, but do as we have practiced and, like any muscle, you will train this one to respond upon your command."

"I will trust you are right on this, Uncle. I have no other choice at this point."

Demok chuckled again as he poured himself another glass of Iresta. "I suppose you don't, dear boy."

Varn rolled his eyes before flopping down into his desk chair once more to wait for the inevitable knock. Varn didn't wait for long, soon anxiety and fear started boiling along the lines that connected him to Mayven. Varn groaned and buried his face in his hands.

What is wrong with me? I'm a man. I don't need this. Just say what you have to say, get it over with, and ignore what she is telegraphing. You have practiced turning down the volume on your connection, just try tuning it out for a little bit. Varn kept running his pep talk through his mind until the rap on the door made him jump almost out of his chair.

Varn glared at his uncle, who started to chuckle, and called out, "Come in."

Mayven stepped tentatively through the door, and two things happened simultaneously. Varn no longer remembered his pep talk, nor did he care that he didn't. Mayven's eyes locked with his as he stood up from his chair, waving mutely to the empty seat next to his uncle. Mayven walked across the room, her head erect and posture unnaturally stiff. She slowly took the seat he offered then stared into his face expectantly.

Varn, however, was concentrating fully on everything her bland expression did not give away. He felt her anxiety like a wave of heat that pounded against his mind. Trying valiantly to remember Demok's advice, Varn broke eye contact with Mayven and turned to stare out the window as he took a long steadying breath and wrestled with the task of muting Mayven's emotional volume.

"Mayven, my name is Demok. I'm Varn's uncle and also a master mage of this guild house. We called you here this evening to discuss some vitally important information with you. Some of which has to do with your guardian, Payin."

Varn felt Mayven's tension ratchet up another notch as the pounding in his head began to feel like his skull would crack.

"I don't understand. You knew Payin?" Mayven's tone was bland, belying the screaming panic she felt.

"We did. We're members of a group called Niesha."

Varn couldn't disguise the gasp of relief that escaped his lips as she instantly changed emotional climate from terrified survival instinct to elated delight. His shoulders relaxed, and he took a slow breath before he finally turned to face Mayven again, nodding slightly to his uncle before he began to speak.

"My uncle placed you with Payin when your parents were murdered. Payin was not a well-known supporter of Niesha and was able to take you in without anyone noticing, due to the fact that his wife was very pregnant and due any day. You could pass as a twin for his natural child since you were only three days old then. Unfortunately, his wife died in childbirth, as did his child, only two days later, and your identity then became that of the child who died. Though I assume you understand you were never his biological child."

Mayven nodded mutely in acknowledgement.

"We had intended you to leave with Payin to Kieshan just shortly after he took you in," Varn continued. "However, Adamdavas was busy sending spies and searchers to Kieshan and every other country they could think of, trying to find you. It was determined until they had given up looking for you abroad, you were safer here, right under the nose of those who sought you so desperately."

Mayven interrupted, "Why did you need to hide me? What does Adamdavas want with me? Why am I so important?"

Varn listened to her questions, all the while reading her impatience through their connection. "Adamdavas is the group that seeks the Language Master. I can't explain now what a Language Master is, for your safety, however, they want you to help them control magic. You have a destiny to correct the problems Adamdavas has created. They want to stop you."

Mayven once again stiffened in her chair at the mention of destiny.

Varn winced slightly as Mayven's resentment and anger began to pound at him once more. "Once it was determined that Payin would remain here with you, for your safety, he dropped contact with us." Varn, sensing her impatience, took a deep breath. "He occasionally checked in, however, we lost contact a few short years later. When my uncle found you both again, Payin was very ill, and he died before your departure time could be arranged. That is when you were taken to the orphanage."

Varn felt anger boiling in her as she demanded, "Why are you avoiding my questions? Why didn't you come and get me? Why did you leave me in that place?"

Mayven glared at Demok, her eyes boring into his.

Demok answered calmly, "I couldn't just walk in there and say you didn't know you had other family. It would look suspicious. I couldn't just go adopt a child who was supposedly deformed, that is even more suspicious, and you needed to learn the basics of adamie. You had no schooling up to that point, am I correct?"

Mayven interrupted again, "So you know I'm not deformed? Why do I have to hide my xodieha? What is my ability, and why must I always hide it?"

Varn could feel a deep anger, resentment, and frustration building inside of Mayven and his head began to pound again. Varn lowered his eyes to the desk and rubbed the back of his neck.

"Mayven, there are several of your questions we cannot answer yet," Demok answered. "Your safety depends on it. I know it's hard to understand. I know it doesn't seem fair. But can you trust me just for a while longer?"

Varn felt Mayven's anger abate slightly as she mulled over Demok's words. Then she asked, accusation still palpable in her voice, "Why did you allow Payin to become lost to you in the first place? He didn't need to die like he did."

Varn slowly sat down to keep from staggering from the onslaught of sorrow that suddenly seemed about to swallow him. Then, as suddenly as the emotion appeared, it was gone, replaced by suspicion and anger. Varn sighed. *Anger is her shield, and suspicion keeps others at arms' length. How am I supposed to navigate this to make her of any use?*

Varn leaned forward, resting his arms on the desktop as he looked into Mayven's eyes. Her features were expressionless as he answered her question, "Payin chose to discontinue contact. The last time he met with Demok, he stated that he had been mysteriously promoted. He said that he was given a raise and company housing. Payin stated that he believed he had been given this because he was being closely watched. He was not sure by whom or what he had done to raise any suspicion but he thought that it was safer to break contact to avoid unnecessary risk until it was safe to move you both. My uncle disagreed."

Varn felt her anger flare and with it his own temper began to simmer. *Why does she have to find fault in everything? Is she so blind she can't see the way things are?*

"I understand Payin's reasoning, I suppose," Mayven replied, her voice laced with sarcasm. "But why did it take so long for you to even start looking for us again? By your own admission, I was very young when this happened. I am now an adult, and over 100 years has passed. What was the delay?"

Varn took a slow breath, trying to calm his irritation but her anger and suspicion fed his roiling emotions and a slow anger began to build within him. "I'm glad you can understand Payin. Demok didn't. Demok urged him not to break contact. He told him that to lose communication could be a vast mistake. Payin refused to acknowledge any communication and soon the engaohnie we had given him was inactive. Payin had moved from his last known location, and Niesha had no way of tracking where he went."

"You seemed to have no problem finding me now?" Mayven arched an eyebrow, crossing her arms beneath her breasts.

Mayven's words pushed on Varn's control, and his emotions broke loose from their weakened restraints and fed veraciously on the anger he felt from her. Without a second thought, Varn lurched from his chair, planted his palms on the desk, and leaned across the table to glare at Mayven. He watched her eyes go wide in shock as she leaned back in her chair to distance herself from him.

Varn glared at her. "I'm so glad you know how hard it is to do our job. I'm glad you are suddenly an expert. Because while you were busy being sheltered and hidden, protected from reality, we were all bleeding, dying, and suffering. We were so remiss not to have just marched in and made your life so much easier. Mayven, open your eyes! Really look at this nation in which you live. You have been out in the real world for only two years, but I'm sure even someone as naive as you must realize how hard it is to avoid being cast with suspicion. We searched high and low for you. Many of us died in attempts to find you again."

Varn straightened from his desk and began pacing, ignoring his uncle's look of warning. "I lost my parents because of you! During the time in which Payin broke contact and we found you again, the search abroad had ceased and Shimiera was searching within its own borders. The laws to register children and their talents earlier had become stricter. Everyone with even the most remote contact with anyone of questionable social status was being followed and watched. The ability to hide in plain sight was no longer as easy. Payin had created what we feared he would, a situation in which we were unable to look and he was unable to contact us due to the high chance of discovery."

Varn's temper ruled him now, his anger fueling his pacing to a manic march as he clutched his arms together across his chest as if holding himself together.

When he spoke again, his voice was a harsh, carrying, whisper. "I will not downplay that your life was hard, Mayven. However, do not judge what you know nothing of. You're not the only one who has suffered. Where you lived your life up to this point was beyond your control. You were a victim of circumstance, but now you must grow up. You must choose to see what really is. There is no place for victims in this world. You will be crushed under the heels of greedy, evil, power-hungry nations, societies, and men long before you ever get anyone to feel sorry for you. You don't have the luxury to wallow in what misfortunes have dictated your life up to this point. You have to choose what you will do."

Varn had stopped his marching and was staring at Mayven, who returned his gaze with anger etched in every line of her beautiful face. Varn took a slow breath, his own anger once again subdued as he continued, "You're the hope of an entire world. However, you can't offer hope if you're blind to reality. There is a time and place for all things. Now is the time to embrace your destiny. We have arranged to get you out of Shimiera in just less than two weeks. You will be leaving with my uncle and myself. When we get to Kieshan, you'll get more answers to your questions. However, for now, you know what is necessary. Knowledge is power, and you are very powerful. Too much knowledge without the ability to wield it properly will lose everything we have been fighting to save." Varn finished speaking, his words fading into silence.

Demok caught Varn's gaze for a moment and nodded, a warm smile on his face. Then Varn turned his attention back to Mayven. He felt the connection between them, however, it was as if his own anger had muted the volume of her emotions. He could still feel her anger, confusion, fear, hope, all of it, but there was no longer the pressure in his head trying to drown out his own thoughts and feelings.

Mayven looked at him a long, time, their gazes locked on each other, then she settled back into her chair and lowered her gaze to her lap. Varn stepped back behind his desk and settled back into his chair, waiting for her response.

At length, Mayven looked up at him. "May I take two friends with me? They are from the orphanage like me. They are my family."

Varn sighed, relief washing over him as he nodded his consent. The rest of their meeting was quiet. Mayven gave them brief descriptions and information, as much as she had, on her friends, Amalayna and Xietak.

When she had left, Demok sat back and gazed at Varn for a long silent moment before saying, "I am glad you've learned to not let her emotions control you. However, I caution you not to drown out her emotions either. The link you share with her is vital to your mission and hers."

Varn nodded without answering and listened absently as his uncle continued to expound on the merits of the connection he shared with Mayven. Varn, however, was miles away from the conversation at hand as he stared out the window overlooking the streets below.

Varn wrestled with the images of his parents laid out on the pak-twatm outside the shen temple in Kieshan. He wrestled with grief that pounded on the walls of his heart as he thought back to that day. Shaking his head, he closed his eyes and tried to concentrate on his uncle's voice. When his mind changed track again, he pictured Mayven, her face swimming in front of his mind's eye as the familiar stirring of lust sped up his pulse and warmed his blood.

Varn shifted uncomfortably in his chair as lust was quickly replaced with anger at Mayven's reactions earlier that evening, which in turn led him back to grief at recalling his parents. Soon Varn was exhausted. Without explanation, he stood and bid his uncle goodnight then left for his room.

As he touched the keypad inside the elevator for the fourth floor, he was immediately reminded of Mayven and her close proximity. Storming into his room, he poured another full glass of Iresta and slammed it down before readying himself for bed. Though Varn was emotionally exhausted, his mind raced. It was hours later that he drifted to sleep, his last conscious thought of Mayven.

CHAPTER SEVEN

Mayven lay in her bed, her mind reeling from the conversation with Varn and Demok. She didn't know what to feel. She was angry that Varn and Demok had admitted that they abandoned Payin. *He died so horribly. How could they have let that happen if he truly mattered to them?*

Then Varn had called her sheltered. *He has no idea what I have lived through. He obviously come from money. His marsa is evidence of that. Oh, and his car and personal driver. Who can afford that? I'm the one who survived Jayben Tavadar. What could he have suffered?*

Mayven rose from the bed and began to pace.

Varn and Demok seem bent on me saving the world. They sound like Payin with his constant talk of destiny.

Then Mayven recalled his remark about his parents dying because of her. *How can he blame that on me? I was a child. I didn't know them.*

Mayven, irritated and restless, began changing her clothing. *And what is with these clothes? The one thing I know for sure is that to blend in you need to be unnoticeable. He says he wants to protect me. Keep me safe. But being invisible dressed like this is out of the question.*

Reason told Mayven she was wrong. In the shop she worked at, everyone dressed very well. In fact, as nice as these clothes were, they were utilitarian by comparison. Mayven ignored her reason.

I won't let him just get away with casually dismissing what happened to Payin or what I have been through.

Reason again, that small voice in her head, told her that Varn was not to blame. That she was reacting foolishly. Mayven again ignored it.

Looking around her room, Mayven noted the thick mattress in her bed. Her hand caressed the crisp white sheets, enjoying the cool feel against her palm. On the desk across from the bed was her engaohnie. In the closet, stacked up or hung neatly, were the clothes she had purchased. Everything was better than she could have imagined.

Then why am I so afraid? The thought flashed across Mayven's mind, then she changed track completely.

I'm leaving this awful place at last, and I can take Amalayna and Xietak with me. The hours of dreaming about this day made the realization of it seem entirely unreal. She knew that Varn had stated he would arrange for them all to meet tomorrow night to discuss the exit plan, however, tomorrow night now seemed very far away.

Mayven now changed into her night clothes and crawled into bed. She contemplated as she lay in her new, warm, comfortable bed how drastically her fortunes had changed in only the span of three days. She looked back at the nights she had slept in an overcrowded dormitory on a hard cot with only the most meager of blankets. The memory alone made her overwhelmingly grateful for this new place and the man who had brought her so much good fortune. *But a moment ago you were angry at him.*

Mayven turned on her side and stared at the wall. *Am I really angry at Varn? Did he do the best he could? He isn't that much older than me.*

Mayven glanced around the room once more, and her mind wandered to all her daydreams as a child in the little apartment with Payin. She had dreamed of a day when they would get to have comfort, safety, and security. She thought back to the orphanage and how much she had longed for warm clothes and decent shoes. *This all seems so unreal. I'm scared. Maybe it's all just a dream.*

Mayven's conscience nagged her with her next thought. *Varn isn't who I'm mad at. I need a way to distract myself from fear so I get angry. Payin always said I let anger rule me.*

Mayven felt her heart skip a beat as she found her mind wandering to Varn. In her mind, she examined at length the thick copper waves that fell so carelessly across his dark olive brow. His sea green, deep-set eyes, and full lips. In her mind, those lips stretched wide in the smile that she had seen the first day she had met him, displaying a pair of deep dimples in his lean cheeks. High cheekbones and a strong square jaw were refined by the aristocratic, slim nose that, though large, was perfectly proportioned to his striking features.

Then she pictured again Varn's broad shoulders, tensed and taut beneath his tunic, his muscled chest and arms straining against the fabric of his shirt as he paced his office furiously. She felt her pulse quicken as she pictured his narrow hips and long lean legs encased in the dark fabric of his tight breeches as he paced like a caged beast inside his office. Her thoughts jerked to a halt.

Is he violent? Am I mooning like a child over someone who could harm me? As soon as the questions raced through her mind, she dismissed them. He was strong. Not someone to underestimate. But cruel violence was not in his nature. Somehow Mayven was certain that she was protected by him, and the thought gave her a sense of comfort.

Mayven found herself examining her emotions, exploring what it told her of him and was shocked to feel desire and anger swirl through her mind. *Where are all these emotions coming from? What is this connection I feel to him? It's like I could find him in the darkest night.*

Mayven thought back to the interview at the orphanage and how she had instantly recognized when he stepped into her classroom that he was looking for her. *Why do I feel like I know him so well? I have never felt this with anyone before. Not even Payin.*

She wandered through the discussion of her life with Payin. Mayven acknowledged a sadness that she would never meet her biological parents and pushed away the grief of never again seeing Payin. Instead, she focused on the one brief sentence Varn had revealed about himself. *"I lost my parents because of you!"*

Mayven sighed and wondered how his parents' death was her fault. She pondered on it a long time before dismissing the thought altogether. Then her mind returned to his accusation of her being naive. *How would he know? He hadn't lived her life. He was not the one everyone despised. He didn't have to constantly hide himself for reasons he didn't understand. How could he say she was naive?*

Mayven's confusion created fear of the unknown, fear created anger and the cycle didn't stop. Mayven lay awake for a long time, then at last drifted into a sleep troubled by dreams of her own face and Varn's, each image eliciting emotions laced with desire and frustration alike.

The next morning, Mayven was grateful that Takmar's shop was very busy. The day passed faster than she had hoped. When Varn personally showed up to take her to the meeting with Amalayna and Xietak, she had to deliberately find something besides his smile to concentrate on. So she made idle conversation about work as the pod car drove rapidly through the busy evening traffic.

Soon conversation faded out completely as she stared out the window at the one part of town she never wanted to return to. The

Fisherman's Wharf was bustling with men unloading large fishing vessels, cargo ships, and freighters. That image didn't bother her; it was the towering mass of the twin giant oaks displaying a sign over the gated, barren, yard in front of them that said *Rashmahava City Orphanage* that made her stomach sink to her feet.

Varn seemed to sense her mood. "We're going down beyond the wharf. It's considered the least desirable part of town, and that is precisely its protection. None of those who wish to keep their reputable stations would set foot in this end of town. This is where all meetings for Rie'hava Ktaya happen."

The pod car pulled to a stop in the warehouse district below the Fisherman's Wharf. Varn cautiously peeked out the translucent fibers that served as windows in the pod car, then, nodding to Mayven, stepped out of the car. "Pull out of sight but stay ready, Laydak. You know the procedure."

Mayven watched Laydak nod then pull into the darkest shadows between two looming oak trees, each displaying signs that read *Warehouse District Block Three*. Beneath the sign were the numbers four and five. Slow moments passed as she and Varn waited, Mayven's eyes constantly searching the dimly lit parking area for a sign of her friends. When at last they walked into view, Xietak clutching Amalayna's hand, Mayven released a breath she didn't realize she'd been holding.

Mayven rushed to hug them both, relief and delight making it hard not to dance with joy at the news she was about to share. Varn, she noted, hung back, though his face seemed to hold an odd sort of smile as if he knew the delight she could barely contain. When at last she introduced Varn to Xietak and Amalayna and then explained the reason for their secretive visit in the empty warehouse district, she immediately caught the look of relief flash across Xietak's face and gave him a slight nod and knowing look.

Amalayna was ecstatic. In her customary fashion, Amalayna bubbled with delight and acerbic wit that charmed Varn, who questioned about her talent and Xietak's, the jobs Xietak and Amalayna did, and what guild they were assigned to.

"So are you both willing to leave this place? Do you want to go with Mayven to Kieshan?" Varn glanced from Amalayna to Xietak.

Amalayna instantly answered in the affirmative. Mayven, however, watching Xietak intently, did not miss the brief expression on Xietak's face. Xietak glanced at Amalayna, his expression filled with longing, then quickly covered the look with a stoic mask of indifference. Mayven waited for his answer, all the while reading the expression in his eyes that flickered between fear and resignation.

At length, Xietak answered. "Exactly, can't wait to go. When are we leaving?"

Mayven frowned slightly, determined to corner him later and discover his reasons for reticence, then turned to face Varn. Mayven noted Varn's intent expression as he darted glances between herself and Xietak but cut him off before he could question her, "When are we scheduled to leave?"

Varn raised an eloquent brow in question. "We're leaving exactly ten days from now."

Relief flooded Xietak's expression. "I assume that we continue with business as usual until then?" he questioned, now completely engaged in the conversation.

Mayven focused on the emotions playing under the surface of what Xietak portrayed as enthusiasm and interest. *He's lying. What is he hiding?* Mayven studied the little group and was thankful that once again Amalayna's vivacious personality gave her the opportunity to fade to the background in order to watch those around her.

Mayven felt an inordinate amount of suspicion toward Xietak building inside her. She also read an unfamiliar protective feeling against herself. Mayven looked around the group for a long moment and it was after another long moment of watching that it occurred to her. *I'm feeling someone else's emotions. Varn? But how could that be? I've never been able to read anyone like this before.*

Mayven struggled to distinguish more from the emotions she could readily recognize as not her own. *I could be wrong, maybe I'm just jumpy. I'm just reacting strangely to everything changing. It's not like I've been very fair these last few days. It could just be my own guilt talking.*

Mayven studied Varn surreptitiously, deciding that she really need to apologize for her behavior the last couple days. Mayven decided to do that just as Amalayna's happy hug and enthusiastic questioning drew her out of her own thoughts.

Xietak wrapped an arm around Amalayna and then Mayven as they listened to Varn detail the plan.

Varn stated that in exactly ten days they would meet up again under the cover of darkness at this same location and leave Shimiera behind them. Varn went into the details, explaining they were not to have any further contact until that night. No calls, messages, or meetings.

Varn finished speaking and looked at each of them intently for a long heartbeat. "It has to appear as if you all are not in contact and far too busy to go out of your normal routines. As hard as the next days will be, you must do this. Any slip up can lead to any or all of you and those who are risking their lives to get you out of here being in the hands of some very bad people. Do you understand?"

The quiet agreement of all of them seemed to set Varn at ease. Then, after their quick whispered good-byes, Varn cautioned one more time, "Do not change your routines. Keep everything as normal as you can for the next ten days."

Mayven watched her little family disappear back into the night and felt her heart grow heavy as she watched them go. She tried to comfort herself from the anxiety that seemed to be weighing her down like a dark heavy blanket.

Varn seemed to sense her unease. "It won't be long. The next ten days will go faster than you can imagine."

Mayven smiled at him then turned toward the alley and the car concealed in the shadows.

"I'd like you to go with me to a place I like to hang out," Varn stated, once inside the car. "Would you like to come? I have some friends I'd like you to meet."

Mayven's first instinct was to decline but then, knowing she had nothing else planned, she shrugged. "Sure, sounds like it could be fun."

The rest of the ride was quiet, and when they stopped outside a modest-sized, shabbily pruned, oak, its windows glowing with light, she smiled. This place, even from the outside, felt like home. Above the door hung a rustic sign etched in elegant lettering declaring the establishment as *Hardak's Pub.*

They entered the wide door and were instantly greeted by the largest man Mayven had ever seen. "Hey, Varn, welcome home. Who is your guest?" he boomed from his place behind the bar.

Mayven felt her jaw go slack as her eyes took in the proprietor. He was almost seven feet tall. His head was wreathed in bright red, straight hair and decidedly disheveled. His skin, freckled and pale, was stretched across the squarest head she had ever seen, and the face wreathed in the warmest smile she had ever experienced. The laughter in his voice was mirrored in the twinkle in the deep sapphire blue of his eyes.

Mayven had just managed to remind herself to shut her gaping mouth when, from the door behind the bar, presumably leading to the kitchen, emerged an equally tall, willowy, full-figured woman, her features just as striking. Her head came to just beneath Hardak's chin, and her mahogany hair fell in soft curls around her face and shoulders, accentuating the warm golden brown of her eyes and the full pink lips stretched in a wide smile.

Mayven blinked, as if she had stared at the sun too long, as Varn's voice drew her attention. "Hardak, Layla, this is Mayven. She is the new apprentice I've been telling you about. We're here early because I wanted her to meet you. Mayven, this is Hardak and... his wife Layla. They own this bar."

Mayven noted a hesitation in the introduction and a questioning look pass between Hardak and Varn.

Hardak snorted. "Pub, it's a pub. When are you ever gonna get that right?"

Mayven was taken aback at the rich warm laugh that escaped from Varn's smiling lips before he answered, "When it stops bothering you!"

Mayven shook her head trying to adjust to this new side of Varn. "Isn't it kind of late for this place to be closed?"

Varn smiled at her briefly, and she felt her stomach fill with butterflies. "No, they open here in just a little while. The place never gets busy until after all the other businesses are closed."

Mayven nodded mutely, unable to find her voice. Layla stepped around the bar and shoved Varn gently in the direction of Hardak as she wrapped an arm around Mayven's shoulders, which came roughly to just beneath Layla's rather impressive bosom.

Layla's melodic soprano rang across the bar as she told Varn, "Why don't you boys go talk shop like always? Mayven and I'll wait here and get to know each other."

Mayven watched Varn smile warmly at her and head through the door behind the bar with the giant known as Hardak. Then she looked up into Layla's smiling face and was promptly made speechless again.

"I can't believe how tiny you are. I thought Varn's match would have been more physically impressive." With that, Layla retrieved a bottle of Iresta and two glasses from behind the bar and led the way to a table.

Mayven settled into one of the chairs, and Layla took the one across from her. Mayven gave her a tentative smile and acknowledged to herself it was much more comfortable not to be constantly looking upwards to speak to her.

Mayven let a small sip of Iresta slide down her throat. "What did you mean by 'Varn's match'?"

Layla smiled. "I mean it was foretold he will find his match and they will share a connection. It's obvious to me that the connection exists. I just pictured you differently is all."

Mayven instantly recalled her observations from earlier. *Maybe I'm not just making it up. Maybe I can read Varn's thoughts.* But that thought was tabled in the presence of another word. *Foretold.* Mayven sighed. *I suppose this is more of that destiny Payin always told me about.*

Mayven felt apprehension bloom in her stomach, making it difficult to swallow the liquid in her mouth. "What do you mean foretold?"

Mayven watched Layla's features intently as Layla's warm smile faded slightly and she gazed at Mayven intently. Layla shrugged. "I suppose Varn will tell you all about it in time. There must be a reason you don't know the prophecy yet."

Layla dropped her eyes to the liquid in her glass as she swirled it absently then, as if deciding on a course of action, she took a large gulp and finished her drink, setting down the glass with a decisive thump. "If the time comes that you need to know of the prophecy and he hasn't told you, come to me, and I'll tell you the prophecy. I know my brother. He listens to my uncle far too much and keeps information that is better shared to himself. He has learned some bad habits from Niesha."

Mayven's mouth fell open again for the second time since meeting this woman. "You're his sister?"

"Yes, he didn't tell you?"

Mayven felt another stab of unease as she contemplated what else he may have left out. She gulped down the last of her drink as well and set the glass on the table. "Nope, didn't tell me that either. Maybe he is waiting for good reason. But I'll keep your offer in mind."

Layla nodded in acknowledgment, her face brightening. Then, returning to her former demeanor, she asked, "So do you want to know all his embarrassing secrets?"

Mayven giggled and nodded. Soon Mayven found she was learning a great deal about Varn. In Mayven's mind formed a picture of a very young, athletic Varn, who was far too serious for a child. Mayven smiled, *He really hasn't changed much then.*

At length, Layla's head turned to glance at the crystal wall display behind the bar, and Mayven followed her glance.

"Time to open," Layla stated as she rose.

Mayven nodded as she offered, "Anything I can help with?"

Layla handed Mayven the decanter and glasses. "If you would like, you can wipe down the tables."

Just as Mayven and Layla finished preparations, Varn and Hardak emerged from the kitchen. Hardak unlocked the door and took up residence behind the bar.

Varn leaned a narrow hip against the wall at the end of the bar. "Have you been busy lately? Any new faces come in?"

Mayven sensed a deeper meaning to the question and watched intently as Hardak responded with a grin. "Nope, but I thought your trolling-for-women days were behind you. Looks like Mayven here has you all tied up. But if you don't want her, I bet I could find her a nice man. I know a couple."

Mayven felt her face flush, and her breath caught as Varn's green gaze caressed her face for a brief moment before he turned to face Hardak and replied, "I never said that."

Mayven's teeth clenched as she felt first anger then possessiveness followed by rejection and hurt flash through her chest. *I'm acting like some scorned school girl with her first crush! My emotions are all over the place.*

Mayven recalled her earlier emotions at the meeting with Xietak and Amalayna. In hind sight, she clearly understood why her emotions over the last several days had been intense and erratic. There had been a lot of changes, Mayven reasoned, still not certain her suspicions of being able to read Varn were accurate.

Mayven ground her teeth together and slid her glass toward Hardak to have it refilled as her mind raced through the events of the last several days. As Mayven wrestled with her questions, she studied the group clustered around the bar waiting for the first customers to arrive. Hardak made a low ribald comment, and Varn's head tipped back in a boisterous laugh. Mayven felt a rush of delight. The reaction fueled Mayven's certainty. *It's Varn!*

Mayven stood absently clutching the glass in her hand, mouth gaping open, and staring at Varn. Her surprise seemed to stop Varn in mid-laugh, and he turned to stare at her, a guilty and knowing look decorating his far-too-comely features.

Mayven snapped her jaw closed, slammed her glass on the bar, and marched over to Varn. Reaching up, she grabbed him by the ear and marched him, bent nearly double, into the kitchen, leaving the others staring after them in open-mouthed surprise. As soon as the kitchen door closed behind them, Mayven released Varn, who stood erect as he studied Mayven, rubbing his ear, a bemused and sheepish expression his only response to her tirade.

"What is this? I have spent the last several days wondering if I had suddenly become horribly self-absorbed and sickeningly attracted to my own physique. You did something. You fix it right now."

Mayven watched without sympathy as Varn winced under the force of command and authority that rang in her voice. She knew exactly the amount of power and coercion she had used. Mayven tapped her foot impatiently, her hands planted on her hips, and her head cocked to the side as she waited for Varn to respond.

"I'm waiting."

Varn winced, rubbing his temples gingerly. "I can't undo it."

He held up his hands palms out in supplication as Mayven eyed him fiercely and opened her mouth to speak.

Varn interrupted her, his features pleading, hands still up in surrender. "I didn't initiate this connection. I can't undo it. I can have you speak to my uncle. He seems to know what the connection is and how it works. I promise it wasn't my doing." Varn looked embarrassed and apologetic. "I've had the same problem the last several days."

Mayven felt embarrassment, then anger as she realized some of her dreams and his had mixed. Embarrassment and consternation warred as she realized that this unbelievably distracting man had heard, or rather felt, some of her most private feelings. Worse yet, even now he could read her wayward, betraying emotions like a book. Mayven felt the blood rush to her cheeks and then drain to her toes in the span of only a few heartbeats. Suddenly feeling mortified and light headed at the same time, Mayven blindly reached out to find a handhold to steady herself.

When her hand encountered nothing, she started to stumble. Varn's arm suddenly wrapped around her as he led her to a seat near the kitchen door. At once, she recognized her body's volcanic response to his touch. Then she realized Varn could feel it as well. With a groan, she fell forward and buried her face in her lap to hide the blood-red shame heating her face to crimson.

"I can't believe this." Mayven's voice came as a muffled groan from the vicinity of her knees.

Peeking up at Varn through her hair, now covering her face, shoulders and a sizable portion of the floor, Mayven noted Varn's look of perturbation.

"I know exactly how you feel."

Mayven turned her gaze back to the floor for another moment. Then, gathering her courage and taking a deep breath, she sat up. "Why didn't you have the decency to at least let me in on the joke?"

Varn's gaze slid away from Mayven's as he shuffled his feet nervously. "What was I going to say? Would you mind too awful much not being so suspicious, afraid, oh, and, by the way, attracted to me? Would you have believed me if I had said anything? You would have, and I can almost quote, called me a self-centered, egomaniacal mogatie. Am I wrong?"

Mayven started to open her mouth to negate his argument then snapped it shut. Her brows drew together in a frown, and the breath she had drawn to argue left her in a defeated huff. *He is right. Almost to the word.* She smiled slightly. *Except he left out the part about being a know-it-all windbag.* Then Mayven blushed furiously as she heard Varn's strangled laugh and looked up to find him staring at her, one eyebrow cocked and a completely sexy and insufferable grin plastered across his very kissable lips.

Varn's other eyebrow shot up, and Mayven groaned as again she buried her heated cheeks in her lap. "I can't believe this."

"Tell me about it," Varn responded, his voice laced with the distinct sound of laughter.

Mayven decided to table the discussion between them for the time being. She stood up, squared her shoulders, and gave Varn a long steady look, trying hard not to think anything thing other than what she had to say. "I think for now this issue is of secondary importance."

Varn seemed relieved at her change of demeanor. "I agree. I also agree with your assessment of Xietak earlier. He is hiding something. I will let you deal with that. But deal with it you must. It could endanger his safety and everyone else's as well if he is up to something none of us know about."

Mayven was jolted by the reference to their meeting with Xietak and Amalayna and instantly jumped to Xietak's defense. "He is probably worried about protecting Amalayna or myself. I doubt it's anything wrong."

Varn didn't argue. "I'm not questioning his loyalty. I just want to make sure we start this mission with everyone's cards on the table."

Mayven snorted as she raised an eyebrow in Varn's direction. *Like he has all his cards on the table.*

A sheepish look crossed Varn's face for a fleeting moment. "I think we should rejoin the others before anyone comes looking. Don't you?"

Mayven turned to go.

Varn paused before opening the door. "We need to meet with Xietak again. It's against protocol but he is hiding something, and we need to know what it is for the safety of everyone involved."

Mayven nodded without turning around. "I agree. I'll contact him tomorrow. We can meet after dark tomorrow night at the same place."

CHAPTER EIGHT

Varn held the door open for Mayven as they exited the kitchen. Noting the pub now had several people seated at the bar, Varn guided Mayven with a hand against her lower back to a table near the kitchen door as heat from their slight contact seemed to sear his hand and muddle his brain. As they took a seat, Mayven's thigh bumped his under the table. He felt a flash of heat coil and spread, making him uncomfortably aware of her soft, intoxicating scent and the sultry sound of her laugh. Varn ground his teeth, trying to follow the flow of friendly banter around the table as Hardak and Layla joined them. However, it was the overwhelming feeling of awareness now pouring from Mayven as she laughed at Hardak's abominable jokes that kept him glowering at the glass he held, which never seemed to empty.

The evening quickly passed, and Varn watched as Hardak and Layla bustled around serving customers and greeting friends. When at last the bar closed, Varn lurched to his feet, noticing at once that the room seemed to tip precariously on its axis as he did so. Varn shook his head, trying to clear it, and the room only twirled faster.

"Mayven, I think you should get me back to the guild. I think I drank too much." Varn scowled at the slurred sound of his own voice.

Mayven regarded him with a smirk.

"I don't think this is funny. What are you smiling at?"

Mayven raised an elegant ebony brow. "It's interesting to know you need my help."

Varn's fuzzy thoughts jumbled together, and he sensed her amusement across their connection. "I don't need your help. I just need you to show me how to get out of here. The room won't stay still."

Somewhere in the back of his mind, Varn registered he was being foolish and may well regret it tomorrow. However, when Mayven stood and offered him a steadying arm around his waist, he didn't object. He did vaguely register Hardak making suggestive comments as he tried to keep himself steady on the way out the door and made a mental note to get even later.

The car ride was quick and uneventful, Varn just wished getting into his room was as easy. He leaned heavily on Mayven while she struggled to remove his engaohnie stone from his pocket. He felt her small hand slip into his snug-fitting breeches as her palm left a fiery trail along its path against his thigh. Varn felt her breath rushing warm and quick against the thin fabric of his tunic, increasing his awareness of her warm full breasts pressed against his ribcage.

Varn groaned as he tried to shift away from her and only managed to make himself dizzy in the process.

Mayven, mistaking his discomfort for something else entirely, looked up at him. "If you vomit on me, I will drop you right here in the floor."

Varn registered the look of indignation on her face and the tenor of disgust in her voice and laughed despite his whirling head. The movement of his laughter shifted his weight farther onto Mayven's slight shoulders. She stumbled under his weight, and her hand slid further into to his pocket and brushed against the evidence of his discomfort. Varn groaned and looked down into Mayven's face. Her cheeks flushed crimson as she curled her fingers around the engaohnie stone and yanked her hand from his pocket.

Varn knew that it would be best if he could get into his room as quickly as possible as soon as his next words tumbled from his mouth. "I wasn't worried about vomiting, as you can tell. But you are welcome to assist with the problem I do have."

Mayven thrust the engaohnie into his hand. "Open the door, you lecherous mogatie. I would like to go to bed sometime tonight."

Varn knew he should keep his mouth shut, in fact he determined he would, his lips just didn't agree with him. Varn grinned down at her. "You can go to bed with me!"

Mayven's angry gaze bored into him. Varn heaved a sigh and squinted at his engaohnie screen and, with his tongue between his teeth, used his index finger to punch in the unlock code to his room door. The door slid open, and they stumbled through it to the bed, where Mayven gave him a slight shove. He flopped into the warm, soft comfort.

Varn turned his face toward Mayven and thumped the bedding next to him. "There's plenty of room for you."

Mayven rolled her eyes, turned on her heel and left without looking back. Varn sat up, muttering as he tried to remove his boots. The room gave a violent twirl at his sudden unsteady movements, then he fell back unconscious, one boot only halfway off.

Morning is never merciful, Varn decided, *today even less so.* It pounded through the windows with an annoyingly cheerful glow, and Varn could swear he heard the chirping of some far-too-cheerful bird outside his window.

"Oh, shut up!" he growled as he rolled over and promptly fell onto the unforgiving floor.

Varn moaned as his head bounced off the floor and went from throbbing to skull-cracking pounding in an instant. A short while later, after a very lengthy shower and a nauseating whiff of breakfast, Varn leaned heavily on the edge of his desk and cradled a stone mug of parfie at which he gazed with almost slavish intensity. The sound of the door opening drew his attention as he took another sip of the scorching liquid that filled the room with a rich savory aroma.

Varn scowled. "What do you want this early, Uncle?"

Demok, minus his usual buoyant manner, took a seat across from Varn. "You may want to have a couple more of those. We have work to do. Adamdavas is on the move. They seem to have found someone they believe will take them to the Language Master. He seems to have been sabotaging a device he was designing to read people's talents. Seems he is a technology mage with the rare gift of being able to harness and duplicate a person's gift in a device."

The cup Varn was holding stopped in mid-motion, halfway between his lips and the table as he suddenly sat erect, staring intently at his uncle. Varn swallowed convulsively and set the mug down with a thud. "I think I know of whom you speak. His name is Xietak. He not only knows the Language Master, she is his personal friend. What are they planning to do to him?"

Demok gazed at Varn, his expression grave. "Vayshatka."

The single word, spoken so softly, resounded like thunder through the room as Varn collapsed back in his seat and stared in horror across the desk at Demok.

"I didn't know that was actually possible. I thought it was only a myth. Forced possession by Tarlens. If he is possessed by demons, they will know everything about him, about her. We have to find out what he actually knows and perhaps move up the time table, a lot. I am supposed to meet with Mayven and him again tonight in the same place as before. I'll do my best to see how much time we have."

Demok nodded and rose from his chair. "It seems destiny has come knocking sooner than we'd planned. Be careful. I'll start planning an exit strategy. Keep me informed of any changes."

Varn nodded then watched silently as Demok left his office.

Within hours, Varn had confirmed the meeting with Xietak through Mayven and began setting up a contingency plan for evacuation and coordinating their arrival in Kieshan. *No matter what that boy says, I'm getting her out of here. It has to be done.* Varn exited the guild house, his mind whirling with all the plans he had yet to finish.

Moments later, Varn sat in the back of his pod car, mulling over the situation on his way to pick up Mayven and escort her to the meet with Xietak. *I can't tell her about Vayshatka because she will endanger herself to save Xietak. But she will know I'm hiding something from her. How am I ever going to get her to trust me? I can't tell her everything until she is away from here and getting her away means not telling her even more. Would I trust someone like that?* Varn heaved a sigh as Laydak stopped in front of Translations & Authentications, Inc. Mayven stood on the curb, waiting, her expression calm and face impassive, though he could sense the unease she concealed artfully beneath her calm demeanor.

She is very good at letting her expressions lie. Can I trust her? Varn felt the tension in his body ratchet up another notch as everything seemed to be spinning out of his control faster than he could grasp it. The door to the car opened and Mayven stepped inside, taking a seat across from him as the car pulled away front the curb.

"I need to know all the information you have on what might be bothering Xietak. Anything he has ever told you about the work he does at his guild and things he may have found out while working there. I need you to be honest, Mayven. Amalayna's and, most importantly, *your* life may depend on your truthfulness with me."

Varn waited for his pronouncement to sink in as he monitored her reaction through their connection. He felt her confusion first, then her customary anger and, at length, her resignation.

Mayven's shoulders slumped. "I'll start from the beginning, though I suspect you know most of what I am about to tell you."

Varn listened as Mayven outlined her time at the orphanage and all her conversations with Xietak up to and including last night. He monitored her feelings through their connection as she explained her feelings toward Xietak and her reasons for suspicion about Xietak's less-than-delighted response the night before.

When at last she finished speaking, Varn stared out the window of the car for a long moment, his hands absently rubbing his thighs as he reviewed the information. Then, turning back to face Mayven, Varn announced, "We'll see what Xietak has to say tonight and go from there."

Varn instantly felt her suspicions rise and the customary anger that followed.

Mayven glared at him, her gaze intense and brows drawn together. "What aren't you telling me, Varn?"

Varn breathed slowly and tried to shield her from his thoughts. "I have information that I can't give to you until I know what Xietak has to say. That is all I can tell you for now. Will you trust me, please?"

The frustration and suspicion he sensed from Mayven needed no connection to detect.

Mayven leaned back, her brow furrowing. "I have no choice, for now."

Varn said nothing further as they waited in silence to reach their destination. Long minutes passed and then at length Xietak appeared from the shadows alone, his face etched in worry and shoulders slumped. Varn watched Mayven study her friend, her eyes fastened on Xietak, and Mayven's expression filled with concern. Mayven's obvious concern stirred a protective urge within Varn fired more by jealousy than noble intention. Varn consciously shut it down as Mayven turned to face him, anger dancing like lightning in a summer sky from her thunderous amethyst eyes.

Xietak cleared his throat, interrupting Varn's staring contest with Mayven. Varn shifted his attention and intently monitored Xietak's reaction.

Mayven laid a small hand on Xietak's arm. "What are you hiding from Amalayna this time?"

Varn shuddered slightly as he felt the crackle of command charged by adamie laced in Mayven's question. *I'm glad I'm prepared when she tries that with me.*

Xietak didn't lower his gaze or attempt to fight the coercion in Mayven's question. "I have to undergo a test for my guild. They are trying to find the person who sabotaged the device I made. They want to know why the project has been undermined."

Varn watched as Mayven's face erupted in a relieved smile. "Nothing to worry about. You'll be gone before they test you."

Xietak shook his head, his face etched in fear and worry. "I'm scheduled to undergo the test before we leave."

Varn felt Mayven's panic race across their connection and heard her breathing catch as she shook her head in denial. Varn's teeth ground together as he felt Mayven's love for Xietak create in her panic and a blind need to protect.

Varn listened to Mayven plead with Xietak and felt the monster within rumble. "No! I can't lose you. You're my family. I won't let them hurt you."

Varn squelched the jealousy that seemed to always bubble just beneath the surface lately as he studied Xietak's face. He knows exactly what the test is, Varn realized as he witnessed the despair etched in the lines of Xietak's face.

Varn saw the tears in Mayven's eyes and watched her shaking her head in denial as he felt her come to the same conclusion he did from Xietak's expression.

"It's set to happen unless we can leave sooner." Xietak's voice was bleak and toneless.

Mayven shook her head, unable to speak. Turning tear-filled eyes on Varn, Mayven silently pleaded with him for another alternative.

Varn shoved his hand through his hair. "I'm working on it."

Varn felt Mayven's fear ratchet up another level as her desperate need to protect Xietak assaulted his senses.

Mayven's lips trembled and her eyes blinked rapidly. "How long before you can have a plan to get us out of here?"

Varn ground his teeth together. "I'm working on it."

Varn's hands clenched at his sides as Xietak smiled at Mayven tenderly as he took a hand from hers and gently stroked her face from her forehead to jaw. Varn watched Xietak's crystal blue eyes and was floored by the love and devotion he saw there.

"I'll be fine."

Varn watched as silent tears coursed down Mayven's face as she stared into Xietak's chiseled features. Varn felt something close to physical pain as Mayven's heart broke and helplessness enveloped her.

Xietak crushed Mayven to his chest and whispered fiercely in her ear, "We have survived this long. We will make it out of this, too. I promise."

Irrational anger and jealousy raged through Varn, heating his blood to boiling. Varn's hands trembling, he forced himself not to rip Mayven from Xietak's tender embrace. Without thinking of what he said or the impact of his words, Varn demanded, "We need to go. We can't risk being caught out here tonight."

Mayven turned in Xietak's embrace, her brows drawn together in a frown.

Varn, completely absorbed by his own anger and disregarding Mayven's emotions entirely, stepped toward Mayven menacingly. "Let's go."

Varn watched the proprietary way Xietak placed a hand on Mayven's waist as they stood next to each other. *I don't know what Xietak is playing at. First he claims concern for Amalayna and then he touches and gazes lovingly at Mayven. The man is a womanizer and is keeping Mayven on the hook if Amalayna doesn't work out.* Varn's frown deepened as he shook his head to clear his confusing emotions. *What do I care? She isn't mine.*

Varn stifled a growl of aggravation as Xietak kissed Mayven on the cheek before turning and disappearing into the darkness, leaving a weeping and distraught Mayven in his wake. Varn didn't speak to Mayven on the way back to the guild house as she stared silently out the window, tears pouring down her face.

Guilt nagged at Varn, along with the slightest wish to confess he was just being jealous. However, Varn pushed the thought to the back of his mind, more determined than ever to see Mayven safely away from this place as soon as possible.

Storming through the door of his office, Varn ignored Demok, who gazed at him inquiringly from his customary seat in front of Varn's desk. Instead, Varn marched silently to his cabinet and poured a drink, downing it in one gulp that left him gasping for breath.

"Didn't go well, I take it," Demok drawled, a hint of amusement lacing his words.

Varn glared at Demok silently as he poured another drink then, walking around his desk, collapsed into his chair to stare morosely at his drink. "I just need to get her out of here."

"For her protection or for your own reasons?" Demok inquired, diving instantly to the heart of the matter.

Varn felt anger boil to the surface and released all his pent-up emotions on Demok in one vicious sentence. "I'm charged with her protection, am I not? You made sure of that."

Demok's shrugged. "That wasn't the question."

"I don't trust Xietak."

Demok's face remained impassive. "Why? Because he has done something or said something to make you feel he's untrustworthy? Or maybe because he cares for Mayven?"

Varn ignored Demok's remark. "Xietak says the test is to be held before we are scheduled to leave. He doesn't know when for sure. I think we have time. We need to make sure there are no problems with our exit from Shimiera. I think leaving tomorrow isn't a good idea."

Demok raised an eyebrow. "That is the worst justification I have heard in my life. You're jealous. You never listen, Varn. I told you to quit trying to see your relationship with Mayven as only business and admit you are attracted and perhaps even falling in love with the girl. You'll see things much more clearly that way. Your motivations for dawdling put Mayven in more danger, not less. They only serve to clear from the field what you view as competition."

Varn gulped the rest of his drink and slammed it on the table before standing to pace the perimeter of his office. *I wouldn't do anything that selfish.* However, he instantly recognized the lie for what it was and, instead of changing tactics, he spun to face his uncle, hands clasped fiercely behind his back.

Varn stared a Demok for a long moment. "If Xietak suddenly disappears, Adamdavas will instantly know he had reason to sabotage the device. They'll tear his life apart, looking for the connection to the Language Master. It won't take them long to find Mayven."

Demok calmly clasped his hands in his. "And we will all be safely away from here when that happens. Adamdavas does not have free reign or right in Kieshan. They would have to look for her the hard way there. You and I both know how difficult that can be. We'll have plenty of time to inform and prepare her for what comes next by the time they even get close."

Varn acknowledged silently the validity of Demok's argument but in his mind he pictured Xietak with his lips on Mayven's cheek and his hand on Mayven's back. "I'm doing this my way, Uncle. As you have repeatedly told me, I am in charge now and this is a game for younger men. Let me do what needs to be done. You need not concern yourself here."

Demok rose from his chair, his eyes narrowed on Varn's face. Anger radiated from Demok in waves as he marched across the room to face Varn, their faces almost touching. Demok's finger jabbed Varn in the chest. "You need to face your true feelings and get them out of the way. Then you need to get her and her friends out of here tomorrow. I have already arranged everything. You will do this."

Varn stumbled back from the force of magic used in Demok's declaration. Varn shook his head, anger burning through the compulsion laced into every word Demok had spoken. "I have also arranged passage for tomorrow. We'll discuss the better options in the morning. I'll do as I see fit. You're dismissed."

Demok's parting words, spoken quietly, cut Varn to the core and poured ice water on his boiling temper. "For the first time in my life, nephew, I find myself ashamed of you. How different are you from all the others who wish to control her life without her permission?"

Demok exited the office, leaving Varn staring after him in silence.

CHAPTER NINE

Mayven bolted from the car and raced to the elevator, blindly seeking refuge in her room. *I have to make sure there are plans to leave. Xietak is not going to sacrifice himself for me. Varn said he is working on plans, but he was more occupied with jealousy than Xietak's safety.*

Something in the emotions Mayven had read from Varn told her Varn knew the test Xietak was to undergo and that it wasn't good news for Xietak. Mayven racked her brain, trying to find a way around Varn in order to help Xietak. For a brief moment, nothing came to mind as Mayven paced futilely around the confines of her room. Then a face flashed through her memory as she recalled meeting Varn's Uncle Demok.

Without hesitation, she grabbed her engaohnie from where she had carelessly tossed it on the bed and looked up the number for Demok in the guild members' registry. Mayven's breath came in short rapid gasps as her fingers flew over the lighted screen.

Punching the last button, Mayven held the device to her ear and waited for an answer on the other end. Demok's message box answered Mayven's call and she left a brief, urgent message and hung up. Mayven paced the room for a long while before falling into bed to stare unseeing at the ceiling while admonishing herself that she may not even receive a return call until the morning.

A brief thought of applying herself to her homework as a form of distraction occurred to Mayven but she quickly pushed that aside. Instead, Mayven reviewed the events of the last two nights, going over every detail she could recall. The effort left Mayven more uneasy than before, and she sprang from her bed and began to pace once more when her engaohnie chimed loudly in the silent room, indicating an incoming call.

Mayven grabbed the device from the bed once more and jabbed her finger at the screen. "Hello!?"

Demok's voice replied from the other end, "I need to meet you downstairs in the library. Please hurry."

Mayven didn't question anything, she simply hung up and raced from her room, headed for the elevator and the ground floor. When she walked into the library, moments later, she found Demok pacing restlessly in the center of the room.

Upon hearing her enter, Demok looked up. "Lock the door behind you and come have a seat."

Mayven did as requested and settled into a chair at one of the round tables in the center of the room next to a large pile of books on which Demok rested his hand as he leaned against the table.

Demok began without preamble, "I assume Xietak is the reason you called me, much as he is the reason I called you. Because we have little time, I am going to be direct. I need you to research a ritual known as Vayshatka. I will go and speak to Xietak while you are doing so."

Mayven instantly opened her mouth to object, but Demok interrupted her before she could speak, "I can go to his guild without being questioned. You cannot. I'm going to relay my evacuation plans for tomorrow. I need you to research the test Adamdavas is going to do on your friend in case, for some, reason they have already conducted it. In addition, I need you to be waiting to receive a guest from the transportation guild. She should be here tonight. I believe you may know her. Her name is Amalayna."

Mayven felt a rush of relief and nodded agreement.

Demok nodded in return. "I need you to use every natural ability you possess when going over these books. If you find even the smallest thing that might be helpful, file it away in your brain. Do not write it down. Lock this door behind me. Answer only to Amalayna; she will let you know she is here. I will be back as soon as I can."

With that, Mayven watched Demok exit the library, locking the door behind him. Mayven, following Demok's instructions, turned to the pile of books in front of her and dug in. The first book was histories on religious points of view, outlining the theology and differences of the two most practiced religions, Jaysha, the followers of a god known as Dsohoay and Hsayda, the followers of a god known as Hsdaie.

Mayven read quickly, recognizing much of the rituals of Hsdaie were practiced daily in the life she had observed since living in the orphanage. It was the religion of Jaysha that drew her attention, however. It outlined a religion that followed Dsohoay and whose followers dedicated their lives to service of others. Mayven found the information enlightening and the theological differences made it clear why clerics of Dsohoay were often persecuted in Shimiera and the shen tree temples left empty. Her first hint of the ritual that Demok mentioned was actually found in that first book.

Jaysha described the Vayshatka ritual as a forced possession by demons known as Tarlens. The Hsayda religion outlined the ritual as a way to control wayward followers. Mayven shuddered, instantly recognizing the description of Tarlens as the blessings she had watched people purchase during the Hsayda festivals held during the first week of summer each year. She wondered how many truly understood what they were allowing to invade their minds and bodies.

It was then she recalled seeing the clerics in white in alleys outside temples at the Hsayda festivals. *Clerics of Dsohoay, this describes the people helping the ones left in the alleys outside of midie temples at the Hsayda festivals.*

Mayven devoured several more pages, learning that the light she had seen the clerics of Dsohoay use were actually angels or messengers of Dsohoay, called Nifen. They used them to banish the demons. For a moment, Mayven was delighted, believing she had found the answer until further reading revealed that Vayshatka was a far more insidious form of possession.

Mayven's heart was in her throat and fear turned her blood to ice as she read the description of Vayshatka and its literal translation from the ancient language. She was so involved in her research that when a knock sounded at the door she jumped from her seat to face the door. Hands trembling and her breathing rapid, it took her a moment to register it must be Amalayna as Demok had promised.

Running to the door, Mayven pressed the panel for it to open, then waited impatiently for Amalayna to enter and the door to close and lock once more. Mayven absently brushed by Amalayna and headed back to the table and her stack of research, desperate now to find a way to save Xietak.

Amalayna stopped Mayven with a hand against her chest. "What's the matter? I haven't seen you like this since the incident in the nursery at the orphanage."

Mayven stepped around Amalayna, her first thought to not tell

Amalayna the situation or her concerns on the matter. Then a thought stopped Mayven in her tracks. *I hate the secrets. I hate the lies. I hate the half-truths that are told supposedly with my good in mind. I won't do that to Amalayna, not any more.*

Mayven slowly turned back to face Amalayna. Taking her hand, she led Amalayna to the table and sat her down. "I have a great deal to explain."

The abbreviated version of the last two years and the resulting situation with Xietak left Mayven sitting in her chair, staring up at Amalayna, who towered over her, livid and berating Mayven in very colorful language.

Mayven calmly allowed the diatribe to continue for a brief while, knowing she well deserved it, then at last held up a hand. "I understand I've done and been all those things. I give you my word and all the considerable power behind that as promise I'll not keep any more secrets from you, no matter how painful. That being said, we have work to do and, so far, what I've discovered is not in our favor. You have two choices, help me or fume in silence."

Amalayna stood in open-mouthed silence for the breadth of a heart-beat then dived into the nearest chair and grabbed a book. "Now there's the girl I love, straight to the point. What's taking you so long? Get busy already, you've wasted enough time with this talking thing, highly overrated, believe me."

Mayven smiled as she shook her head and returned to the book she had previously been reading. "Commit all you find to memory, don't write it down. If you aren't sure if you'll remember something you deem important, I'll read it. Understood?"

Amalayna nodded her agreement, then for a long time the room remained silent, punctuated only by the intermittent sound of rustling paper. Mayven searched every page of the text regarding the two religions for an antidote for the Vayshatka, the only hope a brief reference to a mythological item known as the Tears of Dsohoay. It didn't take long before she had gone through several more large volumes, unaware of the speed of her reading until the sound of pounding on the library door jarred Mayven back to awareness.

Mayven glanced at Amalayna, who regarded her with wide, frightened, silver eyes. Motioning in their silent language, Mayven instructed Amalayna to hide out of sight behind the bookcases as she approached the door.

When Amalayna was safely out of sight, Mayven called out, "Who is it? I've reserved the library for tonight, and you are disturbing my study."

"Let me in now, Mayven."

Mayven's breath released in a sigh of relief as the furious, barely audible voice of Varn answered from the opposite side of the door.

Mayven did as directed and opened the door, then locked and closed it behind Varn once more as he stepped into the library. Mayven turned to face Varn and instinctively took a step backwards.

Varn advanced on Mayven, his tone furious, his face hard in anger. "What were you doing in here? I felt the shift in the flow of adamie like a tidal wave."

Mayven's eyes flickered to the table behind Varn. "I thought you knew."

Varn spun on his heel, marching across the room in four long strides. "Why would I know what you were doing?" Perusing the table's contents at a glance, Varn's face went from livid red to deathly white.

"Demok told me to come here. He gave me instructions to research the ritual of Vayshatka, memorize all that I learn, and to wait until he returned."

Varn lowered his chin to his chest as he raked his fingers through his hair. "How long ago did he leave?"

Mayven glanced at the crystal clock display above the library door. "Almost four bells ago now."

Varn's engaohnie stone beeped, and he yanked it from his pocket, glancing briefly at the screen. Shoving it back into his pocket, he began scooping up the books on the table.

"Get over here and help me. We're about to have company. Your use of your gift created a disturbance and payjiks are on their way to find out who is using unsanctioned magic."

Simultaneously, Mayven raced to the table to gather books, and Amalayna bounded out from behind the bookcase. Varn, not aware of Amalayna's presence, jumped, dropping the books he held on the floor.

Amalayna raised a brow as she bent down to help him retrieve them. "Don't let a little thing like me scare you, handsome."

Mayven paused a brief moment to roll her eyes at Amalayna then continued gathering books. Turning to Varn, Mayven waited for instructions, her arms filled to capacity.

Varn said, "Follow me and hurry."

A brief time later, the books were once again stacked in the vault, a new pile positioned on the table, the library door wide open with Varn, Amalayna, and Mayven sitting together diligently reading the texts.

Varn spoke low, his voice barely carrying across the table to Mayven and Amalayna, "They'll be here shortly. You will need to learn how to lie inventively to get out of this one. If something happens, go with them peacefully. I'll come for you."

Mayven gave Varn a tight, angry smile. *Allowing someone to think up their own lie has become my specialty.*

Moments passed in silence as they waited, then the sound of several voices, one of them Demok's, approached the library. "I assure you all our students are accounted for. Please come see for yourself."

Mayven slowly turned in her seat as Demok, accompanied by two payjiks in their copper tunics, entered the room. Demok's eyes momentarily widened in surprise as he caught sight of Varn at the library table.

The payjik's quick eye caught the expression, however, not the target, and he quickly took a closer look at the table's occupants and zeroed his questioning in on Amalayna. "What are you doing here, young lady? It's after curfew, and you're not supposed to be out of your dorms. It's against regulations to use your abilities for personal use without the proper permits. Come with me this instant."

Amalayna didn't miss a beat. She stood, making a brief obscure hand gesture to Mayven in the process. "I haven't seen my friend in a very long time, and I've missed her. What is to happen to me?"

The payjik leveled an angry gaze in Amalayna's direction. "I'm taking you to your guild house, and your guild master will decide your punishment. I suggest you be properly apologetic. You have caused a great deal of trouble this evening."

The payjik turned to Demok and, giving an obsequious and oily apology, escorted Amalayna from the room without noticing the parting nervous movements of Amalayna's hands on the way out the door. Mayven mirrored the gesture as the group turned away, then waited until Demok closed the library door and locked it once more to demand, "What will happen to Amalayna?"

Demok raised a hand. "She'll be fine. I was aware that something might happen and must admit to a bit of subterfuge in my reasons for having her present tonight. Amalayna will most likely get a stern talking to and a written reprimand. She is much too powerful and valuable to have any permanent damage done to her for such a seemingly minor infraction as what they assume happened here tonight."

Varn advanced on his uncle. "What *did* happen here tonight? Why did they assume Amalayna did it, and where have you been?"

Demok raised an eyebrow. "My usually observant nephew missed the xodieha on her forehead? Amalayna is a remarkably talented transportation mage. She has an amazing and very powerful teleporting ability."

Demok calmly took a seat at the table, glancing casually at the contents, before asking, "Did you find anything useful, Mayven?"

"That only answered one of my questions, Uncle," Varn interrupted, not allowing Mayven to speak. "You put this entire guild in jeopardy, not to mention Mayven. She used her gift. She could have been caught, and you have still not explained why you put her in such danger."

"I had business that needed attending to." Demok artfully avoid answering the question. "I needed to find the answer to the pressing matter at hand. I made sure to have an alibi in place should the moment arise that something unfortunate might occur." Demok reclined in his seat, calmly flipping through a large volume entitled *The Basics of Adamie*.

Mayven listened incredulously to Demok. *Now I understand where Varn learned to lie. Tell the truth, just never the important part.*

Varn slammed his hand on the tabletop, causing a loud crack that echoed through the room. "I'm not interested in your lucky avoidance of disaster, Uncle. Where were you?"

Demok's normally congenial demeanor vanished as he rose from his seat to his full six-foot three-inch height to glare at Varn. "I was busy doing what you should have done, had you listened to me in the first place." Demok's tone was laced in contempt. "Xietak has been informed of our departure plans. We're all set to leave tomorrow at nine bells. I'll tolerate no further childish behavior from you, Varn. It's time you listened to what I said. There is more than business involved in the connection you share. Deal with it before pointless emotions blind you further and create a situation you cannot remedy. I'm going to ready myself for departure. Amalayna and Xietak will both be ready. I advise the two of you be prepared as well. Goodnight." Demok left without looking back.

Mayven turned to face Varn. "Explain."

He sat down and smoothed his breeches in his now familiar procrastination gesture. For several long moments, Varn examined and picked at nonexistent lint on his pant leg. "What were those hand gestures you and Amalayna were doing?"

Mayven balked at his avoidance. "It's a secret way of communicating we came up with at the orphanage because we couldn't speak aloud to each other or communicate where others understood." Mayven's tone sharpened. "What did your uncle mean about taking care of what you should have? What does this have to do with you and me?"

CHAPTER TEN

Varn listened to Mayven's questions, wanting to run from the explanation he was loathe to give. *Uncle is right to be ashamed of me. I'm jealous she isn't just my charge. What have I done? How do I explain now?*

Varn stood and started picking up books and putting them away. He remained silent for a long while, hoping Mayven might give up, but he felt her silent presence like an accusation against him as he moved quietly around the room. Varn smoothed the soft, worn fayen fabric cover of the last volume, breathing in the smell of oil and parchment before carefully placing it on the shelf and turning to face Mayven, who regarded him with barely restrained impatience.

Varn cleared his throat, then walked back to the table. He motioned for Mayven to sit and followed suit, folding his hands in front of him on the tabletop. Varn unclasped his hands, running them across the cool smooth surface of the pale maplewood table.

"My uncle has explained to me that the connection between us is more than just a connection for your safety. He implied that it was meant to be a more intimate connection."

Varn felt the back of his neck heat as he recalled his reactions to her thus far. *It's lust at least. That is a fact.*

"I'm, according to the prophets, not only your protector but your soul mate. I don't know if that's true." Varn stood up and turned his back toward her, all the while feeling her eyes burning into his back. He felt her surprise and disbelief, along with her customary reaction, anger.

Varn turned back to face Mayven, hands raised in surrender. "I understand, you don't want this. You don't believe it. You just want to be free to choose for yourself. I have all those same feelings, but the fact remains that when it comes to you, I have to admit a certain lack of clear judgment on occasion."

Surprisingly, Mayven remained silent, but the raised eyebrow and her expression clearly demanded clarification, as did the suspicion she telegraphed across their connection.

Varn took a deep breath and decided to just say it. "I may have been less than concerned about the consequences when it came to Xietak. I let my feelings for you cloud my judgment."

The anger in Mayven notched up another level, but she remained silent. Varn watched her struggle to keep silent as he rushed on while he began to pace the perimeter of the circled tables, "I wasn't in a hurry to expedite our departure because I was jealous."

Varn groaned and fell into a nearby chair and, resting his elbows on his knees and holding his head in his hands, muttered, "I didn't look at the obvious point; we're all better off away from here, sooner rather than later."

The final words had barely left his mouth as he raised his head to look at her and received the flat of her palm across his face. Then, without another word, she left the room. Varn's first reaction was anger. She had struck him! His next was the shock at the unbelievable grief and shame he felt rolling across their connection. Varn felt as if someone had tied an iron band across his ribs.

Varn pressed a hand against his heart and gasped as grief and guilt slammed into him in waves that drove him to his knees on the floor and left him gasping for breath. He forced himself to focus and breathe, trying to dampen Mayven's emotional volume. The effort was physically exhausting and when at last he succeeded he was drenched in sweat and his own anger was completely gone. Instead he felt a shame he was sure mirrored Mayven's.

Varn stumbled to his feet and blindly began to walk, his mind numbed by effort and emotion. When he stopped walking, he stared blankly for a few moments at the door to his uncle's room. Then, taking a deep breath, he pressed the panel next to the door and waited for an answer.

The door slid open, and his uncle stood there, a knowing expression on his face. Demok wrapped an arm around Varn's shoulders and escorted him into his small apartments. "Well, how did it go?"

Varn groaned and fell into a chair, gratefully taking the glass of Iresta his uncle offered him. Varn didn't answer for a long time as he sipped his drink and looked around the small apartment packed full of crystal displays that flashed photos of himself, Layla, Hardak, and Demok. He looked at the mementos displayed on various shelves of adventures that stood like monuments to the times he and his uncle had spent together, joined not just by a cause but by love and loyalty.

Varn gasped as understanding dawned on him in a blinding flash. *Mayven blindly trusted me because someone she trusted instilled in her the belief that I would do nothing to harm her, and yet I put those she loves and protects at risk. I was willing to sacrifice her family over jealousy.*

Varn slammed down the remainder of his drink and looked at his uncle. "I don't know how to help her now. She may never trust me again."

Demok smiled encouragingly. "Protect your connection to her. Nurture it. Admit how you truly feel about her to yourself, if no one else, and filter all your decisions through that lens. Never assume your answer is always right, and respect her choices, even if you don't agree. The rest will just take time and patience."

Varn sat quietly with Demok for a long while. "I think I best get prepared for tomorrow," he said at last. "Is there anything I need to know?"

"You meet me in your office with Mayven at precisely seven bells in the morning. We'll briefly discuss the details then."

Varn nodded and rose, accepting gratefully a tight hug from his uncle before departing for his own rooms. Sleep eluded him for a long while as he constantly monitored Mayven and tried to send her every apologetic and contrite feeling he felt. When at length his eyes drifted closed and he slept, he dreamed of a violet-eyed beauty who stared at him with pain-filled eyes and tear-stained cheeks.

Restlessness, rather than his alarm, woke him as the gray light of dawn peeked in his windows. Turning his alarm off, he rushed through a shower. On his way out the door, he grabbed his gym bag and headed down the hall to Mayven's room. Mayven answered before he had pressed the call button on the door, and they walked to the elevator in complete silence.

Varn offered Mayven a cup of fayen juice and a roll from his customary breakfast tray that waited on his side cupboard. Mayven took it without comment and settled into a chair to await Demok's arrival.

Varn looked up expectantly as the door slid open moments later. Demok stepped in and, without a single word of greeting, stated, "I need you both to go to the main otal station. Take the portal to the uptown business district and meet me at the guild council house at precisely nine bells. I have a way out from there. Varn, you know the location I am speaking of. Don't be late. I will arrive with Xietak, and Amalayna will arrive via another connection. Follow all protocols. Don't veer from the routine. If anything goes wrong, protect Mayven's identity at any cost."

Varn nodded understanding.

Mayven simply looked up at them both from her seat. "I'll do what I need to do."

Demok gave Mayven a questioning look, then turned to Varn. Varn read the unspoken question in Demok's expression but realized for the first time that morning that Mayven wasn't telegraphing her emotions or intent to him at all. Her emotions were as closed off as the expression that turned her exquisite features into a blank alabaster mask.

Shock must have registered on Varn's face, because Demok wrapped an arm around Varn's shoulders, leading him out of the office. "You aren't able to read her, are you?"

Varn shook his head. "I can only sense her faintly across our connection."

"You need to not mute anything she is feeling or thinking. Read whatever she leaks through, She has learned to block you out. That could be dangerous and painful if it lasts."

Varn opened his mouth to inquire but Demok shook his head. "I don't have time to explain. Just fix it, Varn, quickly."

Then, with another fierce hug, he left. Varn reentered his office and carefully took a seat. "I understand your reasons for being angry at me, Mayven. I know you feel betrayed, rightfully so."

"I'm so glad my emotions are so acceptable to you," she replied, her voice a cutting monotone. "I'm sure you understand if that doesn't change my opinion of you at this point."

Varn, having let down his barriers, was surprised at the relief he felt when her anger reached out and assaulted him, if only weakly. Varn nodded and did not try to engage her again as they waited mutely for the clock to continue its steady march forward. When eight bells chimed, they rose in unison and headed out of the guild house for the otal station.

The bright morning light assaulted Varn's senses like an accusation as the smell of springtime flowers and the cool light filtered through the swaying verdant canopy above his head. People traversed the limb walkways intertwined above the streets. Small green gardens dotted the spaces between towering trees, displaying the bright colors of flowers that announced the full arrival of spring. Everywhere he looked, he saw painted in nature the impressions of hope, life, and new beginnings, making Varn all the more aware of the silent, closed creature walking beside him.

The otal station was packed with the customary early morning traffic commuting to work. He and Mayven blended right in and arrived at the guild council house about ten minutes early.

Varn escorted Mayven inside the ancient tree. "This is the oldest tree in Rashmahava. It's been the guild council house for countless generations."

From the corner of his eye, Varn watched Mayven, pleased to see that her feigned disinterest did not extend to subjects other than himself. Encouraged by her interest, he led Mayven to the elevator and pressed the down button. "The guild council manages the affairs of the guilds. They regulate the rules and approve all membership requests for apprentices who wish to become permanent members of their individual guild. The stained glass windows represent each of the four clans and the totems that belong to each clan."

She examined the windows before asking, "Where is the totem of the Language Master? Where do I belong in all this?"

Varn felt yet another stab of guilt as he recognized the longing to belong. He replied without evasion, "The Language Master totem is a tree. It signifies the connection between all the elements that govern the other clans. The roots of the tree are anchored in earth and water and its branches stretch into the sky, connecting to air and the sun, which represents fire. Through the Language Master, the complete power of all the elements are combined in harmony and when truly mastered can be an unstoppable force for good or evil."

Varn waited for a response but Mayven didn't comment as she looked at each window and examined the intricate imagery magically carved in vivid detail around the four stained glass windows arching above the door in the cavernous foyer of the council hall. The windows were placed so that they appeared in the carving like brightly colored fruits hanging from the massive limbs of a shen tree. The enormous tree occupied the entire front of the council hall.

The roots of the carving spread out from the wall onto the floor and stretched giant fingers toward a small raised planting bed. The bed was filled with flowers and a delicate living wood sculpture of a pump that poured water out of a spout into small wooden bucket. Mayven examined it at length, and Varn registered satisfaction for a brief moment along their connection before she once again became unreadable.

The elevator silently arrived and they stepped inside and plummeted into a rock room located beneath the base of the council tree. Inside the walls of the smooth rock room were two pillars that held crystals that anchored the portal suspended between them. Several long minutes more of silence passed, then the elevator again arrived and Amalayna stepped out.

Varn watched as Mayven rushed forward and embraced her friend in relief. Glancing up at the clock, Varn noted the hour for the third time since they had arrived. *Uncle is never late. What is going on?*

As if in silent answer to his question, the portal between the posts snapped closed. *This portal only closes when the otal stations are being monitored.* Varn instantly registered a problem. *Adamdavas is closing the peripheral otals connected to the network. They are hunting someone. It won't take them long to get here. They'll lock down the elevator first. We better take the stairs.*

Varn sprang into action. Without explanation, he grabbed both girls by the arms and raced for the door next to the elevator. The door slid open at the press of a button, and Varn dragged the women behind him up the staircase two steps at a time.

Varn was grateful that neither one bothered to pepper him with inane questions as they raced out into the foyer of the council building then out the front door, quickly melding into the milling morning crowds. Varn slowed, keeping a casual hand on each of the women's elbows and matched his speed to the bustle of the others around them.

Varn released them after a short distance. "Stay close."

Varn pulled his engaohnie stone from his pocket, punched several buttons on the touch display and held it to his ear. "I need my car immediately. I have guild business I can't be late for. I'll send the co-ordinates."

Varn disconnected the call and then typed in another message before shoving the device back in his pocket. Then, casually linking his arms with the women, he strolled up the street, stopping occasionally to look into window displays. Varn used those occasions to scan the crowd around him through the reflection and noted, impressed, that Mayven and Amalayna seemed to be doing the same thing.

The women also would occasionally make small talk and point out random things, as if the three of them were simply out on a shopping trip. At a corner transportation station nearly three blocks from the council tree, they met with Laydak and were whisked into Varn's pod car.

Once safely inside and hidden from outside ears and eyes, Varn turned to the women. "Something has gone wrong. We're retreating to our secondary exit plan. Continue as you have been. Am I clear?"

Neither woman spoke but nodded in understanding before turning to look at each other. Varn felt a moment's frustration at the fact that he recognized the almost imperceptible nervous hand movements of the women.

I picked a bad time to let lust run my life. I really need her to listen and trust me right now. Varn groaned inwardly at the virtual silence registering along the connection that still tugged at him insistently.

The pod car picked up speed as they cleared the city traffic and raced up Bomar Pass on the way out of Rashmahava toward the Baksadie Mountains. Varn watched anxiously outside the windows, observing each car they passed with keen interest as he repeatedly checked his engaohnie.

Where is the message? Why hasn't he signaled that he reached the secondary location? Varn's thoughts raced frantically around his head as he reasoned with himself. *I haven't had time to reach the location yet. There is still time.*

Varn noted Mayven clutched Amalayna's hand and stared impassively out the window, each of the women's hands now completely still, their expressions completely neutral.

What have I done? I need to know what she is thinking, now more than ever, and she has completely shut me out.

The silence inside the car was interrupted by Laydak. "We've arrived, Jayben Amalvadar."

Varn looked intently at the women. "We're at my uncle's estate. We should be meeting Demok and Xietak here. If, for any reason, you must escape, there is a door leading to a passage beneath Demok's property and out into the mountains beyond the gated estates. Once out there, find any path you can back to the city and reappear at your guilds with whatever story you can tell without lying. Am I clear? Do not, under any circumstance, allow anyone but Xietak, Demok, or to I see either of your faces until you have reached a safe location. You cannot be sighted in order to keep your anonymity."

Varn was impressed that neither woman asked a question. They simply nodded in unison and followed him out of the car and into the towering expanse of the willow that was Demok's ancestral home. Inside, the home was sweet smelling and silent. Varn felt worry and fear clutch at him as he prayed silently. *Dsohoay, please let him get here!*

As if on cue, the front door opened and Demok entered, alone.

Demok didn't allow anyone to speak. "I was followed. Get out of here."

Just then, a blinding light filled the open doorway behind Demok and pierced his body like a sword. The light poured across the room, burning a scorching circle in the opposite wall through the hole it created in Demok, who stood on his tiptoes, suspended, his face frozen in agony and eyes devoid of life.

Varn felt horror and grief mushroom inside his chest. Squashing the pain, Varn reacted as trained and spun, leading the women down the hall to the secret passage and out beneath the grounds of his family estates. At length, the long, dark, close rock passage gave way to light. Beyond the tunnel mouth, the forest seemed to stretch interminably into the distance, the close-packed trunks of uncultivated trees and brush nearly drowned out the morning light filtering down from above the treetops.

Varn turned to Mayven. "I need you to get the two of you safely back to Rashmahava. If I'm captured and I'm not with you, I can't give up a location I don't know. Go now and don't look back."

Varn received a brief silent nod from Mayven, then the two promptly darted into the nearest thicket, disappearing from view. Varn took a few moments to conceal their trail then headed on a path parallel to them, not bothering to cover his own tracks.

CHAPTER ELEVEN

Mayven clutched Amalayna's hand as they rushed through the undergrowth. Mayven pushed Amalayna onward for a long time in silence, then at last Mayven slowed to walk. Mayven's breathing was heavy, her muscles trembling with exertion. Her mind, however, still raced. *Where is Xietak? Why did Demok show up alone? Demok is dead! Does that mean Xietak is dead?*

Mayven kept replaying the scene over in her mind and it kept leading her back to one thought. *Demok is dead, and he arrived alone. That means that either Xietak is also dead or Adamdavas discovered their attempt to get him away and made him undergo the test early.*

Mayven shook her head, trying to focus on the task at hand. She knew they were headed down the pass toward Rashmahava, but their exact location she didn't know. Deciding that downhill would eventually lead them to Rashmahava, Mayven forged ahead as the minutes turned to hours. The dense forest made traveling slow as they had to push their way through thick hedges and densely packed brambles. Soon the low light filtering through the canopy above began to dim and change as the air grew heavy with the smell of rain.

Mayven tried to get her bearings as she muttered, "It didn't take this long to get up here."

Amalayna groaned. "You do realize we were riding in a pod car traveling well above the limit to get here, right?"

Mayven rolled her eyes, ignoring Amalayna as she pushed past another thicket as its longer branches tangled in her now ragged braid and ripped at her tunic. They traveled quietly again for a long while as the dim light turned to dark gray, making the densely packed forest almost as dark as night. The rain started falling in a steady mist that quickly turned into a torrential downpour, and soon they were both drenched.

Mayven shrugged, uncomfortable from the constricting cling of her sodden tunic. Her wet breeches chaffed her thighs and her sodden feet felt like cubes of ice inside her mud-covered boots. Shivering, teeth chattering, and soaked to the skin, Mayven curled close to Amalayna, trying to conserve their body heat as they huddled beneath the branches of a very large maple. Though its large leaves and considerable bower slowed the rain some, it didn't stop it, and the rain had not slowed. Mayven studied Amalayna's face, noting the blue tint to her chattering lips.

How are we getting out of this one? Can it get any worse? Mayven mentally chastised herself as the sound of voices from not far away answered her question. *Never ask that question if you don't want to know the answer!*

Grabbing Amalayna's hand, Mayven pulled her carefully around the base of the tree, away from the sound of the approaching voices. Once out of sight of the others' approach, they turned and ran again. But running is much more difficult when half frozen, exhausted, and the ground is slick with mud.

Mayven struggled to stay upright and failed miserably, as did Amalayna, and soon they were both covered in caked-on grime. The last fall they took left Amalayna with an ankle that would no longer support her weight. *I could heal it. But they may have a payjik and out here any use of adamie would be out of place and easily trackable.* Mayven reconsidered, remembering the incident with the payjic at the guild house.

The sound of their pursuers grew loud enough to be heard over a peeling roll of thunder. *They are far too close in order to be heard over this storm. I have to find a place to hide.*

Mayven felt fear tighten around her chest, making it hard to breathe as she searched, desperate for a hiding spot. Supporting Amalayna with one arm, she turned slowly in a circle, assessing one hiding spot after another before discarding each in turn. Then Mayven spotted what she hopped would be her salvation, a midie tree.

The midie tree stood in a tight cluster of weeping willows. In the darkness of the forest, its black reflective leaves and trunk created a visual illusion that it, too, was a weeping willow. Mayven watched the storm stir the branches and the effect was an illusion of flickering light and dark that made discerning what was beneath those branches impossible. She had found their refuge. Studying the ground behind them, she was grateful to note that the deluge that was giving them hypothermia was also washing away signs of their passing.

Mayven looked at Amalayna. "Get on my back. I'm going to do my best not to leave any tracks."

Amalayna scrambled awkwardly onto Mayven's back, then Mayven began to move forward, one careful step at a time. Another voice rang out over the storm, even closer than the last. *Please just let them be as slow as we are!* Stepping from root to root, Mayven made her way beneath the midie tree and prayed that the rushing stream of water flowing downhill would wash the roots clear of their footprints before their pursuers grew closer.

Mayven listened to the sound of mud sucking at boots and voices calling back and forth. Then, a voice she had only heard once in her life pronounced, "I don't see anything out here. If they have gone this way, Captain, their tracks have been washed away."

Mayven clamped a hand over her mouth as the brutal face of the boy who had killed her teacher on her first day at the orphanage peered intently in the direction of the midie tree under which they crouched. Mayven knew he would have to get much closer to see them through the visually disturbing branches of the tree, especially since they had hunkered down behind some low bushes that grew around the base. However, that knowledge didn't squash the unreasoning fear that gripped her as she trembled violently from cold and shock.

The boy stepped closer, peering into the branches, carefully inching closer to their hiding spot with every step he took. Mayven knew they were trapped. Moving now would immediately give them away, so she waited, her heart hammering in her ears.

Then chance gave them a break as another voice called, "I think I found a trail over here."

The brutish boy stared intently at their hiding spot a moment longer before turning on his heel and leaving. Mayven held Amalayna in place as they waited long after the sounds of pursuit had grown silent. During that time, the rain slowed down again. Mayven murmured a quick prayer of thanks as she hoisted Amalayna onto her back and headed down the mountain once more.

Nearly an hour later, exhausted and barely able to stand, Mayven gratefully glimpsed the edge of Rashmahava. They had come out at the lower end of town, down below Fisherman's Wharf and not that far, she noted, from Hardak's bar.

Pub, she corrected mentally, a bit of hysterical laughter bubbling from her lips as she recalled Hardak's comment to Varn. Mayven stumbled into an alley and made her way along the back of the living buildings away from the prying eyes of anyone on the street. When she reached the back of Hardak's, she pressed her hand against the entry pad and waited anxiously for the door to open. Which it did, not a moment too soon.

At the far end of the alley, Mayven heard the tromp of Gayied boots marching in formation.

A man's voice called out, "Check all the alleys. If anyone came out of the forest down here, I doubt they would risk being seen on the streets."

Mayven slipped gratefully into the back of the kitchen, her body shuddering from cold as Hardak reached out and plucked Amalayna from her back like a child.

Hardak's broad smile lit up his features. "I'm glad you two showed up. Varn called, saying you might."

Mayven interrupted what he might have continued saying as she announced, "We need to get dry, clean, and settled in the bar. The Gayied are in the alley looking for anyone who looks like this."

Mayven indicated her filth-encrusted, soaked attire and matted hair.

Layla stepped into the kitchen. "Lucky for you, Varn has lots of friends. Help me get them upstairs, Hardak. Varn sent over clean uniforms for our young friends here."

Mayven gratefully followed Layla up the stairs out of the kitchen and into a small bedroom. Hardak exited, and Mayven stripped down as Layla unceremoniously undressed Amalayna and pitched all their clothes directly into the recycle shredder, then bustled them into the shower. Reminded of their first day at the orphanage, Mayven made quick work of showering off first Amalayna then herself.

Layla had just helped Amalayna into her clothes and Mayven was buttoning the last of her blouse when Hardak knocked on the door. "You ladies better hurry up. The Gayied are now going through the store next door. They'll be here any moment."

Mayven eyed Amalayna's wet hair and swollen ankle that she was struggling to stand on. Taking a deep breath, Mayven drew in the energy pooled within the tree then willed it to warm, dry, and heal herself. Then, in a rush, she transferred the rest to Amalayna. In a moment, they were both warm, dry and Amalayna's foot was back to its normal size. The welts that had decorated any exposed patch of skin were gone as if they'd never been.

Amalayna, observing Layla's look of disbelief, shrugged. "You'll get used to it. She does this weird sort of thing a lot."

Layla barked a strange, slightly strangled laugh. Leading the way out of the room, Layla showed them the way down the front stairs to the bar just as the Gayied pounded on the back door. The women slipped in from the side hall, unseen. Mayven and Amalayna settled themselves at a table in a dim corner near the kitchen door. Layla casually circled the room and began speaking to customers and taking their orders.

Mayven waved Layla down and ordered a drink. Layla picked up the two glasses already sitting on the table in front of them. Just then, the contingent of Gayied searching the businesses marched out of the kitchen, led by Hardak. They brushed by Mayven and Amalayna's table with only a slight glance at Layla, who stood, empty glasses in hand, waiting to reach the bar. Mayven watched the men walk around the tables, examining each of the occupants cursorily before moving on. The Captain, satisfied that none of the patrons seemed to match what he was looking for, gathered up his men and exited out the front door.

Hardak took his place behind the bar and announced in a booming voice, "Well, that was the entertainment portion of our evening. Anyone need a drink?"

There were several nervous laughs then people began raising hands and Layla began making rounds taking orders. Several more hours passed without incident. The Gayied came and went twice more, but still found nothing that seemed to fit the description of what they were looking for.

Sometime later, Mayven looked at Amalayna. "We need to get back to our guild houses."

Amalayna started to protest this decision.

Mayven raised a hand to silence her. "I need to find Varn. Being here makes it look like we were dodging our duties to hang out. After the incident last night, it's plausible. I need to find out what happened. Varn will most likely be at the guild house. Go back to your guild. I'll contact you as soon as I safely can, I give my word."

Mayven felt a tight cord of magic connect herself to Amalayna and knew somehow she had used her magic again. Amalayna seemed to recognize it as well and was satisfied. They left the pub together. Outside, the evening sky, now clear of every cloud, displayed a brilliant canopy of stars and the bright, full, twin moons of Emwen. The two women walked in silence through the brightly lit night then parted ways at the transportation station at the corner near Hardak's pub.

CHAPTER TWELVE

Varn worked quickly, covering the girl's trail. Then he, too, departed his uncle's home, following a parallel path a short distance from Mayven down the mountainside.

Drenched to the skin and shivering, Varn remained close to Mayven's path. When the Gayied began to close in on her, Varn called their attention to him, making ample noise and leaving an obvious trail as he raced ahead of them down the mountainside.

Barely reaching Rashmahava ahead of the Gayied, Varn met Laydak in an alley near Fisherman's Wharf. After he arranged for Mayven and Amalayna to be received at Hardak's, he headed to the technology guild house in search of Xietak.

Contacts in the technology guild welcomed him without question. Liberal use of his talent, luck, and considerable stealth led him to the observation deck above the research chamber where Xietak was being held. In the darkened room of the observation deck, through the one-way glass, Varn watched, helpless, as Xietak underwent Vayshatka.

Xietak was laid on a table, his body immobilized by a restraint shield, as a small black crystalline device was placed against his neck. The leader of the guild house nodded to the man holding the device. The man tapped the device once, and Xietak began to struggle violently against his restraints, screaming.

Varn took an involuntary step forward, his hand balled into a fist as he raised it to pound on the glass. Then he stopped. *I can't help. Revealing myself would be pointless. I can't protect him. I can't save him from this without risking Amalayna and Mayven.*

Varn recalled his uncle's words on examining his motives and reconsidered his last thought, looking at every option. Still, the fact remained, he could do nothing. So instead he stood as a silent witness and watched the horror a man could endure for those he loved.

Hours passed, and Xietak didn't break. Xietak never spoke a name. He only screamed in pain and defiance. Before long, Varn had crumbled to his knees, his tear-streaked face resting against the glass as he prayed quietly for Dsohoay to protect Mayven's friend.

Varn struggled to keep silent as he witnessed Xietak's torture. His nails dug into his palms, leaving bloody half-moons on his palms, his knuckles bleached white from the strain of his grip. *How can he endure this? Surely he must break and go mad soon. He'll give them up eventually. Then what will I do? Will I be able to protect Mayven and Amalayna as he has?*

Varn felt determination blossom in his breast. *I'll do no less than Xietak. Mayven and Amalayna have suffered enough.*

Humbled by Xietak's sacrifice, Varn vowed he would find a way to be as unselfish in his protection. Then, at last, the room below grew silent. Varn felt an almost perceptible chill fill the air.

The men below were suddenly scrambling to release Xietak as a voice, sounding nothing like Xietak, spoke with Xietak's mouth. "Release me. This mortal has found a way to hide from me. I haven't broken him yet. But when we share the same mind and body, there is nowhere for him to run. In time, I'll know all his secrets. In the meantime, I may as well make use of his remarkable talents."

Varn felt fear slice through him, leaving ice in its wake. *I've heard of a master Tarlen, but I never knew they had learned how to harness one.*

The guild master addressed Xietak obsequiously. "The boy has not given us the important information. Shouldn't we press him further?"

The demon turned to face the guild master, glaring at him with Xietak's now cold eyes. "If we 'press' him further, he'll break. Then we'll not be able to attain anything useful."

The guild master nodded reflexively as everyone backed away. Xietak's body, now operated by a demon who glared out of Xietak's once kind, handsome face with cold indifference, rose from the table. Varn watched the new Xietak exit the room and the room below grew dark. Then he too quietly exited.

Back in the comfort of his office, Varn paced as he struggled with his newest dilemma.

I have to protect Mayven. I can't tell her the truth or she'll race off and endanger herself to save Xietak. That would make all he is suffering for nothing. I can't keep what I know from her. Our connection will tell her everything I manage not to say. How do I fix this?

Varn paced, weighing each option, then promptly discarding it before trying another.

Varn slumped into his chair, resting his head in his hands, at last coming to his decision. *She's already angry at me, that anger has allowed her to almost close our connection. If I push her just a little more, she may break it entirely. If I can to get her to completely break our connection, she won't be able to access my thoughts or emotions. I certainly won't be able to keep her out of my mind any other way. It's the only way I can protect her.*

That thought alone made Varn want to change his mind. The idea of not sharing the connection to Mayven he had come to cherish left him feeling empty. *What have I got to worry about? Look what Xietak has suffered. Certainly this small sacrifice is not anything compared to that.*

Convinced of his decision, Varn paced his office as he waited anxiously for Mayven to arrive. Upon feeling her presence, his thoughts began to race as he turned to face the door. *I have to tell her something. I have to provoke her to shut me out completely. I have to find a way to get her to sever the last cord. I don't know where to start. Uncle would have the answer here.*

A fresh wave of grief over Demok and Xietak made him suck in his breath and sink into his chair. Trying to control his reaction, Varn took a slow breath and turned from Mayven, who sat down across the desk from him. Varn could feel her barely contained anxiety as he stared out his office window but for once she remained silent and undemanding. Varn rubbed his temples, then raked his fingers through his hair and straightened up squarely in his chair before turning to face Mayven.

Mayven watched him from across the desk, and he read her emotions. In a flash, he felt resentment and an old anger born of grief assail his senses.

Before he could rethink his decision, Varn said, "I suppose your only care is that Xietak was not with my uncle. You're simply here in order to know where he is and how to save him."

Varn felt her react to his provocation as she leaned back in her chair, her face flashing a look of surprised hurt then altering to an unreadable mask. Across their connection, he felt a strange vibration, as if tension was stretching a string too taut. He could feel Mayven's grief, anxiety, anger, and concern. There was a brief moment where he heard her clearly as she mentally shouted, *I've had enough.*

Then the line snapped, and pain pierced through Varn, radiating out from his heart to the rest of his body. First a wave of ice, followed by scorching fire that left him breathless and frozen in its wake.

Mayven seemed not to notice his discomfort, her face placid and unreadable. Varn sucked in several deep breaths of air as he tried to control an unreasoning fear that overtook him. When the pain was gone, there was silence. He read nothing from Mayven. Varn's head was reeling, his emotions and body in shock. For a heartbeat, nothing crossed his mind; then his uncle's words repeated themselves like a whisper. *She has learned to block you out. That could be dangerous and painful if it lasts.*

Varn unconsciously raised a hand to his chest, rubbing his breast-bone just over his heart. Mayven continued to stare back at him, her face impassive and not the slightest emotion emanating from her. The thread that had connected them through two years of his constant protection and grown so much stronger from the moment they met felt lax, as if it were still connected to him but severed before it reached Mayven. If there was a pain to describe how it would feel if you lost half your heart and it was still beating, Varn was sure he had just found it.

"I need you to keep up the research Demok had you begin. We're going to need it." Varn struggled not to try and repair their connection through apology as he spoke, though speaking seemed to take more effort than he planned.

Mayven cocked an eyebrow, her expression unyielding. "I planned on continuing my research. I'm just surprised you didn't suggest that we find another opportunity and leave immediately, without Xietak."

Varn heard the rancor in her tone. The anger under her words, grating like stone on glass, jarred him but the emotion he usually got from her was absent. *Yet again I have to find out the hard way that Uncle was right. However, pain doesn't even describe this feeling. I can barely breathe.*

Varn cleared his throat and forced his hand back to his lap, though it remained clenched in a fist. "It wouldn't have done any good, even if I had suggested it. You wouldn't leave, and now Adamdavas is surely tipped off that Niesha is up to something. Better to just lay low and let this look like a Rie'hava Ktaya escape gone wrong."

Varn watched a flicker of interest cross Mayven's expression. "Rie'hava Ktaya?"

Glad for a neutral subject, Varn struggled to breathe as he forged ahead with an explanation. "Rie'hava Ktaya is a byproduct of Niesha's work here in Shimiera. We help those who wish to leave, due to persecution, find homes elsewhere. The project has served as a way to help and a distraction for Adamdavas in order to cover Niesha's other work."

Mayven offered a tight smile, her expression closed. "You mean your search for me."

Varn began to reply to her statement, but she cut him off. "Could I use that as a way to still get Amalayna out of here?"

Varn felt like someone had suddenly put a noose around his neck. *No matter how I answer this, she will not like my response, no matter how well reasoned.* He felt the weight of her broken faith in his motivations like a stone around his neck.

"We could, if she'll go, however, not right away. Rie'hava Ktaya will be under surveillance now. We have to protect everyone involved."

Mayven crossed her arms over her chest. "I am aware of that. I wouldn't put anyone in danger for my benefit." Varn flinched involuntarily at her accusation as she continued, "However, shortly it should be able to be accomplished. Correct?"

Varn nodded in reply.

Mayven stood up. "I suppose your request for me to continue the research means Xietak underwent Vayshatka?"

Varn nodded mutely, his hand unconsciously rubbing his breastbone as in his mind flashed on an image of Xietak strapped to a table.

Mayven nodded in return. "I'll continue the research. In the meantime, I want to participate in Rie'hava Ktaya, once it's safe to begin transport again. When it is safe, I want Amalayna away from here."

"Understood, I'll let you speak to Hardak and Layla about it. They operate Rie'Hava Ktaya. They'll know where you're needed."

Varn noted a slight surprise register on Mayven's face before her expression once again became impassive. Then, turning, she walked out of the room without looking back. Varn watched the door close then leaned back in his chair, feeling tears sliding down his face. He didn't bother to wipe them away or try to control the pain and grief that caused his body to tremble with silent sobs. All of Varn's attention was focused on the pain that seemed to open up a hole in front of him, threatening to swallow him alive.

Grief for his uncle's loss, horror over Xietak's suffering, and a physical pain that scorched Varn's senses, pummeling him until he could barely breathe, left him unable to move. Sitting there in his chair, tears streaking his face and body shaking, was where Layla found him hours later.

Without much conversation, she folded him in her arms, hugging him close, then without words led him to his room, made him lay down and covered him with a blanket before leaving him in silence. Varn found that the silence tortured him even more, reminding him continually of a connection he could no longer feel. When at last exhaustion claimed Varn, his dreams started where his thoughts left off so that even rest eluded him.

CHAPTER THIRTEEN

Mayven immediately headed to the library after her confrontation with Varn. She ignored a strange ache and emptiness in her chest, while trying to block out the reaction she had registered on Varn's handsome face when she cut his connection to her completely. *He has the audacity to question my motives when he would have dawdled, endangering my family's safety over jealousy. As it is, everything is a mess anyway. If we had left last night, Xietak would be safe. He has no one's interests in mind but his own. I won't allow his pain to stop me from finding a way to save my family. Without him in my head, he can't stop me from taking care of Xietak and Amalayna.*

She refused to acknowledge her sudden fear. A fear created by the absence of Varn's mental presence. In place of their connection, she now felt a gaping chasm that threatened to swallow her whole if she contemplated it too long.

Mayven went to the librarian and asked for the books from the vault, almost expecting to be denied access. When the librarian opened the vault and retrieved the volumes, Mayven reverently caressed the aged covers before seating herself to begin reading. Mayven worked for several hours before going to bed.

Sleep came quickly, however, her dreams were soon filled with images of chasms that kept opening beneath her feet. The constant dreams left Mayven feeling uneasy and unable to sleep. Mayven returned to the library before the sun had even changed the horizon to lavender in preparation for another day.

Mayven soon discovered that nearness to Varn made her unease worse and dreams more vivid so she avoided him. Rest became a remembered pleasure. In between her job at Translations & Authentications, Inc., research on Vayshatka, and keeping Amalayna abreast of her progress on finding a cure for Xietak, Mayven hardly noticed the month slip by.

Late one spring evening, Varn entered the library, taking a seat across the table from her. "Rie'hava Ktaya is operating again. There is a group for transport being assembled. You need to speak to Hardak tomorrow. Go to the pub after work. He'll know why you're there."

Without another word, Varn rose from the table and left. Mayven felt the pull toward Varn as if he had reached out and grabbed her. Not calling him back to her took all the effort she possessed as she listened to his footsteps retreat through the open doorway of the library.

The next evening, Mayven stepped into Hardak's pub and was welcomed heartily, as if it hadn't been nearly a month since her last visit. Avoiding Varn had become an exercise in burying herself in work and avoiding places he might show up. Mayven pasted on a smile and stepped up to the bar. Using the bar rail for leverage, she hopped onto the barstool and sat down, her feet dangling above the foot rail beneath the bar as Hardak poured her a two-finger measure of Iresta.

Mayven palmed the drink, swirling the dark red liquid slowly. "You planning on getting me drunk?"

Hardak smiled jovially. "No, I'm just certain you'll need that when Layla is done grilling you over why you've been avoiding us."

Mayven sketched a smile in Hardak's direction and gulped the contents of the glass then handed it to him for a refill.

Hardak poured out another measure. "I see you agree with my assessment. Well, I have other customers. I'll speak to you later."

Mayven nodded silently and focused on the drink in her hand as she reviewed all her research of late. *Everything leads back to the Tears of Dsohoay. Where do I even find information on that? None of my research is giving me anything to go on so far.*

Mayven chased her thoughts around for a long time, hardly noticing the amount of drink she ingested in doing so. Before long, she was consumed with plans to get Amalayna away from Shimiera. That occupied her attention for the rest of the evening as she drank, paying little heed to the comings and goings of fellow patrons.

When the last person had left and the doors were locked, Hardak approached. "Are you now too drunk to talk?"

Mayven, surprised at the hour and Hardak's question, quickly assessed herself. She was intoxicated but not overly so. "I'm not sober, if that's what you're asking. But I do have my wits still. What did you wish to see me about?"

Hardak laughed. "I have it on good authority you wish to help with Rie'hava Ktaya. We are, by that I mean Niesha, fairly certain we're as safe to do so as we ever were. I need someone with contacts in the upper part of the city. Someone who can interact without suspicion with upper caste people and not be noticed and still be able to come to this part of town without drawing attention. Your apprenticeship makes you ideal. I also understand you have a passenger of your own you'd like transported."

Mayven felt adrenaline pour through her system, burning off her clouded thoughts and muddled concentration. "I do."

"Good, then we'll get started. Though I think your first order of business is dealing with Layla. She's been waiting all night to speak with you."

Mayven heaved a sigh and turned to face Hardak's imposing wife, who stared down at her. The expression of hurt displayed in Layla's eyes belied the indifference on Layla's face. Mayven gazed up at her and waited.

When Layla finally spoke, her tone was cool. "Where've you been? We haven't seen you since your journey through the woods."

Mayven winced at Layla's reference to their last exodus attempt. "I apologize for not coming to see you. I've been busy."

Layla raised a brow in question. "So busy you couldn't spare even one evening to come visit?"

Mayven looked down at her hands as she tried to come up with an answer. "I've been busy researching information on Vayshatka."

Layla snorted. "Learning from Varn, I see. You had time. You've been avoiding us. The question is why?"

Mayven felt the sting of Layla's accusation. "I didn't wish to be around Varn."

Layla opened her mouth to question further but Mayven raised a hand to silence her. "I don't wish to discuss the matter. I'll come visit more often. I have missed your company. I apologize for avoiding you."

Layla's brow rose again but she didn't question further. Hardak cleared his throat from behind the bar. The next two hours involved going over the details of Mayven's new position. When at last the discussion turned to Mayven's passenger and she mentioned Amalayna, the room grew silent. Neither Hardak or Layla looked directly at her or spoke a word.

Mayven looked back and forth between her friends. "Now who's taking lessons from Varn?"

Layla was the first to speak. "Amalayna has been working with Rie'hava Ktaya since your last little journey. She has no interest in staying in Kieshan."

Mayven felt anger rush through her, followed by fear as she looked back and forth between Hardak and Layla. They didn't attempt to apologize or try to appease her in any way. Mayven sat for a long moment, letting her mind adjust to this new knowledge. Then a thought occurred to her that set her mind at ease. *It's not like she would have gone without me. I knew that already. I guess that this is the best I could ask for. At least there are plenty of people who will help keep her safe.*

Then another detail of what Layla had said caused Mayven to ask, "Stay in Kieshan? She's been there?"

Hardak bellowed a short laugh. "You're aware that your friend is a very powerful transportation mage. What do you think she has been doing?"

Mayven once again felt fear race through her. "You've been letting her pop open portals. That can be tracked. What are you thinking?"

Hardak and Layla rolled their eyes in unison as Layla said, "We've been doing this for a long time. We wouldn't put ourselves or anyone else in danger. Amalayna is not only our friend, she is a very valuable asset. She has been helping us set up a new network of portals that are not traceable or connected in any way to the network here in Shimiera."

Mayven nodded in understanding. "So this new network cannot be shut down or controlled by the government here in Shimiera. Nice."

Layla started talking, going on and on about all of Amalayna's great ideas, as if Layla were the proud parent of a very gifted child. Mayven smiled. *At least I know she is valued by Layla and Hardak. They would never put her in danger on purpose. More than I can say of Varn.*

The last thought made Mayven flinch when suddenly she felt a familiar pain in her head. Mayven took a deep breath and then made her excuses, saying she was tired and needed to get back to the guild before she was noticed missing. Hardak advised the best route to avoid the Gayied on their patrol routes. Mayven thanked him before exiting the back door of the pub and slipping through the alley's until reaching the guild nearly an hour later.

Varn let her in. Mayven nodded her thanks and, without a word, went to her room to stare sleeplessly at the ceiling until the gray light of dawn started to light her window. That day and each that followed became a routine. Long days of work. Nights of burying herself in study at the library or meeting Amalayna at Hardak's.

Mayven found that frustration became her constant companion. Her days were spent in research that led her to many references to the Tears of Dsohoay. In the video files stored in the library, Mayven found one that documented the Vayshatka ritual. The horror of that was burned into her brain, making the urge to find a way to save Xietak even more pressing.

Long, restless nights were spent with her mind creating new nightmares where the face of the victim changed from Xietak to Amalayna then to Varn. The final and most promising clue came just a week before the month of Yen began.

Yen represented the first month of summer and the first week of Yen marked the celebrations of Hsdaie, called Hsayda. This year, more than ever before, Mayven found herself repulsed by the thought of the ceremonies. Before, Hsayda made her feel uncomfortable. This year, after all her research, she had a new understanding of what everything meant and it horrified her that hundreds of thousands of her people were being led blindly into ceremonies that could damage not only their bodies but their minds and their souls.

As the scarlet and black banners were raised throughout the city and the squares began to set up for vendors in preparation for the celebrations, Mayven found herself growing increasingly tense. Then, just days before the celebrations began, Hardak called Mayven to the pub for a meeting.

Mayven stepped into the pub just after it opened and took her now customary seat at the end of the bar, facing the door. She hopped onto the stool and let her cloak fall from her shoulders and hang around the seat of the bar stool like a table cover. When Amalayna joined her moments later, Mayven was not surprised. When Varn walked in, Mayven suddenly felt the room become much smaller and herself far too aware of his presence.

Mayven watched as Hardak greeted Varn with a rib-cracking hug and back pounding that staggered Varn. Then Varn took a seat at the opposite end of the bar. Soon patrons filled the little pub and the room hummed with conversation, bawdy jokes, and booming laughter. The loudest among the crowd being Hardak.

Mayven, however, kept finding her attention riveted on Varn. Every move he made seemed to draw her attention like a magnet. Even above the clamor around them, Mayven found herself intently listening to every word he spoke. Mayven watched as first Varn then Amalayna left just before curfew. Then she watched as Hardak entered the kitchen to retrieve more glasses just moments later.

When Hardak exited the kitchen and nodded to Mayven, she swallowed the last of her drink and hopped down from the barstool, wishing Hardak good evening and exiting the pub into the rain-heavy, cool, night air. Adjusting her hood, she used it for cover to make sure she wasn't followed as she walked to the corner and at the transportation station turned the corner then dodged down the alley to stop outside the back door of Hardak's.

Tapping twice on the entrance panel, she waited for the door to open, and she stood face to face with Varn. Skirting him carefully to avoid any physical contact, Mayven entered the kitchen and took a seat next to Amalayna at the tiny table next to the alley door.

Mayven felt Varn's eyes boring into her and turned to Amalayna. "What's this meeting about?" Mayven locked eyes with Amalayna, deliberately concentrating on her to the exclusion of all else in the room.

Amalayna cocked her head to the side, her brow furrowing in question as she regarded Mayven. "The date for the next transport has been set. We're just getting together our passenger list. I think there are several that you need to use your job to contact."

Mayven nodded. Avoiding Amalayna's mute question, she turned her eyes to the tabletop. Mayven diligently studied her fingers that were twined together so tightly she could see the whites of her knuckles.

When Hardak and Layla entered the kitchen a few moments later, Mayven jumped at the sound of Hardak's voice as he inquired, "Why is it so quiet back here?"

"I think Varn and Mayven are having a contest on who can ignore the other the best," Amalayna answered, her voice laced with humor.

Hardak's laughter boomed in the small confines of the kitchen. "Since they're both stubborn as a matched pair of darhsen mares, I guess the winner will never be determined."

Mayven was grateful when Layla interrupted Hardak and Amalayna before they could encourage each other further. "We have plans to finish. Varn also has some news that's important. I say we stick to the topic at hand."

Hardak seemed surprised by the last announcement and looked at Varn. "Why don't you go first then, Varn?"

Varn nodded in response, then glanced briefly at Mayven. "I've heard from some of my sources that there've been some traces activated in regards to the research Mayven has been doing."

Mayven knew exactly where Varn was headed and cut him off before he could finish. "I won't quit searching for a way to help Xietak, Varn. There isn't enough coercion in the universe for that. I'll keep searching until I find an answer."

Mayven watched a tired, almost pained expression pass fleetingly across Varn's handsome face before it settled again into an unreadable mask.

"I'm not asking you to stop. I'm asking you to change where you're looking for a while." Varn's tone was soothing and calm, as if speaking to a skittish animal. "Something you've recently looked into had a tracer put on it. My contacts in Adamdavas have made me aware that the trap was triggered. If you continue with whatever you've recently been researching, you'll lead Adamdavas straight to you. Then you won't be able to help Xietak at all."

Mayven ground her teeth in irritation at his tone but nodded curtly, unwilling to speak for fear of regretting what she might say.

Hardak turned to Mayven. "Where have you been researching lately?"

"I know that Vayshatka is basically a forced possession by a high-level Tarlen. I know that in order to counteract it, you need some artifact known as the 'Tears of Dsohoay' but I don't know what that artifact actually is yet or where to find it. Which is what I was researching yesterday. I found the most recent information in the video files at the guild."

Mayven suddenly felt tension coil up her back and begin a dull ache in her shoulders and neck as she watched a shared look pass between Varn, Hardak, and Layla. Leaning on the table, her palms pressed flat against the warm smooth surface of the wood, Mayven demanded, "What? Why did you look at each other like that?"

Varn cleared his throat, then looked at Mayven, his expression guarded. "That means there's a spy in the guild. Only someone from the guild is allowed access to the vault's contents."

Mayven sucked a breath in between her teeth as understanding dawned. *I may have given myself away already.*

"They may not know who was looking into it yet. If they did, wouldn't they have already come for me?" Mayven's voice was desperate, even in her own ears.

"Perhaps, but that also means that they're closer than we can risk at this point. Start researching elsewhere for a while. Avoid the guild library unless it is required for your class assignments," Hardak answered, his voice unusually quiet.

Mayven nodded. "What are the plans for the next transport? I hear I have work to do?"

The next hour was spent going over the list of passengers and procedures for contacting them and arranging the details for departure. When the meeting was over, Varn escorted Amalayna and Mayven out the back door. The three of them walked together, dodging from alley to alley. When Amalayna was safely inside her guild house and Mayven found herself alone with Varn for the first time in weeks, she found herself suddenly, acutely aware of every move he made.

They each remained silent, but Mayven found that her eyes kept wandering to the large man at her side and admiring his catlike, silent grace. A short while later, in the hallway outside her room, Mayven found herself watching from behind the curtain of her hair as Varn opened his door and slid silently inside.

Mayven huffed out her breath in frustration with herself and jabbed her finger on the keypad on her engaohnie to unlock her own door. Once inside, she flung herself on the bed and stared up at the ceiling, her mind far too occupied with the handsome features of one very tall, copper-haired man, and his captivating sea green eyes.

Mayven rolled over and punched her pillow, her thoughts racing. *What is wrong with me? A handsome face, that is all he is. A handsome face that is far too distracting.*

Flopping onto her back once more, she stared up at the ceiling again as she scolded herself aloud, "Get yourself together, Mayven! You don't need to be bothered with school girl crushes. There are more important things to worry about right now!"

The last declaration seemed to calm her racing thoughts, but in her heart Mayven felt an unease begin to grow as Payin's gentle voice wandered through her mind. *Never lie, Mayven, not even to yourself.*

The next morning, Mayven rose from another sleepless night, determined to distract herself the only way she knew how, work. Translations & Authentications, Inc. was closed for the day and that left her with only research for distraction. With the understanding that the guild library was temporarily off limits, Mayven decided to find a cleric of Dsohoay to answer the questions all her book research had left her with.

All this business with Vayshatka and the Tears of Dsohoay seem to be about religion. The only answers I don't have are from the religion following Dsohoay. Seems like a good place to start. Mayven reasoned with herself as a strange unease began to make her neck ache with tension.

Mayven greeted the cool spring morning with a mixture of unease and anticipation as she stepped out of the guild house after just narrowly avoiding Varn at breakfast. Looking right then left, Mayven decided to avoid the bustle of the surface streets and made her way up the broad branch walkway of the guild house to the intertwining bower of pathways made of the branches of the buildings below. From her lofty vantage point above, she walked slowly along the intertwining paths as she made her way toward the center of Rashmahava.

All the while, thoughts chasing through her head as she scanned the bustling streets below. *Where do you find a cleric of Dsohoay?*

Suddenly, looming before her, was the black reflective bower of a midie tree. Its shiny surface changed from the movement of light through its leaves, causing its image to waver between the lush green of the trees around it and the ominous black of its natural form. Mayven instinctively backed away from contact with the tree and changed course, heading down to the streets below. As she did so, Mayven recalled the last Hsayda festival and the man dressed in white outside the alley door of this very temple.

A cleric of Dsohoay! Mayven felt the rush of adrenaline as her feet touched down on the solid smooth stone of the surface streets. Quickly settling into a bench across from the midie tree next to the transportation station, she pretended to read through her engaohnie as she watched the alley from beneath lowered lashes.

The air grew gradually warmer and the sun now filtering down through branches directly overhead warmed her back, causing her to become sleepy. The feeling quickly passed as at last a movement in the alley across the street drew her attention. Mayven sucked her breath through her teeth as she waited to get a better look. The man, covered from head to foot in a long brown cloak, settled himself next to the dumpster opposite of the alley door to the midie tree. Only through keen observation did Mayven observe a slight glimpse of white collar and the telltale glow emanating from the lapel.

Trying to look casual, hoping not to scare the man away, Mayven rose from her seat slowly, then crossed the street at what felt like a snail's pace. Once gaining the walk on the opposite side, she cautiously advanced into the alley. "I have need of a cleric of Dsohoay. Do you know one?"

The figure next to the dumpster remained motionless for a long moment then replied in an elderly voice, "I may know one. What's your business?"

"I have questions about Vayshatka."

With an agility that belied the age in his voice, the man on the ground rose instantly to his feet. A hand snaked out and snapped closed around her wrist, yanking her to his side as he demanded, his voice just above a whisper, "What do you know of Vayshatka, and why are you asking questions?"

Mayven remained silent for a heartbeat in shock, then replied honestly, "I have a friend who needs help."

The hand around her wrist released, and she heard a deep sigh. "Follow me, child. I'll answer all the questions I can."

The unease Mayven had felt all morning cranked up another notch. Mayven ignored it and the tension that threatened a massive headache later. She followed the cleric further down the alley. They walked in silence for several blocks before the cleric stopped behind a small oak and opened a door before stepping back to let her enter.

Mayven hesitated a moment, then stepped inside to find a plainly appointed kitchen and modest furnishings that reminded her achingly of the apartment she had shared with Payin. Mayven's throat constricted, and her breath caught. Stopping just inside the door, she didn't move.

The cleric waved a hand, indicating a seat at a small table. "Please sit down."

Mayven took a deep breath to compose herself, then sat down at the table and looked the cleric fully in the face for the first time.

The man was old, ancient in fact, his face so pale and paper thin it looked as if a stiff wind might tear it. Dark, midnight black eyes regarded her with a mixture of curiosity and excitement that she found unnerving, and so she turned her eyes to the rest of his features. He sat quietly and allowed her to examine him at length.

Pale silver-white hair was cropped close to his scalp, revealing the age spots beneath. On his wide forehead, his silver xodieha revealed a purple diamond at its southern compass point that looked more like an aging bruise than the symbol of his clan. Around his neck was a finely wrought marsa that indicated a high caste, which seemed out of place in such modest surroundings. Across his thin features she observed thin silvery white scars and noted that they disappeared beneath the collar of his shirt.

Mayven lowered her eyes to disguise her shock and horror, only to be confronted by gnarled aged hands with the same pale scars that disappeared beneath his tunic sleeves. Fixing her eyes on the table for a long moment, Mayven took a deep breath before looking up at the cleric again.

He smiled kindly at her. "Why do you ask about Vayshatka?"

Mayven cleared her throat before answering, "I have a friend who needs a cure."

The cleric's eyes were sad but kind. "How do you know there is a cure, child? Vayshatka is a horrible trial."

"I've done research that says there may be one." Mayven felt her unease ratchet up another notch as the cleric's eyes seemed to brighten and become more intense with each word she spoke.

"What do you know of this cure you speak of?" he asked, his gaze locked with Mayven's.

Mayven shifted in her chair. "I know that Vayshatka is a forced possession by a master Tarlen. The research I've done suggests that something called the Tears of Dsohoay will release the subject from the Tarlens control. I don't know the ritual required or the location of the Tears of Dsohoay. That's why I came looking for you."

The cleric regarded her, his eyes bright and face flushed. "I have an answer and an explanation. Do you have time for both? I cannot give one without the other."

Mayven nodded cautiously as she straightened in her chair, crossing her arms over her body.

The cleric seemed to note her discomfort and immediately mastered his expression into a polite smile.

He rose from his chair. "I'd like some parfie. Would you care for a cup?"

Mayven nodded as she watched him bustle efficiently around the small one-room apartment. After taking two cups from the cupboard and filling them from the tap over the sink, he spoke one quiet word and the water began to steam as he added in the small bag of herbs that flavored the water. Soon the room filled with a rich savory aroma that relaxed Mayven slightly, and she leaned back in her chair. He then took out a small tray of rolls from another cupboard and again spoke one word and they, too, were steaming, releasing a mouthwatering sweet scent.

The cleric settled down across the table from her moments later, passed her a cup of parfie and set the tray of rolls between them.

Mayven accepted the parfie. "May I ask your name?"

"I'm Karshadem. My friends call me Kar. You may also."

Mayven nodded. "I'm—"

The cleric interrupted by raising his hand. "I don't wish to know your name, child. I'm certain I already know who you are but names are things that can be tracked. It's better I not know yours."

Fear lanced through Mayven, making her knuckles turn white from her grip on the stone mug she held.

Kar glanced at Mayven's white-knuckled grip. "I don't wish you harm. You're safe here. I just don't wish to know your name. I can't be forced to reveal what I don't know." He elaborated with a casual display of his scarred arms.

Mayven shuddered. "I'm so sorry."

"Don't be. If you're who I believe you to be, I'd suffer it all again and be grateful."

Mayven felt her unease increase and changed the subject. "What can you tell me of the Tears of Dsohoay?"

Kar regarded her with wise dark eyes for a long moment. "There is more about Vayshatka that is vital for you to know because it will determine if you'll be able to save your friend or if he is lost forever. The first thing is to know that Vayshatka is a ritual where the subject is imbued with a master Tarlen against their will."

Mayven nodded and began to speak, but Kar held up a restraining hand. "Unlike those poor souls who willingly take in a Tarlen during the festival of Hsayda, the possession during Vayshatka is forced. It's painful for the recipient and can even permanently damage the individual who is being possessed. They may be altered after being released if their body can survive the ritual that will free them."

Fear and horror curled around Mayven's heart, and her face must have reflected her emotion for Kar reached for her hand across the table. Instinctively, Mayven recoiled then tried to cover her action by clutching at her mug of parfie as she tried to wrap her mind around the new information.

Mayven furrowed her brow. "But how is possession at Hsayda festivals any different? Most of those people don't have any clue what they're allowing into their body and minds."

Kar pulled his hand back across the table and, wrapping it around his own mug, caressed the rim with his thumbs. "Unfortunately, child, making a choice in ignorance is still making a choice. Because they willingly allow the Tarlen into their bodies, it's harder for them to be removed, if ever."

Mayven recalled the alley where she had located Kar. "But I've seen clerics like you free people of Tarlens. I watched every year."

Kar nodded then explained, "Yes, we can free those in the alley of Tarlens because they rejected possession, and it was driving them mad. Once the Tarlens entered the bodies of those people, they realized what it was they ingested. Instead of accepting it and thinking it was good, they sensed the evil and rejected it. They fought against it, which is why the clerics of Hsdaie throw them out the side door. The inner struggle of the subject to free themselves of the possession is violent and often leads to death if not treated. The clerics of Hsdaie do not wish their loyal followers to witness that, it may change their mind."

"But if they willingly accepted it, how can you free them?"

"Because in the brief moments before their minds are lost forever and their souls destroyed by their possession and claimed by Hsdaie, they have an opportunity to cry out for repentance. They can reject that which they accepted. If they do, and a cleric of Dsohoay is near, they can be freed as long as they struggle for freedom. Once the demon has fully possessed them, however, they are lost because they willingly accepted the Tarlen."

Mayven stared into her cup and murmured, "Then my friend is lost. He has been possessed for weeks now."

"No, child, he isn't lost. You miss the point. He never willingly subjected himself to possession by a Tarlen, did he?"

"I don't know. He knew he was undergoing some test. But I don't know if that means he willingly accepted a Tarlen. I know he has never wanted to attend the Hsayda festivals or have anything to do with Tarlens, but I'm not sure."

Mayven looked up at Kar, her eyes filled with tears. "Besides, you said he may not even be in his right mind if he survives the ritual to free him. How can I save him now?"

Kar ignored Mayven's rigid reaction to his touch and clasped his hands over hers around the mug she cradled in her palms. "From what you just described, he underwent a true Vayshatka. The test was not to see if he was loyal but to get information. Those who have the power to perform such tests do not let their subjects choose to be tested. They require it. He was not asked to take the Tarlen, and he was not offered an option to refuse. He was forced. It sounds as if your friend is a very strong man and with you performing the ritual he has a better than average chance of emerging unharmed from the ritual. But even if he doesn't, would you leave him trapped inside his own body a prisoner to be tortured by a demon for the rest of his life?"

Mayven felt helplessness give way to anger and frustration. "No, never. I'll free him if there is any way. But how do these Tears of Dsohoay help?"

Kar smiled, in a way that reminded Mayven of Payin whenever he humored her more erratic moments. "The Tears of Dsohoay are simply crystals like the ones that make up our engaohnie stones, displays, computers, televisions, and numerous other devices."

Mayven opened her mouth to speak but Kar, once again, held up a hand. "However, they're much rarer. Harder to find. Difficult to harvest, and when used in the manner needed for your purpose, extremely more powerful than any other crystal."

Mayven took a sip of parfie and tried not to fidget as Kar chewed thoughtfully on a mouthful of fayen roll. "The crystals you seek can be found in the highest, deepest, mountain lakes. In fact, the conditions that are right for their growth make them accessible in only two known locations that I am aware of. Both are in the Baksadie Mountain Range. There is a problem, however."

Mayven snorted. "Isn't there always."

Kar offered a knowing smile. "The magic required to power the ritual to activate the crystals is no longer available. I know you've seen it. The lights flickering, the unusually early curfews to conserve what the government says is a crystal shortage. The sudden rash of illness that is reaching epidemic proportions. All those things are caused from magic being out of balance. It's being redirected and redistributed. That's what is causing the illness. Our life force in this world is magic. The crystals that we use to harness our magic are not the problem. There is no shortage of crystals, and they are not wearing out. The world is dying because it's out of balance and only Lapahoniesh can save it."

When Kar spoke the word Lapahoniesh, Mayven felt electricity spike through her body and her breathing become rapid.

Kar, now staring at her intently, leaned across the table. "You're the one the prophecy spoke of. I could feel it the moment you mentioned Vayshatka. You have the voice of truth. The voice of the Language Master."

Mayven bolted from her chair. "I need to go. Thank you for the information. It has been helpful."

Kar rose to his feet but didn't restrain her as she made a hasty exit. His words, however, followed her out into the alley. "I'll find you again, Lapahoniesh. You need to know exactly who you are and what must be done. You cannot hide. If you want to save your friend, you must also save our world."

Mayven bolted down the alley, then gratefully blended into the mid-day crowds. After hours of aimlessly following in the currents where the crowd led, she ended up outside of Hardak's pub. Eager for distraction from her whirling thoughts, Mayven entered the welcoming dimness to a hearty greeting and a cool, stiff drink.

The next days were spent pouring over maps to locate high, deep mountain lakes like the one the cleric had mentioned. Mayven found, as he said she would, two in the central uncharted portions of the Baksadie Mountains. Mayven scanned the maps and coordinates into her engaoh-nie and began to discuss the info with Hardak, Amalayna, and Layla. Several times, Mayven avoided revealing where she had gotten her new information, however, her encounter with the cleric was not the last.

Mayven noted that now she seemed to be seeing clerics everywhere. Whenever they noticed her, they would call out Lapahoniesh and start toward her. Soon Mayven found herself hiding, even in midday, beneath the cowl of a cloak to avoid being seen.

It wasn't long before even Varn noticed her strange behavior and she had to explain.

When she was finished, Varn nearly shouted, "What were you think-ing? You might as well have announced yourself in the square. The clerics here are fanatics. Did you give him your name?"

"He didn't want to know my name," Mayven replied, her voice equally as forceful. "He said he couldn't give what he didn't know. And what am I to announce, Varn? My name means nothing, and I have no idea what I am. Just that I am supposed to be powerful, that I am a Language Master, whatever that is. You wouldn't mind enlightening me, would you? It would make it so much easier to avoid getting in trouble if I knew what I'm supposed to be hiding."

Varn's face was livid, the pulse in his temple hammering and his jaw clenched. "I guess we can be grateful at least he had some sense. Perhaps it would help to tell you this. Xietak's abilities have been put to great use by the Tarlen that possess him. He has fixed the device Xietak invented. He is using it, and it works. They're passing them out at centers for testing children and at hospitals throughout Shimiera. If you keep drawing attention to yourself in such a careless manner, Xietak's sacrifice will be for nothing. If you won't protect yourself for the good of anyone else here, including yourself, do it for him. He has done far more than that for you."

The group around them fell silent as Mayven audibly sucked in her breath through her teeth. For an instant, Mayven recognized a look of pain and regret flash across Varn's features before his face became a mask of bronze granite and sea green eyes. Then, without another word, Mayven turned her back on him and marched to the other end of the bar. Slamming her glass on the bar, she hopped onto the barstool and brooded silently.

The rest of the evening at Hardak's was tense among their little group, and Mayven did all she could to be as far away from Varn as possible until the pub had closed. Just before closing, Mayven watched Varn speak briefly in private to Hardak and Layla then leave.

Layla stopped Mayven before she left. "You've learned something important from the cleric. That's good. My brother thinks you're not ready yet. I say you need to pay attention to what you are hearing in your own heart. You have learned a lot in the past few months. I think it's wise to keep learning all you can. When the time comes that a decision must be made, you'll have a better chance of making the right one if you have all the facts."

Mayven frowned at Layla. "What facts? Why so cryptic, and what choice must I make? What am I?"

Layla smile apologetically as she patted Mayven's shoulder. "I cannot say more without betraying a trust. But I'll say that the clerics are not your enemy, but you can't have them draw attention to you. I'd think that speaking with your cleric friend may be a wise choice, even if Varn thinks otherwise."

Mayven shrugged, a frown making her forehead ache with tension. "I'm tired of all the cryptic messages and secrecy. I'll decide what needs to be done. But not tonight. Tonight I'm going to try and sleep. I'm exhausted."

Layla hugged her quickly and then Mayven left. All the way back to the guild, she pondered Layla's words and long into another sleepless night. When at last day broke, she rolled over and looked at the calendar.

Time to put my personal issues aside. Two more days, and I help with my first transport with Rie'hava Ktaya. I have work to do.

With that thought clearly planted in her mind, Mayven jumped from bed and dressed for work at Translations & Authentications, Inc, at last finding a reason to be happy to be in Takmar's slimy presence.

On her way to the otal station, Mayven began to make a mental list of the passengers she needed to contact today for final arrangements. So engrossed was she in her personal thoughts, that it took several blocks before she realized that a man across the street from her was keeping an oddly similar pace to her own.

CHAPTER FOURTEEN

Varn propped his feet on the corner of his desk, his body angled so he could stare out the window of his office as he sipped a steaming cup of parfie, its rich aroma filling the room and invigorating his senses as he contemplated his next move. Time ticked quietly by unnoticed and Varn remained motionless as he chased his thoughts in circles.

There's a spy in the guild. It could be anyone. I need to find them. Mayven has to stay protected. Varn pressed a palm against his breastbone at the thought of Mayven, then his thoughts veered away from her completely. *I need to get in contact with my own network. Maybe they know who the spy is.*

Varn dropped his feet to the floor and sat up, his shoulders square. Purpose propelled him forward, giving him direction and distraction. Varn gratefully dove into both as he gulped the last of his parfie before beginning a long list of brief messages he typed on the crystal display inlaid in his desktop. When the last missive was sent, he grabbed his gym bag and charged out his office door, his mind set on the one place he could blot out completely any thought of Mayven; the maygis ring.

Varn distracted himself in practice at the arena for the remainder of the week. Distraction, however, was a wasted technique on occasions when Mayven managed to give him yet another thing to protect her from. Upon finding out about her meeting with the cleric, Varn pulled Hardak aside and directed him to speak with Kar and several others about staying away from Mayven. That didn't seem to be working. Now, in addition to his already many duties, he found he was running interference for Mayven with every cleric in town.

That job required he follow her almost everywhere. The constant contact with her and the ease with which she seemed to go through life without him was like putting salt in open wounds.

He was grateful she never suspected he followed her, because often he found himself unable to look away when she would smile or laugh. The pain of her nearness was too much.

Every night, she invaded his dreams. Guarding her safety served as a daily reminder of the pain he felt at her loss. Hardak's was no longer a comforting refuge, instead it was another place where he constantly had to avoid her.

Varn was confronted daily with the irony that now, without his connection to Mayven, he found she was more at the center of every emotion he possessed than when he could hear her every emotion and thought. In desperate need of distance, he assigned her a guard.

Varn dove into his other duties with a vengeance. When not working, he was at the arena or concentrating on avoiding Mayven, except to deliver messages required because of her research or their shared work on Rie'hava Ktaya. It was during the first day of Yen, two days before Rie'Hava Ktaya was ready for the next transport, and Varn was once again gratefully burying himself in the mind-numbing effects of physical activity.

Varn felt the burn of hard working muscles as he wiped sweat from his face with one hand while he clung to the rope suspended by magic in the middle of the arena. Maygis practice served once again as a welcome distraction. *This is one place I can have some peace and get rewarded for my effort.* Bodies launched themselves gracefully below him from balance beams to parallel bars and then to rings only to leap back again to the balance beams that lined the outside perimeter of the maygis court. Like the rope he hung from, each apparatus was suspended by magic and none of them were closer to the thick padded mat that lined the gym floor than twenty feet.

From his lofty vantage point, he hung, his weight resting on legs twined around the rope, and one hand clutching the rope as the other waved wildly. "Up here. I'm open."

A teammate below on a beam to his left launched a heavy leather ball at him. Leaning out, his body almost horizontal to the floor below, Varn snagged the ball from midair and tucked it under his arm. Then, righting himself, Varn launched the ball toward a suspended ring just above him in the center of the court.

As the ball left his hand, he saw the door to the gym open as a short, stocky man entered. *What is Arrok doing here?*

The momentary distraction cost him dearly as a defender on the other team connected with him in midair, catching him unaware. He hurtled nearly thirty feet to the padded floor. The impact knocked the wind from his body. Though the impact was cushioned, Varn felt pain shoot through him as his shoulder absorbed his weight and popped out of socket.

Varn blinked as lights danced in front of his tear-filled eyes. Then his vision cleared and Arrok was standing over him as the team doctor chanted under his breath and mended his damaged shoulder.

Varn waited for the team doctor to finish, then sat up, gently rolling his shoulder as the pain ebbed away along with the tingle of magic that ran across his skin.

Looking at Arrok, he asked, "What are you doing in a closed practice?"

Arrok's face was serious as he held out a hand to help Varn from the floor. "I have news and it's urgent. Got somewhere we can talk?"

Varn nodded as he led the way toward the back of the gym. Leaning against the wall by the mens' locker room, Varn rubbed gently at his magically mended shoulder.

Varn waited a moment for a teammate to pass the glanced down at Arrok. "What's the problem?"

"Shimiera's government is losing favor with Adamdavas and, specifically, Kalohdak because they haven't been able to deliver a new Language Master. Adamdavas' previous Language Master just died yesterday, and Shimiera is offering up Niesha as a distraction. It seems Shimiera has known all along about Rie'hava Ktaya and Niesha's connection to it. Shimiera was saving the knowledge for just such an occasion."

Varn stood up slowly, his arms dropping to his sides and his hands balling into fists. "How does this information save Shimiera? Those we help escape this country don't solve their problem."

Arrok leaned in close. "Shimiera is looking for a way to gain favor and distract Kalohdak from their failure to procure the Language Master. They're hoping to gain time to find her by creating a distraction over Rie'hava Ktaya. The added bonus, of course, lots of insiders into Niesha who also have information on finding the Language Master."

Varn waived Arrok ahead of him into the locker room and began to change.

Arrok leaned in close, his voice barely loud enough for Varn to hear.

"You and I both know if they succeed with this distraction technique, they'll inadvertently get the answer to both problems at once."

Varn heaved a sigh. *Well, so much for the playoff game tonight. Coach is going to be furious. I'm going to have a hard time getting Mayven out of Shimiera. How do I convince that defensive little kata I'm trying to save everyone, not just her?*

Arrok leaned closer to Varn. "I think it's time you told me who the Language Master is. It would make protecting her a lot easier."

Varn snorted as he finished lacing his boots. Raking a hand through his hair, he turned to Arrok. "I'm so ready to be done with secrets, I can't even tell you. But the time to reveal them all isn't now."

Varn slung his bag over his shoulder as the two men exited the locker room. He waved Arrok ahead of him and watched until he exited the main doors before he pulled his engaohnie out of his pocket and dialed Mayven. Her engaohnie rang twice before she picked up.

Varn delivered the standard emergency message they had rehearsed, "I've got us on the last transport out. We have a long journey ahead, so you better start saying your goodbyes before we leave for vacation."

Varn clenched his teeth as he waited for her response. There was a brief pause before she answered, "I'm looking forward to it. I'll see you later at the station."

The engaohnie went dead, and Varn heaved a sigh of relief. *That was easier than I thought.*

Varn exited the building into the warm afternoon light that filtered soft but bright through the canopy overhead and walked up to Arrok. "It's taken care of. Follow procedure. We'll meet up as planned. Keep everything as normal as possible for now."

Varn and Arrok shook hands then turned opposite directions on the street. Varn stepped around the corner to the parking lot and a waiting pod car. Laydak stepped out to open Varn's door.

Varn settled into his seat, his eyes locked on the crush of people bustling along the sidewalks outside the vehicle. *Mayven is going to think I planned all this. I hate keeping secrets.*

Varn's engaohnie rang, pulling him back to the present. *Time to start getting everyone organized.* With a sigh, he answered the call and pushed thoughts of Mayven and secrets to the back of his mind.

CHAPTER FIFTEEN

Full sleepy docks and a few stragglers who hurried homeward along the west side recreational beach of Genatmtie Bay gave the pristine forest nestled against Baksadie Mountain Range's green and white granite cliffs the appearance of being untouched and lushly verdant.

However, beneath the lush green canopy of trees, the streets bustled with activity as a myriad of people jostled and pressed past each other. Even above the streets, in the lush bower with its elegantly entwined walkways that formed a living pathway, on the tree's largest branches, people pressed close together. Among the throng on the smooth rock sidewalks beneath the trees, Mayven marched with a rapid stride through the bustle around her.

Mayven crossed the street from the quay to the transportation station on the corner, narrowly dodging a pod car silently gliding down the glass-like rock streets of Rashmahava.

She slid her engaohnie stone from her pocket and, clicking on a section of symbols, glanced at the time displayed on the face. *Takmar kept me late at work again. He sensed I wanted out of there. I wonder if he overheard my call from Varn.*

Mayven's thoughts raced as she stuffed the device back into the pocket of her lightweight summer cloak. *Getting around down here is going to be impossible. Only twenty minutes to get to the other side of the bay.*

Mayven walked so quickly now she was just short of jogging through the crowds that milled around her. *This crowd is great cover for an exit. But it is also a complication I wish we didn't have right now. Yen, the worst month of the year. The first month of summer and the entire week of Hsayda festival could be better spent than on these barbaric rituals.*

Mayven pulled some rumpled cash from her pocket, thumbing through the bills, revealing twenty venay and change. Stepping to the window of the steward's station, she inquired about a ride, her soft voice barely rising enough to be heard through the glass.

The woman behind the glass took Mayven's money, gave her change, and replied without visually acknowledging Mayven at all, "Due to the festivities, we're running a little behind. It will be about five minutes for me to get you a driver. I'm sorry for the inconvenience."

Mayven withdrew from the window and stepped to the corner of the station, where she once again tapped a column of writing on the face of her engaohnie stone. The screen changed as she slipped her last venay into the media station and plugged the engaohnie into the port provided as the state-approved news loaded onto the device.

Beyond the steward's station and all along the street, shen street-lights, buildings and even people were decorated in streamers and cords in crimson red and black. The frantic dancing of such cords around the neck of a Hsdaie cleric drew Mayven's attention to the temple further down the street as a cleric's arms waved wildly about as he called to the passing horde of people, "Come purchase your Tarlens, two for fifty venay. Repent your sins, show your faith and receive the blessings of Hsdaie."

Behind the cleric, like a specter of death, rose a massive midie tree, its leaves and trunk a shiny reflective black that seemed to flicker in and out of sight. The tree's limbs and leaves hung so low it appeared those who entered into the temple housed inside its ominous girth disappeared behind a curtain.

The cleric held out one hand palm up as he waited for an aged cripple to hand him the required payment as the other held aloft a clear glass bottle that housed an inky black creature hovering inside. The Tarlen writhed weakly in the light of full day.

A demon can't stand the light. Mayven swallowed hard at the sight of the vile creature. *I can't believe these fools believe something so evil is a blessing.*

When the cash landed in the cleric's hand, he deftly tucked it away into a pocket and unstopped the bottle, holding it to the man's open mouth. Mayven stared in wide-eyed horror as the man willingly accepted his "blessing" then stumbled toward the temple door.

Her small hand clenched the engaohnie still plugged into the news port so hard her knuckles were white, only the loud beep of the device dragged her eyes away from the scene before her. Shaking her head as if to clear away a bad dream, she unplugged the device and stumbled to the bench next to the steward's station, collapsing onto the rock seat as her eyes were once again drawn to the temple down the street.

Mayven felt the blood drain from her face as several passersby murmured concerned words. She waved them on with a vague motion of her hand. Wiping a sudden cold sweat from her face with her sleeve, she squeezed her eyes shut for a moment then opened them again, searching for what she knew she would find in the alley next to the temple out of sight of worshippers directly in front.

Ravaged individuals, some bloody, others mad with terror or still possessed by that which they paid to bless them, were shoved out a side door. Left to crawl away on their own power or be trampled over by other crazed believers, they fell unconscious into their own vomit. Hsdaie's faithful followers were reduced to mindless animals once their purse was clean.

Mayven clamped her hands over her ears, though she was too far away to hear the cries she was sure came from those left in the alley. Tears streamed unheeded down her face. Then her eyes settled on a man in a pristine white tunic. Even from far away she could see the glow of shen thread from a symbol she knew would be embroidered under the lapel.

Dragging her shaking hands from her ears, she wiped her face hastily with her sleeve once more as she watched the man move quietly and carefully from one person to the next. He leaned over each individual and whispered a few words and a black cloud would lift from them as the Tarlen vanished into the air, the demon no longer able to possess those who the cleric blessed with the words of Dsohoay.

The person would rise and, touching the man reverently, would disappear down the alley, giving the temple a wide birth. Then he would move on to the next person writhing on the ground.

As the last of the latest group vanished, the man raised his eyes and they met with Mayven's. Mayven felt a prickle run up her neck, standing her hair on end as a smile of recognition spread across his face, and he started up the block.

What is it with clerics? I can't see even one of them without them following me and calling for Lapahoniesh like that is my name and I should know them. I don't need that attention right now.

Mayven dropped her eyes and rushed to the steward's window.

Before she could even ask and still without looking directly at her, the steward stated, "Your driver has just arrived."

Mayven looked up in time to see the portal's blue light snap out of existence as the driver stepped to the curb and removed his pod from its bag. She stood back, watching as the driver placed the pod on the street. Before her eyes, it expanded, leaves stretching and enfolding into a larger version of the plant the man had just recently held in his hand.

Hearing footsteps rapidly approaching from behind her, she stepped up to the driver. "I need to reach the lower end of the bay as fast as possible."

"Address please?" he inquired.

Mayven hastily relayed the address as she heard a voice behind her call, "Lapahoniesh?"

She didn't look over her shoulder but said to the driver in a low tone, "I paid for a private ride, please."

The driver, glancing past Mayven, nodded. "Understood."

He spoke a brief word under his breath and the side of the pod opened, allowing Mayven to step inside and disappear from view as it sealed closed behind her.

Sitting down on the fibrous seats within the vehicle, she glanced up to make sure the partition between her and the driver was closed. Mayven removed her engaohnie from her pocket, selected the news download then briefly scanned the headlines until she reached a small article in the health pages.

Orphans are believed to carry a virus that may be causing the rash of illness now sweeping through Shimiera. All orphans are being asked to report to Rashmahava's National Research Hospital for testing.

Mayven's teeth clenched, her hand rubbing at her throat and the choker there with its plain onyx stone. *It's always orphans. That is always the answer if something goes wrong. The orphans did it.* Then Mayven recalled Varn's comment about the Tarlen making ample use of Xietak's abilities and knew exactly the reason for the sudden excuse to corner all orphans.

Orphans were not deemed worthy of medical care unless plenty of money switched hands. However, if they were deemed unclean or diseased they could be rounded up and surreptitiously examined without questions. Caressing her marsa absently, Mayven recalled Amalayna's words from a long ago conversation. *"Being invisible has its advantages."*

Mayven sighed as she looked down at the screen of her engaohnie again. *That was true until now, little sister. I wish you could have left years ago with Rie'hava Ktaya and never joined Niesha.*

Mayven shook her head to dispel her wandering thoughts. *No time for chasing paths not taken. I have to get us out of here now.*

Mayven felt her brow furrow as she stared at her engaohnie. "Call Amalayna."

A brief silence, then a beep and the stone glowed a faint blue light as a feminine detached voice said, "Hello?"

"Ama, its Mayven. Has your shopping list been taken care of?" Mayven recited the coded message, her voice as casual as the tension making her head throb would allow.

Silence for a breath and then, "Yes, my order is full. Did you need to add anything?"

Mayven glanced out the window of the pod, checking her location. "I'm finishing the last of my shopping now. I'll see you later tonight then?"

A sigh preceded Amalayna's answer, "Yes, see you at home. Be careful."

The last statement was brief but the tremor in the voice delivering it was audible.

"You as well," Mayven responded before disconnecting the call.

The car was silent now except for Mayven's breathing, which whistled through her clenched teeth. Mayven took a long, slow breath, relaxing her jaw as she watched the view outside change from the well-manicured wide lanes of the upper side of Rashmahava's affluent district and business center to the narrow crowded lanes of the older rundown section near the Fisherman's Wharf.

There was no sound as the pod raced along the street; only the faint tingle of magic that curled over Mayven's skin announced her car was moving under the power of adamie. Quietly the partition lowered and the driver said, "We're here."

Mayven nodded, exited the car, watched the pod drive down the street, and round the corner before she turned and stepped into the shadows of an alley. The alley ran between two massive willow trees that housed apartments. Mayven leaned against the wall next to the garbage bin in the darkest shadows, feeling the familiar comfort of the energy that flowed from the trunk of this willow she had visited so many times of late.

From the alley, Mayven's eyes could travel the wide curving view of Genatmtie Bay. Shifting from one foot to the other, Mayven took in the view of the green and white granite cliffs draped in garlands of bright blue shmara vines that curled to the pristine white sand of the recreational beach almost nine lils from where she stood. In the gold red light filtered through the pregnant clouds of the late summer evening, the ocean's hem danced along the white sandy beaches, twirling and curling its ruffled skirt down the beach, drawing her eyes onward.

Beyond the beach, the cliffs of the Baksadie Mountain range rose so high that, though the light shown beautifully along the far beach, the inner curve of the bay was already bathed in the soft purple of early twilight. There the faint glow of shen sapling streetlights brightened spots of the wide avenues of Rashmahava's business district. Beyond the wide expanse of thick canopy, the cliffs split in a gap almost three lils wide, allowing a wide view of rain-darkened sky beyond Bomar Pass in the deeper reaches of the Baksadie Mountains. The south side of the gap nearest Mayven displayed a massive waterfall's frothy white curtain billowing over the cliff's edge.

A gust of salt-filled breeze drew Mayven's attention back to the bay. Her eyes were drawn to the sailor's harbor where small graceful sailboats and thin knifelike wind runners bumped dreamily against their moorings. Onward, she watched the waves travel, curling and dancing along the curve of the bay, until they reached the master harbor where the freighters and cruise liners lumbered awkwardly at the quay while tied to stalwart posts of granite. Like sentinels bathed in the fading rays of the summer evening, tug boats waited watchfully from the deeper water of the bay. The last section of the wharf was a rocky beach and run down quay, which was the home of Fisherman's Wharf.

Mayven smiled as she watched the last of the fish market close down for the evening. Under her breath, Mayven murmured a soft word of thanks that the wind was blowing the storm out toward the bay, along with the smell from that dingy end of the docks. The sky slowly grew darker as minutes marched by. Mayven turned her eyes skyward, then glanced down the alley as the flash of metal drew her attention.

Two men huddled close together at the opposite end of the alley, their long black cloaks making their only distinguishing features their height and the shape of their head. Mayven saw an expensive marsa and rather full bag of money exchange hands. The dealer of the altered marsa noticed Mayven and began to advance, but with a quick hand gesture from Mayven, which he returned with one of his own, he turned on his heel, vanishing into the darkening night. His buyer gave a furtive glance in Mayven's direction, then disappeared around the corner, tucking the item into an inside pocket on his cloak.

Mayven checked the time on her engaohnie again and stepped away from the wall, anxious to be on her way as she noted the time. Just then, the door near her opened and a tall woman, shoulders hunched and face drawn, exited the apartment.

Mayven reached out a comforting hand. "Are you ready?"

"Yes," she replied, patting Mayven with a large hand.

Mayven shifted slightly, removing herself from the woman's touch, "Get your family together. Take nothing with you. The cab will be here in an hour."

The woman nodded wordlessly, then stepped back into the apartment building. Mayven glanced again at her engaohnie stone, then turned up the alley further away from the wharf. The night had turned from dim light to deep twilight. The streets were rapidly emptying as people ducked into houses and businesses to avoid the oncoming rain. Recalling the time and the marsa she had seen change hands earlier, Mayven's hand strayed to her throat, caressing the plain band of her own marsa with a polished onyx crystal at its center point.

Lost in thought, Mayven ran into a man in a dark cloak. He reached out to steady her. Their eyes met. Then her eyes were drawn to the glow beneath his collar; a cleric of Dsohoay.

His eyes lit with recognition, and Mayven jerked from his tightening grasp as he whispered fiercely, "Lapahoniesh, you need to come with me!"

For a moment, Mayven stood stock still as she felt the pull of adamie race across her skin. With a jerk, she wrested free of his grasp and rushed past him, right into the path of a payjik.

"Stop now," the payjik demanded. "I need to speak with you."

The cleric had vanished from sight. Mayven stood frozen in mid-stride, her face rigid as much from his command as from fear and fury. Short quick gasps of air whistled between clenched teeth as a tall narrow-featured man in a payjik's copper-colored tunic stepped into her line of sight. "Well, haven't I found a pretty one tonight," he gloated, as he looked down his long narrow nose at her.

His hand reached out and long fingers closed around Mayven's neck, just tight enough to restrict her breathing, causing her face to flush as he leveraged her chin up with his wrist to scan her marsa with his engaohnie stone.

A brief blink of blue light and then a beep, and he grunted. "You're an orphan."

Mayven felt a knot settle in her stomach. Her rapid breathing came almost to a complete stop as his thumb caressed the pulse rapidly beating in her throat. The sensation of his touch, combined with the suggestion in his gaze, made tears prick her eyes and fear snake down her spine, then settle its lead weight in the pit of her stomach.

His leering face drew closer, and his hot breath washed over her. "Have you seen the news? You're supposed to report to the hospital for testing, lovely."

Mayven swallowed hard, feeling her throat move against his palm as she rasped out, "I made an appointment for in the morning. I just got the news tonight."

The payjik looked doubtful, but not inclined to question Mayven or cause himself unnecessary work. Though still not inclined to release Mayven, he suggested, "Well, then I can't detain you, but that doesn't mean I can't enjoy your company a moment."

Anger suddenly rushed to Mayven's rescue. She felt adamie curl around her until the air around them vibrated. "Release me, leave, and forget you ever saw me."

The air seemed to crackle. The payjik's hand jerked back from contact with Mayven's neck as if he had been prodded with a knife. His face went slack, and his eyes glazed over. Mayven raced away from him down the street, leaving him standing there, stupefied, as she checked her engaohnie stone again. Two hours from curfew.

Glancing around, Mayven noted the streets were nearly empty. The frenzied atmosphere was gone and the dim glow of shen streetlights revealed a scarce few brave enough to be out so late under the watchful gaze of living buildings towering overhead.

Mayven rushed up the street, pulling the light summer cape she wore tighter around her shoulders as the cool air of late evening and the fog from the bay gathered closer. She took a quick look around, watching as lights from several windows along the street disappeared.

Mayven stopped momentarily outside Hardak's Pub and glanced over her shoulder just before entering. Normally Mayven felt relaxed in her place of refuge, finding comfort in entering behind other regulars who greeted the proprietor by name.

However, tonight the atmosphere inside her palace of refuge was every bit as tense as Mayven had been all day. The regulars huddled in quiet groups along the bar. Tonight not a single repetitive question from fellow business owners was fired across the bar at the hulking red-haired brute. Tonight Hardak's face was tight and his grin a subdued smile.

Mayven stepped to the bar. "Iresta, Hardak."

Taking a seat at the bar, she unclasped her cape and let it pool in folds around the stool on which she sat. Mayven said nothing but quickly palmed the drink Hardak slid down the bar. Taking a sip of the deep red liquid, Mayven savored the sweet heavy taste and the sharp after bite. She let its warmth pool in her stomach while she watched other patrons from beneath lowered lashes through the bar mirror. Her gaze settled a brief moment on her own reflection as she hastily adjusted the silver headband around her forehead from beneath which a sliver of silver light had escaped. Artfully, she played with her bangs as she examined her reflection to ensure the glow no longer showed.

As Mayven took in her reflection, a heavyset middle-aged man with a balding head sat down next to her, his eyes looking a little too long in the direction of Mayven's tunic where it was stretched taut across her full bosom. She glanced briefly at him, noting his xodieha, displayed openly on his forehead, marked him as a member of the air clan. Mayven gave the man a tight smile and leaned against the bar to block his view, only to realize it only enhanced his view of her backside, which he seemed to admire as well.

Her new bar mate pointed with his drink at the group in the corner. "I don't suppose that bunch is lost after too many Tarlens at temple."

Mayven shuddered inwardly at the mention of the inky black demons she had seen earlier that evening and curled over her drink without responding to his invitation to conversation. Meanwhile, her eyes continued to examine the reflection of the other patrons. At length, her eyes traveled to the tight knit group of large men in the corner.

They all wore plain black tunics with identical gold chain symbols embroidered around their shirt cuffs, identifying the hard-eyed group as mercenaries. Mayven felt her blood run cold and her palms grow damp as she took another careful sip of her drink to calm her suddenly jangling nerves. *Why are they here?*

Everyone else in the room seemed to wonder the same thing but no one looked at them directly, not even Layla. Instead, Layla silently got them whatever they requested. Mayven felt her heart hammering in her throat. Pretending to stare into her drink, Mayven watched the group's reflection from beneath lowered lashes. Then the leader of the group raised his head. He seemed to feel her eyes on him. His eyes locked with hers a brief moment in the mirror as she raised her glass to her lips, taking another sip.

Careful to set her glass down without her hand trembling, Mayven let her eyes slide away from his in the mirror and turn as if interested in two women conversing far too loudly just down the bar. Mayven glanced for the fifth time since she had entered at the clock above the bar, then reminded herself not to yet again.

Just then, the door swung inwards, blowing in a cool rain heavy breeze and Kar leaning heavily on a staff. His cloak was dripping. His pale thin face revealed fresh bright pink scars against the age-lined cheeks that spoke loudly of a torture that was not long ago.

Mayven stared at Kar's reflection in the mirror, her eyes unblinking. Her gaze locked with his in the mirror, and she felt a new layer of tension draw her spine straight and tighten her shoulders. Kar leaned heavily on his stick, and his cape fell open to reveal his tunic of white. *Please, not tonight!*

Mayven's thoughts were frantic, and her eyes strayed to the men in the corner as the group stared at Kar. As Hardak started to speak, her eyes were drawn to Hardak while passing the reflection of the group in the bar mirror. Mayven quickly noted the entire group now seemed very interested, not in Kar, who stood leaning heavily on his staff and dripping water in the middle of the bar, but in her. Fear knifed through her.

"Please not tonight, old man." Hardak's eyes strayed to the mercenaries in the corner. "You've been dragged out of here twice now and it hasn't been good for you, as all can see. Just take a drink and go home."

"I come to bring a message to Lapahoniesh," Kar said, as though he hadn't heard Hardak. His voice was resonant in the now silent pub. "Tonight is the night you must choose. Our world is dying. Listen to the world around you. Don't let others make you blind and deaf. If magic dies, so do we."

His voice rose in pitch with each syllable, his fervor coloring his pale face a vivid red that made its newest scars nearly disappear. Midnight black eyes drilled into Mayven's back as she clutched her glass. Her hands remained perfectly still, trying to resist the urge to rub her aching temples.

Mayven watched Kar through the mirror. His eyes continued to bore into her spine. "You must come forth, Lapahoniesh. All will be lost without you." His voice increased in force as he used adamie to coerce a reaction.

Mayven felt adamie draw a cord around her and jerk. It took every effort of her mind and body not to move a muscle. Mayven radiated strain that drew attention from her leering bar mate.

Mayven gave him a tight smile that even she could tell by her reflection looked more like a snarl, and her eyes darted to Hardak imploringly. He picked up the remote, saying loudly, "I almost forgot the maygis playoffs are on."

The giant crystal screen behind the bar leaped to life and the room's attention once again shifted, this time to the game. Mayven, however, still eyed Kar's reflection, her body stiff as he continued to stare at her back. Only when he finally turned and shuffled back out into the now rainy evening did she relax even a moment.

Her eyes traveled to the corner, and she relaxed a little more, noticing they were now watching the game. Checking the clock again, she noticed thirty minutes to curfew and took another sip of her Iresta as her eyes focused without interest on the game. Varn should be playing, but she doubted he was.

Suddenly her engaohnie stone vibrated from her cloak pocket, making it dance against her stool's leg. Mayven quickly retrieved it and checked the screen. *Takmar, now, what does he want? I better find out. He, of all people, can't be suspicious.*

Mayven stood up, her feet landing on the floor with a soft thump and all but her head and shoulders disappeared from the mirror behind the bar. As she donned her cloak, the women down the bar began to cheer and her new bar friend muttered in Mayven's direction. She didn't acknowledge him as she examined her reflection in the mirror.

Mayven appeared to be adjusting her cloak in the mirror as she checked her headband. Her eyes drifted to the back corner, only to notice that somewhere in the last few minutes that deadly little group had left. Surprise caused her to suck her breath in through her teeth. Mayven instinctively shifted her weight to the balls of her feet. "Goodnight," she called to Hardak. "See you tomorrow. Got to beat the curfew home."

Hardak smiled a thin-lipped grin, his eyes staring straight into hers. "Be careful."

Mayven acknowledged his warning with a tight smile and turned, trying not to leave the room at a run. Outside, the rain came down in a steady, soaking pace as Mayven marched quickly along the street. At the next corner, she took a left, rounded the corner, then, reaching up as if adjusting her hood, she glanced over her shoulder to ensure no one watched before dodging into the next alley where she broke into a ground-eating jog. Dashing from alley to alley, she made it the three lils to the town square in record time, her breathing only slightly faster than normal. Slowing to a walk again before she crossed the square, she felt the familiar anxious tug of magic as she passed near the ancient, abandoned shen tree in the center of the square. Her eyes rested sadly on the paktwatm, the alter for the dead. She balled her hand into a fist, pressing her knuckles to her breastbone above her heart as she recited the quick blessing for the departed Payin had taught her so long ago.

The knell of bells from the town hall, Menrieahfiet, caused Mayven's now slowed pace to pick up as she dodged into the alley on the opposite side of the square. The sound of marching feet pulled her up short just before exiting the alley to cross the street to her destination, Translations & Authentications, Inc. She ducked down into the shadows near the garbage bin, pulling her cape around her to further hide her from dis-covery.

At the entrance to the alley, a group of Gayied, the city guard, stopped as the leader of the group spoke gruffly, "Radiea."

A light with no discernible source appeared above his head, and he stared down the alley for a long moment. Then, with another gruff command, he marched his men further down the street.

Mayven stepped around the rubbish bin and started out of the alley, when a pale hand snaked out of the darkness and closed with an iron grip around her arm. "That was close," said Kar's familiar voice from the darkness. "You got away again but tonight you must choose, child. Make sure you choose carefully."

The pale hand released and vanished back into the shadows as Mayven stared for a heartbeat longer where it had been clamped around her wrist. Then, shaking her head, she dashed across the street and rap-ped three times on the door and leaned close against the wall, listening for footsteps on the nearby street. When the door, at last, opened, she slipped inside.

Takmar greeted her on the other side, his face inches from her as he shoved her against the now closed door with the proximity of his rail thin body and rancid breath. "Where've you been? I got priority business from your guild waiting on you. I've been calling you for hours!"

Mayven shoved against him and angled her body past him and into the hallway. "Don't exaggerate, it's not been that long. I just got your message fifteen minutes ago."

Takmar stepped in close to her again, grabbing her arm in a claw-fingered grasp. "He's impatient and demandin' you! I don't need any trouble from the guild!"

Mayven jerked her arm from his clutching bony fingers and felt her heart sink to her stomach as she walked toward the office door, thoughts racing. *What if it's the spy from the guild! Maybe they figured out who I am. Maybe I should leave. Where would I go? The Gayied is out in force tonight, not to mention those rather large men from Hardak's.*

Mayven ignored her racing thoughts and the ball of ice that had settled in her stomach at her last thought and started down the hall, when Varn stepped out of the office. Mayven looked up and felt her heart jump to her throat. Picking up her pace, she brushed by Varn and stepped into the office. He followed, and Mayven closed the door on Takmar.

Mayven spun on her heel to face Varn. "What are you doing here?" Her voice was low and fierce as she glared into icy sea green eyes.

Varn towered over her, clenching his jaw. "I had you brought here because they have Gayied and mercenaries coming to the guild house. I have to get you out of here."

"Why are you here? Are you trying to blow my cover?"

Varn stepped in close. "Didn't you hear me? It's too late for that. You're already discovered. Let's go!"

Mayven's stomach dropped to her feet. "Wha—?"

Mayven's question was interrupted as they heard Takmar in the main shop, his voice raised. "I'm sorry, we're closed. Come again tomorrow."

Takmar's voice had barely ceased when the sound of splintering wood and shattering glass echoed through the shop. Mayven sidled to the door, glancing through the crack. Her hand pressed instantly over her mouth to stop the sound that almost escaped as she stared wide eyed at the men in the main room. One of the men had his back to her, but she recognized the black tunic and embroidered design on the cuffs of the sleeves. Mercenaries. She understood the implications immediately.

"Where is she?" a low harsh voice demanded.

Mayven assumed it must be from the man with his back to her, since no one else in the room spoke. Her heart slammed against her ribs as she stared, horrified, through the crack in the door.

"Get out now," Varn said.

Mayven stared into his eyes. "Don't compel me! They're staring right at the door."

Takmar's voice filled the silence with a strangled whisper, "Who do you want?"

Varn insisted, "He is only going to play hero for a few more seconds until he realizes giving you up may save his life, which it won't. Get moving."

Mayven felt the inevitable compulsion on her will as she tried to resist him. Then a large hand closed around her upper arm as he shoved her out the door in front of him and wheeled her around to face the rear exit. Their rapid exit from the office drew the attention of the giant holding Takmar suspended in midair. In the frozen second in which the mercenary recognized them, his hand convulsed, snapping Takmar's neck with a crack loud enough to fill the shocked silence. Varn, still clutching Mayven's arm, took advantage of the split-second delay for the merce-naries to react and shoved Mayven toward the door. Mayven lurched in surprise, then her feet took flight as adrenaline charged through her system. She and Varn burst through the back door, bowling over the sentry at the back entrance.

A car waited at the end of the alley. Mayven turned to look back.

Varn shouted, "Get to the car."

Mayven didn't even try and resist his command as she raced toward the pod car. The side of the car opened up, and she was shoved through as Varn jerked away from one of their pursuers and fell through the opening on top of her. The car accelerated so fast she saw the buildings flashing by as nothing more than blurs through the slowly closing side of the pod car.

Mayven looked up into his sea green eyes. "I breathe much better when you aren't on top of me."

Varn stared down at her a moment, eyes flashing emerald, then lifted himself off of her and settled into a seat. Mayven rose from the floor, taking the seat across from him and watched as he shoved long-fingered hands through his hair before raising his eyes to hers.

"What just happened, Varn?"

Varn returned her steady gaze. "I got information that we were compromised. The spy in the guild figured out who was researching. It looks like the intelligence was right."

Mayven studied his immaculately clad figure a moment as he picked at a piece of imaginary lint on his form-fitting breeches, which encased long, leanly-muscled legs. His wide shoulders were stiffly straight, his square jaw clenched, and thick brown lashes lowered to conceal his eyes as he tried to decide how to speak next. Mayven sighed. *What is he trying not to tell me now?*

The car sped silently along the street as Mayven looked out the window. Then, through a crowd of black-clad men, Mayven glimpsed a small woman with a waist-length shock of silver white hair. Two things flashed through Mayven's mind simultaneously. *That's Amalayna! We need to get her out of there!*

Mayven lurched across the car, her eyes wide as her small hands clutched at Varn's muscled thigh. "We have to stop now! I just saw Amalayna! Mercenaries have her."

Varn's face paled, and his head snapped to the left to look out the window, his eyes searching the darkened streets outside but the group was already out of sight. Turning back toward Mayven, his expression grim, he said, "We can't. It's too late, and you're too important."

Mayven felt the color drain from her face as she shrieked, "What? We can't just leave her here! Turn around now!"

Varn's features also paled slightly but he set his lips in a hard line and leaned away from Mayven as he shook his head then tapped on the speaker next to him to speak to the driver. "We have to get to our departure site fast. Can you speed it up?"

Mayven felt dread curl around her and settle in her stomach as if she'd swallowed a fayen fruit, shell and all. Then adrenaline shot through her veins as she lunged for the speaker, her hand reaching for the button as she screamed, "Turn around now! You have to turn around!"

Varn shoved her back against her seat as the pod started to slow and held her there with one long muscled arm as he punched the button again. "Disregard that last order and get a move on. Pay no more attention to any order unless it is from me directly."

"Understood, Jayben," answered a man's disembodied voice.

Mayven struggled angrily against Varn as she watched him release the speaker button. As he turned to face her again, Mayven's hand came up, her fingers curled into claws and she raked them across his face and deliberately commanded, "Release me! Turn this pod around now. We are going after Amalayna."

Mayven felt the adamie her words released gather around her and tingle across her skin then hurl itself toward Varn. Then, just as rapidly, it recoiled on her and slammed her against her seat. Mayven gasped in surprise, then asked, "How did you do that?"

"I've known what you are your entire life. I took precautions for just such an occasion." Varn's reply entered her consciousness just as the recoil started to fade her world to black.

Mayven's muddled brain managed to wonder what that meant. Then the world faded out.

CHAPTER SIXTEEN

V arn watched Mayven crumple sideways onto her seat. Her expression faded from surprise to confusion and then her eyes drifted shut as she fell unconscious. Kneeling on the floor in the narrow space between the two facing seats, Varn gently lifted her legs and tucked her onto the seat of the car. For a moment, his hands gently caressed the silken strands of raven hair back from her forehead, his heart aching and thudding against his chest in a strange unsteady beat as if it were missing half of its parts.

I suppose it is. The other half lays here in front of me and may never speak to me again. Varn felt a furrow form between his eyes as he considered his last thought. *Is she the other half of my heart? I know that, since our connection severed, it feels like I've lost half of my heart.*

Varn sighed as he recalled his uncle's warning, *"She is more than just business to you."*

Varn forced himself to return to his seat and lower the window to speak to the driver. "How much farther to the otal location?"

"About ten minutes, Jayben."

Varn pressed his lips together in a tight semblance of a smile. "If you make it in five, I'll double your pay for the month."

Laydak nodded. "No need, Jayben, I understand."

Varn nodded and raised the partition again and stared out the window. His mind anxiously ticking off the seconds, Varn scanned the forest of Bomar Pass, whipping past the window so fast it blurred into a solid wall of dark green in the pale light of the two half-moons hanging overhead. When the car at last slowed to a halt, he scooped Mayven unceremoniously over his shoulder and ducked out into the night to be greeted by Layla, Hardak, and Kar.

"We need to go, Amalayna won't be joining us. I'll explain when we're safely away."

Layla looked askance at Mayven's limp form draped over Varn's shoulder and he answered her silent question brusquely, "I'll explain this later, too. Someone grab the crystals we need to get out of here and close this behind us."

No one said another word as Hardak unearthed the two dark argit crystals buried in the ground on either side of two trees in between which hung a large wavering blue portal. Layla, Kar, and Varn's driver stepped through the portal first, then Varn handed off Mayven's limp form to Hardak and, taking the crystals from him, turned to look back.

The dark forest was silent, much too silent on such a night, and just before he stepped through the portal, Varn glimpsed the faintest movement of something very large creeping through the trees. Varn blinked, not sure what he'd seen, but it was gone.

Turning on a heel, he stepped through the portal. On the other side of the portal waited Hardak, Layla, and Kar, along with several others.

Varn spoke quickly, "Is everyone who met with you all through the portals?"

There was a nod of agreement from everyone.

"Hardak, help me please. Gather the crystals. Layla, you and Kar take everyone upstairs. Take our guests to the dining room. I'll meet you in my study."

Hardak handed Mayven's still-limp form to Layla and began collecting crystals and piling them on the table in the center of the massive room.

When the last crystal was dumped into the pile, Varn held a hand over the pile and murmured, "*Dactoh argit.*"

Beneath his hand, the crystals vibrated for a brief moment, then dissolved into sand. Around the perimeter of the room the portals, all but one, snapped closed, leaving seven sets of wooden pillars with empty crystal sockets standing like guards around the remaining portal.

Varn glanced briefly at Hardak, then turned to head up the stairs. "I don't know what I'm going to do to get her to trust me now, Hardak. I just had to leave Amalayna behind."

Hardak grunted but did not respond until they reached the top of the staircase. When the door to the kitchen slid silently open to reveal the large kitchen beyond, Hardak said, "I think you best not keep any more secrets. You want her to trust you. Give her no more reasons to wonder what you are really up to."

Varn felt the stab of accusation in his friend's words but didn't react. *He isn't wrong. Would I have trusted me if I was her?*

Varn looked forlornly around his kitchen and wandered over to the island in the center to pick up a large green fruit from a crystal dish sitting there. He examined the gieda for a moment, smelling the sweet tart aroma wafting toward him and feeling the supple firmness in his palms before placing it back in the bowl uneaten.

Leaning a hip against the bar, Varn turned to face Hardak. "I didn't lie to her to hurt her. I had to keep her safe. I never meant for the things I didn't say to cause her pain."

Hardak smiled kindly back at Varn and thumped him with a massive paw on the shoulder, causing Varn to stagger slightly. "I know you didn't. But she doesn't know that. She doesn't know a lot of things. And if you don't start telling her all the truth, you won't ever get her to trust you. There are no more valid reasons to keep who and what she is from her. She is as safe as she will be until everything is set right again. You are running out of time. She is running out of chances she is willing to give you. I think you are down to the last one. Be honest, Varn, and let Dsohoay handle the rest."

With that, Hardak exited the kitchen, leaving Varn standing there staring at the immaculately clean countertops that gleamed in the early morning light falling through the kitchen windows. The bright light jarringly contrasted his exhaustion, reminding him just how far the otals Amalayna had constructed had transported them.

It's nice to be home at last. A world away from the darkest part of my life, Varn went to a cupboard and pulled out a tray and several large mugs, filling them with water.

Sounds of shuffling feet could be heard behind him and Varn turned to greet his aged servant and friend with a smile. "You didn't have to get up and help so early, Rohtak."

"I'm your Shemla, it is my job, Jayben. One I happily do and for which you pay me handsomely. It is an honor."

Varn smiled kindly at the older man. "Then I will leave you to it. Please serve my guests in the dining room parfie and rolls. I will have someone here to collect them shortly."

"As you wish, Jayben."

Varn shook his head and exited the room headed for his study. When he got there, Kar had already taken the others to the dining hall. Those remaining in his study were Hardak, Layla, and Mayven, who still lay sprawled unconscious on the settee by one of the windows.

Varn flung himself bonelessly into the nearest chair and waved an arm at Layla and Hardak, indicating they should sit as well. Then, leaning forward on his knees, head in his hands, he asked, "Have either of you heard from Arrok? I think we should call him and see if he may be able to tell us news on Amalayna."

"I sent him a message just after I arrived," Layla answered. "He should be answering shortly."

Varn glanced up in time to see the worried glance that passed between Hardak and Layla.

Mayven stirred restlessly on the settee, and Varn rose to cover her with a blanket before setting down behind his desk. Looking across the wide expanse of wood that almost mirrored exactly his desk at the guild, Varn said, "I think it is best we all rest. When Mayven wakes, there will be a lot of questions to answer. I would like you both here so that at least she will trust and believe someone."

Layla nodded understanding, her smile apologetic as she rose from her seat. Hardak followed suit, but before exiting the office said, "Remember what I said, and if you need us we will be upstairs."

Varn smiled at his friend and nodded, then shifted his gaze back to Mayven as the door closed. A short while later, Varn's engaohnie stone chimed and he opened the message, reading it briefly. Varn felt unease curl in his stomach and his forehead crease. *Will she ever forgive me?*

Varn heaved a sigh then glanced up to check on Mayven, who still lay sleeping soundly, her expression relaxed and unguarded. Deciding facing her when she woke would be easier rested, he called in Rohtak. After instructing Rohtak to keep an eye on Mayven and notify him the instant she awoke, he, too, went upstairs to a warm shower and soft bed.

Several hours later, he awoke to find that for the first time in many weeks he had managed to get several hours of deep dreamless sleep.

Ironically, all it took was total exhaustion and the fear of telling Mayven I haven't gotten Amalayna back yet. Who knew it could be so simple? Varn, laughing aloud at his own caustic humor, then dressed quickly and headed for the kitchen. *Even men sentenced to death get a last meal.*

CHAPTER SEVENTEEN

Mayven heard voices somewhere near her as her mind struggled toward consciousness. Her eyes opened as she focused on the ceiling, blinking several times as she tried to recognize her surroundings. Panic made her heart race, and Mayven lurched upright, her head turning right to left as she looked around the room. Her eyes landed on Varn's face, and everything came rushing back in heart-stopping clarity. "Where is Amalayna? Where am I?"

Varn looked at her, his face impassive. "I have people working on it. We don't have her back yet. You are in my home. We are in Kieshan's capital city, Lirie."

Mayven ignored his answer to her second question. "What people?"

Varn's lips were set in a thin hard line. *He can't tell me, it would be admitting something!*

"What people, Varn?"

"Niesha is working on it. We have other matters to discuss."

Mayven glared at him, her jaw clenching. *He is telling the truth in pieces. Ever the artful liar. At least the basic principles of adamie stuck with him. You can never lie, but you can avoid the truth. I won't allow the mogatie to lie by asking him questions. I'll get my answer later.*

"What is it you want to discuss that is more important than my family, Varn?"

"You need to learn about your real family, Mayven. The reason you are so important. The reason Rie'hava Ktaya was targeted was in order for Shimiera to distract Kalohdak and Adamdavas while they searched for you. Adamdavas power for ages has relied on their ability to gain and control the Language Master. You are the Language Master, Mayven. You are the reason Rie'hava Ktaya was raided last night."

Mayven felt her heart stop momentarily as her mind raced wildly. *I caused this? How? Is Amalayna another name to add to the list?*

At that thought, a brief flash of images she had seen of Vayshatka filled Mayven's vision, the subject, unlike in the film, Xietak. Her stomach lurched into her throat as sweat suddenly dampened the hair on her brow. Her heart pounded in her ears as she blinked rapidly, trying to dispel the image. What brought her back to the present was Varn's arm suddenly encircling her shoulders as he spoke soothingly into her ear, "Mayven, I'm sorry. That was not how I meant that. It isn't your fault, but being who you are has everything to do with all that has happened."

Rage instantly replaced terror. Mayven turned to glare into Varn's sea green eyes, disregarding the concern she saw mirrored in their clear depths. Her breath, emerging from behind clenched teeth, disturbed the loose, copper, hair falling across Varn's tan forehead. "Get your hands off me. What is this information you say we need to discuss?"

Mayven registered dimly a change from concern to resignation. Then in his eyes a glimpse of something else she couldn't quite grasp before his face once again became its customary stoic mask. He rose gracefully from beside her and straightened into a stiffly erect posture as he clasped his hands behind his back. Mayven's breath caught a moment when the sun pouring in the window caught his copper waves and highlighted his angular features with a soft halo that made his brilliant eyes shine as he stared down at her.

Just another pretty face! Mayven stood up and walked across the room she now recognized as a sizable library an office.

She leaned a shoulder against the bookcase by the window as Varn addressed the other occupant of the room; the owner of the second voice she had heard upon waking, "Please get Mayven some food and drink, Shemla."

Mayven's eyes narrowed at his polite request of the servant. *This man makes no sense, all orders and commands are requests to those who by their station he should ignore.* Sighing, she pushed the thought aside and observed him a moment longer.

The elderly man, clearly a servant in his silver gray tunic, vest, and black breeches, nodded and left the room as Varn turned back to face her. Varn cleared his throat as he paced a few short steps toward the wide desk rising in seamless shape from the very wood that composed the floor. Stopping behind his desk, he leaned onto his balled fists and stared down at the wide expanse of the desk for a long moment before raising his eyes to meet hers. "I guess the best place to start with your family history is where it all began.

"At the beginning of recorded history, your family produced the first Language Master in that time and then the second. From that auspicious beginning up until modern times, your family line has had the most Language Masters. In fact, your family line is the only one that has repeatedly produced Language Masters. All others seem to occur randomly and have never been consistently repeated. In addition, your family line has the distinction of being the only one in our history where there have been born two Language Masters on the same date repeatedly. This knowledge has been safe guarded and kept secret by Niesha since Niesha began. Adamdavas has always sought to control the Language Master, believing that by controlling the ultimate power of our world, they can thereby control the world. My family has been tied to yours since the beginning. As co-founders of Niesha, our families swore a pact to protect the secret of your family line."

Mayven turned from the window when Varn paused for a long moment. Varn's expression was vulnerable as some inner pain darkened his eyes to jade.

Varn noticed Mayven's attention and cleared his throat. "My family has been your family's guardians from the beginning. Our story, yours and mine, became entangled when we were only infants. Adamdavas had control of the current Language Master, but from information gleaned from that Language Master and a prophecy older than the Vanishing War, Adamdavas assumed a new Language Master was destined to be born soon. Since those Language Masters who have fallen under Adamdavas' control have an abominably short life span, they knew they needed another Language Master soon and that, according to prophecy, the next Language Master would be the most powerful Language Master in our history. They desperately wanted control of that child from the very beginning. When your mother became pregnant and the physician explained your approximate date of birth, all of Niesha suspected you were the one everyone was waiting for, but the twist was that another of your family line, your uncle's wife, was due at the same time. Only Niesha knew the power would be with two children of your family line, according to the cycle in your family history, so both mothers were secreted away and protected until the date you were born. You were the answer to the prophecy, for the prophecy spoke of a female Language Master, not a male."

Just then, the servant entered again, bearing a tray holding two tall glasses of chilled fayen juice and a plate of sandwiches. Mayven moved away from the window where she had been staring out as she listened to Varn. Taking a glass of the chilled purple liquid and sandwich from the tray that now rested on the desk, she sprawled her length in the chair across the desk from Varn.

He now sat in the large padded chair behind the desk, his feet prop-ped on the corner of the highly polished wood, sipping fayen juice as he regarded her through a hooded gaze. Mayven sipped the energizing purple juice, letting the cool, tangy, sweet drink moisten her throat as her mind reviewed the information. *So there are two Language Masters alive now. And he is related to me, interesting.*

Before taking a bite of her sandwich, she commanded, "Continue."

Varn lifted a dark winged eyebrow and then leaned back in his chair. "You and your male counterpart were well protected and safely hidden away until you were the age of five, then somehow Adamdavas disco-vered your parents' location and sent a mercenary squad to collect you. Your parents were killed and mine barely escaped with you. Knowing that you would be searched for in every home in Kieshan, they secreted you away to Shimiera, hoping to hide you in plain sight. Unfortunately, they were quickly discovered. Right before my parents died to protect you, they left you with Payin, where you remained until his death. To this day, fortunately, Adamdavas doesn't know of your male counterpart, and he remains hidden. However, with your existence and with Adamdavas' desire for power, you are the only one they really wish to control."

Mayven washed down her sandwich with a gulp of juice. "Is that why this is my fault?" she inquired, her tone caustic.

Varn ignored her question. "The Shimiera government and Adam-davas have been linked since the Vanishing War. Just days ago, the last Language Master Adamdavas was able to control died. Shimiera, appar-ently, has known for quite some time that Niesha ran Rie'hava Ktaya. In order to distract from their failure to find you, they offered up the capture of several Niesha operatives to distract Kalohdak and Adamdavas while they continue to look for you. Unfortunately, they inadvertently picked up the one other person in this world who gives them a hold over you. And perhaps the information they need to find you."

Mayven shoved herself from her chair and stalked to the window to glare unseeing to the street below. "They can't use her against me if I get her back."

"Any attempt to rescue her yourself will put you at risk and will do nothing to save Amalayna. You'll be too careless and could cost Amalayna her life. If they discover who she is to you, no harm will come to her while they try and find you. You have to let Niesha handle this. Amalayna knows you're more important."

"She knows no such thing. And what if they don't discover what she is to me?" Mayven said, her voice a low snarl. "Do you just want me to concede and leave her there so you can keep me here for your own plans? What are those, Varn? We both know your loyalties have always been allied with Niesha. Not even your own wants or needs come before your devotion. So what do you have planned for me? What is a Language Master, and how do you think that I am such a person?"

Varn exhaled sharply. "I forgot you have never lived outside Shimiera. You have no idea who you really are."

"Who am I really? Quit being so cryptic." Mayven stormed back to the desk, leaning across it, her balled fists supporting her weight. "Out with it! What am I supposed to be? Who am I really?"

"You happen to be the most powerful adamie mage among the Hato. A Language Master power is so rare it most generally appears only once in any generation. The fact that your family frequently and consistently produces Language Masters and has produced the only times in our history where there have been more than one in a generation makes you a very powerful and sought after person."

Mayven raised a skeptical brow. "Adamdavas, Kalohdak, a link to Shimiera. You're speaking of things I don't understand. I was told of Niesha and others who sought me. I assume that is Adamdavas and this Kalohdak. I know I'm a Language Master, but have no idea what that is or how to use it."

Varn dropped his feet to the floor and laced his fingers together in his lap. "Kalohdak is the current head of Adamdavas. Adamdavas has control of the majority of the Shimiera government and that government answers to Kalohdak. No one has ever discovered who this person is or where he is located. His identity has been kept, like that of all his predecessors, top secret. I, like all my family before me, swore to protect you. Niesha and I decided that you were best protected through ignorance. Payin didn't tell you about your gift to protect you. If you didn't know who and what you were, you would be protected from detection because you couldn't use your gift as it was meant to be used."

Mayven stood erect and slashed her hand through the air. "Get to the point, Varn. What gift?"

Varn shifted in his chair, leaning forward, his shoulders tense. "You used it every day at Takmar's shop, but not to its full potential. It's the gift to read and decipher all languages and, most importantly, the language of creation. The language of Dsohoay."

Mayven locked her arms across her body, feeling her brows creasing in a frown. "That's it, Varn, I'm done with this conversation. I won't be sucked into religion with you and your precious Niesha. I have researched what religion did to Xietak. I have watched what happens to those who serve Hsdaie. I want nothing to do with capricious gods. I served Niesha all this time because my service wasn't about religion. But I will not stay around to hear how I owe some religion my loyalty due to a gift I did not want."

Mayven spun on her heel and stormed out of Varn's office, rushing headlong out into the late morning light. Outside, the sun was muted and the air heavy with impending rain. Mayven glanced up to see thickening clouds roiling and converging into a dark gray curtain that was slowly blocking out what feeble light was threading through the clouds. Mayven turned her attention back to the street. Tall trees, all carefully manicured, with large lush lawns marched in orderly rows down either side of the wide lane. *Of course he lives in the rich district. Nothing less for Varn. That just wouldn't do.*

Mayven started west along the wide lane and watched with interest as the homes slowly gave way to businesses and then the wide square of Lirie's town center. Beyond the square, the lane continued to Abhie Bay, and docks that were busy with organized chaos. Mayven skirted the town center and traveled toward the bay as she watched payjiks directing citizens this way or that and gathering around a group of eight men and women dressed in scarlet tunics, identifying them as weather mages, each of them with their hair woven with multiple braids to show their years of service as a mage. *None of them have less than twenty braids in their hair. That many masters means this is a bad storm.*

Mayven watched a moment longer as the group turned to face the violent sea and their hands reached up, palms out, as if to hold back the storm itself as their voices rose in a staccato two-part cadence that charged the air around them with the tingle of adamsah. With the chanting of their combined singing magic, a bubble seemed to form around them and slowly spread outward toward the edge of the docks and back toward the town behind them. Mayven stood transfixed, staring at the awesome sight until a payjik shoved her shoulder. "You need to get back at least as far as the town square to be safe. We need all citizens away from the docks."

Mayven nodded mutely, her eyes fixed on the mages a moment longer, then turned back toward the town square. All along the wide boulevard, men, women, and children hurried in groups toward the town center. The rain, now falling steadily, drenched them and plastered clothing to their bodies. In the center of the square stood a massive shen tree, glowing warmly beneath the darkening sky. The magic that fueled its glow seemed like a beacon to those around her as they hurried to the shelter of its massive branches, then reverently filed inside.

Mayven watched anxiously, her eyes darting from the payjiks to those entering the temple. Suddenly, the presence of payjiks jogging her memory, her hand flew to her forehead as she thought of her headband covering her xodieha and was relieved to find it still in place. She watched a payjik take an elderly woman to the shen tree and finally decide to acknowledge the gentle call of its magic to come and visit the one place she had avoided her entire life. The shen temple, her talking trees. Mayven considered her decision as she watched people file into the temple. *These people are not afraid to enter the temple. The payjiks don't arrest them for going there but take them there for shelter. Maybe I can finally see why these temples always call to me.*

Mayven followed the crowd up the hill and entered beneath the circle of the tree's massive limbs. The tingle on her skin was the unmistakable touch of adamie. Shivers chased up and down her arms, adding to the chill from her rain-soaked clothes and making the damp hair at the back of her neck stand on end. Her eyes wandered over the tree, noting the care with which this temple had been treated. The limbs were all neatly trimmed, the streets around it neatly cared for and the paktwatm, a large white marble alter, stood polished to gleaming in front of the wide doors. Mayven balled her hand into a fist and pressed her knuckles to her breastbone above her heart as she recited the prayer for the departed on her way past, then she paused at the wide doors.

Mayven looked through the open doorway to the cavernous interior. She shook her head slightly as she heard something inside her mind, as if a voice was calling to her. The tingle on her skin increased and enveloped her entire body. Her legs, moving of their own volition, marched her forward, and she found herself inside the threshold of the temple.

"I give you this place that you may have knowledge and reverence for that which created you," said a voice that resounded within her head.

Mayven blinked, disoriented, as she stared mutely down at her booted feet and watched the mirror-polished surface of the floor seem to ripple and brighten to an iridescent bright blue, then ripple outward from where she stood. Adamie seemed to be drawn into her body until she felt like a crystal that had stored too much and was overheating. Then her head rocked back on her shoulders, and her mouth fell open as Mayven felt the release of the adamie from every pore on her body. Standing locked in place like a lightning rod in a thunderstorm, she watched, unblinking, as the temple around her rippled and brightened to an almost blinding light. Mayven felt the adamie slowly releasing her. The flow of magic was now considerably reduced.

Just before her eyes slammed shut and she passed out, she heard a voice say, *"Thank you, Lapahoniesh, for saving the Ohkie'en."*

CHAPTER EIGHTEEN

Varn watched Mayven storm out of his office, her slender form disappearing around the corner. Then, rubbing his temples in aggravation, he decided he needed to let her calm down before he tried to repair the latest rift between them. *One step forward, two steps back with her. It is so exhausting.*

Just then a knock at the door sounded, and Varn looked up.

"Arrok is here, Jayben," Rohtak said. "Would you like me to show him in?"

"Yes, please," Varn answered before leaning back to wait for his guest to arrive.

Moments later, Arrok strode through the door. Varn stood and stepped around the desk to embrace the short, stocky, dark-haired man. "I'm glad you got out. The Language Master is worse than a tkhoda at mating season. I suppose it's lucky she doesn't have its more terrifying attributes. I would probably be dead now because I wouldn't go back for Amalayna. You did get my message about Amalayna?"

Arrok's dark brown eyes twinkled slightly. "You are lucky she doesn't know how to use the power she possesses. And, yes, I received your message."

Varn nodded slightly. "What information did you get on Amalayna before you got out?"

"I have a location where they are holding her. I don't know more than that. Though I'm sure you are able to guess as well as I what she must be enduring right now."

Varn stared down at his hands for a moment, his thumbs tapping an absent rhythm as he collected his thoughts.

Arrok leaned a hip against the desk. "How did you get out?"

Varn looked up. "We were all ambushed just after your call of warning. We narrowly escaped. Mayven saw Amalayna being arrested and tried to compel me to do as she wished. Thanks to my wards, she didn't succeed and it recoiled on her, knocking her out. That made her much easier to deal with," Varn rubbed the back of his neck. "Hardak, Layla, Kar, Mayven and I managed to make it to one of Amalayna's secondary exits. I unanchored it, and we stepped through, ending up here. Mayven slept for some time. When she woke, I told her how everything happened and now she is furious with me because I told her that she and I are not going back to get Amalayna."

"Where is she now?"

"She stormed out the door half a bell before you came in."

Suddenly the screen on the far wall of the library came to life, displaying a weather warning as a disembodied voice said, "All citizens are under a hurricane warning level three. Please take all necessary precautions."

Varn bolted from his chair. "We need to find her. She is so angry I doubt she is paying attention to the weather."

The two men exited Varn's home, pulling their hoods up on their capes to shield them from the rain that already pelted them relentlessly. Just as the two men stepped to the curb, a surge passed through the air, the unmistakable ripple of powerful adamie. Varn and Arrok turned in unison to face toward the town square, watching in open-mouthed disbelief as a column of light burst up through the cloud-darkened sky, burning blindingly white for the space of two heartbeats then blinking out of existence.

"Finding her didn't take long," Varn said sarcastically.

Arrok nodded as the two broke into a run. "Why don't we take the car?"

Varn glanced at him from beneath his hood. "I don't need to endanger my staff for her stupidity. You, on the other hand, signed up for this and neither of us can drive a pod."

Arrok nodded curtly as they raced ahead through the gathering storm. The town square soon came into view, and Varn headed for the temple, where a crowd had gathered, talking loudly. "My guess is we found her."

Pushing their way through the crowd, they reached the door. Varn pulled a white robed cleric aside. "Was there a girl here, raven hair, violet eyes, about this high?" He held his hand out about chest high.

The cleric nodded. "She stepped in, and the temple lit up. Everyone heard a voice saying, 'Thank you, Lapahoniesh, for saving the Ohkie'en.' She passed out. A payjik came and gathered her up and was going to take her to the hospital, but he was called to the docks by another payjik. He said to tell anyone who was looking for her that she would be at the jail."

Varn thanked him and started to turn away when the cleric reached out to grab his arm. "Do you think it is true she is Lapahoniesh? Who are the Ohkie'en?"

Varn felt a strange twist in his stomach and shrugged absently, muttering his apologies before pushing back through the crowd. Just as he reached Arrok, the crackle of lightning rent the air as a bright bolt of light split the jail across the square in half from the top cradle of branches down to the massive roots buried beneath the smooth surface of the bedrock paved square.

The formed inner core of the tree broke into pieces and careened inward as the outer shell fell apart, the nearest half of the towering tree falling toward the spot where Varn and Arrok watched in horror. Varn shoved Arrok, and they broke into a run, gathering others ahead of them, trying to clear a path for the massive trunk and branches that fell in a graceful but rapid arc. The majority of the crowd raced to the shelter of the temple. Varn and Arrok reached the door just as the body of the jail crashed against the temple. The hsieleng shield held, but barely, as the temple shuddered under the weight of the load. When the last noises had settled, Varn and Arrok stepped outside to find the upper half of the temple tangled up with the upper half of the jail and the trunk and lower branches blocking their path.

Varn started climbing over branches that were larger around than he was tall as he worked his way toward what had once been the base of the tree. Arrok followed in his wake along the ground, occasionally calling out to Mayven. Varn shook his head in distraction, searching frantically for a way through the debris. He looked at Arrok, his voice a snarl as he said, "Where is that screeching coming from? It sounds like someone dying, and I can't think it is so loud in my head."

Arrok frowned as he stood on the stone surface of the town square. "I don't hear anything."

"Come over here. We have to help. You will hear it better over here!"

Arrok stepped over fallen limbs and scattered leaves and then, stepping up onto a thick unbroken branch, froze as if someone had nailed his feet in place. Arrok's face bleached white and his eyes grew huge, then gingerly he stepped to the ground and then back onto the branch. "It's the tree, it's screaming!"

Varn gaped at Arrok. "How can a tree scream? Have you been knocked on the head?"

Arrok shook his head, his face filled with disbelief. "No, I swear. Step down from where you are."

Varn looked at Arrok, his eyes narrowed. "I don't have time for this," he said through clenched teeth.

Arrok motioned to Varn. "Just do it."

Varn launched himself gracefully from where he stood and, landing lightly on his feet next to Arrok, turned to face him with his mouth agape. Then he jumped back up onto a branch and back down. "Okay this is a mystery I don't have time for right now but go to the town hall get the master masons down here and get the repairs underway immediately. I'll see to Mayven."

Arrok nodded and dashed off as Varn, carefully avoiding touching the tree, made his way out into the open and broke into a run toward the mass of debris that made a mound of broken splinters and planks where the jail had just recently stood. Loathe to touch anything associated with the tree, Varn took a deep breath and, shielding his mind as much as possible, started pulling debris from the pile as carefully as he could. Soon payjiks and masons had joined him, and there was a confusion of exclamations as they started to help, only to jump back at contact and stare at each other.

"The tree is screaming, most likely in pain. I don't know how, I just know it is. Masons, get to work doing what you can to help until we have cleared the survivors. Payjik, let's find anyone who may be in here," Varn commanded.

Masons of every level gathered in a circle as they began to sing, the sound of the Adamsah they wove rose like a soothing balm. The song magic curled over Varn, and he felt the pressure against his mental shield relax. Many hands made light work, and it didn't take long before the magic woven by the masons and the work of moving debris by Varn and payjiks had cleared the ground. Four people lay on the ground floor of the once majestic building. Two were dead, Varn briefly glanced at the third as a payjik gathered a stretcher and carefully lifted him onto it, then he turned to examine Mayven.

She lay on the floor, her complexion white and bloodless, her lips tinted blue, and blood bubbling from her mouth with every shallow breath. He searched her neck and found a thready pulse as he turned, his voice loud and demanding, "I need a stretcher over here."

"It's on its way," a payjik assured him.

"I don't think she'll make it. There is blood coming from her lips, I think she's punctured her lungs. Is there a medic close?"

"I am," a tall, reed-thin woman said as she knelt next to Varn. She closed her eyes, holding her hand over Mayven's back. Then, in a low vibrato, she began to sing softly just above a whisper. The bubbling from Mayven's lips stopped as the woman stopped singing and said, "I've done what little I can."

Varn looked up to see the stretcher being lowered next to Mayven. Raking his hands through his hair, he growled, "Be gentle. Do we have a transport pod?"

Neither stretcher bearer looked up from their patient as they carefully transferred Mayven to the stretcher. "It's waiting. Will you be going with her?"

Varn grunted assent and followed behind as they filed to the waiting transport. Once inside, they were flying along the streets to the hospital as Varn listened absently to the medic and the stretcher bearers converse in low tones while working furiously over Mayven.

"It was like all the magic decreased at once, and the master weather mages couldn't hold back the worst of the storm. I've never seen anything like it. So much damage."

"Just concentrate on her," Varn snarled as he clenched his hands together in white-knuckled frustration.

The others fell silent and, moments later, they exited the transport at the hospital's emergency entrance. The huge willow tree smelled soothing, its branches hanging low to caress those who passed inside. The touch of the tree seemed to make the many passing beneath them flinch in surprise, and Varn braced himself as he followed the stretcher beneath the swaying branches. The light touch of leaves sent a voice into his head, *"Thank you for bringing Lapahoniesh to me. I will gladly help to heal her."*

Varn's eyes jerked upward a moment, then he continued behind the stretcher inside the open doorway to the emergency room. Doctors were already surrounding the bed on which Mayven now lay, and they none too gently ushered him back to the lobby to wait. Varn collapsed into an empty seat, his head in his hands and sighed heavily.

A hand touched his shoulder, and he jerked away as he looked up. Arrok stood there, his palms up in surrender as he asked, "How is she?"

"I don't know yet. They just took her in. We just got here."

"There are some really strange things going on outside, my friend. Have you seen?"

"I guessed, but I'm busy at the moment. I have more important matters to concern me."

Arrok clenched his teeth together and slowly sat in the chair next to Varn, his back stiff, not touching the back of his seat, as he stared unblinking at the space between his boots.

Varn looked at him a moment then muttered, "I'm sorry."

Arrok nodded slightly and relaxed back into his chair, crossing his arms over his chest as they both settled in to wait. Varn alternately paced the floor and sat in the chair, watching the clock as the hours ticked by slowly, one, then two, then three finally the doors to the emergency department opened and a doctor stepped out. Speaking briefly to a woman at the desk, the doctor looked toward Varn. The woman nodded, and Varn rose from his seat to meet the doctor as he approached. Varn greeted him brusquely.

Introducing himself, the doctor said quietly, "She is stable, but in very bad shape. She is in a coma and, due to her injuries, I'm not sure how long that coma will last or if there is a possibility of her waking up again. The next twenty-four hours will determine more."

Varn felt the knot in his stomach sink to his feet, and he staggered back to sink into his chair. The doctor sat next to Varn as Arrok looked on, his muscled arms clenched across his chest. Varn felt the warmth of the doctor's hand on his shoulder before he acknowledged the quiet calm voice at his ear. "Are you okay?"

"I'm fine. When can I go in to see her?"

"In an hour, we will come and get you. She is recovering now and then being moved to a room. I will send a nurse for you when she is settled."

The doctor rose and disappeared back into the interior of the hospital. An hour passed and, as promised, Varn walked into Mayven's room to find her remarkably unmarred. The crystal display above her bed monitored her breathing, her heart, and brain waves and a restraint shield was in place, marked by the hsieleng crystal inserted in her headboard. Mayven looked unharmed and, except for her unusual stillness, one would have thought her to be only sleeping.

Varn turned to look at the nurse. "Why the restraint?"

"She has massive internal injuries. If she wakes, we don't want her moving until we are certain her body is healed enough to allow her to do so without causing further injury."

Varn nodded mutely and settled into a chair next to the bed to wait.

Arrok cleared his throat quietly. "Do you want some food or clean clothes? You may be here a while."

"Sure, you know where I live. Rohtak will let you in. Tell him what you need. He'll see to it."

Arrok nodded and left without another word as Varn stared silently at Mayven's pale profile. Mayven's forehead, now bare of its customary band, revealed the bright, glowing xodieha on her forehead. The intricate design with its delicate scrolling created a tree instead of the compass that represented the xodieha of others. The delicately knotted and vibrantly glowing mark tied each of the compass points together with the sign of earth nestled in the roots of the tree, the signs of air, water, and fire curled in its branches. Unlike most xodieha, each compass point was illuminated, representing her unique ability to access any of the magic associated with each of the four points. The tree glowed and pulsed, matching Mayven's heart rate line on the monitor above the bed.

CHAPTER NINETEEN

Mayven lay perfectly still, eyes closed, as she felt air rush easily through her lungs when she sighed. *I should be dead. I know I was under the bench in the jail when it collapsed on me.* Her hands caressed her ribs. *My ribs don't hurt. Perhaps I died. I remember pain, a lot of pain.* Light filtered through Mayven's closed eyelids. Blinking, she opened them to stare up at the dappled light filtering through the towering tops of a grove of trees. She slowly pushed herself upright as she looked around her, feeling her brow furrow in confusion.

Looking down, she noticed her clothing was undamaged. "I must be dreaming or dead."

The wind picked up, caressing Mayven's face and blowing waist-length raven locks over her shoulder. A voice, soft and whispering like the wind around her, entered her mind. *"You are not dead, Lapahoniesh. But you are, in a way, dreaming."*

Mayven raised her hands to feel the wind as she looked up through the treetops. "I am where, then? What is this place?"

"This is the beginning and the end of a story that has linked our peoples for generations longer than can be counted."

"Am I supposed to interpret riddles to find the answer to my question? Are answers to my questions as elusive as your identity?"

Laughter, the wind increased, the sound from the trees magnified in her head, laced with a soft harmony of water over rocks. *"Children are so impatient. It has been so long since I spoke to one so young."*

Mayven felt resentment rise in her as she spun on her heels, looking for a face to speak to. "I am not a child. Where are you? Face me and answer my questions! I'm tired of all the cryptic speeches and Lapa-honiesh."

"You are looking at me. Look at the center of this glen, the center of this cathedral. I am right here."

Mayven turned to face the center of the glen. A massive shen tree, its breadth far greater than the width of the open space between her and the tree, towered at the center of the trees surrounding the glen. It's canopy towered overhead so far above her that the uppermost branches were further up than she could see. The branches spread out, making the majority of the lattice that formed the top of the natural cathedral in which she stood. "I see no one there."

"I am here. You see me, but do not know that I am speaking. You and generations of your people have not heard my voice or that of any of my people. But I see from the world around that the Hato have honored our bargain, even without knowing why they do so. It is a testament to a race so young. Your people have much honor."

Mayven stared at the shen tree as she slowly walked forward. Reaching out her hand and placing her palm against the smooth, softly glowing bark of the magnificent tree in front of her, she asked, "You're the shen?"

"I am. Though my people are called Ohkie'en. We have been asleep since the vanishing war. There is much I must explain. But we have some time. So I will start at the beginning, if you would like to make yourself comfortable."

Mayven gasped and stepped away from the tree a moment to stare once again up toward the towering height of the softly glowing tree, its silver white leaves reflecting bright dappled light against softly bending waves of the tall grass around her legs. Looking down at her feet, she watched as the roots of the tree moved and changed into the shape of a cradle-like chair on which she sat. Consciously closing her mouth, she waited in stunned silence for the ancient to being to speak.

"You are right to think of me as ancient. In fact, I am the first tree to speak with your people. I am the first of the Ohkie'en to see the advantage we could be to each other. I see, now that I am once again awake, that my thoughts were true."

Mayven's contact with the tree against her body seemed to magnify her senses. She felt the flow of sap and water through the being like a pulse and warmth on her skin as if exposed to the sun shining directly above the canopy.

"My name is Radiea. Though not my name given by my people, it is a

name I cherish. It was given to me by your oldest ancestor. By that, I do mean your direct ancestor, child. She called me light when she first saw me, and I was honored by her comparison, so I kept the name. Each of my people have a name of our language and those who serve your people have a name given by your people."

Mayven caressed the silken bark beneath the palms of her hands and heard a soft hum, followed by a sudden brief rush of wind through treetops. "I can see why she would have called you Radiea. It fits. But how do you mean 'serve my people'?"

"We are your shelters, temples, places of gathering, and worship. We offer our fruits to your health as food. We service you."

"And how do we do anything for you? You spoke of an advantage to each other. What could we do for one such as you?"

"It started long before I met your first ancestor. When your race were only infants, you did not harm us. But as you grew and learned the dangers of this world, you discovered the need for shelter. Not knowing that we were sentient, just as you, your people began to cut us down to create shelters to protect you from dangers that fragile creatures such as yourselves need protection from. As you began to survive longer, you increased in number and the numbers of my people that were sacrificed to your people's safety became ever greater. I knew then it would be only a matter of time before we would be far too few to serve you or us. So, against the wish of the Ohkie'en, I contacted your ancestor. She, like you, was also very special, I believe your people call you Language Masters. She was surprised that I was speaking, just as you have been. But I showed her, as I will show you, how the forces that bind this world are connected and how the magic of her people and mine could be combined to benefit us all."

Mayven sat in silence as the tree's voice trailed off in a breezy sigh. Looking around the glen, she took in the perfect circle created by the trees on the outside of the glen. Mayven watched the grass bending in gentle waves beneath the wind then felt a horrified jolt send shivers chasing down her spine as a group of stumps not far from where she sat revealed themselves beneath the tall green stalks.

"What are those?" Mayven already felt the horror at knowing those represented Ohkie'en who had died most likely at the hands of Hato.

"Quiet yourself, child." Mayven smiled, for the reference to her being a child no longer angered her, and listened as Radiea continued, *"I will explain on that in due course. Your ancestor's name was Tama, meaning bridge in your language, a fitting name for the purpose she fulfilled in her lifetime. Tama quickly grasped the problem but the solution was not as*

easily reached. It took a very long time and practice for the two of us become proficient at understanding each other, then at being able to explain to each other the needs of our two peoples. Longer still to come up with a solution to the problem."

A sigh ran through the surrounding trees as the breeze rustled leaves softly in its wake. There was a sadness and tension in the sound that caused Mayven to squirm anxiously in her seat.

"By the time Tama and I had defined and agreed to a way to solve both our problems, the Hato had made immense progress into the forest, cutting down trees for shelter and clearing land to plant for food. The Ohkie'en were loath to listen to our plan, and the Hato believed Tama's wits had been taken by Dsohoay. Months passed as she and I continued to meet and talk and then talk to our separate people."

Mayven felt her heart pounding in her chest, her mouth dry as her breath rushed past parted lips. Her eyes remained glued to the stumps in front of her. It wasn't until her fingers began to ache that she realized she was gripping the tree's roots so hard her knuckles were white. Taking a deep breath, she slowly forced her body to relax but her eyes wouldn't leave the stumps as Radiea continued, *"Our world met in a clash not far from where you sit."*

Mayven's head lowered to her chest, the sound of the breeze growing faint as Radiea began to speak, *"Tama and I felt helpless to stop it. The Hato refused to believe Tama that trees could speak or feel. The Ohkie'en refused to believe that the Hato even cared that they were hurting beings who knew what was happening and could feel the pain the Hato's actions caused."*

Mayven felt a sadness surround her as Radiea's voice in her head softened to a reverent whisper, *"Tama did what many in your ancestry have done. She gave not a thought to her own safety. She linked to me through touch, much as you feel my emotions and the sensations of my body now, and using her considerable magic ability, cast a work of our magic, Adamha, and Adamie like has not been seen since. She transmitted the thoughts, pain, fear, anger, and grief of all the Ohkie'en at once toward her people, who gathered close by clearing another field for planting."*

Mayven felt the wetness of her tears sliding down her face but paid no heed as she continued to listen in stunned silence.

"The pain transferred through Tama, scorching her mind and body, burning her alive from the inside out. But the Hato heard. The Hato stopped in the midst of what they were doing. Tama managed to survive long enough to teach someone else how to speak to me, and we helped our people

to come to an agreement known as the Great Accord. Tama was honored by your people and ours and still is, among ours. You, child, have joined her ranks."

Mayven took a shuddering breath. "Don't thank me or esteem me so highly yet. While our people have obviously kept that accord, I'm not so sure the spirit of it remains with all my people for there is something going on much larger than I can grasp. It has something to do with this Lapahoniesh."

The wind burst through the trees in quick succession, racing around the glen, starting a furious rustle that matched the chuckle in Mayven's head. *"You are this Lapahoniesh. I am getting there, little one. There is so much that has been forgotten since we were put to sleep."*

Mayven sighed heavily and leaned back into the comforting cradle of the tree's embrace, causing Radiea to chuckle as she continued, *"The Hato and Ohkie'en learned to help each other. Ohkie'en provided education in the use of Adamha, our natural magic, which is what all plants and animals possess to some degree, whether they are sentient or not. Hato taught us how they use Adamie and Adamsah, your speaking and singing magic. We agreed to provide shelter and the Hato agreed to allow us to do so while not killing us to attain said shelter. We taught your people how to harvest the food our kind provided and things progressed nicely. However, in our world is another race that found our arrangement very inconvenient to their desires. The Aniwie are older than the Hato but not as old as the Ohkie'en. They were part of the danger your people needed protection from. They eventually caused the Vanishing War."*

"So there is yet another race on this world our people have forgotten about?"

"Not all your people have forgotten about them but, because the Aniwie are so patient, Adamdavas believe they have the Aniwie under control. They, unfortunately, are very wrong about that. The Aniwie are large carnivorous beasts. There are three tribes in their race, the Katawie, or great cats; the Osowie, or great bears; and the Wasawie, or great wolf people. To these people, the Hato were food, to be eaten. In fact, they are the inspiration behind you curse, mogatie. To the Aniwie, it means 'nothing more than a meal'."

Mayven swallowed hard, her stomach churning slightly. "Adamdavas knows of the Aniwie. Do they also know of the Ohkie'en?"

"No, the Aniwie decided that having Adamdavas without options, should they ever discover the Aniwie's true intentions, was a sound strategy.

They forbid those who knew of the Ohkie'en to pass on the knowledge, and eventually we were forgotten."

"And what are the Aniwie's true intentions?"

"The Aniwie have no desire to share this world with any other race. They want to have all the power of magic and the control of the world to themselves. They nearly succeeded during the Vanishing War and, if it hadn't been for the last minute change of heart by the Language Master they had under their control, they would have."

Mayven stirred uncomfortably in her seat as the magnitude of her position in this began to sink in at last. "How did they almost succeed?"

"The Aniwie needed to learn how to use the Adamie and Adamsah, speaking and singing magic, of the Hato so they could master it. Just as the Ohkie'en learned from the Hato your use of magic, so did the Aniwie under the guise of the treaty they put in place. The treaty stated that they would apprentice some of the most powerful users of magic in your people and teach them the use of magic by the Aniwie in exchange for knowledge of magic use from the Hato. They also agreed to stop hunting Hato as a food source. They did not agree, however, to free the Hato who were their slaves."

Mayven felt bile rise in her throat at the implications of that statement.

"The agreement was upheld by the Hato and your people showed them. But when it was time for the reverse to be shown, the Aniwie evaded the exchange and began the second half of their plan."

Mayven felt the tension in her body slowly increasing and her heart beat slamming against her chest. "This is where the Language Master comes in, am I right?"

"Yes," Radiea's voice whispered in her head and a soothing rustle of the trees surrounded Mayven. *"Language Masters are central to the problem created by the Aniwie and central to the solution of that problem as well."*

Mayven shifted in her seat as her hands rubbed absently over the fabric stretched tautly across her thighs. "What is that problem?"

"The second half of their plan, once they understood the basics of how your people used your connection to magic, was to gain control of a Language Master. The Aniwie discovered they would never be able to do with Adamsah or Adamie what your people are able to do, so they opted to try and control one who could wield all those powers. The Aniwie felt to eliminate the other races, they needed to eliminate their access to magic. They were correct and wrong all at the same time."

Mayven shifted slightly as she contemplated the statement. "How is that possible?"

"There is a circle that is created by our world. Eliminating one portion of that circle breaks it and then throws off the balance. Aniwie would not listen to the council of the Ohkie'en, who discovered their plan. Instead they declared us their enemy. They coaxed the greedy and powerful of the Hato to help them. Then created the secret society known as Adamdavas. The Ohkie'en who knew of their plans created Niesha. The struggle only escalated from there."

"That is still not the answer to how they can be both wrong and right." Mayven, now restless with anticipation, rose from her seat and began to pace between the stumps and Radiea as she listened.

"They will destroy our people, the Ohkie'en and Hato, if they remove us from our connection to magic. Magic is as much a part of how we function as the blood in your veins or the sunlight that feeds me. In that, they will succeed. But in destroying us, they will ultimately destroy themselves and our world, Emwen."

Mayven stopped and planted her feet shoulder width apart as she stared up at the canopy above her as she clasped her hands behind her back. "I understand it will destroy the Ohkie'en and Hato but how would it destroy the Aniwie and Emwen? Wouldn't the magic just transfer to the Aniwie and Emwen then only have one inhabitant race?"

"In theory, but perhaps it is best to explain the spell was altered and put the Ohkie'en to sleep. The spell was simple but magnificently complex. I admire their ingenuity, if they had only put it to good use. The Language Master they controlled came up with the spell. It was to be activated during a pitched battle when all the Ohkie'en and Hato were otherwise engaged fighting the army the Aniwie had amassed. The spell was to strip the magic from our people and then transfer it to the Aniwie during the highest point of the battle, allowing them to destroy us at will."

Mayven heaved a sigh. "Brilliant but deadly."

"Indeed, as I said, ingenious if not kind." Radiea was silent for a long breath as the trees around her rustled anxiously, the noise causing the anxiety in Mayven to increase as she began to pace a path in the high grass once more.

When at last Radiea spoke again, her voice was low and filled with sadness and the glen grew unnaturally calm. *"They began the battle. The Language Master was at the back of their forces and had the words memorized. The spell was ready to spill forth at the height of the battle. Niesha reached the Language Master as the Aniwie guard was otherwise* occupied with a more furious attack than they expected, led by myself and a large group of the Hato. Niesha were trying to convince the Language Master of what would really happen and not making any progress until one of the Ohkie'en showed what happens when the circle is disrupted and the balance thrown off."

Mayven suddenly saw in her head what was shown to that Language Master.

When the magic was cut off from the Ohkie'en and the Hato, the winds fell silent, the air grew thick, unbreathable, and the Hato fell dead in their tracks. Then, a giant surge of power focused like a tidal wave against a shallow shore on the Aniwie and, because they could not contain or control all the magic at once, they too were struck down. Emwen trembled, the world shuddering in a death throes as it tried to balance the power pouring out from its core. But there were no longer reservoirs to contain it, like a tkhoda with a fatal wound, Emwen bled out the magic that sustained it and became dead as the non-sentient inhabitants, one by one, lost their connection to the life force that sustained them. As the last pictures faded from Mayven's mind, her knees gave way and her stomach revolted, spilling bile into the grass in front of her.

A soft breeze cooled the tears that streamed down her face and then it became silent again as Radiea continued, "*The Language Master agreed to leave with Niesha, but was then recaptured by the Aniwie and forced to perform the spell. But the knowledge that Language Master now possessed changed him, and he changed the spell though he spoke it. Instead of eliminating the magic from the Hato and Ohkie'en and severing their connection to the magic, he reduced our connection and put the Ohkie'en to sleep, for he understood that having both awake would eventually kill off the weaker of the two, since the reduced magic would flow toward those who required more to survive. The Aniwie left the battle, believing they had won. The land where the magic was performed was scorched beyond recognition and became known as the Hareshtava, the forest made ruin.*"

The unnatural silence stretched on as Mayven once again paced furiously, the tension within her balling her hands into fists at her side.

"*On return to their lands, the Aniwie waited for proof of their victory in the deaths of their Hato captives. It never came, and when they went to the Language Master to find out why, he had poisoned himself. He spoke a prophecy, a spell, saying that the strongest line of Language Masters would produce one who would break his spell and restore the balance and the Aniwie would have to face their reckoning. Then he died. The Aniwie then withdrew from sight, to be forgotten by all except the highest among*

Adamdavas. They have a plan in place, I am sure. I do not know it yet. But our people will work on it as fast as possible. You must lift the spell completely. The exact wording of that prophecy is written in the documents of the Language Master's Library. You will need it to finish your work."

Mayven stopped moving as something was stirring in her head. Her small slender hand rubbed her forehead as she processed all she had been told then her head snapped up. "You're awake, the power balance has shifted. What is happening to the Hato?"

The glen once again filled with a furious rustle, breaking the un-natural silence as Radiea continued, *"That is where you come in, Lapahoniesh. Your ancestry is important. The power in your line is what will restore balance, and it must be done soon or even you will lose the strength to alter what has been done. Your line is what the prophecy spoke of, and you have the power to set the balance right but there is only a limited time to get it done. The balance can only be restored where the damage was done, at Hareshtaivah. You are standing now in the place where it must be set right. This glen was once known as Narenashie, it means sanctuary. It can be restored to that, but you must break the spell."*

Mayven looked around. "If I'm where I need to be, why can't I just fix it now? How do I do it?"

"You are only here in your mind. You must be here in your body. This place no longer looks like this, though I still am alive, barely. Your body is too weak. You have been badly injured. You need the information from the original spell. All these things must be right. The Ohkie'en are going to heal you as our gift to you, so you may continue your path. Please hurry, Lapahoniesh, there is not much time."

Mayven felt another rush of power like the one she had felt in the temple. Her mind raced with questions but she had no time to ask them before Radiea whispered in her head, *"Remember what we have spoken of and hurry."*

Then a warmth flooded her body, her eyes opened, and she was staring up at Varn's furrowed brow and worried green gaze.

CHAPTER TWENTY

V arn stood and leaned over Mayven as she stirred restlessly on her bed. The crystal display beeped faster and the lines jumped with her movements. As he leaned over her and spoke her name, her wide violet eyes, framed in long ebony lashes, sprang open and stared up at him, filled with fear and anxiety.

Varn placed a hand on her wrist and felt the tingle of the restraint shield run over his skin when he made contact with it. "It's okay, you're at the hospital. They have you restrained so that you won't injure yourself further. You were badly hurt."

"I'm fine." Mayven's gaze cleared of confusion, and her eyes filled with determination. "The Ohkie'en healed me. I need out of here. I have things I need to get done."

Varn frowned at her reference to the Ohkie'en. He watched emotions play across her expressive pale face as her eyes studied him intently.

"What is it?" he asked when she began to struggle again.

"I need you to explain my family history. I know now how important Lapahoniesh is, but I need more information. Do you know what a Language Master Library is?"

Varn smiled as he felt his heart race. *Finally, she understands.*

Taking his hand from her wrist, he touched her forehead. "In due time. The doctors are coming in. They want to make sure you're okay. It may be a little while before you can get out of here."

Varn frowned as he watched panic race across her finely etched features.

Mayven struggled against the shield. "I don't have time. We have to get moving."

Looking up, he watched the doctors come bustling into the room and pushed him to the side as they touched the monitor. Beeps and clicks filled the room as the display flashed the message, *scanning*. Then the doctors examined the results and looked at the screen again and ran the scan twice more. All the while, Mayven grew more impatient with every passing minute.

Varn sensed her agitation and even he, without medical training, could clearly read the screen that said she was in perfect health. "I think it is safe to let her go. You have scanned her three times now. She is fine. You were better healers than you thought. Obviously she is well, let her up. I know there are many others who need your help."

Mayven chimed in, saying, "I'm fine. I need to get out of here."

The doctors conferred among themselves and at last agreed to release her based on her obvious health.

Nearly two hours later, Varn walked out the front door with Mayven at his side. They walked in silence for several blocks and at last he looked over at her. "Who are the Ohkie'en?"

"They are the trees." Mayven stared at her feet as she walked. "They're not just plants. They're alive. They told me there is more to do. I'm trying to remember all of it."

Varn stepped into the town square alongside Mayven and realized that though his time at the hospital had seemed like days, only a very short time had passed and it was evident in the wreckage of the jail that still lay strewn around the square. Varn heard Mayven gasp and turned in time to see her go rushing toward the tree.

"Oh, he is in such pain. What can we do to help?"

The mason's guild masters, their multiple tiny braids denoting their rank, stood in a group and looked at her in question. "What do you mean, he is in pain?"

Varn watched as Mayven turned, her small frame straight and stiff as polished granite. "Tell me you haven't been ignoring the cries of this poor being. I know each time you touch him, you can hear him."

"I've heard sounds when we touch the tree. But no being is here."

Varn concealed a smile behind his hand as he looked on.

"The tree is the being, you mogatie." Mayven stomped her tiny booted foot. "The tree is a member of a race known as Ohkie'en. They're awake again. He needs your immediate help. Don't delay any longer. He's suffering."

Varn saw the master mason advance on Mayven, his jaw set in a stubborn, angry line.

Varn stepped in quickly. "She is Lapahoniesh. She knows of what she speaks. Do as she says as quickly as possible."

Varn watched the mason's face change instantly at the mention of Lapahoniesh. Then the mason's gaze darted to the xodieha on Mayven's brow. His eyes grew wide, and he turned to his group, giving several abrupt orders. The group gathered in a circle and, raising their hands outstretched toward the fallen leviathan, began to sing.

The song of the guild masters was low and rhythmic, as if to the beat of pounding hammers, at the end of each line of song, rhythm increased. Varn felt the magic around them seem to rush forward, crawling over the surface of his skin like ants. He watched Mayven's face for a long moment as she stared, wide-eyed, at the work being done. Her ruby lips parted softly, her pale cheeks flushed as her entire body leaned forward, balanced on the balls of her tiny feet.

Varn turned his eyes back to the work at hand as he felt his pulse begin to increase. Like rewinding time, the tree and its multiple pieces rose from the stone paved town square and began winding themselves back into the body of the colossal tree. The mighty trunk once again stood in front of them, whole, but showed a monstrous scar down its center where its body had been cleaved in half. The sound of the mason's song decreased in speed, the rhythm becoming more deliberate as the bark healed over the scar and the glittering shards of glass coalesced in the air, approaching the empty sockets where the windows had been. Then, in multiple bright flashes, the glass was once again in place. Several more short pounding phrases later finished the last of the work and then the music stopped.

The magic that prickled over Varn's body stopped. He watched as Mayven launched her body like an arrow at the tree. Placing her palms on the rough bark and resting her head against it, she closed her eyes briefly then pulled back, a contented smile on her face.

"He says thank you, honored ones, for doing your work so well and thoroughly," Mayven addressed the masons. "He can hardly tell the damage was done."

Varn watched the head mason walk forward and place his hand on the tree. He closed his eyes, then a moment later pulled back as he stared up in wonder.

Mayven came toward him, bouncing on her feet, happiness etched in the wide smile on her face. "It wasn't a dream," she whispered, "they're real."

"The Ohkie'en?"

Mayven nodded. "They're the allies of the Hato."

Mayven went through the story as they walked together through the town square. Her face filled with wonder and excitement, and she infected him with her enthusiasm. Varn felt the connection between them thrum as her enthusiasm and excitement allowed her iron guard to slip. Afraid she might withdraw again, and enjoying the meager connection that served as a cooling balm for his aching heart, Varn said little, letting her explain all she had heard. When she had finished speaking, he motioned to the door of his home, where they had arrived while they talked. "Then you will understand what I am about to show you."

Varn ushered Mayven into the foyer and a soft deep voice entered his head as he stepped onto the polished familiar surface of his floor. "*I am glad to see you still live in your ancestral home.*"

Varn looked up to see who had spoken, but no one was there. A smile played across his mouth as he remembered Mayven's tale. "You're Ohkie'en. I'm sorry I don't know your name. You haven't been heard for many generations."

"*I am called Sharieana by your people.*"

Varn looked at Mayven in wonder and saw a smile stretching across her features as her eyes stared unfocused at the ceiling. "You're talking to her."

Mayven's eyes focused on him again. "She said she didn't mean to be rude. She just wanted to thank me for helping her people."

Varn nodded and smoothed his shirt with his palms. "I understand. I need to show you something very important. Sharieana may wish to be included when we discuss it. I need to check on some things. Why don't you get you something to eat? The kitchen is at the back of the house. Then meet me in my study."

Mayven nodded, and Varn turned and headed up the stairway to the second floor. Opening the door to Arrok's room, Varn noted it was lit by the still gray light of the storm-clouded sky and completely empty. Varn heaved a sigh. *Arrok must be working on something. I'll have to catch up to him later.*

However, worry clouded his thoughts as he descended the stairs. *Arrok doesn't usually take off without explanation.*

Hearing Mayven call to him, Varn increased his pace. "All is fine. I'll be right there."

As he started back down the stairs, Varn pulled his engaohnie stone from his pocket. Scrolling down the list on the screen, he tapped on Arrok's name. Varn stepped onto the foyer just as the answering message for Arrok's device started to play. He listened impatiently and, when allowed, left a message. "I need you at my home now. There have been some unexpected developments. I hope you are safe, old friend. Call or get here quickly."

Removing the engaohnie from his ear, he continued on to the library, taking a deep calming breath before stepping through the door. Mayven sat in the chair in front of the desk, her diminutive stature dwarfed even more by the size of the chair that was created for someone more his size. He watched her tiny booted feet swing absently as they dangled several inches above the floor. Her raven hair fell like a curtain, shielding her face from his view. One tiny hand held a glass of fayen juice as she bent intently over a large book in her lap.

Varn licked his lips as he watched slender fingers caress the moisture gathering on the outside of the glass. Running a hand roughly through his hair, he cleared his throat to alert her to his presence as he stepped into the room, shutting the door behind him. "I'm sorry for the delay. Is there any way you can have Sharieana listen and speak to both of us during this conversation? I think she may have even more information than I do on what we're about to discuss."

Mayven looked up at him and the impact of her deep amethyst eyes caused him to suck in his breath, distracting him briefly and leaving him unprepared for her caustic reply. "She heard you. I don't need to translate. Speak to her, and she'll answer."

Varn sucked his breath through his teeth, clenched his jaw, and lowered his eyes as he gathered himself then strode to his desk, taking the seat opposite of Mayven. "I apologize for the misunderstanding."

Turning from Mayven and facing the bookshelf, he expelled his breath in rush as he removed several books and opened a hidden compartment behind them, pulling out an intricately woven neckband. Turning from the safe, he laid it upon the desk in front him, carefully unwrapped it from the cloth that protected it and struggled to compose himself.

The wide band was finely wrought, braided, silver inlaid with amethyst chips. Around the band above the chips, in the delicate vine-like letters of their language, was engraved a quote, and from the center of the band hung a large amethyst stone. He felt his lips twitch. *Unfortunately the same color as her eyes.*

Shoving his hands through his hair once again, he squared his shoulders and braced himself as he leaned back in his chair and looked into Mayven's now guarded gaze. "This is your family marsa. It belongs to you as the only living member with the family surname."

I can't read her again. What has her guard up now? Varn waited, his hands relaxed in his lap but his shoulders aching with tension as he waited for her response.

Mayven took two long breaths and then she asked softly, "What is my surname?"

Varn once again felt his equilibrium tilt off balance at her softly spoken, guileless question. *She is always doing this! I never know how to react to her, one minute a kata, all claws and teeth the next a lamta, all soft eyes and gentle voice.*

"Tiramahaba is your surname. The other Language Master born in your family line is not of your surname and doesn't possess the power you do. Though, he is talented in his own right."

He watched Mayven eye the marsa on the desk as if it were about to bite her.

Mayven's confused amethyst gaze locked on Varn. "What's his name?"

Varn answered before thinking, "Rohodak Xeptira."

Varn had barely finished speaking and registering the excitement on Mayven's face before he regretted his monumental lapse of judgment. Varn felt anger rush in as his hands clenched into fists. *Mogatie, give her the most dangerous bit of information you have besides her own identity.*

Sharieana spoke, *"Only you can hear me right now. You must trust her if you want to her to believe in you. Trust is how you will get one as guarded as her to listen. Tell her what all this means, but be honest."*

"I have real, living, family of my blood? Why didn't you tell me? Why make me believe I was an orphan?" Anger, Mayven's ever present shield, colored her cheeks a rosy red.

"I had to, for his protection and yours. Please pick up the marsa. Look at it closely, and I will explain."

Mayven launched herself from her chair and her feet hit the floor with a barely audible thump. Varn sighed as he relaxed back in his chair, watching her pace in front of his desk.

"I can't believe this!" Mayven gesticulated wildly as she marched in front of the desk. "You want me to just go along with all your plans for me, while keeping secrets every time I turn around..."

Varn tuned her out as he let her vent until she had worn out her anger. He watched her slender form pace and her pale cheeks flush with color as her eyes flashed first violet then amethyst.

Varn sighed as he thought on all the times he had felt her put her fragile frame in harm's way to save some poor soul in the two years she had struggled through life in the orphanage. Every time her efforts had been met with cruelty and neglect. He watched her frantic pacing and knew her fear of trusting him was justified. Not only for his own actions but from the actions of every one she had ever met in her entire life. Varn knew that her distrust of him had a lot to do with the botched transfer in which his uncle had lost his life.

He leaned forward and rubbed his temples and pulled his thoughts back to the present as Mayven sank into her chair and faded into silence as a mental shout issued from Sharieana, *"You children need to focus on the here and now. You can worry about the past when you have the luxury of reflection. Lapahoniesh, listen to him. He has information you need to know and time is running short."*

Mayven's face colored pink all the way to her hairline as a worried look flashed across her countenance before she nodded and her face once again became an impassive mask. Varn sat up straight, looked Mayven in the eye, and picked up the marsa from the desk. "This is not a marsa as you know them. This is not a device to rank you in society. It is what it was designed to be, a history of your family. This is your genealogy from the first recorded member of your family tree."

Sharieana interrupted in a quiet voice both of them could hear, *"It was a gift of honor given to your people from mine. After the great accord, the marsa was created and imbued with magic as a way for each family to trace their lineage. The Ohkie'en have something like it transferred in our memories, and we thought it would be a way for you to have your histories, too. It was done originally to honor Tama's family so that all her prodigy would know of her story, but all your people wanted to have such a treasure so we taught them how to create their own. But the one before you is the one created for Tama. It is the only one created by the Ohkie'en. It tracks your family all the way back to your first ancestor and is passed down through the family to those who have the same surname as Tama. You, child, are the last of that line. Your people have tracked their lineage from the females of their line since the creation of this marsa."*

Varn held it out to her. Mayven reached across the desk and gingerly took it in one hand. When the amethyst touched her skin, a graphic of a tree in golden lines appeared in the air in front of her. Varn watched

Mayven's face as her eyes went wide, a frown line appearing between her brows as her tongue flicked out to wet her lips.

Varn felt the tension inside him crank up another notch at that familiar nervous gesture. Taking a slow breath, he leaned forward on the arms of his chair. "This is what a real marsa is meant to depict. The family history of every person you are directly related to. There is nothing in a real marsa, like the ones here in Kieshan, that put a label on your caste or rank in society. They don't track your movements or monitor you in anyway. But this marsa has been sought after for generations now. It is legendary. The first marsa created for the very first Language Master. Adamdavas believes it will tell them where to find the most powerful of the Language Masters and when that master will arrive."

Sharieana's voice whispered into the conversation, *"They are right if you know how to use it. Read the inscription aloud, child, and then place the marsa around your neck. When you have memorized that inscription, you won't need to read it to produce the same effect."*

Varn felt first wonder, then concern, make the hair on the back of his neck stand on end. He leaned forward, reaching for the marsa.

Sharieana commanded, *"You have no right to hold this secret, Varn. She is the only one who can activate the marsa in this way. Adamdavas is right in what it does but not in how it works. Only those of her main blood line, with her surname, who are Language Masters, have the ability to activate the marsa at all, much less attain this information."*

Varn felt his face grow hot and dropped his hand as Sharieana correctly judged his motives. *Can Sharieana read all my thoughts?*

"Only those that are unguarded when we are in direct contact," Sharieana answered him, *"and since I'm speaking only to you right now, she doesn't know. But it is my advice that you keep fewer secrets if you want more than just an uneasy truce with Mayven. No one cooperates well with those they know are not telling the entire truth."*

Varn felt the heat on his face grow and lowered his head as he took a long breath. Mayven shuffled restlessly in her seat, and Varn looked up as she placed the book she had been reading on the desk then cradled the marsa in both hands and examined the writing on the wide band. As she studied it, Varn rose and removed the plain state-issued marsa she had received at the orphanage in Shimiera. Varn held it up by one end and muttered, *"Kit'ivahtkiet."*

The marsa vibrated so hard if fell from Varn's grasp and dissolved into dust before it hit the floor.

Mayven looked up at him, her large eyes questioning. "Why did you do that? It was deactivated and there could've been a use for that later."

"If ever you enter Shimiera again, it won't serve as a way to hide you any longer. You may as well wear the one you were intended to wear since birth. It's your heritage."

Varn watched her examine her marsa again.

"Is that a real marsa then?" Mayven asked, indicating Varn's marsa.

Varn felt the muscles in his neck knot. "Yes, it is. Since I was technically in Shimiera not as a citizen but as a professional athlete, I never had to wear one of their marsas."

Mayven lowered her head. "Yet another privilege you garner and keep for yourself."

Varn heard the grinding of his teeth as he marched around the desk and resumed his seat. Smoothing his leggings with his palms, he took a deep breath and looked up. "I thought after our conversation of earlier that you understood your identity was kept from you to preserve your safety. Not to punish you. The best way to do that was to let you be who you thought you were."

Mayven's head snapped up, and Varn instantly recognized the petulant set of her jaw.

"You trusted me to protect myself in the orphanage. But not to protect myself as a Language Master known as Lapahoniesh with a destiny to save the world." Mayven rolled her eyes. "Obviously, Emwen would be in better hands if you left the job to someone more trustworthy."

Varn opened his mouth to defend his decision yet again, when Sharieana broke into the conversation, her tone stern, *"Mayven, you are being childish. Through our contact and inclusion in this conversation, I know what you both are speaking of. You have survived numerous inquests by the Gayied in Shimiera expressly because a tarlen can only take from your mind what you know, not what you are capable of. Otherwise, you long ago would have been discovered. As it was, you were lucky tarlens, Gayied, and adamdavas never thought to ask the proper questions during your years at the orphanage. I must say the Hato have a very inventive way to lie. Never can you speak a direct untruth but you can avoid speaking of what you are not directly asked about."*

Several emotions crossed Mayven's face before she dropped her head.

"Varn and all the others did what was best for you," Sharieana continued. *"What he is trying to get you to help with now is not only in his best interest, but yours and everyone you care about. The time for childish*

behavior is past. You must now do for others what they have all sacrificed to do for you. Protect Emwen from destruction by Adamdavas."

Varn watched as Mayven ran her thumb over the marsa once more, then she held it out to him. "It's best this stay hidden for now, along with the knowledge it possesses. Sharieana is right, what I don't know keeps me and others safe."

Varn felt the tension ease from his shoulders and the knot in his stomach uncurl as he carefully retrieved the marsa, wrapped it back in its cloth, and placed it back in its hiding place. When the bookcase was once again in order, he turned to face Mayven. "You asked earlier about the Language Master Library. I would like to take you there."

Mayven pushed her ebony, waist-length waves over her shoulder. "I'd be glad to go."

Varn led the way through his home, along the hallway toward the kitchen and down the stairs to an underground room. Eight sets of pillars stood like sentinels around the perimeter of the room, all but one pair guarding nothing. Directly across from the door was the only otal in the room. On either side of the disk were two pillars, on top of which each were inlaid blue glowing crystals with a mark etched on each of them.

Mayven walked over to the anchor pillars and traced the mark on the crystals that held the magic allowing the portal to stay open. "Amalayna has been here? She knew about the library? She knows what I am?"

A tear slid down Mayven's cheek before she roughly wiped it away with the back of her hand. Varn reached toward her, but when her shoulders tensed, he lowered his hand and smoothed his palm across his thigh. "She knew about the library. But for her protection and yours, she didn't know about you."

Varn flinched from the impact of Mayven's stormy violet gaze. "It didn't protect her enough, obviously."

Sharieana's voice addressed them both, *"I feel it would be safer if you took down this portal and destroyed your crystals. I have a way to get you to the library that your people have forgotten about and Adamdavas doesn't know of."*

Varn looked at the portal a moment as he shoved his hands through his hair. "Are you sure you can do it? It has been a long time since you have tried, and things have changed since the Vanishing War."

Sharieana was silent a moment then answered, *"Point well made. Perhaps your way is best until things are set right again."*

Varn nodded and looked at Mayven, who examined the additional sets of pillars. "Those are the pillars that held the portal to our locations in Shimiera. I destroyed them when we came through this morning."

Holding out his hand, palm up, Varn looked directly into Mayven's eyes and felt his breath catch at the pain she tried to hide by blinking back tears. "I'm sorry. I'm working on getting her safely back, I promise. She is safer if you don't go after her and let me get her back. Please trust me." Varn felt warmth spread through his body at the contact of her tiny calloused hand with his own. "Shall we go see your library then?"

Varn waited for Mayven to nod approval, then he clasped her hand firmly and they stepped through the portal as one.

CHAPTER TWENTY-ONE

Mayven felt the rush of adamie flowing over her skin and the sensation of a string having tied itself to her spine then jerking her forward. Then the tingle of adamie subsided and the world steadied as Mayven arrived on the opposite side of the portal. Still holding Varn's hand, Mayven immediately registered the sharp sweet scent of a fayen tree that made her mouth water for the taste of its sweet purple fruit. Mayven turned to Varn as excitement and delight caused her to bounce on the balls of her feet. "The library is in a fayen tree!"

Varn's wide grin and low chuckle caused Mayven to blush as she realized she was acting like a child on Vaktmha. Fayen fruit was certainly nothing as grand as gifts on the first day of spring or as important as the celebrations of Dsohoay that marked the gift of life. But still. She released Varn's hand then turned to conceal her childish delight. *It's fabulous that knowledge and my favorite fruit are all in the same place.*

Mayven looked around the massive room in which she stood. She stood in the center. The wide open circle had a large desk with a comfortable-looking chair and several large couches with plush cushions, beside which stood low tables that held small glowing bapas made of shen fabric, though the light from the delicate-looking lanterns did little to add to the light of midday. Beyond the center circle, bookshelves were lined up in neat rows, forming the outer border. Directly above her head was an intricate stained glass window that allowed multicolored light to fill the cavernous room. Off to the right was a wide set of double doors. Just to the right of the doors, a staircase curved up the outside wall of the library, disappearing at the ceiling, which marked the second floor.

Mayven took a deep breath, enjoying the sweet familiar scent. Then, like sitting in a tub slowly filling with warm water, a tingling warmth worked its way from the soles of Mayven's feet to the top of her head and the subsequent chill that followed caused her to rub her forearms as if she were cold. Mayven didn't even flinch at the sound of a voice in her head.

"Lapahoniesh, at last you have found me." The voice was soft and husky. *"I have waited so long for you. I am Tamaryn, so named in honor of your ancestor. I am the library created by her to house the knowledge gained by her, the very first Language Master, and every one that has been since."*

Varn stepped up beside Mayven. "It's nice to meet you, Tamaryn. I'm Varn."

"I am glad to meet you, Varn. Lapahoniesh—"

Mayven's eyes traveled around the room as she interrupted, "Please call me Mayven."

"Mayven, I think we should get started right away. May I direct you to the stacks marked prophecies."

Mayven strode across the room, her eyes scanning the markings on the ends of each shelf then heading down the aisle. Without further instruction, she pulled from the farthest end of the shelf a leather-bound volume that read, *Workings of Language Master Daymar Xeptira.*

Mayven read the cover and, recalling the name of the cousin Varn had mentioned earlier, she nearly dropped the book as she looked up. "Is this man my ancestor?"

Tamaryn didn't answer for a long moment, then replied, *"Yes. Do not judge harshly, child, until you have read what you hold in your hands. You, like all other Language Masters before you, have a volume in this library. That volume will record your works throughout your life. One page of a person's life cannot measure its entire worth."*

Mayven felt dread coil around her heart a moment, then suddenly something occurred to her. "How did I know exactly which book to pull from the shelf?"

Tamaryn's voice rustled through her mind. *"By agreeing to come here, you have embraced your power. Acceptance leads to knowledge, and knowledge will lead you to your destiny. What you do with that destiny will determine your story. You will learn from that book just how much a destiny can change by a single choice. You have a lot to learn and none of these books leave this place. I suggest we get started."*

Mayven caressed the cover, examining the thickness of it. "I don't have time to read this entire volume. It's enormous."

"I think you are about to get a crash course in what it means to be a

Language Master." Tamaryn's voice held reassurance and a touch of amusement.

Mayven heaved a sigh then returned to the open circle and curled up on a couch directly across from Varn, who had sprawled his length along another couch in the room. Beneath her palm, the cover felt smooth and warm as if alive. "How is this cover so warm?"

"Each book is a tale that is written about the life of each Language Master. The book itself is like the person for whom it records, it is alive. Since sometimes actions taken by each Language Master during their lives won't see fruition until long after the Language Master's passing, the story remains alive and changing. So it is even with your book, Mayven."

Mayven's brows drew together above her slim straight nose, but she didn't say anything further as she slowly opened the cover of the book in her lap. The air around her seemed to charge as adamie curled over her skin and trailed delicate tickling fingers along her arms. Then the scent of a warm winter day wound around her, and the chill of winter air caressed her cheeks. Mayven looked around, her eyes wide with wonder and mouth slightly agape as she stood in a vast evergreen forest. Before her stood a man who stared at her with sad brown eyes. "I am Daymar Xeptira. I am going to walk you through my life and ask that you withhold too harsh a judgment on me until the end. I am your ancestor, and I am responsible for whatever has become of the world in which you now live. This is how all you know has come to pass."

Mayven felt a rush of adamie curl over her once more, then she stood in front of large sprawling oak tree that was obviously the home of a very pregnant young mother. Mayven heaved a sigh of frustration. *I don't have time for every little detail of his life.*

But Mayven's fears were ignored and allied in the same breath as she watched a baby born into a loving and welcoming family quickly grow into first a boy then a man. As he grew before her eyes, Mayven realized though she was only seeing the highlights, she somehow had gained the knowledge of an entire lifetime. She had shared in his schooling and his experiences from the day he was born. Her brow furrowed as she tried to reconcile this bit of information. The rush continued until at last the end of his life was reached. Instead of witnessing his death, the story seemed to pause. Once again, Daymar Xeptira stepped forward.

"I know the experience you have just had. If it is not your first, then hopefully what I did has not changed our world much but if it did and this is your first experience, know that it will take you a while to completely appreciate all you have learned. You are the one I spoke of in my final prophecy. I know this because this message was meant only for you. I have done our heritage a great disservice, and it is you who must set it right. The spell I cast must be reversed. All I can say is that the basic first lesson we ever learn as Language Masters applies here. Every spell is a lie. It changes what is to what we say it is. Dsohoay be with you."

Suddenly Mayven was jerked from her book then deposited once again in the library.

Varn sat staring at her, his feet now planted on the floor in front of him as he rested his elbows on his knees. "That didn't take long. What did you learn?"

Mayven blinked, her mind reeling as she processed all she had just seen. "I don't know for sure, it was so much. My head feels overstuffed. I need a while to think about everything."

Mayven stood and rubbed her temples absently, her brows knit in thought as she mumbled, "Did you know there are giant animals known as Aniwie and they like to eat us?"

Varn covered a momentary look of concerned shock as he rose from the couch and rushed to her side. He took her elbow, staring down into her face. "Are you okay? I think that book messed with your head."

Mayven stared up at him, her eyes searching his concerned green gaze. "I'm serious, Varn. I told you of them before, remember, but I didn't realize then what they were. They are huge beasts, three tribes apparently, bears, cats, and wolves. Their shoulders are above even your head. I promise I'm not crazy. Ask Tamaryn."

Varn stared down into her face. "Tamaryn, is it true?"

The sound of rustling leaves preceded her response. *"Yes, it is. They have stayed hidden for many generations in hopes that the spell they forced the Language Master to create would eventually take effect. Unfortunately, when the Ohkie'en awakened, the Aniwie decided hiding was no longer an option. They are mobilizing an army."*

"How long do we have, Tamaryn?" Varn's face paled as his eyes widened.

"There is time, but not much."

Mayven heaved a sigh, adrenaline making her heart slam against her ribs. *What do I do? There is so much I need to get done. I don't know where to start.* Varn held her hands, and she clutched his in return, her mouth dry. *I have to think.* Mayven's breathing sped up as her mouth dried out. *I need to get out of here.*

Mayven backed away from Varn, releasing his hands. "I need to think. I'll be back later."

Turning abruptly, Mayven stepped through the portal. She kept going all the way out of Varn's home until she found herself once again down by the docks of Lirie, watching the waves roll placidly against the beaches. *I wonder where the library was? The sun seemed so much brighter and warmer, pouring through those windows.*

Mayven stood at the end of the dock, a hip resting against a stone pylon and rubbed her palms against her arms. A gentle breeze caressed her face, causing tendrils of hair to obscure her vision. She tucked stray strands behind her ear and watched the clouds move sluggishly as they began to break apart to allow more light.

Mayven watched as large ships began to make a line and tug boats, two at a time, guided them through the harbor to the docks. The docks were bustling as payjiks, weather mages, masons, and healers scurried back and forth in organized chaos.

Mayven turned at the sound of nearby voices and listened as a healer and payjik spoke.

The payjik, a gray-haired, stalwart man spoke in an authoritative tone. "I can have all these freighters at the docks in under an hour. They have been notified they are being reassigned to be used as hospitals for the time being. I assume you have healers ready to be assigned to the vessels as they dock in order to organize the casualties?"

The reed-thin woman nodded "Yes, we have two per vessel, waiting the ships' arrivals. We also need to get the wards and shields working again. This storm has abated some, but is not gone. According to the weather mages, it may return tonight."

"The weather mages and masons are working on it," the payjik replied, his voice laced with concern. "However, whatever happened seems to have created a vacuum in the flow of adamie. There doesn't seem to be enough to sustain any additional shields. They are trying to come up with a way to compensate. I'll keep you informed of our progress."

The healer sighed. "I'm aware of the problem, Jayben. I think that is also why we're suddenly being flooded with the ill and dying. Whatever happened is draining the life force from the people who are weakest. If it isn't corrected soon, the stronger ones will be next, until there is nothing left."

Mayven sucked in her breath as images of a dying Emwen flashed through her mind. The conversation she had while asleep in the hospital came rushing full force into her mind as her stomach churned with dread and fear. *It's happening just like Radiea said it would, and all I know is that fixing it has to do with a lie.*

Frustration and tension caused Mayven's shoulders and neck to ache and her head to pound as she tried to go over every detail she had gleaned from the book in the library, the conversation with Radiea, and her limited understanding of the prophecy. Mayven stared unseeing out over the rolling waves of the bay as she tried to untangle the prophecy she had witnessed at the library.

The sudden touch of a hand on Mayven's shoulder made her stiffen. Mayven jerked away from the contact, then wheeled around. Behind her stood a man.

His mahogany features wrinkled with smile lines and dark brown eyes laughed as he stood with his hands raised at shoulder level, palms out and a grin on his face. "I didn't mean to startle you. I was just looking for you. My name is Arrok. I'm a friend of Varn's."

Mayven clenched her teeth as she turned to face out toward the ocean once more. *Can't Varn give me just a few moments of peace? I will do what he needs. I just need to figure out how.*

"Varn needed to send someone to collect me, is that it?" Mayven spoke brashly, her tone harsh.

Arrok's smile changed to a look of questioning surprise as he lowered his hands. "Why would you say that?"

Mayven turned back to face Arrok. "Varn always wants what is best for Varn."

A flicker of anger rolled across Arrok's face before he schooled his features into a pleasant smile. "I think you misunderstand, a lot. First of all, I volunteered to come and escort you on some errands that Varn felt you might need help navigating because I wished to meet you. Secondly, you have no idea what Varn always wants."

Mayven, already tense and frustrated, felt her anger ratchet up a notch but, tamping it down, she raised a brow. "I would think I would be the perfect one to know what Varn always wants. His life revolves around what is best for Niesha and himself. His main goal is to see that I stay in line and do what I'm supposed to so he will look like the hero."

Arrok's expression went from tolerance to anger in a flash. "I think you need to open your pretty eyes and your petty closed mind. You know what, I'll be more than glad to help you with that."

Mayven bristled, her hands clenching at her sides. "I doubt there is much that you could teach me about the things I am living."

Arrok snorted. "I think there is plenty I can teach you. While I'm busy making your life more comfortable today, I plan to see that I do. Why don't we start with you looking around and telling me what you see?"

Mayven's eyebrows raised almost to her hairline at his sarcastic and mocking tone. Indulging his little tirade, she looked around carefully. The storm was clearing and the sky, brighter now, revealed a lovely, well-maintained city, though the storm had wreaked havoc on several buildings. The city boasted huge trees, well-trimmed; wide lanes, well-manicured; and in between the buildings vast shaded areas of grass and flowers where children gathered to play. In the center of the square, just up the spacious avenue from where she stood, the shen temple towered, its massive bower stretching out over the entire perimeter of the square. The trunk, leaves, and branches glowed softly even in daylight and warmed the city square with welcome light beneath the shade of the wide canopy above.

The wharf was once again buzzing with the sound of voices calling back and forth. Pod vehicles, some passenger vehicles, others delivery, flowed silently along the wide busy avenues. Mayven found she couldn't help but notice the atmosphere here was so much more open and inviting. People called out greetings to each other on the street corners and stopped to visit in the wide gardens between buildings. Even through the desperate activity of the payjiks, healers, and masons weaved an air of congeniality and cooperation.

Lirie was a prosperous and happy metropolis. Mayven felt a flash of anger. *Like I don't already know the pampered easy life Varn has had. But why not play along? I'm sure it will be amusing.*

Mayven returned her gaze to Arrok's impassive expression and hard gaze. "I see a very wealthy city with lots of happy people. Why?"

Arrok's mouth sketched a full-lipped but hard smile, one that never reached his eyes. "What do you think Varn's life has been like?"

Mayven paused as she searched Arrok's face for a clue on the trap she was sure he was laying. "He has had all this luxury, happiness, security, safety. He has been handed everything he wants. Varn has had the privilege to be anything he chose."

Arrok's face became impassive, his enunciation precise and tone nonchalant. "I suppose he has had a lot given to him in his life."

Mayven sensed the trap was about to spring but anger pushed her. "Yes, he has. He has never known what it's like to suffer anything. How could he? Look at where he got to grow up!" Mayven's reply ended on a shout, drawing attention from passersby.

Arrok simply smiled at them before turning back to her. "I think you're a blind, self-centered, and unsympathetic child. I don't see why Varn has any faith that you would be able to save anyone. You can't even see reality when it's right in front of you."

"What would you know about reality?" Mayven scoffed as she turned away from Arrok to stare back out across the bay.

Mayven was jerked around by her elbow as Arrok's hand closed tightly around it. Mayven spun, off balance, and collided with Arrok's broad chest.

"I am going to forgive you this one time because you are ignorant and can't possibly know what you are speaking of," Arrok said, his voice a low snarl of barely restrained wrath. "But, my dear, this is the last time I will ever allow you to blindly accuse anyone in my presence without first taking a look at things from their point of view."

Mayven, face flushed crimson, opened her mouth to snap a scathing reply.

Arrok held up a hand, silencing her. "I think it is time you got a history lesson. One, I'm sure, Varn didn't enlighten you of, because he is far more generous than he should be, or than you give him credit for."

Arrok's grip tightened to almost painful as he dragged Mayven along with him to the bench on the edge of the dock and forced her to take a seat. Then, standing over her, Arrok glared at her. "I have known Varn his entire life. We have been best friends since we were children. His family and mine have known each other for generations. So I am going to educate you on everything you think you know."

Mayven felt adrenaline fueled by anger pound through her system as she moved to stand up.

Arrok roughly shoved her back to her seat. "I think you owe me this much. You seem bent on judging a man I consider my brother. Since he won't defend himself against you, and your narrow outlook on life, I think it's about time someone did. You will sit here and listen. When I'm done, you may leave, if you choose. But I will get to finish, and you will not speak or move until I am done."

Mayven felt adamie curl over her skin like heated bands and tie her to her seat. Her voice silenced as she tried to formulate a retort. He had used his magic to tie her to her seat. A captive audience.

Arrok's full wide lips twitched in a hard smirk. "I am powerful in my own right, Language Master, as are many of those who surround you. It would be wise not to forget that."

Then Arrok paused to take a seat and lean back on the bench, spreading his arms wide across the back of the seat as Mayven sat ramrod straight, silent, and immobile beside him.

At length, Arrok began to speak again, his tone now calm as if relaying a story to a child. "Varn's parents died when he was a child of ten. He and his sister were raised by his bachelor uncle, Demok, after their passing. Demok, bless him, had no clue of children or how to raise them. Demok's entire life had been obsessively devoted to finding you, the Language Master. Demok knew the entire prophecy and the very important role you played. However, he was also privy to the role that Varn played. In essence, Varn's childhood ended when Demok became his parent."

As Arrok's last words fell into a brief silence, Mayven's anger stopped instantly. Intrigued, she rolled her eyes to the side, straining to see Arrok's face as he leaned forward, resting his elbows on his knees.

Mayven could barely see the top of Arrok's head as he stared down at the ground between his booted feet for a long moment. "I went to school with Varn. Throughout school, he was a dedicated and diligent student. The best grades and the best maygis player in our entire school. By the time he was old enough to graduate, he had earned a full scholarship to any college or guild of his choice if he would play maygis for them. After school each day, his education continued. He spent hours of time honing his magic or locked away, studying in the library with his uncle. He was taught that your safety was his sole responsibility. That you were to come before anyone else, including himself."

Arrok paused, turning Mayven to face him. He looked directly into her eyes. "He gave up college and his dream of being an archeologist and historian to follow after Demok and protect you. When he reached the age of majority, instead of staying here in this beautiful country and pursuing a life he wanted, he went to Shimiera and signed as an apprentice to the historians' guild. For ten years, he has worked unceasingly to gain a position in that guild so he would have the power to help you when he found you. When he found you, he used his magic to protect you. Having never seen your face until the day you met him in the orphanage, not long ago he consigned himself to suffer every torture and interrogation you ever underwent. His magic bound you to him so intimately that every physical pain you have ever suffered since your first day at the orphanage he has also suffered."

Mayven felt her stomach clench as nausea from recalling her first days at the orphanage rolled over her.

Arrok took a deep breath as he released Mayven's arms and looked past her at the city bustling around them. "Varn took on an identity of no one in Shimiera. He was frequently interrogated and constantly watched. His sister, Layla, followed him there and married Hardak. Varn still carries the guilt for what happened to her."

Mayven felt her heart stop. *Layla? What had happened to Layla? Why did Varn blame himself? Why did it suddenly matter?* Mayven, still unable to speak, raised her eyebrows in question her expression, pleading to know the rest of the story.

Arrok studied her face a long moment as if deciding whether to divulge the knowledge he possessed. "What I'm telling you is private. You will never speak of it." Mayven felt the command in his words. "Layla became pregnant not long after she and Hardak wed. But because Hardak had no caste in Shimiera, he had no money or ability to pay for medical care when Layla suddenly became very ill. Varn tried to get Layla back here but was unable to. She lost the baby. When she was able to return here later, she discovered that she no longer had the ability to become pregnant."

Mayven felt her throat close off at Arrok's last declaration, *Layla would have been a wonderful mother.* In her mind, Mayven pictured Layla's shining smile and Hardak's hardy build and laughing eyes and mourned for what they had lost.

Arrok drove the last piece of reality home in a soft voice. "You see, Varn feels responsible because Layla followed him. Layla has always followed him. She has always been the balance between Demok's single-minded devotion to the prophecies and Varn's need to please his family. She knew Demok loved Varn but that in his devotion he would push Varn, perhaps to the breaking point, if not held in check. That is how she came to be in Shimiera. Now Demok is gone, and Varn blames himself for that also. He feels it is his failure that cost his uncle his life. Though he will never admit it out loud. You, in your childish self-importance, are confirming all his self-condemnation."

Mayven felt a wedge of guilt start to splinter her stone image of Varn.

Arrok drove the wedge home with precision. "You think you're the only one who has suffered. You're so completely wrong. Payin and his wife were loyal followers of Niesha. They were set to come back to Kieshan when his wife became pregnant. But your parents were killed, you were left an orphan, and Adamdavas made it impossible to bring you back here. No one else was available to take you, so Payin and his wife stayed and took you in. She died in childbirth, along with his child, to save you."

Payin's dear face on his last day flashed in front of Mayven's eyes and a tear slid silently down her face.

"I don't say these things to hurt you, Mayven," Arrok continued. "I just wish to point out that there are far more ways to see the story of your life than just from your own point of view. If you learn nothing else from those who have loved and protected you over the years, learn this. Life is short. You only get one chance to do what is right, and sometimes what is right costs you more than you can imagine."

Guilt flooded through Mayven. For the first time since meeting Varn, she saw him not as a blind fanatic, a selfish, pampered socialite, or someone else destined to deliver her to her destiny, but as a person. Mayven felt her anger at him dissolve and grief for his pain take its place. The thought of him hurting made her ache. *I need to talk to him. I need to tell him I'm sorry.*

Arrok heaved another deep sigh. "You're released, Mayven. I'm sorry I let my anger rule me. I hope you will forgive me."

Mayven felt remorse flood her but, unwilling to admit it to Arrok, she asked, "What was it you needed me to do?"

Arrok raised a brow slightly. "I need to get you to the bank with your birth certificate so you can access your family's accounts. You are far removed from poverty, Mayven. Then Varn asked that I take you to a clothier. He is having a dinner party tonight in order to conduct some business and thought you might like appropriate attire."

Mayven felt a bubble of joy and laughter fill her. *He is always thinking of what I need. I love that about him.* Guilt made her cringe. *I should remember that more often.*

Mayven suddenly froze in place, her heart in her throat as she reexamined her last thought. *I love him? I think I do! I do! I love him. Can he forgive me after all that I have done to him?*

Mayven's hand went to her heart, and she closed her eyes, recalling the link that had joined them together only a few short weeks ago. Then she recalled how she had severed the link in her anger after Demok's death. Her heart ached when she remembered the look on Varn's face when the cord had snapped. Mayven's hand absently rubbed her breastbone as she turned from Arrok's questioning gaze to stare out over the water for a long moment.

Can I repair the damage I've done? Will he even want me to? Mayven lowered her head and forced her hand down, then turned to face Arrok. "Then I suggest we get started. We have much to do."

Arrok regarded her with a questioning look but, to his credit, didn't pry. Taking her elbow gently in the palm of his hand, he steered her toward the bank located on the outside edge of the main square.

Hours later, after paperwork and shopping were completed, Mayven chatted comfortably about minor things with Arrok as they walked arm and arm toward Varn's home. When they reached the door, Arrok parted ways with her, heading to the study as she made her way to the kitchen.

Varn's shemla, Rohtak, was busily preparing a snack and drinks and arranging them on a tray when she entered.

Smiling at Rohtak, she asked, "May I get something to eat?"

Rohtak's dark silver eyes lit up. "Here, have one of these. I made too many." Rohtak handed her a sandwich and a chilled glass of fayen juice as she took a seat on the counter. Mayven noted that Rohtak's hand trembled slightly, and his face seemed drawn and pale. "You remind me of Varn. He used to come in here and do the same thing, not so long ago. I miss him being that relaxed."

Mayven imagined what Varn would look like completely relaxed and felt her breath catch. Rohtak, watching her closely, gave her a questioning look, to which she answered with a brief smile before gulping down the last bite of sandwich.

Hopping down from the counter, she started for the kitchen door and then paused. "Where is my room at, Rohtak? I assume I have one I will be staying in."

"Yes, indeed," Rohtak replied as he lifted the tray deftly onto a palm. "Second floor, third door from the landing, Miss. If there is anything you need, just let me know. I did prepare everything for you I could think of, however, it has been a while since a lady was in the house. Your packages arrived just a few moments ago. I placed them on the bed."

Mayven thanked Rohtak, noting the trembling hand he tried to steady as he passed her on the way out of the kitchen. Then Mayven headed up the stairs, all the while her mind whirling. *I love Varn!* Mayven felt a foolish smile spread across her face at the thought. Then her mind wandered to Rohtak's comment, and she felt her heart thud oddly in her chest as she recalled the mental picture she had envisioned. *I hope someday to see him that happy.*

The door to the guest room sliding open paused Mayven's musings as she took in the elegant, costly decor. The bapas were intricately embroidered, the shen thread glowing brightly even in daylight. The raised, dish-shaped bed occupying the center of the room held the thickest madra pod mattress she had ever seen. Mayven lay down on the mattress, her hands caressing the silken fabric of the sheets and comforter before she curled herself in a ball around the comforting softness of her pillow as a wide smile pulled up the corners of her mouth. Then a knock sounded at the door. Mayven sat up in the middle of her bed, the pillow across her lap as she called, "Come in!"

Layla stepped through the door, and Mayven bounced out of bed and ran across the room, enveloping Layla in a bone-crushing hug.

Layla, smiling slightly, extricated herself from Mayven's exuberant embrace and took a seat on the bed. "To what do I owe this enthusiastic greeting?"

Mayven twirled in a circle then flopped onto the bed and gazed up at Layla with a smile so wide her cheeks ached. "I love Varn. I just realized I love him."

"You suddenly love him, despite all the reasons you say you have not to?" Layla responded, her words laced with doubt.

Mayven's smile all but disappeared as she felt a frown begin to tighten her forehead and a knot form in her stomach. "I do have reasons to be mad at him but Arrok explained more about Varn's life than I used to know. I guess I realized all he has done for me."

Mayven turned her head in time to see Layla raise a brow.

"So now that you know all he has done for you, he is worthy." Layla's mocking tone cut Mayven to the quick. "You couldn't discover on your own how valuable and wonderful he is; someone had to point it out. You don't really love him, you just love that he has his entire life centered on you."

Mayven felt hurt turn her heart to ice as tears pricked her eyes. "I thought you were my friend, Layla. I thought you wanted Varn and me to be together?"

Layla heaved a sigh before standing up and turning to face Mayven. "I'm your friend, but I'm also Varn's sister." Layla spoke softly, her voice barely carrying across the room. "The last thing he needs is someone who needs him for their own validation. Varn hides his scars better than you but that doesn't mean he doesn't have them, Mayven. He needs someone who loves him for all that he is. Not because he can do or be something they need. Love is not about what someone else can do for you, but what you can do for someone else."

Layla started for the door, then paused. "I want you to be with him if it is best for both of you. Not just for one of you. Love is never selfish, Mayven. I want to make sure you love him for the right reasons."

Mayven sat up and watched the door close behind Layla as tears slipped silently down her cheeks. Mayven didn't really enjoy getting ready for the dinner party, though she had hoped to look especially attractive in hopes to catch Varn's attention. Instead, her mind replayed every word Layla had spoken to her. Mayven also replayed the conversation with Arrok. *Am I really selfish? Do I not really see Varn for who he is?*

Mayven was so occupied with her thoughts, she didn't even notice Varn's reaction as she walked down the stairs. All she saw was Layla standing next to Varn, her arm laced through Hardak's. Mayven caught Layla's eye for moment, in which Layla raised a brow as if to ask, *Do you really see him?*

Mayven turned her attention to Varn and noticed his palm rubbing against his chest over his heart and something inside her broke. She had caused the pain he hid. She recognized the ache he unconsciously soothed whenever he was in her presence. She felt the same pain but had blocked it out, now it hit her with a vengeance. The impact of realization nearly caused her to stagger as she gained the foyer. Taking a deep breath, she closed her eyes and focused on the connection between them, willing it to come alive again as the pain in her own chest grew. Nothing happened, and suddenly the gulf that its absence made opened beneath her feet and threatened to swallow her whole. Heartache took her breath away, and her balance felt off, as if she stood teetering on the edge of some vast abyss.

Mayven, staggering slightly, opened her eyes to find Varn standing directly in front of her, his eyes searching her face, his hands hovering in the air between them as if afraid to touch her.

Mayven grasped his hands in hers and smiled as she answered his question with as close to a lie as she had ever come, "I just got a little dizzy. Are your guests here?"

CHAPTER TWENTY-TWO

Varn watched Mayven descend the stairs. She walked erect, her shoulders straight and head so high that her posture made her seem far taller than she really was. Mayven moved down the stairs one graceful step at a time, her eyes seemingly focused on thoughts that drew her far away from those around her.

Varn admired the way the silken black dress clung to her frame. The sleeves were black but split open from the shoulder seam to just above the elbow and tied together with royal purple silk that matched the flowers and ribbons that adorned the mass of hair piled atop her small head. Tonight she didn't hide her xohdieha. It adorned her head in brilliant silver light, the colored symbols of each clan glowing like gems that accentuated her deep amethyst eyes and highlighted their intense color.

Varn's eye was drawn to the neckline of her dress. The neckline plunged over her lifted breasts. Beneath her ample bust, an embroidered leather corset laced with purple satin made her slender waist seem impossibly tiny. The full skirt was four panels of black satin that joined to just below her hip then separated to reveal the glow of shen fabric beneath, embroidered with starlight lilies in the same purple of the satin on her dress and in her hair. Tiny feet encased in delicate-looking black satin slippers peeked out from under the skirt as she walked.

The overall effect was breathtaking and yet Mayven seemed unaware. Varn heaved a sigh. *How I wish I knew what she was thinking.*

Mayven paused, her eyes locked on Layla next to him. Varn glanced between the two before looking again at Mayven and noticing her looking at his hand, which he hadn't even realized rubbed absently at his chest. Varn thrust his hand to his side and waited for her to finish her descent to the foyer.

When Mayven closed her eyes for a moment, he felt a stirring, as if she were reaching out to him. He felt the ache in his heart lessen, but then her eyes sprang open as she swayed unsteadily on her feet. Afraid to touch her and break the small resurgence of their connection, he stood with his hands extended between them. When she grasped his hands, the impact of her touch rocked him to his core. The line between them vibrated, and he felt sadness radiating from her.

Varn heaved a sigh, at once equally grateful for the renewed connection, no matter how small, and sad because she was still hurt and hadn't forgiven him.

Mayven looked up at him.

"Are you okay?"

Her magnificent eyes flashed something unreadable. "I just got a little dizzy. Are your guests here?"

Varn stared at her a moment. "Oh, yes! We should join them in the dining room."

Placing a light hand at Mayven's elbow, he led the way as he escorted her into the dining room. When they entered, Varn immediately found himself surrounded by friends and family he hadn't seen for a very long time and every one of them had their eyes fastened on the woman at his side.

Varn introduced her around the group, and she smiled, greeting each person in turn. When it seemed like Mayven began to become overwhelmed by their attention, he quietly steered the subject by signaling Rohtak to announce dinner.

Varn sat at the head of the table with Layla to his right next to Hardak and Mayven to his left next to Arrok. As Rohtak began to serve dinner, Varn found himself distracted by Mayven. Every time he would look her direction, he found her eyes on him. When the young woman next to her, for some reason he couldn't recall her name, would become overly chatty and giggle at his every comment, Mayven would all but demand the girl's attention.

Varn found the interplay amusing and, to his slight embarrassment, very enjoyable. *She acts like she's jealous. I didn't think she cared.* Soon Varn found himself antagonizing Mayven's response as dinner broke up and they adjourned to the living room to have drinks. He would seek out the young lady, letting her bombard him with questions about his career as a maygis player, and watch as Mayven found a way to insert herself into the conversation.

Soon, however, it was time to get down to business, so Varn had everyone find a seat as he stood in the center of the room to address their group. "First, I would like to thank you all for coming this evening. We have all been waiting for this day a very long time."

Varn let the murmurs over his last statement die down before proceeding. "I need you all to get your groups active. We need to get everyone connected and the word out. The next days and weeks are not going to be easy. The Language Master has already awakened the Ohkie'en. Their renewed presence is changing the balance of a lot of things. Communication must be up and running. I don't have a lot of details as of now, however, I brought you here to see Mayven. To offer you all the chance to see for yourself we have made the first step."

Nods of agreement followed his statement as Varn continued, "We still have more to do. I think our first order of business is reports from each of you. I would like to start with Arrok."

Arrok stood and took his place at the center of the room. Arrok's usually jovial expression was absent, his dark eyes even darker with concern as he began to speak. "I have spent most of the day out working with masons, payjiks, and healers to coordinate the recovery after the storm. The preliminary reports are as follows. Since the Ohkie'en have awakened, there seems to be a power drain on the weaker among the Hato. The magic that is our life force is being drained from the weakest of us to sustain the stronger. Those who require more magic include the Ohkie'en. I have gone over reports from contacts in every nation joined to our cause and have discovered the increased numbers of sick and dying to be staggering. We're looking at days, not weeks, before even the most powerful of us begin to feel the effects of the wasting sickness."

As Arrok's voice faded into silence, the murmurs of concern rose around the room. Then questions began to bombard Arrok. Varn rose to rescue his friend but was surprised when Mayven rose to stand next to Arrok. When Mayven raised her hand, the room fell silent and Varn, like everyone else, waited breathlessly for her to speak.

Mayven's beautiful eyes scanned the room. "I have been to the Language Master Library, I've spoken to the Ohkie'en myself, and I've heard the original prophecy from the lips of its creator. I know what must be done, and I will work as quickly as I can. I'll need to have passage back to Shimiera arranged and someone with knowledge of my ancestral home's location to guide me. According to all I have learned at this point, everything must be set right where everything went wrong. I don't know the details of how as of yet. I'm working on that. Please know that I want this to be over as quickly as all of you do. I will do my best to make it so."

Varn released the breath he hadn't known he was holding as pride and delight filled him. *She has finally embraced her destiny completely.*

The room remained silent for a long moment then questions began to be launched at Mayven in rapid succession. Varn watched as she deftly handled several before he noticed her beginning to tense under the scrutiny. Clearing his throat, Varn called for order as he stood and asked Arrok and Mayven to resume their seats.

Then he scanned the once again silent room before he spoke. "Before we end this meeting tonight, I would like you all to raise your glasses in a toast to my uncle, Demok. He sacrificed his life, as so many others we all love have, to make tonight possible."

Varn noted a strange expression briefly flicker across Mayven's face before she raised her glass as everyone said, "To Demok."

Varn was occupied seeing his guests out and didn't notice Mayven had left until the last of his guests had exited. When he started looking for her, he came across Layla in the kitchen.

Varn set a silver tray of empty glasses down on the wide island in the center of the kitchen. "Have you seen Mayven?"

Layla sighed and turned to face Varn, her expression a mix of determination and sadness. "I believe she went to her room."

Varn nodded his thanks and turned to go.

Layla called him back. "Varn, wait. I need to talk to you."

Varn paused, turning slowly to face his sister, a sudden heaviness settling upon his shoulders. "What's the matter?"

Layla fidgeted with the silverware she had been polishing as she collected her thoughts.

Varn shifted anxiously from one foot to another before leaning a hip against the island, shoving his hands through his hair and demanding, "Out with it."

Layla looked up at Varn and asked bluntly, "Are you in love with Mayven?"

Varn's mouth gaped slightly, then, snapping it closed, he stared at Layla a long moment. His heart sped up as he rolled the word over in his head. *Do I love her? Is it possible?*

Varn wasn't even conscious of his own answer until he spoke aloud. "Yes, I am."

"Does Mayven know that? Have you told her?" Layla persisted, now ceaselessly turning the knife over and over from palm to palm.

Varn sighed and reached out a hand, stilling Layla's nervous movement. "I know you have something on your mind. Please tell me."

Layla looked at him a long moment, her expression a mixture of sorrow and regret. "I think if you haven't told her how you feel, you shouldn't."

Varn instantly dropped his hand from Layla's, standing to his full height before demanding, "And why is that, sister?"

Layla flinched but Varn ignored her reaction as he raised a brow in question and crossed his arms across his chest, waiting for a reply.

"She is young, Varn. In so many ways, she is far younger than you. She hasn't seen life like you and I have. She doesn't even know all that is expected of her to fulfill the destiny she was born into. Love her if you must. But don't tell her."

Varn felt an unreasoning anger simmering just beneath the surface and tried to reign it in as he demanded, "Is it now your turn to dictate my life and choices, Layla? You are now the one who gets to tell me what I should and shouldn't do? Demok must have handed you some great assignment on running my life after his death, is that it? I can't love or be loved? My life is nothing more than duty and sacrifice for the cause?"

Layla's eyes filled with tears that spilled down her cheeks as she shook her head, denying Varn's accusations. When she spoke, her voice trembled slightly but resolution gave her words substance. "You and Mayven are different than the rest of us. The fate of our entire world rests on the choices the two of you make. You already know that. You have been raised knowing that your entire life. She doesn't. She thinks that whatever you need her to do is a simple task. Then, when it is completed, her journey with destiny is done. She doesn't know what is ahead." The tears on Layla's face now coursed unceasing. "I don't wish to dictate your life. You, more than anyone I know, deserve love and to be loved." Layla paused a moment to wipe her face with a sleeve and take a deep breath. "I just don't think Mayven is ready for that. Love is a distraction. Neither one of you have the luxury of playing out a great love story between you. There are other more pressing matters at hand."

Varn ignored the sorrow etched in Layla's expression. "I thought if you cared nothing for me that at least Mayven was a friend. Someone you loved and valued," Varn continued, his voice a low demanding snarl. "What if she loves me? Would you tell her the same?"

Layla squared her shoulders, her eyes flashing at Varn's accusation.

"I care for both of you. I already told her loving you is more than a game, and I don't believe she loves you for the right reasons."

Varn slammed his hand down on the counter and leaned across it, bellowing in Layla's face, causing her to take a step back, "I don't care what you believe. I have had enough of you, Demok, and the entire world running my life. I don't need your advice, and I would appreciate it if you stayed out of mine and Mayven's private affairs."

Varn registered the look of fear that momentarily flashed across Layla's face and for a second regretted his outburst.

"You and Mayven have no private affairs, Varn. Everything both of you choose matters to more than just the two of you. The entire world needs you both to be focused on what is best for everyone."

Layla's response washed away his regret, fueling his anger to white hot. "I'm tired of the world coming first. I'm tired of life being about what everyone else wants and needs from me. I choose what I want. I choose what I need and if you, destiny, and the world doesn't like it you can all—"

Suddenly, inside both Varn and Layla's head, Sharieana shouted, *"Silence, both of you. Your anger will cause you to say words you can't take back. Your tongues be silent in anger. You know this, children."*

Varn was pulled up short and snapped his mouth closed. "I'm sorry, ancient one. I know better. Thank you for keeping me from doing something I can't take back."

"You are welcome, child. Perhaps this is a conversation for another time. I do suggest, however, that you consider this, Layla. What good is doing good if you can't do it with love? And consider carefully this, Varn. If love is selfish, is it truly love at all?" Sharieana's voice trailed into silence as Varn and Layla stared across the island at each other.

Varn took a deep breath then, without a word, turned on his heel and left. *Layla said Mayven loves me!*

Happiness bubbled inside of him as he considered the thought, his heart and imagination running away with him but then Sharieana's warning came to mind and his feet slowed on their way up the stairs. Outside of Mayven's door, Varn stood for a long time, his hand suspended halfway between the entry pad and his heart. At length, he gave one more longing glance at the door, then turned and headed up the last flight of stairs to the third floor and his room.

CHAPTER TWENTY-THREE

Mayven left the living room, grateful that the party was over and no one else was there to tell her how grand her destiny was and how much she must sacrifice for the good of everyone.

Mayven, though still not fond of the sacrifice portion, was surprised to find, instead of the old resentment, acceptance. She sighed. *I've spent far too much time being angry about destiny and taking it out on Varn because he was the messenger.*

She mounted the stairs one heavy step at a time. *The best part, however, is that I no longer have to watch Varn and that girl flirt with each other.* Mayven felt her heart pound an uneven measure in her chest as her eyes filled with tears. *Maybe Layla is right. I don't know what real love is, and Varn knows it. He is seeking out someone who knows who he really is. Not some silly girl infatuated with her savior.*

Sinking into her bed, Mayven curled into a ball around her pillow, not even bothering to change from her gown. Tears soaked the soft smooth fabric beneath her cheek as she replayed every smile and laugh Varn shared with the girl with the brilliant auburn hair and flashing green eyes.

"I think perhaps you need to find some answers, child," Sharieana's voice interrupted her tortured memories at length.

Mayven wiped at her face, sitting up and looking up at the ceiling. "Sharieana?"

"It's me, child. You need not speak aloud, unless you prefer it. You can just speak to me from your mind," she answered.

Mayven smiled as she thought, *"Are there really male and female in your species, Sharieana?"*

A brief laugh sounding like wind through treetops filled Mayven's head.

"I suppose," Sharieana answered. *"But not in the way you have separate genders. We cross pollinate to create seeds for the next generation."*

Mayven sighed. *"Love must be much simpler for you than us."*

"Love is never simple or easy, child." Sharieana paused on a long soft breeze of a sigh before she continued, *"Love comes in all forms and serves many purposes. But perhaps the best authority on love is the Creator. Why have you not sought Him out to find His answer to your questions? On love, He is the expert."*

"Love doesn't concern Him," Mayven pronounced with a grunt of disbelief. *"It's a matter for mortals. He only concerns Himself with destiny and souls."*

"How would you know what concerns the Creator?" Sharieana questioned in gentle reprimand. *"Have you asked Him? Has His name crossed your lips at all?"*

"I want nothing to do with religion. It's not for me." Mayven flopped back onto her tear-stained pillow and glared up at the ceiling.

"What do you think religion is? Why do you dislike it so?"

"Religion is a way to control the masses," Mayven answered promptly. *"To get everyone to conform and be a certain way. It's a way to make some feel like they are above others. Religion is poison. It makes people do horrible things in its name and then be proud of them."*

Mayven finished speaking by punctuating it with a fist to her pillow as an image of Vayshatka filled her mind.

"I cannot disagree with your assumption," Sharieana admitted with sadness.

"Then why would you ask that I seek out the Creator? He is religion."

"No, child, He is not," Sharieana said before Mayven could continue. *"He is the Creator. He does not call us to religion. He calls us to faith. He calls us to a relationship with Him. Faith is but another word for trust and love. Religion is another word for rules and divisiveness. You cannot have religion and faith. They cannot exist in the same body. Religion separates and faith joins together."*

Mayven remained silent a long moment as she considered Sharieana's argument.

Sharieana interrupted her thoughts, *"Perhaps you should speak to Kar. He is the expert on such matters."*

Mayven groaned, rolling her eyes. *"He is all about religion and following Dsohoay. He, of all people, probably knows the least about faith of anyone."*

"You are very quick to judge things you know nothing about." Sharie-ana's tone was now hard, laced with a touch of anger. *"How do you think you can help anyone if you are not able to see beyond your own narrow view point? If your mind could conceive all the answers on its own, what need would there be for love, faith, religion, friendship or needing to save the world at all? You would merely be able to speak and the answers you gave would set all to rights."*

Mayven's teeth ground together.

"The point I'm making is this, child, you're hurt and seeking a way to stop that pain. There are things you don't know or understand that are proof that faith is necessary and vital. You need to stop judging based on only your experiences and become a student. Learn all that you can because choosing something without knowledge and understanding does not make you any less responsible for the consequences of your actions."

Sharieana paused a brief moment. *"I have Kar outside your door if you would like to let him in."*

Mayven briefly considered denying him access but then capitulated, saying aloud, "Enter."

The door slid open and Kar walked through, his aged and scarred countenance wreathed in a smile as he took a seat beside Mayven on the bed. "Isn't Sharieana magnificent? I'm so glad you have brought them back to us. I have learned so much since the Ohkie'en have awakened."

Mayven's only response was a groan as she sat up to face Kar. He looked back at her, saying nothing, his smile still firmly in place.

At length, Mayven asked, "Well, what is this great revelation you and Sharieana have for me?"

Kar laughed out loud, throwing his head back in abandon. Then, collecting himself once more, though his eyes still twinkled merrily, he asked, "I had nothing planned to say. Sharieana simply said there were things you might like to know about faith and Dsohoay."

"I think she would like to hear your views on faith and religion," Sharieana answered for Mayven. *"She seems to think that as a cleric of Dsohoay, it is your duty to push religion. The child is quite opinionated."*

"I see," Kar replied aloud. "I'm opinionated myself. It can be quite inconvenient at times, at others quite useful."

Mayven rolled her eyes again as she roughly pounded her pillow into a ball in her lap. "If you two wouldn't mind not discussing me like a potted plant, it would be nice."

Sharieana and Kar both laughed, then Kar began to speak, his tone light but serious. "I happen to believe religion is for those who lack the faith to just believe. Religion is a set of rules that makes people more comfortable with something they can't possibly understand. Religion makes Dsohoay smaller, more like us. For those with no faith, it is necessary, perhaps. I have in my life relied on religion but it was never as fulfilling as faith."

"I think you both have left out the most popular religion in our world." Mayven sighed, then pointed out, her tone that of an aggrieved student, "What of those who follow Hsdaie? They have a religion. Should they have faith?"

The room fell silent for a long time. Mayven stared at Kar, waiting for his response, her fingers absently drumming on the pillow in her lap.

When at length Kar spoke, his tone was somber, his eyes filled with sadness that etched itself in the lines of his ancient countenance. "I fear, child, that those who follow Hsdaie have a remarkable lack of ability to have faith in anything but themselves and power. That is why they follow him. They don't understand how to have faith or how to love. Hsdaie does not engender faith or love. He supports the belief that self is all powerful and can attain through aggression anything the heart desires. He is a god of anger, hate, and selfishness. He only purports to love his followers because at our core we are created for a relationship."

Kar's expression grew grim. "Hsdaie draws in his followers with promises that appeal to their basest nature. Then holds them captive with lies that he loves them and will give them everything they want. But love is not about getting everything you want. It is about doing what is best for someone, whether they want you to or not."

Kar struggled with the next thing he had to say before he turned to face Mayven, his earnest gaze filled with sadness. "Love is like raising a child. Children will say they don't need you or want you, they will demand you leave their life alone. Children will scream for their independence and for you to not check up on them. But the truth is a parent who really loves them will not give in to their demands. They will demand their child obey and learn to follow rules and adhere to boundaries because one day, even though that child may resent it today, those rules and those boundaries will be needed and remembered then passed on to their children." Kar let his words trail into silence.

Mayven waited, sensing he was not finished.

"Those lessons must be adhered to and passed on," Kar said, his voice choked with tears. "Love is not about what the person you love wants but what is best for them."

Mayven contemplated what Kar said and then compared it to Layla's statement from earlier. "So love is not about the person who is in love but about the person who they love and doing what is best for them whether they appreciate it or not?"

"Succinctly put, child," Sharieana answered. *"I think you may at last have a grasp on this. Now how do you think this conversation relates to religion, or your destiny?"*

"I feel like a child at school," Mayven groaned as she rubbed her forehead. "What is all this teaching on love and the best thing for others about? What does all this have to do with religion or my destiny and the prophecy? Is it because I love Varn? Because no one wants us to be in love. Because I don't get to have love. I don't understand the point in this lesson."

Kar answered her, his voice once again calm and reassuring, though sadness still thickened his speech. "The point is there is a difference between fulfilling your destiny with duty or with love. It is not about not letting you have love, but teaching you the proper way to love."

Mayven bristled as she stared at her hands, twisting the fabric over the pillow in her lap. "I suppose that I don't know how to love. Is that the point?"

"Quite the opposite," Kar sighed, his tone now one of long-suffering patience. "You have an incredible ability to love despite all you have been through. You're guarded, but you love and when you do it's fierce. The point is much finer than that."

Sharieana interrupted, *"The point is the manner in which you fulfill your destiny."*

The room fell silent as Mayven waited for the continuation she knew was coming, though inside a small light of understanding was beginning to dawn. Several long breaths passed as Sharieana allowed Mayven to reflect on her statement.

"Consider this, Jayben Tavadar was assigned the duty to run the orphanage," Sharieana continued. *"She did so, considering it her destiny to teach orphans their proper place in society."*

Mayven's teeth ground together at the mention of Tavadar's name and an unreasoning anger filled her. Mayven opened her mouth to speak.

Sharieana interrupted, *"If Jayben Tavadar's destiny was that job, as* she believed it to be, how would have it changed if she had approached her destiny with love instead of duty?"

Silence again reigned, and Mayven felt as if she were being led down a path. Though the end of that path was near, she still couldn't clearly see it.

Sharieana waited several moments for Mayven to consider her words. *"In her duty, Jayben Tavadar was cruel and heartless. She left scars on you, Amalayna, Xietak, and every other child she touched. She did teach you all lessons that were valuable to your survival but in the cruelest way possible. Some she caused not to even exist. But if she had approached that destiny with love in the attitude we have explained, what then would have been the result? Would you not all have learned the same skills to survive without the scars? Wouldn't some of those she taught to be cruel and to follow in her path of evil been changed for the better?"*

Mayven sucked her breath through her clenched teeth as understanding dawned bright. "Destiny done without love is duty and can be corrupted. Destiny done with love is sacrifice for the good of others and while misunderstood by some will never be corrupted." Mayven understood but fear prodded her to ask, "Does that mean that I am only destined to sacrifice for others but have no love or comfort of my own?"

"I know you are afraid that with all this you do for others there is nothing for you in your future," Kar answered, his voice filled with certainty and deep understanding. "Rest in this, child, what we sow we will also reap. That promise is of Dsohoay, not only as a caution but as a blessing. You cannot plant good and reap evil. It is against the laws of the Creator."

"And that is where faith comes in, right?" Mayven questioned softly. "I have to have faith that though for now what I want is last in line, someday it will be first. There is where my faith sustains me and not religion."

Sharieana's laughter filled Mayven's thoughts, and she was sure Kar heard it as well for he smiled brightly.

"And now, the child has grown," Sharieana stated. *"The rest of your journey is yours to take. You must reach out to your Creator. In order to have faith, you must have relationship and love. I think for now you have learned enough, but I caution not to ponder long. Think on what you have learned and decide your course. Much hangs on your decisions, and time is not in your favor."*

Kar now spoke, his voice ringing with authority, "I think perhaps it's time you revisited your library. Clerics have long been aids to the

Language Master, and perhaps there is something I can assist you with. I would be honored if you allowed me to aid you."

Mayven sighed, her shoulders feeling lighter, less burdened with duty. With a nod, she stood from her bed before assisting Kar to his feet. "I have two things I need your help with. The first is to find the exact manner in which to prepare for and perform the reversal of Vayshatka and the second is to help me unravel the exact manner in which I set the balance of adamie right again."

Kar nodded agreement, and Mayven smiled. *Not long ago, that aged scarred face frightened me and now I find I hardly notice the scars.*

Mayven and Kar slipped out into the silent hallway and made their way downstairs and toward the kitchen to the basement entrance. Upon entering the kitchen, Mayven was surprised to find Hardak and Layla leaning against the bar, eating leftovers of the night's meal as they conversed in low tones.

Mayven cleared her throat to alert them to her presence.

They turned in unison as Layla questioned, "Where are you off to so late?"

Mayven felt a flash of anger and shoved it down with a sigh. "I'm going with Kar to the library. You're welcome to come, if you wish."

Layla raised a brow, and Hardak shrugged a massive shoulder, then both followed Mayven and Kar to the basement and through the portal.

Entering the library, Mayven headed across the room. "I need to know where to find information on the Tears of Dsohoay, Tamaryn."

The ancient voice of Tamaryn rustled through the mind of each person present as she replied, "There is a section on ancient artifacts, and I believe you will need the cross reference under rituals as well."

Mayven instantly understood where Tamaryn was directing her and collected the volumes from the shelves that were indicated. Then, setting down at the chair she had occupied earlier, she looked up at the others. "Give me just a moment."

Several quiet minutes passed, in which Mayven simply opened each book and absorbed their contents. Then, once Mayven was aware again, she noticed that Layla lay pale and still on the couch opposite of her. Rising, Mayven closed the distance between them in two rapid steps and fell to her knees beside the couch.

"Layla, Layla, can you hear me?"

Mayven's cries drew Hardak and Kar's attention from across the room where they were studying the book containing the prophecy.

Hardak shoved Mayven aside as he knelt in her place, his large hand tenderly caressing Layla's face as tears splashed from his eyes onto Layla's pale cheeks. "Layla, Layla, wake up! Please wake up!"

Mayven suddenly felt the constraints of time shoving her forward. "Kar on the shelf over there is a map of the location of Radiea, my ancestral home. I need that. Then get Varn a map of the locations for the Tears of Dsohoay."

As Kar raced across the room for the maps, Mayven spoke several short sentences and in her hand appeared two books.

Hardak stared up at her in grief and anger. "Layla is dying, and you're doing research and working on saving your friend. How can you be so selfish? Layla loves you."

Mayven sighed as once again a new understanding of Varn made him even more precious to her in the seconds it took to answer. "I'm doing what is best for everyone, Hardak. I hope to save them both. But I need your help."

Mayven looked at the two books in her hands, one was a small journal, the other a larger volume. The cover of the larger book read *Prophecy*.

Mayven handed the journal to Hardak. "I need you to give this to Varn. It is the instructions to collect and set up for the reversal ceremony. Then I need you to take care of Layla until I return."

Hardak raised a brow in question. "And just where do you think you're going without Varn? He'll never allow it."

Mayven looked up at Hardak. "If he wants to do what's right, he'll do as I ask."

Hardak's face lit with understanding. "I don't suppose Varn will like that you suddenly embraced your destiny and are calling the shots. I think I'll have to pay close attention." Hardak paused, looking down at Layla's still, pale form. "Layla will be mad if I don't give her all the details."

Mayven felt a lump fill her throat as she tried to speak, her voice coming out a choked whisper instead. "I promise you'll get to tell her every detail. But we have to get going."

Mayven, now accustomed to the magic that accompanied such statements, ignored the tingle across her skin as she turned toward the portal.

Hardak stuffed the journal in the waistband of his breeches and scooped Layla off the couch. Kar stepped through the portal, carrying the maps Mayven requested, followed by Hardak, who was carrying Layla.

Mayven paused a moment before leaving as she asked Tamaryn, "The lie is what we have believed. The truth is what we have denied ourselves. Is that correct?"

Tamaryn's jubilant voice filled Mayven's mind. "You have reached your path. Follow it wisely, Language Master."

Mayven smiled but didn't respond as she stepped back through the portal and into the basement of Varn's home.

CHAPTER TWENTY-FOUR

Varn sat up with a jerk, his eyes still blurry and ears being assaulted with the sounds of chaos coming from the main floor. Hardak's voice bellowed his name again, and Varn bounded out of bed. He hastily donned his breeches before racing down the staircase two at a time. The sound of his bare feet slapping against the smooth wood of the staircase was lost in the cacophony of sound emanating from the general direction of his study.

Varn raced down the hall and burst through the door to his study, just as he pulled his shirt over his shoulders.

Hardak knelt by the settee beneath the windows, his large frame shaking. "Varn, you mogatie, where are you?"

Varn crossed to the settee. "I'm right here. What has you bellowing like a wounded tkhoda?"

The last words had barely left his lips as Hardak moved aside to reveal Layla on the settee, her lovely face ashen and her breathing shallow.

Varn fell to his knees. "What happened?"

Hardak answered, "We were at the library with Mayven. Layla said she was tired and laid down to rest. The next thing I knew, she was like this. Mayven says she knows how to fix everything. She is on her way back now."

Varn looked up, just as Arrok barged through the study door followed by Kar. Varn noted Rohtak's conspicuous absence from the group gathered in the study. Varn felt unease curl through him. *Rohtak wasn't feeling so well last night either.*

Varn turned to Arrok. "I need you to go check on Rohtak."

Arrok nodded and headed out of the study, passing Mayven on his way through the door.

Varn locked eyes with Mayven. "What's going on? Hardak says you can help Layla?"

Varn watched Mayven's expression change from confident to determined and braced himself for her response. Watching her carefully as she strode toward him, Varn noted the book she carried in one hand and the fact that she still wore the remarkable outfit she had worn at the dinner party.

Mayven came to a stop in front of him. "I need you to follow the instructions in the journal I created and gave to Hardak while I go to my ancestral home and reset the balance of magic."

"I can't do that, and you know it, Mayven." Varn's rose instantly from the floor. "I'll not allow you to put yourself in danger by going to Shimiera alone and unprotected."

Varn felt heat spread through him like fire as Mayven gently placed a small palm flat against his bare chest over his heart. He blinked slowly as he looked into Mayven's jewel-like eyes as she smiled at him.

"I know you want to protect me, but I must do my part and you must do yours. I need to restore balance again, but I also need to free Xietak of the master Tarlen. There is far more at stake than you know if balance is restored and he remains possessed. Please, do as I ask. I'll take Arrok with me, if you wish."

Varn shook his head, trying to clear his senses of Mayven's over-whelming nearness. Her scent was a mix of shmara flowers and starlight lilies and her warm hand against his chest had his mind completely focused on things that had nothing to do with the crisis at hand. Varn cleared his throat, taking a cautious step backward, unwilling to break the physical contact with Mayven but needing his brain to function again.

Varn clasped her fingers that trailed fire down his torso in his hands. "I see you have learned reason at last. I'll do as you ask."

Varn looked up as Arrok entered the room.

"Varn, I'm sorry but Rohtak has passed," Arrok pronounced, his eyes downcast. "I went to his room as you asked. I thought he was asleep, but he wasn't breathing and he is cold. He seems to have been dead for some time."

Varn suddenly couldn't breathe, as if someone had sucked all the oxygen from the room. Varn staggered slightly, unsteady on his feet, and it was the tender touch of Mayven's hand against his chest that reminded him to suck in air for his starving lungs.

Through a fog that seemed to momentarily incapacitate his brain, he heard Arrok tell him to sit down. Varn followed Arrok's command without thinking and sat, resting his head in his hands.

Several long moments of silence.

"I know you're hurting. I'm sorry, for your loss." Mayven's quiet voice was soft. "But right now we need to focus on fixing what is wrong before there is even more to grieve over. Please, Varn, we need to—"

A bright blue flash appeared in the doorway, then vanished, and in its place stood Amalayna. Varn stared at her in open-mouthed astonishment. She stepped forward, her clothes dirty and torn. Amalayna's olive skin was caked in blood and filth, and her face was bruised and bleeding. When she stumbled forward and started to fall, Varn lurched from his seat to catch her.

Lifting her slight form easily, Varn breathed through his mouth in order not to gag on the smell of vomit and urine rising from Amalayna's matted, filth-encrusted hair and ruined clothing. Varn gently sat her down in the chair he had just vacated. Pushing filthy strands of hair out of Amalayna's face, he asked, "Ama, how did you get here?"

Amalayna's voice was weak and shaking as she replied, "I—I transported to Mayven."

Varn relinquished his place as Mayven shoved him aside. Varn watched Mayven's hands flutter just over Amalayna's battered form as her amethyst eyes swam in tears that cascaded onto Amalayna's cheeks, creating muddy tracks.

"Ama, we need to get you upstairs and cleaned up so I can help you." Mayven's voice trembled. "Can you let Varn carry you to my room?"

Amalayna nodded her head weakly, and Varn stepped to her side and gently lifted her, cradling her against his chest. He carefully walked up the stairs, trying not to jar her broken form too much with movement. He entered Mayven's room. Mayven and Arrok followed him as he continued straight to the bathroom, where he stepped into the shower, still holding Amalayna. As Mayven turned on the water, he turned his back to the spray until he felt the water warm, then carefully turned and let the water begin to rinse the grime from Amalayna.

Mayven stopped at the edge of the shower. "Can you get me scissors please, Arrok?"

Arrok handed Mayven the scissors, and she began to cut off the remaining shreds of Amalayna's ruined clothing. Varn watched Amalayna cringe with each movement and small pitiful cries escaped her lips. Mayven began to gently wash Amalayna's hair and body. Varn's arms were aching, even with Amalayna's slight weight, by the time Mayven had finished.

Gratefully, he handed Amalayna off to Arrok, who stood outside the shower. Arrok gently wrapped Amalayna in a thick, warm towel then laid her on Mayven's bed.

Varn asked Mayven, "Would you mind getting me a towel?"

Mayven's cheeks grew red as she took in his dripping form before hastily retrieving a towel from the shelf next to the shower. Varn chuckled slightly as she thrust it at him blindly, then left the bathroom, closing the door behind her.

Looking down at his soaked clothing, Varn decided they were as ruined as the scraps of Amalayna's attire still littering the floor of the shower. He stripped down and hastily washed himself off before drying and wrapping the towel around his waist, then entering Mayven's room.

Arrok stood next to the bed as Mayven lay next to Amalayna. A blanket engulfed Amalayna's tiny form as she lay cradled against Mayven's chest. The room seemed to vibrate with magic.

Mayven gently rocked. "Ama, I can't heal you completely. I have to save some magic to set things right. When we have, I'll come back and make you well again."

Varn felt the magic coalesce then, like a barely running faucet, flow toward the bed where Mayven and Amalayna lay. Suddenly it stopped and flowed backward, dissipating into the surrounding walls of his home.

"*Mayven, you have done all you can for now.*" Sharieana addressed them all. "*I will watch over her. You need to get going. We are down to hours left before the balance shifts too far.*"

Mayven tucked Amalayna's now serenely sleeping form more securely into the blankets. "Give me a moment. I need to change, and I'll meet you downstairs."

Varn nodded and exited the room, closing the door behind him as Arrok remarked, "You might want to change as well there, friend. Quests are a little more difficult if you're naked."

Varn chuckled. "Yeah, I'll see you in the study."

CHAPTER TWENTY-FIVE

Mayven stripped out of her dress, tossing it carelessly on the floor, then went to the closet. Inside, the clothes were all neatly hung and organized. Mayven retrieved a pair of black breeches, purple tunic, light cloak, and knee-high boots, all the while thinking of the kind-eyed man who had so carefully arranged her things.

Shaking her head to dispel a sudden wave of grief she began to dress as she glanced at Amalayna's sleeping form. *I need to stay focused before anyone else pays so dearly.*

Mayven sighed as she finished pulling on her boots. On the way out the door, she slung a bag over her shoulder and fastened her cape around her shoulders.

"Why are you and Mayven not fixing this, if she knows what's wrong?" Hardak yelled at Varn as she entered the study. "You should be gone already and setting things right."

Mayven paused at the desk.

Varn faced Hardak, fists clenched at his sides and shoulders tight beneath his green tunic. "I told you already, Hardak, we had to help Amalayna, and we're leaving as soon as we can."

Hardak began to say something else, then snapped his mouth closed when his eyes locked with Mayven's.

Mayven stepped around Varn and tilted her head back to look into Hardak's face. "We're leaving now. I'll do all I can to make sure she is okay, Hardak."

Mayven watched her usually boisterous, giant of a friend nod jerkily as he blinked rapidly, trying to conceal tears. Reaching out a hand, Mayven placed it on his arm. "Do you still have that book I gave you?"

Hardak turned away, mumbling, "Yeah it's over here."

Mayven felt a tender sadness make her own throat tight as she watched Hardak swipe roughly at his face with a giant paw before picking up the book from the table by the settee and turning to face them.

Mayven took the book without a word and passed it on to Varn. Then, looking around, she found Arrok sitting quietly in the chair behind the desk, his arms clamped tightly across his chest as he frowned at Layla's sleeping form. Kar stood at his side, his hands clasped behind his back as he, too, stared at Layla.

Mayven scanned the room, then, finding the map she had dropped earlier, picked it up and tucked it into the bag on her shoulder. "Kar, I need you to remove the crystals that lead to the library and destroy them. Then stay here and care for Amalayna. Hardak is busy with Layla."

Then she turned to Varn. He stood next to the window, his face cast in shadow from the dim light of the moon outside the window as he roughly shoved a hand through his hair, his eyes locked on Layla's sleeping face. Mayven felt her heart catch, and she closed her eyes a moment, trying to reach out to him across their connection to comfort him. There was a faint stirring, and Varn's head turned as his eyes locked with hers.

Mayven tried to give him a comforting smile but the questioning look in Varn's expression made her certain she had failed. Sighing, she said, "Varn, I need you to take the journal and head to the Baksadie Mountains and one of the two lakes we were researching earlier. Retrieve me the crystals called the Tears of Dsohoay exactly as explained. That is very important. I don't have time to explain everything it will take too long. But once you have those crystals, you need to have Xietak in Niesha's control. I assume you have contacts who can do that for you while you're busy with the retrieval. As soon as the balance of magic is restored, I'll meet you where you are."

Varn raised a questioning brow. "How are you going to manage that? Can you suddenly teleport?"

"I should be able to, but I don't know how yet."

Sharieana's voice interrupted the conversation as she spoke into all their minds, "*That is where the Ohkie'en will come in. We have a means to get her where you are. We will know where that is. When she is ready and we have the necessary power again, we will transport her to you.*"

Mayven smiled at the look on Varn's face, a mix of confusion and disbelief. Mayven said, "Sharieana, I need you to share all the strength you can to sustain Layla until I return. Amalayna is powerful enough, she should be fine, but I fear Layla may need you. Can you do that for us, please?"

"*I will watch over her. You have my word, Lapahoniesh.*"

Mayven smiled. "Shall we go then?"

Varn nodded. "I have a way to get us into Rashmahava. It's one of the other portals Amalayna set up. I suggest we take the crystals from here and destroy them, along with the ones on the other side."

Mayven nodded agreement. Arrok rose from his chair, retrieved two small packs from the floor, handing one to Varn, and together the three of them stepped out into the far too silent night. The night birds didn't call to each other and even the breeze that touched their faces was hushed. Shen sapling street lights barely glowed, while the shen temple in the city square, though still bright, lacked its usual luster. Starlight lilies in the town's gardens were without light and Bapas that hung from the lattice of branches serving as walkways over the streets were dark.

The effect was terrifying and Mayven saw again the picture Radiea had shown her of what happens when the balance shifts. Mayven nervously adjusted her cape around her shoulders as tears pricked the corners of her eyes. *The process had already begun, and I sped it up when I awakened the Ohkie'en. This is my fault.*

Mayven, lost in her own thoughts, was surprised when Varn's large warm hand touched her shoulder. "Are you all right?"

Mayven shrugged. "No, I didn't start this problem but I sped it up and now so many more are sick and dying because I woke the Ohkie'en. We have to hurry. There isn't much time."

Varn, for once didn't argue. He cupped her elbow in his palm, and they increased their speed as they turned up the lane, away from the town square and into the unmaintained forest beyond the manicured lawns of Lirie's city limits. Mayven jogged to keep up with the two men, who marched down a barely visible path off the side of the main, paved road, just a short distance outside of town. The path finally opened into a small circular clearing, barely large enough for two large men to lay foot to foot. In the clearing's center, a large flickering blue disk lit the night.

"This is the last of the portals connected to Ama," Varn stated. "We need to destroy it and allow the adamie that it's using to return to her. She needs her strength."

Mayven watched the disk grow bright then dim as if to the beat of a pulse.

Arrok's tone was rough as he noted, "This may well be a suicide mission anyway. We don't need to leave them open to make rounding us up any easier if we fail."

Mayven felt her stomach twist as she finally spoke the truth she had learned aloud, "If we fail, it won't matter anyway. There will be no one to search or to find. We've reached the end. We either succeed and live or fail and die and there isn't much time."

Varn nodded and dug up the two crystals on either side of the portal. Together, the three of them stepped through and into the confines of a very small room. Arrok retrieved the second set of crystals from shelves on either side of the portal. Mayven watched as Varn set the crystals together on a shelf, spoke two words, and the crystals dissolved into dust.

Arrok shifted uneasily next to Mayven. "I would really like to get out of this room, if you don't mind."

Varn touched the entry pad, and the door opened into the slightly larger kitchen of Kar's home. Mayven took in the surroundings. *I was here and never knew Amalayna had been here also.*

Mayven pushed her thoughts aside as she removed her map from her satchel and laid it on the table. The map had two markings. One point was named Radiea, the location of her ancestral home. The second was high in the mountains that towered over Rashmahava. Mayven planted a finger over the second mark. "Varn, this is the closest and easiest to reach destination for your mission. I assume you have a way you can get there?"

Varn nodded. "I still have a friend who, if not too weak, can get us close to there in a pod. But the last part will be on foot and it will be treacherous. How much time do we have?"

Mayven looked up at Varn. "I have less time than you. But even after the balance is restored, we only have a day, two at most. Will you be able to get there in that limited time and back here by then?"

Varn shoved a hand through his hair, dislodging the braids from the silver clip at the back of his head. "I'll have to, won't I? I have a few quick calls to make. I have some people close to Xietak. They'll be able to get him here and hold him until I'm able to return."

Arrok pointed at the second mark on the map denoted Radiea."Isn't this inside Hareshtava?"

Mayven nodded. "It's the beginning of all this."

"Bomar Pass goes directly through the center of this location." Arrok glanced at Mayven, his expression concerned. "No one has set foot inside it for generations beyond counting. It's said to be cursed."

Mayven looked solemnly at Arrok. "It is. That's why we're going there." She turned to Varn. "Make your calls. Get your driver and, if you can, get us a second. If not, we'll drop you off and he can take us the rest of the way to our destination."

In unison, the three of them spun around and stared in astonishment as Amalayna stepped through a portal as it blinked out of existence behind her.

Amalayna regarded them, her expression bland. "No need to worry about that. I'll portal you there once we get to Varn's drop off. I don't think I'm strong enough to portal you that distance right this moment. It took a lot to get here."

Mayven rushed forward, embracing Amalayna fiercely. "You should be resting. We got this under control."

Then, when Amalayna didn't hug her back, Mayven pulled back from Amalayna, examining her face intently. "Are you all right?"

Amalayna gave a noncommittal shrug. "I think we don't have time to wait."

Varn nodded. "I need you all to wait here. I'll return shortly."

Varn glanced at the clock. "If I'm not back by next bell, you need to leave."

Mayven looked at the clock, noting the time before she nodded. She watched Varn step outside, her heart sinking as the silence inside the kitchen seemed to grow. Mayven sighed. Needing something to occupy her time, she went to the cupboards and began to prepare parfie. "How will we leave if he doesn't return?"

Saying the words aloud made a spike of fear wedge itself above Mayven's heart and spread ice through her veins. With trembling hands, she finish the parfie and set it before Arrok and Amalayna.

Amalayna accepted the mug and stared at its steaming contents. "I think I'll have rested enough to get us most of the way to where you need to go."

Mayven stared for a long moment at Amalayna's bent head. *She isn't acting like herself. I suppose I wouldn't be myself either, if I survived what she has been through.*

Then Mayven asked, "Are you sure? You need to take care of your-self."

Amalayna shrugged again. "I'll be fine."

Mayven locked eyes with Arrok over the top of Amalayna's bent head as the room fell back into uncomfortable silence. The time ticked slowly by as Mayven paced restlessly, first cleaning the glasses they used and carefully putting them away, then washing down counters and straightening knick-knacks on shelves.

Arrok rose and placed a hand on Mayven's shoulder, folding her against his chest. "He'll be back soon."

Then as if on command the door opened and in it stood Varn with another man at his shoulder. Arrok released Mayven and crossed the room to Varn. Arrok grasped Varn's arm, then hugged him, a smile of relief lighting his face.

Amalayna rose mechanically from her chair, smiling halfheartedly at Varn. "Well, let's get going. We have work to do."

Mayven felt a frown draw her brows together over the bridge of her nose and she turned to find Varn looking at Amalayna, his eyes filled with concern. Mayven shrugged as she glanced between Varn and Amalayna. "Then we should get moving."

As they stepped out of the house into the alley, the driver released the pod and made it take form. Once they were inside the vehicle, it began to move sluggishly until it contacted the smooth surface of the main street. Soon the vehicle was speeding along the streets and then beginning its ascent of Bomar Pass. The vehicle remained quiet for a long time.

Varn studied Amalayna intently. "Amalayna, is everything all right?"

Amalayna snorted. "Oh, I'm just peachy, handsome. My love is entombed in his own body by a demon. I was tortured nearly to death before escaping, but other than that I'm great."

Nervous laughter filled the space as Amalayna's sarcastic comment faded into silence. The rest of the trip was spent with everyone diligently staring unseeing out the window. Mayven, however, was acutely aware of Varn's presence next to her and the comforting, if faint, thrum of connection between them once more.

CHAPTER TWENTY-SIX

Varn felt the tension around him but was concentrating more on the stirring of warmth along the connection between him and Mayven. Like the feeling of early morning sunshine warming skin, the connection began to slowly spread and lessen the constant pain that had been his companion for weeks. Varn found himself acutely aware of Mayven, his eyes continually drawn to the delicate features that wavered between worry and relief as Mayven alternately stared out the window of the pod car and then at Amalayna, who sat across from her.

Far too soon, the pod car reached the end of the road.

The driver lowered the divider. "Varn, we're here. I'll find a place to shelter and wait."

Their group exited the vehicle.

Varn pulled Arrok aside. "Keep her safe and watch Amalayna closely. I get the feeling something isn't right with her. I think she isn't as well as she wants us to believe."

Arrok nodded as he glanced at Amalayna. "I will, you can count on me."

Varn squeezed Arrok's shoulder. "I know, my friend. I always can."

Then, stepping up to Amalayna, he looked down at her lowered head. Reaching out, he tipped her chin back so he could look into her black-ringed, clear silver eyes. "Be careful, little one. We just got you back."

Turning to face Mayven, Varn found he had no words to say. He simply stepped forward and enfolded her in his arms before releasing her and stepping into the dense forest. Varn forced himself not to look back as he felt the shift of adamie when Amalayna opened the portal. Varn stumbled slightly, noting the shift of magic made him lightheaded and that the smaller plants seemed to wither before his eyes. Then the flow of adamie returned, his head cleared, but the plants still lay withered and black at his feet.

The blackened corpses of small flowers and shrubs crunched beneath his feet as a constant reminder that time was running out. Varn marched onward, steadily rising higher. The air grew thinner, and snow became a blanket that grew ever thicker as he ascended the steep side of the mountain. Trees, once towering in strength, became smaller, thinner, and twisted, then ceased to exist as he climbed above the tree line.

Stopping to catch his breath, Varn examined the map in the journal Mayven had created. Looking up and to the left, he found a gap that led between the jagged peaks. The clouds now appeared like a thick soft blanket spread across a floor, concealing the world far below him. Moonlight changed the clouds' voluminous bodies to silver as they flowed lazily across the sky.

Varn's thoughts wandered a moment as he stood catching his breath. *I think Mayven would find this place very beautiful.*

Then, heaving a great sigh, as much from the need for oxygen as to clear his head, Varn started to the left across the front of the giant peak. His breathing grew labored, and his muscles were screaming as the hours ticked by slowly and eventually dawn began to light the sky to lavender. At last the rays of the sun fully shown down on Varn as he stared down into a massive valley.

The high mountain peaks were bare for several hundred feet before the stony face gave way to lines of trees spread out like the sentinel forms of gnarled soldiers. Down in the depths of the valley, taller trees concealed the shoreline of a glowing green lake covered in a thin veil of ice.

Varn couldn't see across the length of the valley or the opposite side of the lake, even from his lofty perch at the top of the trail. Starting down the trail as carefully as possible, he reached the first of the stunted trees. Using them as handholds when necessary, he was grateful for the thickening air that fed his oxygen-starved lungs as he descended to the edge of the lake.

Dread, not relief, coursed through Varn as he stood staring down from thirty feet above the surface of the water. The cliff face beneath him, jagged and encrusted with crystals that glowed only a faint green, indicated he had indeed found what he sought, the Tears of Dsohoay.

Varn's eyes wandered left and right along the shoreline. If the cliff edge were any closer on either end to the surface of the lake, that point was far beyond his range of sight. *I don't have the time to wander around and look.*

Kneeling down on the edge of the cliff face, Varn unslung the pack Arrok had prepared for him from his back. Inside, thanks to Arrok's penchant for over preparedness, he found a plethora of useful items. Including the one most needed now, a long sturdy length of rope and rappelling gear.

Taking out the rope, Varn went to a nearby tree and placed a hand against its trunk. "I need to use you to tie off my rope."

"I don't mind. Just remember to remove your rope when you are finished," the tree replied.

Varn set his pack and the cape he had been wearing down at the base of the tree and tied the rope around the tree's girth. Checking to make sure his pockets were empty and the bag and knife needed to retrieve the crystals were securely fastened in place, he uncoiled the rope as he started toward the cliff edge. Dropping the rope over the edge, Varn lay flat and peeked over to find that the rope hung down the face of the cliff, swinging gently just feet above the surface of the water.

Varn rose and returned to the tree, checked the knot that anchored the rope, slipped into the repelling harness, then reread the instruction Mayven had given him.

The Tears of Dsohoay were shed because of the destruction jealousy had wrought that created heaven and hell and left Emwen the prize to be fought over in the middle. The tears, legend says, glow greenest in the cold depths of deep mountain lakes, where they are untouched by direct sunlight. These lakes are like the hearts that breed jealousy, cold and unforgiving. The most powerful of Dsohoay's Tears are the crystals untouched at all by the direct light of day.

Varn finished reading the passage and stared out over broad expanse of the lake. *How do I get that deep? Nearly four hundred feet!*

Varn felt tension tighten his shoulders and neck as he considered the task at hand and the limited time he had to achieve his goal. Swimming was an exercise he was good at, but the water temperature in the lake had to be close to freezing to form even the lacy-looking veil that hung around the edges of the water. Varn considered his options. *I have free dived in oceans up to nearly 600 feet. That is more than far enough to find crystals untouched by direct rays of light. But how long will my air last in freezing water? I also have hypothermia to worry about.*

Varn pondered several moments, then with a smile of decision, he spoke several short sentences aloud. Resting a palm against the tree, Varn bent to tuck the journal back into the bag and the tree's voice entered his head again. *"Inventive way to avoid hypothermia, making your clothes self-heating. Keep in mind, young one, adamie is getting stretched thin. You may not have much time, even with such an ingenious plan."*

Varn nodded. "I know, but perhaps it will be enough."

Varn returned to the edge of the cliff, hooked his rope to his harness and walked out over the edge. Three short drops later, he dangled above the water's surface. Taking a deep breath, he released his harness and plunged beneath the lake's eerily glowing surface.

The freezing embrace of the glowing, green lake activated his enhancement to his clothes and he began to swim down carefully, controlling his oxygen as he had been taught. Counting his depth as best he could in his head, he monitored the light filtering in from the surface and when the glow from around him was brighter than the light above him he continued another hundred feet until he found a large crystal whose intense green light shone stronger than those of its fellows.

Working as fast as limited oxygen and the impediment of water would allow, Varn at length managed to break the crystal loose and tuck it into the black bag at his waist. After tucking his knife into its sheath and sealing the bag closed, he noticed the water around him glowed even brighter.

Varn felt a flutter of current in the water and fear curled up his neck as he cautiously turned and came face to face with the largest pair of white eyes he'd ever seen. The fact the animal was clearly blind was no comfort, because his movements drew its attention as its sightless eyes stared in his direction. The glow of its pale blue green flesh, encasing a body three times the size of a tall man, lighted the area around it. Varn struggled to control the urge to scream as his eyes beheld the almost body-length razor-like teeth of the creature snap open just before it hurtled itself toward him.

Terror and adrenaline mixed as Varn clawed his way toward the surface, following the bubbles that rose lazily around him. Panic caused Varn to lose his control and soon his lungs were so starved for air it felt like they were trying to crack his ribcage. Varn glanced down, finding, to his horror, the fish seemed to lazily follow him upwards, its maw open wide and sightless eyes staring through him. Varn kicked hard, pulling water past him with his hands and trying to save the last of his breath so he wouldn't black out.

The fish continued to advance, growing closer with every stroke of its wide tail fin. The creature taunted Varn, swimming at a leisurely pace;

as if it knew Varn had no chance of escape. Varn reached for the knife tucked in his belt and, clutching it in his fist, kicked faster, pulling for the surface, praying it wasn't as far away as it seemed. Varn's lungs, now devoid of air from his accelerated ascent to the surface, caused him to feel lightheaded and bright pinpoints of light exploded behind his eyes every time he blinked. Darkness started to tunnel his vision as his legs slowed and arms grew heavy.

Several more, much weaker, strokes and Varn was suddenly aware he felt cold. The magic he had cast over his attire was wearing off. One more kick, and Varn's foot touched the monster's face. Varn looked down, noting that the creature was inches away from making him lunch. Adrenaline fired through his veins as he shoved off the creature's snout with both booted feet, launching himself to the surface of the water.

While gulping in lungfuls of air, Varn scanned the water, noting the creature was no longer leisurely pursuing him. Its massive body was cutting through the water like an arrow from a bow, its mouth wide, sightless eyes staring, and aiming to make Varn his next meal. Varn lunged for the rope dangling above the water at the side of the cliff. Uncoordinated from exhaustion and lack of oxygen, Varn missed, his palms scraping over the rough walls of the cliff face as crystals tore through the flesh of his palms. Just as the creature's gaping maw approached Varn's flailing feet, his cold, numb fingers closed over the rope. With his last burst of energy, he yanked himself from the water.

Varn took a moment to catch his breath, then began to fasten his harness back to the rope. His fingers, numb and awkward, struggled to perform the familiar task as sodden clothing only added to the pull of gravity on his exhausted body. Varn, done fastening himself to the rope and setting the brake on his harness, noted the massive fish swimming below had paused, staring at him sightlessly for a long moment then turned and launched itself straight down into the depths from which it came.

Varn, taking a deep breath of relief, however fleeting, mumbled a brief prayer of thanks. Shivering violently, Varn's body made him aware of impending hypothermia, reminding him he needed to begin the climb back to the cliff top. Then movement below him in the water's surface drew Varn's attention as suddenly the creature from the lake launched itself into the air with a screech. Varn reached for his knife, wrapped his free hand in the rope, and swung the knife with all his weight behind it. The blade collided with one of the monster's eyes and its blood drenched

Varn's arm nearly to the shoulder before the creature fell back into the water then disappeared.

Shivering, covered in blood, and barely able to move, Varn struggled several feet up the rope before his muscles could no longer support his weight. Dangling helplessly, halfway between the icy water and the cliff top, Varn closed his eyes in exhaustion as a cold wind began to blow gently across the lake, changing his sodden clothes to a stiff frozen prison.

Varn tried to force his eyes open. *This is not the way you are meant to die. Hanging here like bait on the end of a hook for that monster lurking below.*

But despite his caustic pep talk, Varn's body refused to move. Then the rope began to jerk and Varn groaned. *This is it. I'm being fed to the fish by an angry tree because I can't get up there and untie the rope.*

CHAPTER TWENTY-SEVEN

Mayven watched Varn disappear over the rise just beyond the pod car then turned to face Arrok and Amalayna. Amalayna regarded her with a blank expression, her silver eyes unreadable as Mayven asked, "Are you sure you can do this?"

Amalayna didn't reply but turned away from Mayven as a portal snapped open. Mayven glanced at Arrok to find him studying Amalayna with a questioning look.

"I can't hold this open for long. Can we go now?" Amalayna said, her back still to Mayven and Arrok.

Arrok's eyes met Mayven's, and Mayven shrugged. Taking a breath, she stepped through the portal. Mayven blinked furiously, trying to find a light source to make out her location. Then Arrok's solid form collided with her back, slamming Mayven into a stone wall and causing her to cry out in pain. The portal snapped shut and the faint light it had offered now absent plunged Mayven and Arrok into complete darkness.

Mayven felt dread fill her as she called out, "Ama, are you here? Arrok, did she come through with you?"

Arrok, still pressed against Mayven's back in the tight space, his voice close to Mayven's ear and breath brushing warmly against her neck, answered, "I don't think so. She said she was having a hard time holding open the portal so I jumped through behind you."

Mayven extended her arms to the sides, testing the width of the space and touched cold stone on either side with her arms still bent at the elbow. The width, however, was enough that Mayven and Arrok could stand side by side without crushing each other into the walls. Mayven looked up, trying to find some source of light and noted that above her stars were twinkling like diamonds in velvet and just visible at the edge of the opening above was the moon.

Arrok shifted next to her and Mayven reached out a hand, touching his arm. "Look up there. I'm not sure how far it is, but maybe if I got on your shoulders I could reach the edge and get us out of here. I have no idea where Amalayna sent us."

Arrok shifted, taking both of Mayven's hands in his. "I don't know where we are either but I would wager that Amalayna does. I don't think this was an accident, Mayven."

Mayven ignored him as she tried not to ponder what he said, though it had been running through her mind for several long moments already. Instead, Mayven squeezed Arrok's hands in return. "Hoist me up. I'll see how far up the opening is."

Arrok didn't press her for a response to his statement. "Take off your cape and put it in your satchel. I have a rope in my bag. Put it over your shoulder, if you can get out, tie it off and drop it down to me."

Mayven quickly followed Arrok's instructions and then carefully as possible climbed onto his shoulders. Arrok grunted as he stood beneath her. Mayven reached up, her fingers just short of the ledge.

"Can you push me up, Arrok? I just need a few more inches."

Arrok placed his hands under her feet and then started lifting. Mayven locked her knees and tried to maintain her balance as slowly the rim of the hole came within reach of her hands. Grasping quickly at the edge of the ledge, Mayven supported as much of her weight on her arms as possible while Arrok continued to lift her up until his arms were fully extended. Then, steadying herself for just a moment, Mayven adjusted her grip on the ledge and heaved herself up and over the edge of the pit.

Rolling onto her stomach, Mayven lay quietly, taking in her surroundings and noted not far away a very large fire with shadowy figures gathered around it. Mayven removed the coil of rope from her shoulder and, finding a large boulder nearby, wrapped one end twice around it. Holding her end with one hand and feet braced against the boulder, she tossed the rope into the pit. Moments later, Arrok emerged and they gathered up the rope, stuffing it back in the bag.

Mayven crouched low next to the boulder she had anchored the rope on, shivering from the cool night air. Mayven again donned her cape as she whispered to Arrok, "Should we leave or see who they are?"

Arrok, his voice barely loud enough for her to hear, answered,

"Running blindly will get us nowhere and waste time. We need to know who they are and where we are. Stay here, I'll be right back."

If there was a way to drain color from beneath mahogany skin, Arrok had found it. He crouched down close to Mayven, his frame quaking and face fixed in a look of horror as he whispered, "Didn't you mention to Varn something about a race known as the Aniwie?"

Mayven's limbs began to tremble and bile rose in her throat. "Yes, why?"

"Because I think we just got delivered to them. We need to get out of here now."

Arrok reached for Mayven's hand, and they turned from the fire, making their way slowly in the opposite direction, taking care to conceal themselves in the shadows as much as possible. They had traveled some distance, the light of the bonfire now appearing much smaller, when the sound of branches rustling overhead caused Mayven to look up and a scream to tear from her throat unchecked.

Slowly, slinking down the side of the tree in whose immense shadow they had taken protection was a cat whose emerald green eyes alone were larger than Mayven's body. Long, wickedly curved claws flexed, tearing at the bark of the tree as the cat launched itself directly into their path. Its lips peeled back in a snarl, revealing yellowed teeth. The cat's incisors, Mayven estimated, were longer than she was tall.

Mayven couldn't react, adrenaline raced through her veins but fear had frozen her in place. Her mouth hanging open in shock, Mayven tried to assimilate the information her senses were feeding her as the snarl of the cat could be heard by her ears but in her head a purring rumble of a voice demanded, *"Where do you two think you're going?"*

Then Arrok, seeming to recover more quickly than she did, yanked Mayven behind him as he slowly started backing away from the beast, shoving Mayven along with him.

The cat seemed to chuckle, the sound like a purring cough as it spoke to them. *"Where do you think you can hide, little snack? I can smell you from miles away, hear you nearly as far, and see you like a beacon on a hill top. I suggest you come back to the fire with me while you're still in one piece. I think there is someone who wishes to speak with you."*

Arrok's hand locked on Mayven's elbow as the rumble from the cat increased while its voice continued in their heads, *"I'm assuming by your posture you think to outrun me. Let me help you with that decision. I know where you are. You don't. I can see at night. You can't, and I'm certain you can't run faster than I can."*

Mayven whispered in Arrok's ear, "Let's go along for now."

The rumbling laugh that accompanied the cat's comments made Mayven's blood run cold as it said, *"I think the littlest snack is right."*

Mayven felt Arrok's fingers flex convulsively around her elbow as simultaneously they both realized this creature had probably been watching and following them since they had left the pit.

Then, without further toying, the cat gave a low snarl. *"Let's get back to the fire. My boss wishes to speak with the female."*

Mayven welcomed the protective arm Arrok put around her shoulders as they walked. *Somehow, I think it helps him as much as me.*

When they arrived at the bonfire, Mayven suddenly felt the air leave her body in a rush as she found Amalayna sitting comfortably next to a massive black bear, nibbling at a plate of fruit. The urge to vomit brought bile to Mayven's mouth, and fury launched her blindly at Amalayna before Arrok could stop her.

In a flash, Mayven was in front of Amalayna and her hand smacked Amalayna so hard, Amalayna's head rocked back on her shoulders. When Amalayna looked at Mayven again, she regarded Mayven with cold eyes as she wiped a trickle of blood from her lip. Then, without a word, Amalayna rose and walked away.

Mayven's fury gave way to grief as unheeded tears spilled from her eyes. Then a voice, different from the cat's, lower and more gravelly, spoke into her head. *"If we now have all the drama out of the way, I would like to introduce myself."*

Mayven quickly composed herself. Wiping the tears from her face, she schooled her features into a neutral mask and looked around the bonfire at the massive creatures gathered there.

There were three kinds: cats, wolves, and bears. Each of them dwarfed humans. None were smaller than half the height of the ancient trees in the forest around their fire. For the first time, Mayven contemplated what it took to create a fire and stared at the pit of flickering flames licking at half-burned logs and wondered which of the Ohkie'en had lost their life for these monsters' comfort.

Mayven's eyes drifted around the circle. "Which of you is speaking?"

The bear Amalayna had been sitting by rose to all fours, towering over Mayven as it rumbled low in its chest before replying, *"My name is Kalohdak."*

Mayven instantly recognized the name, and her thoughts jarred to a stop a moment. *So this is the one behind my lifetime of hiding, fear, and pain. Now he has turned my sister against me.*

Rage caused Mayven's voice to shake as she replied, "I would say it's a pleasure to meet you, but you know I'm not allowed to lie."

Kalohdak's massive sides heaved as he emitted a huffing grumble Mayven assumed was a laugh. *"You have audacity. I admire that. Now why don't you have a seat and we will discuss what I need you to do for me."*

Mayven snorted. "I have nothing to discuss with you, and you can't make me do anything."

Kalohdak's rumbling, jovial tone turned to a lower menacing growl. *"Oh, but I think I can."*

The massive bodies of the beasts gathered around the fire shifted as from between each pair, from the darkness beyond the fire, emerged ragged slouching figures. Around their necks were collars that resembled the marsa Mayven had been given at the orphanage and the rags they wore were filthy and couldn't even begin to be described as clothing.

Bare feet shuffled through the dry-packed earth, stirring up clouds of dust in their wake and bodies, emaciated from lack of good nutrition, shuffled along in an ungainly and loose-jointed gait that made them appear disproportionate in the flickering light of the fire. Mayven, horrified and fascinated by the sight of the wretched creatures, was not prepared when a pair of them wrestled her to the ground with amazing strength, given their apparent condition. Containing Arrok required six of the waifs.

Once both Mayven and Arrok lay immobilized on the ground, Kalohdak stepped forward, extending an ebony claw and laying it gently against the center of Mayven's breastbone. He turned his head, so one eye could regard Arrok, who still struggled against those who restrained him. *"You will go with my servants without argument or I will make her wish she were dead."*

Arrok froze in place, his face twisted in fury as he was dragged to his feet and marched to a cage at the edge of the firelight. Kalohdak stared at one of the wolves in the circle for a silent moment. A short while later, Amalayna was brought before Kalohdak.

Amalayna's tiny figure stood stiffly in front of Kalohdak, the hot wind from the fire blowing her silver white hair gently around her shoulders. Tears choked Mayven as she stared up at her friend from her place beneath Kalohdak's claw. *Why did she do this? What happened to her to change her so much?*

Kalohdak spoke again, his mental voice projected so all could hear him, *"You are now free to go."*

Mayven's questions were partially answered when Amalayna's features flushed red as she demanded, "Where is Xietak? I did as promised. Your end of the bargain was to set him free. To return him to me."

Kalohdak's huffing rumble that served as his laugh preceded his reply, *"If you can find him, and figure out how to remove the Tarlen, he is all yours. I won't stop you from having him."*

Mayven couldn't stop herself from yelling up at Amalayna, "You did this to save Xietak without even knowing what it would take to free him. How could you?"

Amalayna looked down at Mayven, her face contorted in rage. "I know, remember? I helped you research the answer. Varn is getting the crystals and all I need to do is do the ritual and he is mine again. You were never really interested in saving him or helping me. Ever since you found out you are this Language Master, you have forgotten about us. I did what I had to do to save Xietak. How does it feel to be betrayed, Mayven?"

Mayven's mouth hung open in shock and horrified sadness at what Amalayna believed to be true. "I hope you realize you will kill him when you try the ritual yourself. Only a Language Master is capable of performing it properly," she said, her tone flat and unfeeling. "I never betrayed you, Amalayna. Every day you were gone from me was torture. Every day I can't yet save Xietak is like a wound and now, because you lost faith in me, it may no longer matter at all. Time has run out. If I cannot fix what these monsters have broken, Xietak, you, them, me, and everyone else will die in a matter of days, if not hours."

Amalayna's face blanched as white as her hair, then she flung herself against the massive leg of Kalohdak, pounding on him with balled fists as she shrieked, "You lied to me! You lied to me!"

Kalohdak's huffing rumble ended in a growl as he ordered, *"Take her to the cell with the other one."*

Then Kalohdak turned, his head focusing one eye on Mayven and pressing down every so slightly on the claw at her breast bone saying, *"Now what is this you told the tiny one about all of us dying? I think you lied to her. I want you to fix the problem and I will let your friends live."*

Mayven laughed, on the edge of hysteria. "I can't fix it. You want me to give you all the adamie. You want the Hato and the Ohkie'en to die. The problem is, you've shifted the balance already and your people don't have enough numbers to hold the power that sustains our world. You're going to die with us. Only balanced distribution of adamie can sustain us."

Kalohdak pressed harder with his claw, breaking the skin open beneath her tunic as Mayven felt the thick warm trickle of blood flow down beneath her breast and across her ribs. Mayven stifled a cry of pain.

Arrok lunged against the cage bars. "Leave her alone. She's telling the truth."

Kalohdak snarled in the direction of the cage as he mentally shouted, *"Silence, mogatie."* He returned his attention to Mayven, pressing harder against her breastbone.

This time, Mayven screamed in pain as her breastbone cracked and her flesh split open between her breasts.

"Fix it," Kalohdak ordered. *"You're the Language Master. You can control all types of magic. You will fix it."*

Pain scorched through Mayven's mind and body as she trembled in shock. "I am not the Creator. I cannot make something work that he has designed not to. I cannot fix what you have done except by undoing it."

Kalohdak raised his paw, his claw now imbedded in Mayven's breastbone, making her momentarily dangle in the air until gravity pulled her free and she landed with a jarring thud on the ground. Then Kalohdak's paw slammed down on Mayven's shoulder, dislocating it and crushing her upper arm as he roared, *"If you care nothing for your life, mogatie, perhaps you care for someone else's more."*

Kalohdak gave a silent order and one of the shuffling minions from before opened the cage as it took six more of them to drag Arrok in front of Kalohdak.

Mayven barely registered the movement that slammed Arrok to the ground and pinned him under Kalohdak's claw. Mayven shrieked as pain lanced through her body when two men dragged her by the arms inside the cell with Amalayna.

Arrok screamed as she was dragged away, "Mayven, I will die with honor. Don't dishonor me by giving him what he wants."

Tears streamed down Mayven's face and the pain in her heart outweighed the pain of her body. "Even if he made me want to, which I do, I cannot."

The sound of the gate slamming shut was punctuated by Arrok's screams as Kalohdak raked a claw down his chest from his sternum to his navel. Blood bloomed in the color of dark red roses through the thin fabric of his pale tunic and Mayven lay, unable to move, on the floor of the cage.

Amalayna's sobs caught Mayven's ear above Arrok's tortured screams.

Kalohdak called out in a mental shout, *"You can stop his pain, Language Master. All you have to do is give me what I want."*

Pain fogged Mayven's mind a moment before what Kalohdak had said registered. Then Kalohdak's words triggered every admonition she had ever heard about her powers. *If I am so powerful, I can stop this. I just have to figure a way out.*

Another muffled sob drew Mayven's attention back to Amalayna and then a plan formed instantly in her mind. Mayven didn't want to waste any adamie on healing herself, afraid that there wouldn't be enough to complete the rest of her plan. Gritting her teeth against the pain, she used her free arm to touch Amalayna.

Amalayna drew back as if she had been scalded. Mayven clenched her teeth together in frustration. *I need to talk to her.* Mayven thought of using their sign language but realized Amalayna could block her out by looking away. Then Mayven recalled the words of the cat. *If I say a word aloud, they will hear me.*

Arrok began to scream again as Kalohdak pierced a claw through Arrok's shoulder, pinning him to the ground as he mentally shouted at Mayven, *"Language Master, how can you let this pitiful creature suffer so?"*

Mayven had to clench her teeth together not to cry out in jubilation as a thought raced through her mind. *I mentally talked to the Ohkie'en and the Aniwie. Why can't I do that with Ama?*

Mayven closed her eyes and thought, *"Amalayna, I need you to listen to me. I have a way out of here. Can you hear me?"*

Mayven heard Amalayna gasp, and her muffled sobs cease with a hiccup. Taking that as signs Amalayna had heard her, Mayven continued, *"I need you to think of the way you access your power to portal. Concentrate on it in detail, but don't do it. I need to learn how. If I can learn it, I can get Arrok out of here. Please help me, Amalayna."*

Mayven's head was suddenly filled with two voices, Amalayna frantically apologizing and Kalohdak threatening further harm to Arrok if she didn't answer him soon. Mayven blocked out Kalohdak and nearly shouted aloud in her frustration with Amalayna, *"I don't have time for your apologies, Amalayna. Arrok is going to die. I need to learn how to portal like you do."*

Amalayna responded silently, *"But I can't create an opening of a portal so far away from me."*

Mayven tried not to sound angry as she coaxed, *"I know, but I may be able to. I'm the Language Master. Everyone says I'm so powerful. I think it's time I tested that opinion. Please just do as I ask, Ama."*

Mayven was relieved when Amalayna finally began. Then, when she had reviewed it, Mayven said, *"I am going to heal Arrok and open a portal directly beneath him. But first I need to get Kalohdak away from him long enough that he won't follow Arrok through the portal. That is going to take all the strength I have left. I will need you to portal us out of here. Can you do that?"*

Amalayna answered, *"I can try, but they may have blocked this cage so adamie won't work in here."*

Mayven answered, *"I don't think they have remembered that yet. Are you ready?"*

Mayven received no answer mentally from Amalayna but she nodded her head. Mayven took a breath and shouted aloud, "All right, leave him alone, Kalohdak. I will help you."

Arrok screamed out, "No, Mayven, don't."

Kalohdak silenced him with a careless backhand by a massive paw that knocked Arrok perilously close to the fire. Mayven smiled in triumph as Kalohdak sauntered toward her, ignoring Arrok's broken form.

Mayven closed her eyes and drew every ounce of strength she could from the Aniwie surrounding the fire. Channeling it through herself, Mayven poured it into Arrok and the formation of a portal directly beneath him. Simultaneously, Arrok rose, a look of astonishment on his face and then immediately dropped through the portal that opened beneath his feet.

Mayven felt blackness beginning to engulf her as the rebounding power rushed backwards through her unchecked into the Aniwie she had drawn it from, leaving the Aniwie momentarily weakened and confused. Mayven screamed aloud, "Now, Ama, get us out of here!"

Mayven's vision, now tunneling to complete darkness, registered the opening of the portal before oblivion claimed her.

CHAPTER TWENTY-EIGHT

Varn felt warmth around him and through his eyelids registered flickering light. Opening his eyes, he stared at a fire. *Heaven has fires. Well, at least it's warm.*

Then his mind registered what he had been trying to accomplish and that led to thinking of Mayven. He sat bolt upright, his heart slamming against his ribs as he hollered aloud, "I can't be dead, I need to help her."

"You aren't dead, and she is capable of helping herself," came a droll reply from the other side of the fire.

Varn focused his eyes on the person speaking. Varn laughed aloud, then rose from the ground, circled the fire and slapped Arrok on the back. "I'm sure glad you got here when you did. I think I might have died. In fact, I thought I had at first."

Arrok's mouth tilted up at one corner. "So I gathered."

Varn's relief gave way to confusion. "How did you get here, and where is Mayven?"

Arrok's expression caused dread to settle like lead in his stomach. Varn sat down next to Arrok and smoothed his now dry breeches over his thighs. "Did she get taken by Adamdavas?"

"She was with Kalohdak when she created a portal beneath my feet and sent me to you," Arrok replied. "I don't know where she is now. I was hoping you could tell me."

Placing a hand over his chest, Varn closed his eyes and concentrated on Mayven. The line to her began to thrum and Varn, desperate for a more definite answer, engaged his power. He began to seek her. The mental shift, from connecting to her mentally and emotionally, to seeking her with his adamie was jarring and left him unusually lightheaded.

"She hasn't restored the balance yet, has she?" Varn asked.

Arrok heaved a sigh, then stood and began packing up the camp site. The fallen branches and twigs that had fueled the fire were easily extinguished, and Varn and Arrok were quickly ascending the steep trail between the peaks.

When they reached the tree line on the opposite side of the peaks, Varn turned to Arrok. "Seeking her is easy enough. How hard is it going to be to rescue her and why didn't Amalayna open the portal?"

Arrok regarded Varn in silence for a short moment before turning and starting down the trail once more. Varn stared at his retreating back for several seconds then, catching up, walked beside him in silence for a while.

"Are you going to tell me what happened?" Varn asked.

Arrok shifted his back pack uncomfortably and then began to tell him. When he had finished, Varn remained silent until they had reached the road where they were to meet the driver.

Then Varn turned to Arrok. "Amalayna betrayed Mayven?"

Arrok threw up his hands in disgust. "Out of all I just said to you, that is all you have to say?"

Varn shrugged and closed his eyes as he concentrated on seeking Mayven. Varn concentrated, but nothing happened. Frustration mounting, Varn tried again. Nothing.

"I can't connect to her. I don't know if the adamie has gotten too weak or if she is—" Varn stopped, unable to finish his sentence.

Arrok looked up at Varn. "I think this time we have to trust that she will find us. We should go to Hareshtava and wait. She will get there."

Varn raised a brow as he regarded Arrok. "Since when have you become so certain of her?"

Arrok shrugged, his expression earnest. "Since she alone saved my life."

Varn stared off into the distance, the road along Bomar Pass lined by forest making it disappear into a wall of green at the point at which he could no longer see. The smell of rich loam and the sound of gentle breeze filled the early morning with assurance that life continued. Varn, however, wondered. *How long do we have until this is all gone? Do I search for her? Do I wait for her? What is the right answer?*

Varn looked up at the clear blue sky bright with morning light.

"What should I do? Everything is counting on her success, and I can't find her?"

A Nifen, bright even in daylight, appeared, bobbing in front of Varn. "Go where it all started."

The Nifen vanished, and Arrok looked at Varn. "I could say I told you so, but I think that already happened."

Varn rolled his eyes as the driver expanded the car. Minutes later, Varn stared unseeing out the window as he drummed his fingers against his thigh and the forest slipped by the window in an unbroken green wall.

CHAPTER TWENTY-NINE

Mayven felt warmth on her skin. Opening her eyes, her first sight was the latticework of a cage. Without thinking, Mayven tried to sit up and pain seared through her chest and shoulder, making her gasp in pain. Small pinpoints of light dotted Mayven's vision, and she blinked rapidly, trying to clear them.

Where is Amalayna? Mayven leaned heavily on her good shoulder, trying to breathe as deeply as the pain of her broken ribs would allow. Adjusting cautiously, she noticed Amalayna was absent.

Recalling the flicker of a portal just before she had passed out, Mayven sucked in her breath. *They killed her before we could leave!*

Beyond the bars of the cage, two emaciated men stood guard, their backs to her. Beyond them, the blackened stumps and ashen remains of the fire still put forth lazy tendrils of smoke that wafted their way slowly to the treetops above.

In the light of day, Mayven took in her complete surroundings with horror. Beyond the cage and fire that had occupied her attention the night before was a field of uprooted stumps. Roots nearly as tall as some of the homes in Rashmahava stretched toward the sky like the reaching fingers of a dying man. The lush grass was trampled flat and among the remains of the trees emaciated, beaten, lifeless creatures Mayven barely recognized as her own kind shuffled listlessly picking up the wood on the ground, dumping it into a pile not far from the bonfire.

The normal sounds of a living forest were absent. No birds sang in the treetops, no voices of any kind could be heard. Even the wind through the trees was hushed. Then the silence was pierced by the sound of pain and terror, and Mayven noted that none of the creatures she was watching even flinched.

Turning her head cautiously toward the sound as quickly as her broken body would allow, a new horror assaulted her vision. Behind her cage was another pen. These creatures were well fed and healthy looking, though in their faces no life or spark seemed to flicker. The one exception was a young woman, who crouched, clinging to a child, as an enormous cat lay outside the cage. A shuffling, emaciated man opened the door. The occupants in the cage grouped in the corner, abandoning the woman and child to the man who had entered.

The man reached down and grabbed the child, ripping it screaming from its mother's arms and walked out of the cage. Mayven grasped the bars of her own cage and, ignoring her own agony, pulled herself up as she tried to scream at the others to save the child. Mayven's cry ended in a feeble cough as her lungs wouldn't fill with enough air to even speak. Collapsing against the bars as weakness made her feel faint, she watched the man, the child under one arm, lock the cage and turn to the cat. He laid the child on the ground. The cat pierced the infant with a massive claw, silencing its pitiful cries as the child disappeared into the beast's gaping maw.

Mayven's stomach heaved, and bile spewed from her lips. The movement caused pain to slice cleanly through her consciousness and send her reeling back into welcome darkness.

When again she awoke, Kalohdak sat outside her prison, lazily licking his lips as he rumbled satisfaction. Two men were diligently combing his fur. *"You don't seem particularly well this morning, Language Master. I was told you awoke earlier but then fainted."*

Mayven listened to Kalohdak's mocking laughter that rumbled deep in his massive body and demanded, "I want to know where Amalayna is."

Kalohdak's ears twitched. *"After all she did to you, you still care for her. Amazing, I would think that the woman who betrayed you then left you prisoner would be the last of your concerns."*

Mayven shook her head in denial. "She didn't leave me here. You took her when we tried to escape."

Kalohdak rolled his enormous head, turning so he could regard Mayven with one depthless black eye. *"I did nothing of the sort. You were both locked inside that very cage in which you sit. I didn't have time to open it before she disappeared."*

Logic told Mayven Kalohdak was right. Amalayna had betrayed her again but Mayven pushed the thought away. *I need to get out of here.*

As if reading her mind, Kalohdak said, *"Don't bother trying to repeat your little portal trick. I have warded the cage in which you sit. You cannot escape."*

Mayven tried to draw in adamie to heal herself, to no avail. Kalohdak had fixed his oversight. She was trapped unless she could get out of the cage.

Kalohdak shifted, rolling his massive shoulders before he stood, knocking over his groomers in the process. He began to saunter away, then turned to face Mayven. *"I'll be back shortly, and we will finish our conversation we started last night. You'll give me what I want or you will die."*

Regarding him with what she hoped was a bland expression, she said, "I don't need to help you. You'll get what you want shortly and die for the effort. Killing me will only ensure your death. Kill me now if you like."

"Don't test me, Language Master," Kalohdak bellowed into her mind so loudly she cringed in pain. *"I can make you wish for death long before it ever comes."*

Mayven was shocked at the agility and speed with which he charged the cage. Mayven felt fear shiver down her spine but, determined to provoke him, she pulled herself up on the bars with her good arm. "I have nothing better to do. You need to be taught that just because you want something doesn't automatically mean you'll get it."

As Mayven waited, staring at Kalohdak, something beyond his shoulder caught Mayven's attention. A shen tree so large and ancient that the lowest branches of the tree were as big around as trees for single homes. The glow of the ancient being was dim, even for something so powerful. Mayven's eyes were glued to the tree, her heart hammering in her breast as she recognized it from her dream. It was Radiea.

Excitement and determination coiled in her breast, and Mayven smiled at Kalohdak. "I'm so glad you're so stupid. At least when I die, I know you won't be far behind."

Kalohdak reacted at last, mentally shouting to everyone, *"Someone get her out here. I want her in front of me now."*

Then he spoke directly to Mayven. *"I'll make you regret those words right before you give me what I want."*

Mayven continued to smile at Kalohdak as the cage door swung open and two men entered, grabbing her arms and dragging her to stand in front of him. Mayven's smile faltered as pain from the rough treatment seared through her, making her vision flicker but she managed to stay standing once they had released her.

Now what? Mayven thought frantically as her heart beat rapidly in her chest. *I don't know what to do next. I'm where it all began. I know the truth has to be revealed.*

Then it dawned on her, and her smile widened. Kalohdak's paw knocked Mayven roughly to the ground, and she struggled to stay conscious. *"Why do you smile at me like an imbecile? You have nothing to smile about. I have the power here."*

Mayven's smile grew wider as she lay there, staring up at him. Kalohdak, infuriated by her response, unsheathed a claw and stabbed it through her thigh, pinning her to the ground as he demanded, *"Tell me what is so funny now, Language Master."*

Mayven screamed in pain but when the immediate pain subsided, her smile returned. "Don't you see, you foolish beast? You don't have the power. We share the power. The only reason we're subject to you is because we allow it. You take what isn't yours because we gave you permission. Not because you won it or because you earned it and definitely not because you deserve it. We, the puny Hato, the humans you despise so much are allowing you to have what you have. You haven't taken anything. Nothing belongs—"

Mayven's words were cut short as Kalohdak ripped his claw from her flesh and this time pierced it through her mutilated shoulder and lifted her by it to his eye level. *"I don't believe you. There is nothing that you can allow or disallow. I take what I want."*

Mayven felt her blood running down her body and her mind fading quickly into blackness. Determined to finish what she started, she forced herself to stay conscious. "What you believe is not the point. What we, the Hato, believe is the point. I don't believe we are weak. I don't believe you are stronger. I don't believe that even if you kill me you have won."

Mayven felt a shift in adamie and suddenly, like a river breaking through a damn, she felt it release and pour through her body. The ground trembled and the wind picked up. Just before Mayven's mind faded to black, she watched as Radiea suddenly began to project light like a beacon. The shen tree glowed so brightly that even in daylight the sun seemed dim.

CHAPTER THIRTY

V arn shifted uneasily on his seat. The pod car seemed to be slowing down. Adamie was fading quicker than he had imagined and getting to Mayven before time ran out seemed an impossibility. Varn pressed a button on the console next to him. "Can you speed it up?" he asked the driver. "How much farther is it?"

The driver's weary voice replied, "I'm going as fast as I can, Varn, and we're still at least an hour away."

Arrok shifted in his seat. "Varn, he is doing all he can. I want to get there at much as you but you've been badgering him for the last two hours and it doesn't make us go any faster."

Varn felt anxiety pouring through him, making it difficult to stay still as his leg thumped repeatedly against the floor of the pod car. Restless and his mind anxious, Varn's head began to pound in time with his heartbeat. Placing a hand over his breastbone, he rubbed gently as he tried to connect to Mayven but nothing happened.

The absence of connection to her now was worse than when she had first severed their connection. Instead of the string lacking connection, it was as if it had never existed. Time continued its steady march, unconcerned over his anxiety.

Varn reached over, about to press the button again to question the driver. Arrok reached up, smacking his hand away and suddenly everything stopped. The car was no longer moving and Varn felt as if his body were locked in place.

Rolling his eyes to see if Arrok felt it, too, Varn noticed Arrok sat rigid, his hand stopped in midair and body tense. There was a sudden outflow of adamie, the air left Varn's lungs in a rush, and his vision started to tunnel to black. Several eternal moments later, the adamie returned, stronger than he had ever felt it before. The car, only moments ago barely moving, was now hurtling down the road at unbelievable speed.

Varn, gasping for air, turned to find Arrok doing the same and then the connection to Mayven was back, stronger than it had ever been. Varn felt physical pain scorching through him as the line that connected him to Mayven seemed to pull taut.

Varn realized he was suddenly on the floor of the pod car when Arrok leaned over him, his face filled with fear. Varn grasped Arrok's shoulder, trying to find a way to ground himself, some way to physically center himself so he could control the information that was overloading his brain.

Varn watched Arrok's mouth move, dimly registering Arrok asking, "Varn, what's wrong?"

Varn opened his mouth to answer and the line connecting him to Mayven jerked and was dragging him forward. Instinctively, he grabbed onto Arrok and moments later the two of them were on the ground in the center of a clearing.

Varn, still reeling, his mind unable to adjust to the overload of sensation, tried to stand but barely managed to sit up. His gaze instantly fell on a massive black bear who stood with Mayven impaled on a claw. With a roar, the beast flung Mayven away from him. She sailed limply through the air then landed hard on the ground. Rolling bonelessly, she came to rest against the roots of an overturned tree.

Arrok, however, was on his feet in an instant and yanked Varn up beside him. Varn stared down the charging animal, trying to figure out how to get to Mayven as he realized that the bear was not alone. Two massive cats and a pure white wolf created a formation as they flanked the bear. The group created a wall of fur and claws that hurtled themselves toward Varn and Arrok with incredible speed.

Varn, still incapacitated, was thankful when Arrok yanked him out of their direct path and into the shelter of the roots of an overturned tree. They crawled into the tangle as far back as they could manage, but the bear's giant paws were making short work of the roots in his way. Varn felt the tree against his skin and heard its screams of pain, then, with a power unlike Varn had ever experienced, adamie gathered in a massive wave and focused itself on the large group of massive beasts beyond the roots of the tree. The wave surged forward, and the beasts were gone. The glen fell silent.

Varn still felt like he was in a fever and watching a strange movie on fast forward. His mind couldn't seem to function. Then, like a cool cloth on a fevered brow, a presence entered his head.

"I am Radiea. I am the shen tree that is Mayven's ancestral home. I can help you control the connection to her until she is conscious again. I need you to bring her to me. She is badly injured, as I'm sure you know. I can help her."

The deafening of Mayven's pain and halt of sensation overload allowed Varn to function once more, and he raced to Mayven's side. She lay pale and limp, her limbs tangled like a child's discarded toy. Her clothes were soaked in blood and a thigh and shoulder displayed gaping wounds.

Varn choked back a cry of grief as he gently lifted her in his arms. Looking up at the beacon of light the shen tree created, he walked as quickly as he dared beneath its immense bower and laid Mayven down at the base of its trunk.

Radiea spoke to Varn again, her voice slow and powerful. *"I will need time with her. I need you to find a way to help those of my people who still survive and make them whole again."*

Varn looked around the glen and found not a single beast left in sight but in among the roots of the trees gathered the most tattered and forlorn creatures Varn had ever seen. He turned, knelt down, and looked at Mayven, brushing her hair from her face, he kissed her forehead. Then, rising up, he went to the group who stood apprehensively in the shadow of a felled tree.

Varn looked at them demanding, "Who are you? What are you doing here? Can any of you help me with the trees?"

A frail ancient being emerged from the center of the group. "We are Hato, as you are, but we were slaves to the Aniwie that were here. We did not do this to them. We refused to. The Aniwie tried to starve us to death for our disobedience. We can help you. There are those of the earth clan among us and we now feel our power restored, thanks to the Language Master."

Varn nodded. "What do you need me and my friend to do?"

The ancient one looked at Varn, saying simply, "Feed us and free the others over there from their prison."

Varn turned, taking in the cage of well-fed Hato huddled in terror in the corner of a metal cage. Varn glanced at Arrok, then at the old man in front of him. "I thought you said you were being starved for not harming the Ohkie'en. Did they do this? They're all well fed."

"They were food. An Aniwie likes his meals plump, not skin and bone." The old man's response caused Varn's heart to skip a beat as the contents of his stomach heaved.

Varn turned to Arrok. "Free those sad creatures. Let's set this place to rights and destroy those cages."

Arrok nodded and soon, in his customary fashion, had everyone in order. Varn left Arrok to that which made him most content, being useful. Varn quietly walked away and went to sit with Mayven, gently lifting her head and laying it in his lap. Leaning back against Radiea's warm trunk, Varn soon found himself asleep, his mind at ease for the first time in months.

CHAPTER THIRTY-ONE

Mayven's last thought before unconsciousness was peaceful and unhurried. *If I die today, it was worth it.*

Then another voice entered her mind, whispering softly, *"You have done well. Your faith is small but it can grow. Seek me when you are well."*

Then all faded gratefully to black as she was flung away from Kalohdak, never feeling the impact of the ground when she landed. Mayven knew she wasn't dead when she woke to pains that, though not as intense as her torture, were excruciating.

Mayven moaned as she tried to move, then a cool hand touched her brow as a tender voice said, "Don't move. You aren't completely well yet. Radiea is working on it."

Mayven licked her lips, and her hand reached up to touch her chest. Though she couldn't see Varn's face, she could feel his love and concern like a river flowing cool and healing into her through their connection.

Mayven rolled her eyes, searching for Varn's face. Varn leaned over her. "I'm right here."

Mayven licked her lips again and patted her chest. "You're right here. Where you belong."

Varn bent down and briefly touched his lips to her forehead. "I'm glad you think so, too."

Mayven smiled as her eyes drifted closed again and sleep claimed her once more.

When she woke again it was dark, the pain in her body completely gone, and light of day with it. Radiea glowed brightly, filling the glen with her light. Around her were groups of Hato, laughing and singing. Their voices were filled with celebration.

Mayven felt Varn's relief and turned to him, automatically finding him in a group of people just behind her. Walking over to him, she took his hand in hers. "These are the people the Aniwie enslaved. What happened to the Aniwie?"

Varn shrugged, his lips curving in a bemused smile. "I'm not sure. The Ohkie'en were angry. They removed them. These people were being starved for not harming the Ohkie'en and the ones who weren't being starved were—"

Mayven raised a hand and placed a finger on Varn's lips, feeling his disgust and revulsion at what he had learned. "I know."

Keeping her fingers laced with Varn's, Mayven gently led him away from the group. "I need to get Xietak here. Do you have the crystal?"

Varn nodded. "How will we get him here?"

Mayven grinned as she felt her new confidence fill her body with determination. She raised a hand, and a disk of blue light popped open and through it tumbled Xietak and two men. Xietak was tied to a chair and the men, apparently guarding him, were cast across the ground like dice in a game of wsieha. Mayven smiled up at Varn triumphantly. Varn stared at her in open-mouthed wonder.

Then, without giving Varn a chance to ask all the questions she felt him trying to sort out, she said, "I need that crystal and Xietak over by Radiea."

Varn released her hand as he and Arrok picked Xietak up, chair and all, and placed him at the base of Radiea's trunk. Then Varn retrieved his pack, took out the small black bag containing the crystal and handed it to Mayven.

Mayven took the bag in her hand and looked up at Radiea. "I need you to help me with this. I've never done it. I need to concentrate all the power of your light into this crystal. Can you help me?"

Radiea's leaves rustled and the breeze around the glen picked up. "*It is done.*"

Mayven nodded then taking the crystal, still in its bag, she stood in front of Xietak. Mayven closed her eyes. "That which was not invited is cast out. In light of truth, you cannot possess that which was not willingly given."

Mayven unveiled the crystal and, pressing it to Xietak's neck, felt the crystal draw from her and from Radiea as it poured adamie through the crystal and into Xietak. Mayven nearly dropped the crystal at Xietak's screams of pain. The crystal in her hand vibrated, and she stood rooted to the ground, her body shaking.

As the crystal grew hot in her grasp, she heard Radiea say, "*It is almost finished. Don't let go! This child has been possessed for some time. It is taking longer than expected to free him.*"

Mayven couldn't find a coherent way to answer but she could feel Varn growing more agitated with each passing second. Mayven concentrated on Varn, trying to reassure him but his concern only increased. Xietak's voice grew silent, and Mayven's eyes flew open.

A dark specter floated between Xietak and Mayven, then Radiea's light seemed to intensify and the creature shrieked then vanished. Mayven fell to her knees in front of Xietak, her hands caressing his face. "Can you hear me? Come on, little brother, wake up."

Xietak's eyes flickered and then slowly opened, revealing a deep crystal blue gaze filled with tears.

Mayven smoothed them away as they fell to his cheeks. "It's okay, you're free. Talk to me. Are you okay?"

Xietak nodded, his voice husky. "I'm okay, thank you so much."

Varn quickly untied Xietak and knelt down in front of him next to Mayven. "Are you sure? What is your name? Do you know who we are?"

Mayven watched in surprise as Varn questioned Xietak and checked him out carefully. She noted the tender way he cared for her friend and suddenly, through the connection, she knew Varn had witnessed what had happened to her brother. In Varn, she registered a love for Xietak that was never there before and a concern for his welfare that touched her deeply. Backing away, she let Varn care for Xietak, unwilling to disrupt them.

Sighing, she stood back and watched, then jumped slightly in surprise as Arrok's arm curled around her shoulders.

Arrok inclined his head. "He is a good man."

Mayven turned to look at Arrok. "Xietak?"

"Yes. He suffered so much just to protect you and Amalayna. I'm honored to know him."

Mayven flinched at the mention of Amalayna.

Xietak heard her name as well. Looking around the glen, he looked back at Mayven. "Where is she?"

Mayven, for the first time, felt her grief over Amalayna's betrayal wash through her like a flood. The pain staggered her so much for an instant she couldn't breathe or speak. Then, stepping forward, she knelt next to Xietak. "I need to speak to you in private."

CHAPTER THIRTY-TWO

Varn watched the two walk off, hand in hand, and noted that not a twinge of jealousy peeked out from his soul. Sighing, he sat down in the chair, his head in his hands as Arrok knelt beside him.

Varn raised his head and looked at Arrok. "I feel sorry for them both. I don't know how either of them will survive that betrayal. They've been through so much."

Arrok nodded as he picked at a long stem of grass. "And there is more to go through, my friend. You don't think that just because balance has been restored everything is fine?"

Varn heaved a deep sigh. "No, we have won this battle but the war is still ahead. We can give them some time but there is much left she must help us do."

Arrok's gaze focused on the ground. "And what about her? Have you told her how you feel? Has she said anything to you?"

As Arrok raised his eyes to look at him, Varn smiled. Then he gave a noncommittal shrug. "I have told her without words. We have time for the rest."

Arrok's expression was solemn. "Don't deny yourselves a love that you may need to sustain you through what is to come. I saw Kalohdak's brutality first hand. You'll need each other. She especially will need you."

Varn felt a shudder as he recalled Mayven's broken body. "I will not withhold myself from her. But it's up to her to decide if she wants me. She has never truly trusted me and, without that, love doesn't last long."

Arrok's smile grew wide, and Varn suddenly felt a tiny warm hand on his shoulder as Mayven pulled him back in his chair and sat down on his lap. "I trust you with my life, Varn. More than that, I trust you with my heart."

With that, Mayven leaned in and placed a gentle kiss on his lips. When she pulled away, there was a smile on her lips and tears in her eyes. Varn cupped her face in his hands and kissed her again, pouring every emotion he felt for her into her through their connection and receiving every one in return from her.

Acie Lynn is a lifetime writer that began her career at the ripe old age of six when she re-wrote the ending of Heidi (granny didn't get treated fairly in her estimation). She entitled the piece 'The Bline Grinmather' (misspellings historically accurate) and that is how the much cherished document became family legend. She then learned to spell and subsequently spent her awkward teen years hiding in school libraries devouring books on everything she could get her hands on (classical literature became a favorite along with westerns by Louis L'Amour). She has a modest collection of published short stories, poems, and several small articles. Journalism was her goal on the way out of high school but life has curveballs so she went into Business Administration for twenty years then followed that up with a degree in Medical Assisting. During those long years she raised two magnificent boys, continued to write several novels (none of which have seen the light of day due to her harsh critiquing skills) and had even more poems published. She has taken several writing courses most notably from a fellow author and mentor Holly Lisle (she highly recommends the course How to Think Sideways by Holly Lisle, it taught her a lot). She resides in Pueblo, Colorado with her phenomenal husband, their children and one very spoiled bark-o-lounger (a.k.a. the family dog, Jayben). The next book in The Prophecy Tales trilogy is RECKONING tentatively scheduled for release in spring of 2015.

You can contact Acie Lynn through her website at:

www.acielynn.com

CPSIA information can be obtained at www.ICGtesting.com
Printed in the USA
LVOW01s0837190914

404873LV00003B/5/P